A TIME AND A PLACE

JOE MAHONEY

FIVE RIVERS PUBLISHING
WWW.FIVERIVERSPUBLISHING.COM

Five Rivers Publishing, 704 Queen Street, P.O. Box 293, Neustadt, ON N0G 2M0, Canada.

www.fiveriverspublishing.com

Edited by Dr. Robert Runté.

Copy-edited by Aerin Caley.

Interior design and layout by Éric Desmarais.

Titles set in Downcome designed by Eduardo Recife in 2002 as a messy display font.

Text set in Lora designed by Cyreal as a well-balanced contemporary serif text typeface with roots in calligraphy. Its appearance is memorable because of its brushed curves counterposed with driving serifs.

Published in Canada

Library and Archives Canada Cataloguing in Publication

Mahoney, Joe, 1965-, author

A time and a place / Joe Mahoney. –First edition.

Issued in print and electronic formats.

ISBN 978-1-988274-25-6 (softcover).

ISBN 978-1-988274-26-3 (EPUB)

I. Title.

PS8626.A417415T56 2017 C813'.6 C2017-900362-3 C2017-900363-1

For my girls
Lynda, Keira, and Erin

CONTENTS

1

BEAUTIFUL STRANGER

I GREETED DOCTOR Humphrey at Charlottetown's modest airport. My old friend had changed somewhat in the months since I'd last seen him, becoming, shall we say, a tad plumper than before. His wardrobe, though expensive, suffered from a certain rumpled quality. The colour scheme was also a bit of a problem: largely grey, with dashes of darker grey here and there. In the dim light of the parking lot Humphrey's heavy-set shuffle and predominantly grey attire conspired to create a remarkably convincing illusion of a small grey elephant lumbering along beside me—an observation I thought best to keep to myself.

In the taxi I summarized for the doctor the notes I'd made—the seemingly innocuous but significant changes in my nephew's personality. How he'd begun making his bed. How the other day I'd caught him washing the dishes, and that same afternoon stumbled upon him cleaning the bathroom. How he'd been brushing his teeth, flossing regularly, combing his hair, smelling too good and smiling too much, and how it all scared the dickens out of me, because it meant that something was horribly wrong with the boy, and I had no idea what.

A summer rain squall hastened the onset of darkness as we neared my house on the north shore, about a half hour drive from the island's second largest city,

Summerside. Our taxi grumbled to a halt in the gravel driveway just as Ridley arrived home. I sat with Doctor Humphrey in the cab to wait out the fierce rain.

We watched as my nephew made his way to the front door. As he carefully negotiated the notoriously slippery steps, he seemed completely unaware of our presence there in the driveway. Such single-mindedness of purpose was characteristic of the boy's increasingly disturbing symptoms.

He halted for a moment on the rain-soaked porch. A stone gargoyle, an original feature of our century-old dwelling, glowered down at him from its perch above the porch. Lightning flared, illuminating the house and a stretch of sandy shore beyond. In that sudden flash I could have sworn that one sunken eye of the gargoyle winked at my nephew.

At least, that's how it appeared to me from my vantage point inside the cab. True, we were parked some distance away from the boy, the cab window was all fogged up, and an errant eyelash had made my left eye water prodigiously—nevertheless, I was quite certain of what I had seen.

The rain let up after a few minutes. I paid the hefty cab fare and helped the doctor inside with his luggage. I looked closely at the gargoyle as we ascended the porch steps. Its absurd, leonine head stared back at me. The raw beauty of the gothic creature had always appealed to me. So expertly fashioned was it that I found myself almost disappointed when it failed to jump into motion before me. Instead, it behaved as all good inanimate objects should: remaining utterly still, twitching not so much as a limestone ear.

Inside, Humphrey made himself comfortable in the

den, smoking one of his malodorous cigars. I lit a fire in the hearth to combat the stench and fetched some liquid refreshments.

Ridley saved me the trouble of hunting him down by appearing in the den of his own accord. If Humphrey had harboured any doubts about my story, before us now stood the proof. Ridley was barely recognizable in slacks and a freshly pressed shirt, his hair neatly combed. He reeked of cologne, a marked deterioration from the morning. The boy was a dapper nightmare.

"Hello, Doctor," he greeted Humphrey. "Here for a few days, are you?"

"That depends. I–"

"Good, good. Well, we'll see you. Don't wait up, Uncle." Ridley retreated down the hallway.

"Don't be late," I called after him, pointlessly. The front door slammed shut behind him.

I shrugged at Humphrey, who stubbed out his cigar. "Wildebear, there's something you need to know. Joyce. She's–well, she left me, dammit."

"What? No... When?"

"Last month."

Humphrey's newfound shabbiness came sharply into focus. "Peter, if there's anything I can do–"

"I just thought you should know."

I nodded. If he didn't want to talk about it, I wouldn't press him.

He sipped his scotch. "About Ridley. You two been getting along lately?"

It was a leading question. Humphrey knew Ridley's tragic tale all too well. Four years earlier Ridley's father had vanished without a trace. Not the sort to run off on his wife and only child, he was presumed dead. Ridley had been only eleven at the time. Two years after that Ridley's mother—my sister, Katerina—had been killed in a motorcycle accident. As Ridley's only living relative, I had assumed guardianship.

Humphrey knew just how well that had gone.

Even as I had grieved my sister's death, I resented the responsibility thrust upon me. Though I would not have admitted it to anyone, I much preferred living on my own. Sadly, I soon discovered that teaching English to kids Ridley's age did not necessarily translate into an ability to parent one.

Kids can smell that sort of thing. Ridley was about as enamoured of me as I was of him. Also he had the loss of his mother to contend with. Oh, I made a few tentative overtures at friendship, but when it became clear that he disdained my company as much as I did his, we began to steer clear of one another. Weeks went by with hardly five friendly words passing between us. Two years passed in this manner, until this past Tuesday, when something changed.

"He's been quite civil," I told Humphrey. "I can't understand it."

"You don't think two people ought to be able to get along?"

"Of course they ought to. But Ridley? Something's not right. I can't explain it."

Humphrey chewed on his bottom lip. "He's cleaned himself up quite a bit. What do you make of that?"

I didn't like it. I didn't like it at all. But I couldn't bring myself to tell Humphrey that. My feelings on the matter didn't make sense. "I don't know. What are you suggesting?"

"Your nephew's sudden interest in personal hygiene

could have a perfectly reasonable explanation. Such as a young lady in his life."

I met Humphrey's eyes. Watery and bloodshot, they looked as if he had recently spent a few moments poking them. "It's possible. Except the change happened so quickly–practically overnight. The boy's entire personality has been turned upside down."

Humphrey nodded. "You're right. I fear there's more to it than just that." He rose to his feet. "I'd like to see his room."

I followed him upstairs mutely, afraid of what we might find.

The tidiness of my nephew's room, so uncharacteristic of the Ridley I knew, jarred me afresh. Not a single undergarment soiled the floor. His bed gave me the creeps, with the blankets tucked up neatly underneath the pillow, every corner just so.

Humphrey leaned over to sniff the linen. "Downy," he remarked, arching an eyebrow.

On Ridley's bedside table there was a fancy-looking book I had never seen before. Humphrey picked it up. Together we examined the cover, which consisted of a lustrous black material heavily adorned with red and gold embossing. A title in flowery script occupied the top third of the cover: IUGURTHA. I found the overall effect compelling, if a trifle gauche.

"I was afraid of this," Humphrey said.

"What, Doctor?"

"You're going to find this difficult to believe." Humphrey held the book tightly to his chest. "Wildebear, this book is dangerous. It ought to be destroyed."

"I do not approve of censorship, Doctor."

Humphrey scowled. "You don't understand. This is no ordinary book."

"I understand perfectly well. The book belongs to Ridley. It almost certainly contains subject matter offensive to people not used to dealing with teenaged boys. It's perfectly normal. I'd prefer to concentrate on–"

"Damn it all, Wildebear. Don't patronize me. Here's the thing. It's not really even a book. It's–" he gestured helplessly, searching for the right words.

I stared at him. "What?"

"Look. Believe it or not, this book–or one just like it–stole my wife from me."

What was he suggesting? I glanced at the book's cover. The title was oddly appealing. I said it aloud to see what it felt like on my tongue: "Iugurtha."

Several things changed abruptly. I found myself facing a different direction. The book lay open on the floor at my feet. Doctor Humphrey sat on the floor rubbing his shin.

I struggled to reorient myself. "What are you doing down there?"

The doctor rose and grabbed the book from off the floor. He slammed it shut, set it none too gently back on the bedside table, and glared at me. "Now you've done it."

"What do you mean? What happened?"

"It's going to be a lot to swallow, Wildebear. A little scotch will help it go down easier." He stepped forward and winced. "Not to mention ease the pain."

He limped out of Ridley's room. I followed him, wondering why I couldn't remember him dropping the book or hurting himself.

At the entrance to the den he halted abruptly. Peering past him, I saw a young woman sitting in my easy chair. She looked to be about eighteen years old, and had the kind of fresh-faced, rosy-cheeked good looks you'd expect to find on a ski hill somewhere in Sweden. Clad in a simple white skirt and blouse, she smiled at our arrival.

I had left a bottle of Lagavulin on the coffee table. The young woman poured herself a tumbler and threw back its contents in a single gulp.

"The devil's own brew," she said huskily.

"Iugurtha, I presume," Humphrey said.

Although slightly piqued to find a stranger sitting in my den drinking my single malt scotch, I strove to keep my tone amiable. "I beg your pardon, miss, but how did you get in?"

"You let me in through the gate, Mr. Wildebear. Will Ridley be home soon?"

"Ridley? Not for a while, I'm afraid."

Her smile made the most of her full, red lips. "Then I shall wait."

I frowned. A few years earlier my house had been vandalised. Ever since then I'd kept every door, window, and vent locked. She could not have entered without having been let in. But I had not let her in, nor had the doctor. Evidently neither had Ridley. Furthermore, my house had no gates.

Humphrey drew me back to the hallway.

"I don't understand how she got in," I whispered.

"Time to bring you up to speed, Wildebear. The demon's right: you let it in through the gate."

"Me?"

"Yes, you. You don't remember because you were in a trance at the time."

"I beg your pardon?"

"Try to keep up, Wildebear." He took a deep breath. "As I told you, the book's not really a book. It's a gate to someplace else. Another dimension. Hell, maybe. It put you in some kind of a trance. You attacked me, took the book, opened it, and let Iugurtha out."

"She came out of the book."

"That's what I'm telling you."

The doctor's story did explain the disorientation I had experienced in Ridley's room. But of only two facts was I truly certain: that his story was an awful lot to swallow, and I had had no scotch with which to down it.

"Are you trying to tell me that the woman in my den is some kind of supernatural entity?"

"Yes. No." Humphrey shook his shaggy head in frustration. "Maybe."

"And you believe the book has something to do with your wife leaving you?"

"I do."

It was too much. I glanced inside the den at the young woman, who offered up a little wave.

"Humphrey, be rational," I said. "I sympathise with what you've been through, but you know as well as I do that there are no such things as demons."

Humphrey limped forward and locked his bleary eyes onto mine. "A few minutes ago you almost killed me."

"I blacked out–"

He raised a finger in the air. To my astonishment he jabbed me square in the middle of the forehead with it. "Ridley's changed. You know it. That's why you called me here. There's a woman in your den you've never seen before. You can't explain how she got into your house or why she's here. I'm telling you: she's either a demon or a damned good approximation of one. Whatever she is, she's after your nephew."

I tore my eyes away from his and rubbed my forehead where he'd poked me.

"I hope you come around soon. Before it's too late." Humphrey limped off down the hallway. "For Ridley's sake," he called back over his shoulder.

I stared after him, flabbergasted. His wife's departure had left him completely deranged. As he fumbled with the latch to the bathroom door, I wondered just how much of his scotch he'd drunk.

I entered the den feeling bad for having abandoned our guest and for talking about her behind her back. "I'm sorry, Ms..." I hesitated, unsure how to proceed.

"Iugurtha."

I stood awkwardly, wondering what it meant that her name was the same as on the book. She offered me her hand. Unsure whether to shake or kiss it, I decided upon the former, and she impressed me with a firm, manly grip. Taking a seat on the couch I struggled to produce some excuse for the doctor's odd behaviour. A decent fabrication escaped me. I decided a little candour wouldn't hurt.

"Doctor Humphrey has it in his head you're some kind of demon," I chuckled.

Iugurtha elevated a pair of well-groomed eyebrows.

"I'm afraid there've been spirits of another sort at work here tonight," I added, indicating the bottle of Lagavulin on the coffee table.

Humphrey's glass remained where he'd set it earlier

in the evening. I noticed with some consternation that it was still almost full.

Iugurtha said nothing.

Afraid I'd offended her, I changed the subject. "So you're a friend of Ridley's, are you?" She looked quite a bit too old for him, in my view.

She produced a most delightful white-toothed smile. Seeing her face light up like that, it was all I could do not to burst into song.

"Ridley is much more than a friend to me," she said.

I wasn't sure I liked the sound of that. Still, I had to admit that if a woman like Iugurtha were to enter my life I might consider some changes of my own. But could she alone account for Ridley's transformation? Maybe. But what if there was more to it? Drugs, alcohol, or a chemical imbalance in the brain?

Iugurtha brushed a blonde lock away from her forehead. "Excuse me."

"Certainly," I said, smiling vacuously, with no idea what I was excusing her for.

She reached up and plucked the left eyeball from out of her head. My smile froze on my face. She began to polish the eyeball with the hem of her skirt.

I let my breath out. A glass eye. Unusual in so young a woman but not unheard of. She followed the same procedure with her right eyeball too. "I don't know how you people see with these things."

The woman was blind. No, she'd made eye contact several times. Could a person see with two glass eyes? Of course not. I felt hot and tried desperately to think rationally. I clutched at a fragile hypothesis. She looked like a television character from my youth, Jaime Sommers, the bionic woman. That was it. She was bionic.

I worked to regain my composure. Iugurtha placed each eyeball back where it belonged. To my horror, her pupils now glowed like twin drops of molten lava. As she fixed me with that volcanic gaze, I knew that these were not the eyes of a six million-dollar woman.

They were the eyes of a demon.

DEMON IN THE DEN

I LEAPT TO my feet and tore from the den. At the door to the bathroom I whispered urgently, "Doctor Humphrey!" but the doctor did not respond.

The door was slightly ajar. I nudged it further and found the bathroom unoccupied. Perplexed, I rushed to the kitchen, thinking maybe the doctor had gone for a bite to eat, but I did not find him there. I searched in the dining room, the office, the rec room, all three bedrooms, two bathrooms, the furnace room, the laundry room, and the attic, but couldn't find Humphrey anywhere.

The doctor was not in the house.

Pacing frantically in the front entranceway, I tried to think where he could be. The closet nearby caught my eye. Something about it tugged at my brain. I realised I hadn't searched in any closets for the doctor. Absurd, of course, the thought of Humphrey hiding in a closet, yet the longer I stood there, the greater became the urge to open that door.

Finally, I could stand it no longer. I eased the door open and stepped inside to take a look. Stuffy air assailed my nostrils. Everything seemed in its place: hats and jackets, boots, shoes, scarves and mittens, and hanging on the wall, my Remington double-barrelled shotgun. But no Doctor Peter Humphrey.

As I began to close the door, the back wall of the closet slid open. A dark form leapt out at me. I struggled against it but my efforts proved fruitless. Seconds later I found myself held fast, with my arms pinioned tightly behind my back.

A male voice whispered harshly in my left ear, "Try anything stupid and you'll regret it."

The threat did not bother me quite so much as the stench of garlic that accompanied it. My captor could no doubt have made good on his threat simply by breathing in my face.

My assailant spun me around and prodded me into a red-dirt tunnel that I was stunned to learn existed behind the closet. I needed to act quickly if I wanted to avoid an uncertain fate at the hands of this ruffian, so I kicked back hard, trying to connect with his knee, or anything else that might cause him to release his hold on my arms.

I hit nothing. An instant later I received a thunderous blow just above my right ear. I stumbled and fell. Cold steel nuzzled my neck. I heard the metallic sound of a gun being cocked.

"We'll have none of that," the thug said into my ear. I gagged at the stench of his breath.

Garlic Breath hauled me to my feet and shoved me ahead of him once more. The tunnel quickly became a cramped affair. I was forced to my hands and knees where I crawled like a baby for what felt like forever. Finally, dirty, fatigued, my head throbbing, I arrived at a well-lit area large enough for me to be able to stand up again.

I recognised my new surroundings immediately—the largest of several caves dotting the sandstone cliffs adjacent to my property. Perhaps two dozen men and women occupied the cave. Half appeared to be technicians, busy monitoring banks of complicated-looking gear. The bearing of the others, along with the daunting weapons they possessed, suggested a more military orientation, though no one was wearing uniforms. My assailant, a well-muscled man with a curiously misshapen head, figured among the latter. Silver brooches shaped like crescent moons were pinned to everyone's shirts.

A great deal of equipment clogged the cave. Aside from paraphernalia that I couldn't identify, there were a dozen full-colour video monitors covering one of the cave's walls and displaying every square inch of the interior of my house. Several of the monitors showed Iugurtha sitting tranquilly in the den applying lipstick. I could not tell from the angles provided whether her eyes still glowed a preternatural red.

Humphrey lumbered forth from one of the cave's many crannies, red-faced and covered in dirt.

"Doctor!" I winced, as speech made my head even worse. Reaching up, I found a large lump over my ear where I'd been struck.

Humphrey was accompanied by a small, wiry man clad in black. A pencil-thin moustache lent the man a dapper air. A tiny earpiece sat snugly in his left ear, connected to an equally unobtrusive microphone suspended before a pair of thin, bloodless lips. As near as I could tell all of the men and women in the cave wore identical wireless gear.

"Kindly keep your voice down, please," the man in black admonished in a clipped British accent.

Having discovered that excessive volume hurt my head, I had been planning to do just that, but being commanded to do so made me change my mind.

"Who are these people?" I demanded of Humphrey.

"This one calls himself Rainer. Other than that, I have no idea. They forced me here at gunpoint."

"Me too. After some convincing." I indicated the growing lump on the side of my head.

Humphrey examined my injury. "Dizzy?"

"No more so than usual."

"We'll keep a close eye on you." He scowled at Rainer. "Do you have any idea how serious head wounds can be?"

"As a matter of fact I do," Rainer said. "For what it's worth, Mr. Schmitz here knows just where and how hard to hit. I assure you, under the circumstances we could not have just up and rung your doorbell."

"Why not?"

"I really must insist that you speak more quietly, Doctor."

"Why is that?" Humphrey practically bellowed.

I winced. Rainer looked pained. "The entity has an extraordinary ability to hear. It must not learn of our presence here."

"And just whose presence is that?" Humphrey asked.

"We call ourselves Casa Terra."

"What does that mean?" Humphrey asked.

"It's Latin, my good man. It means *Earth is our home*."

"Yes, obviously, but that tells me nothing."

"We are humanity's last line of defence."

"Against what?"

"You could not even begin to imagine."

"How long have you been spying on me?" I asked.

"We are not spying on you. We are observing the entity."

"Whoever you're spying on, I think it's outrageous and I won't stand for it." I shouldered my way past the man, only to have garlic-breathed Schmitz and one of his colleagues block my way.

Fuming but with nowhere to go, I found myself forced back to Humphrey's side.

A hint of a smile played on Rainer's lips.

"We are your prisoners," Humphrey observed.

"You are here for your own protection."

"Protection from what?" I snorted. "This entity of yours looks about as dangerous as a pussycat. Except for her eyes, she seems quite–" I struggled to produce the right word "–nice."

Inwardly, however, I could not suppress a mental image of Iugurtha's white, bulbous eyeballs loosed from the confines of her face.

"Nice?" Humphrey grunted. "Get it through that foolish head of yours, Wildebear. It's a demon."

"Nonsense. The entity is extraordinary, but there is nothing supernatural about it." Rainer touched his earpiece and fixed his gaze on the bank of monitors. I followed his line of sight. One of the screens showed Ridley arriving home. I realized that the camera tracking him must have been concealed in one of the gargoyle's eyes.

The breadth of surveillance within and around my home awed me even as it outraged me. I missed nothing as Ridley (exercising none of the caution he had displayed earlier in the evening) fairly capered up the front steps and entered the house. He appeared to be whistling as he hung up his jacket and headed for his room. Perhaps those in the cave equipped with earpieces could actually hear him.

As disturbed as I was to discover a covert surveillance

team monitoring my house (not to mention having been struck in the head and kidnapped in my own front-hall closet), a greater concern gripped me now. What did Iugurtha want with my nephew?

I turned to Rainer. "If this entity of yours is as dangerous as Humphrey believes–"

"There's nothing we can do for your nephew," Rainer informed me quietly.

"You took us out of harm's way. Why not him too?"

"I'm sorry. The boy's fate is sealed. It's too late for him."

I started forward again. "Not if I can help it."

Rainer stepped in my way. "I will not have your blood on my hands as well."

"You risk blood on your hands either way," I told the man. "You'll have to kill me to make me stay here."

Beside me, the doctor began moving purposefully toward the mouth of the cave. Schmitz moved to block him. Rainer waved the thug off.

"You're wrong," Rainer said, stepping aside. "If you wish to face the entity I will not stand in your way. I will, however, not be responsible for the consequences."

I wasted no time sprinting after Humphrey, catching up with and passing him just outside the entrance to the cave. A full moon lit my way as I raced along the rocky shore beneath the cliffs to the section of beach adjacent to my property. I clambered over several sand dunes to get to my backyard. Once there, I groped in my pocket for my keys and let myself in the back door, thinking that although I had fed the boy, housed him, and clothed him, it hadn't been enough. Not by a long shot. Now he was consorting with demons and it was my fault. I had failed my sister and failed Ridley. I only hoped it wasn't too late to put things right.

I headed straight for the front closet and plucked my Remington off its hook on the wall. Handy for warding off skunks, coyotes and door-to-door salespeople, I saw no reason why it wouldn't serve equally well against demons. I inserted two shells into the gun's breach and shoved a handful of others, along with my fears, deep into the pocket of my corduroys.

Peering cautiously into the den, I confirmed that Iugurtha was no longer there. I ran upstairs and kicked the door to Ridley's room open, where I was confronted by the sight of Iugurtha and the boy sitting together on the bed, the book clasped firmly in Iugurtha's arms. I dared meet her eyes, now as blue as a summer sky and devoid of any trace of their former fire. Iugurtha did not look the least bit like a demon to me. On the contrary she looked like an angel. I half expected her to unfold an enormous pair of ivory wings from behind her back. Perhaps she was a fallen angel, like Lucifer.

I heard a rustle from behind. A thrill of fear gripped me and I spun rapidly, ready to blast any demons coming at me from that direction. I removed my finger from the trigger a fraction of a second before blowing Doctor Humphrey's head clean off. Seeing a shotgun pointed squarely at his fleshy face, the doctor looked alarmed but said nothing—perhaps because he couldn't, he was panting so heavily.

Lowering the shotgun, I faced Iugurtha and demanded, "What have you done to the boy?"

She cocked her head to one side. "I took in a little bit here, and let out a little bit there."

Sweat made the shotgun slippery in my hands. "What do you mean? What does she mean, Ridley?"

Emotion played over Ridley's face like ripples on

the surface of a pond. A pond from which, I might add, his nose protruded like the dorsal fin of a shark. "I'll explain everything, Uncle, if you'll just put the shotgun down."

"You'll get nothing out of him," Humphrey panted. "He's under the demon's influence."

Ridley wrinkled his brow. "Demon?"

"It's nothing to be ashamed of, boy. The demon stole my wife and now it's trying to steal you. Fortunately, your uncle had wit enough to call me." Humphrey faced Iugurtha. "You may as well know I won't rest until I get my wife back. And I won't let you steal the boy."

Ridley rose quickly to his feet. "Just hang on, everyone. I'm sorry to hear something's happened to your wife, Doctor, but whatever it is I'm sure there's a perfectly reasonable explanation."

"This is a creature of the netherworld, boy –"

"She's a jinn!" Ridley cut him off.

I narrowed my eyes. "A what?"

"A jinn." Ridley nodded earnestly. "You know, a genie. Except she came out of a book instead of a lamp. I would have told you before except she didn't want me to. Plus, I've been a bit distracted lately."

"Now listen, Ridley–"

"I beg your pardon, Doctor, but maybe it's you who should listen. Maybe you should hear my side of the story."

Humphrey's cheeks reddened.

I had come to accept Humphrey's wild notions of our uninvited visitor. Despite his radical personality change, however, Ridley appeared sane and reasonable. Keeping the shotgun levelled at Iugurtha's pretty face, I said, "Perhaps we should hear the boy out."

The doctor shook his great unkempt head but said nothing.

"Thanks, Uncle. It all started one night when I couldn't sleep. I went into the guest room looking for something to read, and I found this really interesting-looking book, but when I went to read it, I must have blacked out or something because the next thing I knew the book was on the floor, Iugurtha was sitting on the bed, and I was thinking, 'Whoa! Where the heck did she come from?'

"I'm looking at her when she says, 'Make a wish, Ridley,' and I think, right, either I'm nuts or a heckuva lot more tired than I thought. It takes me a second to recover from the shock of seeing her. Then I'm, like, 'What are you, my fairy godmother?' She just smiles this amazing smile. And that's when it hit me—she's a jinn."

"So you made a wish," I said.

Ridley nodded.

"What did you wish for, son?" Humphrey asked.

Ridley blushed. "There's a girl I know in Port Kerry, Rebecca Redwood. I wished for her to like me."

Humphrey grimaced. "You didn't need a demon to help you win a girl. If you'd tried, you might have won her by yourself."

"Thanks for the vote of confidence, Doctor, but Becky wouldn't have wanted a guy like me. Not the way I was."

"Why not?" I asked. "You're half Wildebear, after all. You have a lot going for you."

"Like what?"

I shrugged. "The strong Wildebear chin. The Wildebear height and intellect. The imposing Wildebear masculinity. You have all of that."

"The Wildebear modesty," Humphrey put in.

"Yes. Thank you, Doctor."

"Thanks, Uncle. But let's face it, I'm not the best-looking guy."

I attempted to reassure him. "It's what's inside that counts."

Ridley looked sceptical. I couldn't blame him—the truth was I wasn't much of a ladies' man myself.

"What harm could come from such a wish?"

Our heads swivelled as one at the sound of Iugurtha's voice.

"Only good, surely," she continued. "I tailored the metamorphosis to correspond to what would appeal most to the girl Rebecca. Typical of your species, most of the required changes were superficial. No dramatic physical alterations were necessary. They rarely are. In the end it was a simple affair—more to do with attitude than looks."

Ridley's smile reached his ears. "Becky and I have been seeing one another since Wednesday."

"You are dealing with a creature of the netherworld, son," Humphrey pointed out. "You will be required to pay for the services you've received. The price my wife paid before you, and who knows how many others before her."

"Nothing in life is free, I know that," Ridley said. "If there is a price, I'll pay it."

"You don't know what you're saying, boy!"

"That's very noble of you, Ridley," Iugurtha said. "What price the love of a woman for a man?"

She snapped her fingers. Ridley slumped like a marionette on strings. Humphrey and I looked on in horror as his eyes glazed over and his head lolled loosely from side to side.

"I made a few additional alterations," Iugurtha admitted.

I gripped the shotgun tightly. "Whatever you've done, undo it now."

Iugurtha ignored me. Perhaps she recognized my weakness. That I could not bring myself to shoot a woman (nor, if the truth be known, a skunk, a coyote, or door-to-door salespeople). She licked her thumb and used it to flip through the tome in her hands before selecting a page and allowing the book to fall to the floor. At least, it would have fallen had not it expanded upward and outward, becoming a rectangular slab about twice the size of a refrigerator. Within this slab, dark shades swirled incessantly, and I knew it to be the gate of which Humphrey had spoken.

The colours within the gate began to change. I caught a hint of purple. Seconds later, trees and fields of a sort I had never seen before coalesced into being. A mountain range loomed majestically in the distance against a violet sky. No sound emerged from this alien panorama to disturb the heavy silence that had settled in Ridley's room.

Just when I decided that it was all a trick involving a concealed holographic projector, a preposterously ugly creature swathed in mauve fur emerged from a thicket of extraterrestrial bracken and padded through the gate. After tracking alien mud into my home it stopped and stared up at me with wide, trusting eyes. I stared back.

Iugurtha stroked the creature's head and shooed it

back through the gate. "Off with you! Back to C'Mell. You would not be happy in this world."

She took Ridley by the hand and led him to the gate.

"Where are you taking him?" I demanded to know.

She didn't answer. Nor did she stop. I fired off a warning round. Buckshot blasted a jagged hole in the wall beyond her. It did not deter her in the least.

I lowered the shotgun. "Doctor, we're losing him!"

Looking about as taut as a jellyroll at my side, Doctor Humphrey still managed to convey the impression of a man about to leap into dazzling motion.

He held out his hand. "Here."

I handed over the shotgun, ashamed of whatever it was inside me that prevented me from shooting Iugurtha outright. As she prepared to step through the gate with Ridley at her side, Humphrey took careful aim at her back.

"Stop," he said, "or I will shoot you. I mean it!" He began pulling the trigger.

A slender woman dressed from head to toe in black darted past me. She jostled Humphrey, causing the weapon to discharge. Humphrey cursed. The shot missed Iugurtha. Fortunately, it missed Ridley too, blowing another section of the wall apart.

Still running, the woman in black tossed a silver object about the size of a brick through the gate. Before it could disappear into the tall grass of the alien world, it exploded into hundreds or even thousands of discrete units resembling small silver flies that whizzed away into the distance. Meanwhile, the intruder somersaulted over Ridley's bed and tumbled noisily into the space between the bed and the wall.

Undeterred by the activity surrounding her, Iugurtha stepped through the gate with Ridley in tow. The two of them had vanished into the purple forest within seconds. Dimly, I registered the woman in black climb to her feet and brush herself off, but her well-being was the last thing on my mind.

"She's taken him," I said. "Doctor, we've got to stop her!"

Beside me, Humphrey looked stricken.

I was Ridley's uncle, his guardian. It was up to me to go after the boy and bring him back. I stepped toward the gate—a small, uncertain step, neither far enough nor fast enough.

Before I could muster up the courage to continue, a squad of armed men and women, silver crescent moon pins gleaming upon their chests, stormed into Ridley's room. They streamed past Doctor Humphrey and me like a river flowing past rocks in its midst. The firepower they brought to bear on the gate could have wiped out an army. Rainer entered last. He relieved Humphrey of the shotgun before walking directly to the woman who had thrown the silver object through the gate. He helped her to her feet. She appeared unhurt, and favoured him with a smile.

Satisfied, Rainer turned and addressed the men and women surrounding us. "The gate is anchored. Good show, everyone. I confiscate it now in the name of Casa Terra."

A great bellow of despair sounded beside me. It took me a second to realize that it was Doctor Humphrey, calling out his wife's name. Before anyone could stop him, he lumbered forth and did what I should have done, had I not been such a coward.

He threw himself through the gate.

AN UNUSUALLY COMPELLING NOSE

AS HUMPHREY PASSED from one side of the gate to the other, his cry of "Joyce!" was truncated just before the sibilant end of its single syllable. As a result, those not in the know might have thought that he cried out, "Joy!" and that he made his leap through the gate out of some kind of religious fervour. I knew better, and watched in horror as Humphrey disappeared into the wilds of another world, in what was, in all likelihood, a dangerous and vain mission to find his wife. And no doubt Ridley too.

"Commander Fletcher!" Rainer barked. "Get in there!"

A tall man with chiselled features stepped from the ranks. Fletcher, I presumed. Three other soldiers, two men and a woman, fell in line behind him. Each of them sported an impressive array of gear including camouflage clothing, rugged knapsacks, and arcane equipment strapped to their belts. I shouted silent cheers of hooray as they inspected their sinister-looking weapons. Surely, these trained men and woman would fetch Ridley and Humphrey back.

As Commander Fletcher stepped confidently through the gate, I peered over his shoulder through the gateway. I saw that extraordinary violet sky embraced by a mass of dark clouds. At a glance, I took it to be a cold front moving in, until I realized that not only was the weather changing, the land itself was alive with motion. I watched entranced as mountains levelled themselves, day became night, and fields and trees transformed to lifeless dirt and rock. All this occurred in less time than it took for the commander to complete a half-step through the gate and for Rainer to shout, “Abort, Fletcher! Abort!”

It’s unlikely Fletcher heard the command. He had completed half a step through the gate before becoming utterly motionless, one foot suspended in the air above the roiling surface of the alien world. Fletcher’s comrades, panicked, leapt immediately to his aid, clutching at his hair, his arm, the heel of his left foot, whatever element of him protruded from the gate to afford purchase. They tugged and yanked but failed to get Fletcher back into the bedroom.

The surface of the alien world settled into a rocky monotony not unlike the surface of Earth’s moon. Alarmingly, the gate’s perspective now appeared to be several hundred meters above the surface. Fletcher’s comrades redoubled their efforts to haul their Commander back to safety, but with no luck.

Fletcher unfroze with a violent twitch of his head. He blinked once, threw his head back, and screamed—at least, it sure looked like he screamed, though I could not actually hear it on my side of the gate.

Horribly, Fletcher’s body diffracted and elongated until it stretched hundreds of meters toward the alien surface. When it reached the point of maximum elasticity, the part of him that remained in his fellow soldiers’ grasp slipped free and shot forward with tremendous speed. How fast that part of him was going when it joined the rest of him and hit the ground

I couldn't guess—but it was fast enough to make it one of the most gruesome deaths I could ever imagine.

My knees felt wobbly. I fell into the chair at Ridley's desk. From there, I listened as Rainer spewed profanity and barked instructions to his people with barely suppressed emotion. I watched his team search the room, scouring closets and drawers, and running what I supposed to be scanning devices over the floor, walls and ceilings. A separate team removed furniture from the room, while yet another carried in elaborate racks of equipment. I did not have the strength to protest any of this.

I summoned up just enough energy to get up and go downstairs to the den. I poured myself a scotch, slumped on the couch, and stared dumbly at the wall for God knows how long before Rainer came in and sat down opposite me.

"Sorry about your people," he said. "An unfortunate turn of events. Shame about Commander Fletcher, too. Tragic. But at least Fletcher knew what he was up against."

"And what is that?" I said with sudden vehemence. "Just what are we up against?"

Rainer withdrew a photograph from his wallet and handed it to me.

I stared at the woman in the photograph, at her blonde hair wildly askew. She stood on the deck of a large sailboat, her arms encircling Rainer's waist, a radiant smile illuminating her lovely face. I recognized that smile, having only recently made its acquaintance.

"But– But that's–"

"My wife," Rainer said. "Angelique."

He retrieved the picture and put it back in his wallet, which he slipped in his back pocket.

"I don't understand. Iugurtha and your wife are one and the same?"

"The woman in the picture—my wife, Angelique—does not really look like the creature you know as Iugurtha. If you look closely, you will observe that their facial features are similar, but not quite the same. The entity is quite a bit younger, for example." Rainer spoke calmly. Indeed, he might have been discussing the weather. "The body Iugurtha is using is comprised of several beings. One of whom happens to be my wife."

He allowed that to sink in. Which it did—like an especially buoyant duck.

I shook my head. "I don't understand any of this. One minute she's a demon, the next she's a genie, and now she's Frankenstein. Which is it?"

"We believe that some of the people Iugurtha abducts wind up as a part of her. Literally. Her body, and perhaps even her mind, is made up of several identities. My scientists believe her eyes to be artificial, and I'm inclined to agree. Why they should be an exception we don't know." Rainer reclined in his chair, his arm draped over the back. "Mr. Wildebear, although it may appear otherwise, we actually have the situation well in hand."

"Of course you do," I murmured, though I couldn't see how. One man was dead, Ridley had been abducted by a demon, and Humphrey was— well, God only knew where Humphrey was.

"We must remain positive. We've accomplished something quite tremendous this evening. We've anchored the gate."

"Bravo," I said, though I don't suppose I sounded very convincing.

"You've been through a lot," Rainer said. "Get some sleep. We'll talk about it in the morning." He rose. "Oh—one more thing. I want you to know that you may move about your house and property freely."

"That's very generous," I said. "Considering this is my home."

If he registered my sarcasm, he didn't let on. "Would you like to know why I am able to permit such freedom?"

"Not particularly."

"Because of how closely we are monitoring you."

"Good for you. Wait—how closely?"

"Your every breath. Your every heartbeat."

I assumed he was exaggerating. Still— "That can't possibly be legal."

"This is more important than the law."

I was indignant. "How can something be more important than the law?"

"When it is to protect the law. You see, Mr. Wildebear, if we fail, there will be no law, or much of anything else. You need to know that any attempt to sabotage this operation or compromise our presence here will not be tolerated. Stay close to home, and out of our way."

"Look," I said. "I don't want any trouble. I just want Ridley back. And Humphrey."

"Of course," he said. "I understand."

I was glad one of us did.

He left.

I finished my tumbler of Lagavulin, and poured myself another.

And then another.

I awoke sprawled on the couch in the den. I stumbled to the kitchen and made myself a cup of coffee, which I drank black, the two sips I was able to get down. I tried to make myself believe that what had happened the night before had been nothing but a scotch-induced nightmare. Surely Ridley and Humphrey were asleep in their respective rooms—it wasn't unusual for either of them to sleep late.

Two strangers clad in grey overalls passed outside the kitchen heading toward the front door. They were carrying something between them covered in a brown tarp. One adjusted her grip on the tarp, allowing me a glimpse of her burden. An enormous bloodshot eye peered out at me from within a mass of red ochre tentacles. Beneath the eye was a gaping hole trimmed with several hundred tiny fangs.

The eye locked on me. I leapt from my stool with a cry, my coffee splattering every cupboard and wall within reach. The monster bearers either didn't notice my reaction or didn't care, continuing on down the hall out of sight. The front door opened. A moment later a truck revved up and drove away.

No longer able to deny the events of the night before, my impulse was to flee to Summerside and and arrange to sell this demon-infested house. I took a series of deep breaths. I couldn't leave. Not if there was even the slightest chance that Ridley lived. I had failed him too many times already. I would not do so again.

Also, it was pretty clear that Rainer had no intention of letting me leave.

The door to Ridley's room was ajar. I shoved it the

rest of the way open. It clanged off something metallic that hadn't been there the night before and bounced back at me. I stopped it with my foot and surveyed the changes a single night had wrought.

Not a single possession of Ridley's remained to proclaim the room as his. Every single stick of furniture had been cleared away and replaced with rack after rack of scientific equipment. Several scientist types worked furiously, monitoring equipment and tapping rapidly on elaborate-looking consoles. Two soldiers stood in the centre of the room, directly before the gate. Another one kept an eye out the room's only window. Ridley's room was unusually large—it was actually the master bedroom; I'd given it to him because I didn't need the space—still, Casa Terra's redecorating had left little in the way of elbow room.

The soldiers appeared unconcerned by my sudden arrival. None of them so much as blinked when I leaned into the room for a better look at the gate—except for the one looking out the window. That one turned and frowned at me. It was Schmitz, the man with the bad breath and malformed head who had struck me in the tunnel. We locked eyes, and a chill coursed through my spine—I haven't been on the receiving end of such a malevolent glare since my fourth grade teacher caught me carving my name into my desk.

I snapped my gaze away from his and focused my thoughts elsewhere. The gate now led to someplace new. Were I to pass through to the other side now, I would find myself in as harsh looking a realm as I'd ever seen: an endless expanse of ice, water, and snow. I felt distressed. What if Ridley was stuck some place like that? Could he even survive in such an environment?

I was startled by a voice at my side. "Help yourself."

It was Rainer. He motioned toward a small table sitting in the hallway. "They're for everyone."

"I'm not hungry."

"No, I don't suppose. Mr. Wildebear, your nephew's belongings have been safely stored. You can have access to them whenever you like." He took hold of my arm and propelled me into Ridley's room. "I have someone I would like you to meet."

We stopped before a cramped workstation. He placed a hand on the shoulder of the woman who sat there. "Miss Sarah Frey, without a doubt the most brilliant extra-spatial analyst in the world. Sarah, meet Barnabus Wildebear."

The most brilliant extra-spatial analyst in the world was so absorbed in her work that she didn't even bother to look up.

"Sarah believes your people are still alive," Rainer said. "I thought you might be interested in what she has to say."

Sarah brushed a raven lock out of her eyes and leaned in to peer at her monitor more closely. I wondered how long I would be required to stand there. Abstractly, I noted that she had a pretty face featuring an unusually compelling nose: snub at the end, with a smattering of freckles at the top.

"I might be interested," I said. "Were she to actually say anything."

Sarah looked up at me. "I'm sorry." She pushed her chair back. "Look. I won't lie to you. I don't know for a fact they're still alive. All I know for sure is that what happened to Commander Fletcher didn't happen to them."

"How do you know?" I asked.

"Because what happened to Fletcher was a fluke.

The gate doesn't always lead to the same time or place. Fletcher got caught in one of its transitions. Thirty-million years elapsed in a heartbeat. Getting caught in that is what killed him. Mr. Wildebear, how much do you know about the gate?"

"Not much. Just that it appears to lead to other worlds, as crazy as that sounds. Iugurtha's world."

Sarah's eyes widened. "That's not a name you should say out loud."

"Why not?"

"How can you ask that? You've already personally experienced how dangerous the entity's name can be."

"What do you mean?"

"We watched the whole thing on the monitors. You said the entity's name out loud and then let it in through the gate."

"You mean Humphrey's story was true?"

"Every bit of it. It's all in our database. We can play it back for you, if you like."

"No, thank you." I didn't fancy the idea of watching myself beat up my good friend Doctor Peter Humphrey. "Doctor Humphrey thought this entity of yours was some kind of demon. What is she actually?"

"Your friend is a little superstitious," Sarah said. "I don't expect to find any fantasy worlds beyond the gate. Still..."

"What?"

"There have been some transitions that have been difficult to explain."

"Such as?"

"I wouldn't care to speculate until I've gathered

more data." She glanced at her console. "Speaking of which..."

Rainer took the hint. "Sarah is working hard on getting your people back. Perhaps we should leave her to her work."

Sarah shot me a brief sympathetic smile.

It did nothing to lift my spirits.

Feeling sick, I stumbled out the back door of my house where I paced compulsively atop the expanse of crabgrass that constituted most of my backyard. Before I knew what I was doing I was making a beeline toward the woods, Rainer's dire warnings having completely slipped my mind. I forced myself not to think about the disastrous events of the night before and to concentrate instead on the majesty surrounding me. The countryside around my property is among the finest the island has to offer. The path to nearby Port Kerry wends through a forest of towering pine interspersed with poplar and birch. I savoured the soft crunch of pine needles beneath my feet and the twitter of forest creatures hidden from view. In time, the forest did its magic, and I felt capable of breathing again. The wind, whispering in from away, caressed not just the lofty conifers around me, but all in its path, and as it embraced me it breathed a simple truth into my ears:

That a walk in the woods wasn't going to do a damned thing to help Ridley.

Some instinct made me glance off the path to my left. A man was watching me from beneath the canopy of pine. A silver crescent moon glittered upon his chest.

Schmitz.

Abruptly, I remembered Rainer's instructions to stay close to home. Was Schmitz here to drag me back? Pretending not to see him, I hurried on down the path.

"Mr. Wildebear, wait."

Schmitz jogged the handful of steps it took to catch up to me. A dull ache persisted on the side of my head where he had struck me with the butt of his gun the day before—a reminder to conduct myself with caution.

"Nice woods you have here, Mr. Wildebear," he said upon reaching me. "Well done."

I increased my pace.

"Going for a little walk, are we?"

"That's right. A little walk."

"Where you going?"

"What's it to you?"

He grabbed my shoulder, forcing me to stop. "You're not safe here."

I faced him defiantly, adjusting my stance and steeling my abdomen, just in case. Although I am not a small man, this fellow Schmitz scared the bejeezus out of me. He was ugly—damned ugly—having been cursed with a head that looked as if it had been jammed painfully, but firmly, into a piece of farming equipment back in some early, significant stage of development. Although he was shorter than I, his close-cropped auburn hair bristling about level with my chin, he was much stockier. I would have had better luck trying to knock down one of the big pines on either side of us than try to take him.

"I've looped the surveillance satellites," he said, speaking softly. It was all I could do to remain close enough to hear him—did the man not own a toothbrush? "But they'll see through that before long, so we'll need to be quick about this."

"Surveillance satellites?"

"Rainer's a good man," he said. "A little off his nut since losing Angelique, but I wouldn't hold that against him."

"So?"

"He has plans to interrogate you, using Mind Snoop."

"Mind Snoop?"

"He thinks you know something, something you may not even know you know. It won't take him long to figure out what it is using Mind Snoop. But..."

"But what?"

"Here's the thing. Mind Snoop is . . ."

"What?"

"It could leave you . . ."

"What? What?"

"An incontinent husk of a man." He fished in his pocket and pulled out a tiny vial containing a bubbly blue solution. "This is an antidote. Drink it as soon as possible to make sure you're protected. Don't act any differently during the session, just answer like you normally would. Rainer doesn't have a whole lot of experience with Mind Snoop. With a little luck he won't realize it's not working. When you're still okay at the end of the procedure he'll be surprised, but relieved."

I stared at the vial. "How do I know this isn't some kind of poison?"

Schmitz smiled–the first time such an expression had crossed his misbegotten face in the brief time that I'd known him. It sent chills down my spine. "You don't."

"Why are you helping me?"

He shrugged. "Because."

"What kind of answer's that?"

"The only kind you're going to get."

I stared at the vial some more, then took it. "Thanks. I think."

Propelled by nervous energy I started off down the path. Looking back, I was relieved to see that Schmitz wasn't following. He wasn't even looking at me. He was just standing where I'd left him, idly kicking a fallen branch with his boot.

Shortly afterward I deposited the vial in a garbage can beside a grocery store on the edge of the village. No power on Earth could have made me drink a single drop of whatever rubbish was inside the vial. Not for an instant did I believe all this Mind Snoop nonsense. Just the same Schmitz was clearly up to something. Had he been trying to poison me? If so, surely there were subtler ways to do that.

I was just about to turn around and go home when I spotted someone familiar entering the grocery store: Sarah Frey, the world's best extra-spatial analyst. It irked me, seeing her out here. She was supposed to be figuring out how to get Ridley and Humphrey back home, not fetching groceries.

I set out to remind her of this fact. Following her into the store, I spotted her by the fruit and vegetable section, sorting through a sorry lot of wrinkled green peppers. Before I could confront her, the soporific muzak emanating from the store's public address system was interrupted by a voice reverberating through the aisles.

"Will-de-bear. Will-de-bear!"

I jerked my head up at what had sounded like my name.

"Will-de-bear, are you out there?"

I stood transfixed. It was the inimitable growl of none other than Doctor Peter Humphrey. There was no mistaking that voice, though it possessed an odd, halting quality about it now. Could he have returned through the gate and followed me into town? Humphrey being Humphrey, he would think nothing of commandeering the store's public address system in a bid to get my attention. There was a bizarre quality to the sound of his voice, but I chalked that up to the store's poor sound system.

Forgetting all about Sarah, I made for the cashier's station where I supposed Humphrey to be, hoping that he had brought Ridley back with him through the gate.

"Will-de-bear–Help! Quick–"

Good Lord, was Humphrey in trouble at the front of the store? I broke into a mad run. Skidding to a halt near the cashier, I looked wildly about. Humphrey was nowhere to be seen. Neither was Ridley. Was I in the grip of some feverish hallucination, the only one present capable of hearing the doctor's voice? No–like me, the cashier and my fellow customers were staring around them with alarm.

Humphrey's voice ploughed on. "Will-de-bear! Help me!"

"Doctor! Where the devil are you?"

His voice was fading in and out like waves breaking on a distant shore. He was shouting something now, but I couldn't make out the words.

"Doctor, I can barely hear you!"

"Will-de-bear, I need my–"

"What, Doctor? What do you need?"

Suddenly such was the clarity of his voice that it was as if he were standing right in front of me. "My bag, Will-de-bear. I need you to bring me my bag!"

FRIENDS LIKE THESE

THE MUZAK RETURNED to its prominence in the middle of a song featuring heavy strings and a mellow saxophone. I wandered the small store's handful of aisles in a daze, reflecting on Doctor Humphrey's final words. His bag? Bring it where? I didn't even know where the man was. He certainly wasn't in the store. Could he have reached out to me from beyond the gate? Was such a thing possible?

I needed to think, preferably without muzak driving me to distraction. I bolted out through the front door and found a light post in the parking lot to hold me up. I closed my eyes and tried to control my breathing. After a few minutes I became aware of the pleasing scent of a perfume I couldn't immediately identify—something peachy, with a smidgeon of lavender.

Someone touched my shoulder. I opened my eyes to see Sarah Frey standing beside me.

"Are you all right?" she asked.

I let my breath out with a whoosh. "Sure. Fine. I'm fine."

"Seems your friend wants you to bring him his bag."

"It sounded like he was right there, talking to me," I said. "But when I went looking for him, I couldn't find him anywhere."

"That's because he wasn't in the store. We would

have known if he'd returned through the gate. His voice must have been piped into the public address system via the internet."

"But you just said he's on the other side of the gate. How could he do that from there?"

"That," she said, "is the million-dollar question."

We looked at one another and something unusual happened, something that sounds corny now, but that felt quite profound at the time. When I looked into Sarah's eyes, it was as if some kind of energy passed between us—a rush, a jolt of electricity, I wasn't sure exactly what. If you had asked me before, I would have said I didn't believe in that sort of thing. And yet there it was.

"Walk with me?" she asked, hooking her arm in mine.

I allowed her to lead me toward the woods, understanding now that I was in the presence of an unusually attractive woman—not just pretty, but highly intelligent. I told myself that this was interesting, but of no real significance. She was a conduit to getting Ridley and Humphrey back, nothing more.

As we walked, she plucked a Brown-Eyed Susie from the ground and waved it idly about.

"The air smells so sweet out here," she said, breathing deeply of the forest air. "You're lucky to live in such a beautiful place."

"I know it. Lucky to have grown up here." We passed under the shade of the first few trees. "Don't you have lots of work to do?"

"Plenty, but we're running a few tests right now. Thought I'd come out here and think while I waited."

I decided to accept that, and took a few seconds to appreciate our surroundings. "I take my classes out here on field trips each spring. I like them to see what the island must have looked like before most of the trees were cut down last century to make boats. Not many stands like this one left on the island."

Sarah nodded appreciatively "Barnabus, about your nephew Ridley."

I tensed. "What about him? Is he okay?"

"I'm sorry. I didn't mean to alarm you. I don't have any new information. It's just that Ridley is the twenty-fourth person the entity has abducted so far, that we know of. We've done extensive background checks on each of them. Some we even knew personally."

I relaxed a bit. "Angelique."

"That's right, Angelique. I suppose Rainer told you about her. A terrible loss. Barnabus, did you know that Angelique was a fifth-degree black belt in Matsubayashi-Ryu Karate?"

"I did not."

"The thing is this, Barnabus. Every single man, woman, and child the entity has abducted has some exceptional talent. The entity's quite selective. San Chow Ming, for example—a small-arms specialist and an award-winning marksman. Doctor Humphrey's wife? A champion equestrian."

I had known that about Joyce. "You're not seriously suggesting that Ridley has some special talent like that?"

"There has to be something about him. Benjamin Muir, abducted seven months ago, is a specialist in guerrilla warfare. Maybe Ridley has some specialized body of knowledge like that."

"He's only fifteen. I can't think of anything. Unless you consider insolence something the entity might be interested in."

Sarah smiled. "Give it some thought. It might not be something obvious."

"These skills–they all sound martial in nature."

"They do," Sarah admitted.

"Almost as if the entity is putting together some kind of army." The sudden realization stopped me dead in my tracks. What in blazes had Ridley gotten himself into? "Is that it? My nephew's been recruited into an army? He was pretty good at board games when he was younger, now that I think of it. Strategy, that sort of thing."

"Maybe that's it," Sarah said. "Whatever the case, you have my word we'll do our best to get him back."

I believed her, but if Ridley was caught up in some kind of bizarre intergalactic war, what chance did I really have of getting him back safely?

We emerged from the woods near my back porch. I lingered, reluctant to part with this intriguing woman. Despite many burning questions, I found myself at a loss for words.

Sarah, on the other hand, said exactly the right thing. "Come with me to the lab. See what we're up to. Maybe there's some way you can contribute."

I remembered Rainer's warning to stay out of the way. The heck with him.

"Count me in," I told her.

Little had changed in my nephew's room since the morning. Iugurtha's gate remained the dominant feature. Within the gate a lone avian form circled menacingly, silhouetted before a blood-red sun. Enormous rocks, like the discarded building blocks of giant children, cast long shadows on a shrub-encrusted rise. The gate could have been a giant travel brochure for Texas or New Mexico.

Rainer paced impatiently from workstation to workstation, pausing occasionally to peer over shoulders and issue caustic remarks. He spotted me and frowned but said nothing. The stone-faced soldiers were unchanged since I'd last seen them, except for the absence of Schmitz from their ranks. Any trace that my nephew Ridley had ever inhabited the room had been scrubbed away like a stain.

I excused myself from Sarah and made my way to the front hall closet. I found what I was looking for on the top shelf. A lick of orange flame emblazoned the front of the battered old baseball cap—the logo of Ridley's favourite baseball team, the Summerside Silver Foxes. Ridley had worn the cap virtually every day before his personality change.

I brought the cap to his room, where I stood in the doorway and considered where it might best be featured.

Ah, yes.

I strode forward, reached up, and—

"Oof!" A snub barrel of advanced weaponry poked me plum in the belly. "What the—"

"Sir," an incongruously baby-faced soldier said. "No one may approach the gate, sir."

Rainer appeared at my side, hands clasped behind his back. "Problem?"

Baby-face never took his eyes off me. "No one may approach the gate. Those are your orders, sir."

"Mr. Wildebear?" Rainer regarded me with one eyebrow arched. "Not considering a little interplanetary jaunt, are we?"

"Of course not. I just want to hang Ridley's cap up

somewhere. There ought to be something of the boy left in the room."

"We did clean the place out pretty well," Sarah conceded.

Rainer scanned his surroundings as if for the first time, observing the walls, floors and ceiling, now devoid of even a hint of the room's former occupant. "At ease, lad," he told Baby-face. "What did you have in mind?" he asked me.

Baby-face stepped back, but remained positioned to intercept me should I try for a dash through the gate. I made no such move. Instead, I stepped clearly to the side, rose on my tiptoes, and hung Ridley's cap on the top left-hand corner of the gate.

An audible gasp arose from those about me. "Good God, man!" a male voice exclaimed.

The cap sat there perfectly fine, in no way disrupting the operation of the gate. You could see the cap from anywhere in the room. It made me feel better, seeing something of Ridley's up there.

Rainer chewed contemplatively on his lower lip. The index finger of his right hand performed two swift strokes of his moustache. With his other hand, he reached into his back pocket and pulled out something orange and silky. A woman's scarf. He tied the two loose ends into an elegant bow and offered it to me.

"If you please," he said, not having the advantage of my six-foot, two-inch frame.

"Certainly," I told him, and hung Angelique's scarf—for it had to be hers—on the top right-hand corner of the gate.

Rainer nodded. "That's what this is all about," he

announced to the room. "Lest we forget. Thank you, Mr. Wildebear."

"You're welcome," I said, studying Rainer's features, trying to guess his thoughts. Was he just humouring me?

At her workstation, Sarah donned a wireless headphone mike. "Sebastian, let me see an abridged log for the time I was gone." She stepped over to the food and beverage table as an image began to manifest itself before her console.

It was a miniature hologram of Ridley's room. The jaw-dropping realism of the thing left me goggling. I marvelled as tiny, three-dimensional doppelgangers of Rainer's team went about their sundry tasks. If I reached a hand in, I could have clutched the obsessively pacing Rainer and lifted him, wriggling and perhaps crying out, into the air.

I resisted the temptation to try, and accepted a glass of icy cola from Sarah, who had returned to her workstation with drinks and a plate of fresh cantaloupe. I swigged a mouthful of the cola and watched events unfold in the hologram just as they had a few short hours earlier in real life.

A snappy holographic zoom and Iugurtha's gate came to comprise the entire hologram. As Sarah and I watched, the gate experienced a transition quite a bit different from the one that had claimed the life of Commander Fletcher. A gentle ripple passed from top to bottom across the aperture of the gate, leaving in its wake almost, but not entirely, pitch black.

"What's that?" I asked. "Deep space?"

Sarah shook her head. "It's one of those transitions I mentioned earlier, difficult to get a handle on. According to our probes, what we're looking at is almost wall-to-wall organic material. It looks black because there's no light source illuminating it, except for the little getting through from our side of the gate."

"Organic material? You mean we're looking at the insides of something that's alive?"

"That's correct."

"Why the devil would the gate lead to the inside of a living creature?"

"Barnabus, I've been studying this gate for over four years. In that time I've concluded it could lead just about anywhere."

"You told me before you don't expect to find any fantasy worlds beyond the gate."

"That's right. I just meant I don't expect to find anything contradicting the laws of nature." She smiled. "Of course, it's always possible there are a few laws we don't know about yet."

I returned the smile–for about two seconds, after which it dawned on me that I didn't feel very well.

Sarah peered at me closely. "You look a little peaked. Are you all right?"

"Oh, nothing. It's just that–just that –"

Just that I needed to lie down before I fell down.

I muttered an apology to Sarah–something about breakfast having gone down the wrong way–and retreated to the den, where I dimmed the lights and collapsed on the couch. My mumbled excuse was of course just a polite falsehood: breakfast hadn't gone down the wrong way, since I hadn't, in fact, had any breakfast or lunch at all, apart from two sips of coffee and a slurp of cola.

A knock sounded on the den door. Sarah, come to check on me? I struggled to sit up. "Come in."

To my disappointment not Sarah but Rainer strolled in to hover over me. "Not feeling well?"

"I'm afraid not."

"Dizziness? Nausea? Bit of a dry mouth?"

"All of the above, as a matter of fact." I looked up at him. "Why do you ask?"

Rainer settled in my easy chair. "I'm afraid you've been drugged."

"Drugged?"

Rainer scrutinized first one, then two of his exquisitely manicured fingernails. "You are being prepared for a procedure called Mind Snoop. I would have preferred to avoid such an unpleasant, invasive procedure, but sadly I do not have the luxury of time. Please do not take it personally. You are simply a victim of circumstances."

"But I haven't been administered any drugs."

"She put it in the cola."

"I beg your pardon?"

Rainer cleared his throat. "When you wouldn't take the drug from Mr. Schmitz, I had Sarah put it in the cola." He leaned back in his easy chair. "We will begin the procedure shortly."

I sat stunned at the knowledge that Sarah had been my Judas.

V

IGNOMINIOUS PROCEDURES

Schmitz stalked into the den with the poise of an unusually ugly panther and slid gracefully onto the couch beside me. A whiff of his breath almost pushed my stomach over the edge. When I glared at him and moved over, he grinned.

"Thought you could fool me with that bit about the antidote," I grumbled.

His grin evolved into a sneer. "And yet here you are."

I let the matter drop.

"Could I have your attention please, Sebastian?" Rainer said.

Silence.

"Sebastian," Rainer repeated.

"Perhaps we need headphones in here, sir," Schmitz said finally.

"I had imaging installed just today. Sebastian!"

"I'm here, gentlemen," a male voice said, from just to the left of where Rainer was sitting.

The voice had come from out of thin air. My interest piqued, I sat up, my nausea momentarily forgotten. Did Casa Terra have an invisible man in their ranks? Unlikely. Someone named Sebastian had turned on the holographic display for Sarah, I remembered.

More than likely Sebastian was just an ordinary man in a control booth somewhere.

"What took you so long?" Rainer asked.

"What do you expect, asking me to multi-task with the pitiful bandwidth you've given me?"

"You're a field unit, that's all the DSP you get. Still, you should be concentrating as many resources on this session as possible."

"You're getting forty-seven percent of me, which is all I can spare. I wouldn't complain. Downstairs in the lab, Giorgio is only getting twelve. All his samples are taking twice as long. He's fit to be tied."

"Serves him right, always monopolizing the network," Schmitz said. "Okay, Sebastian. Record these proceedings under the filename 'Wildebear interrogation,' please."

"Certainly, Mr. Schmitz."

What was this about a lab in my basement? I slumped back on the couch. Ordinarily, I might have been impressed by all this technology, but just then all I felt was ill, and ill-used.

Rainer turned to me. "Mr. Wildebear, please tell me your full name and your age."

I had already decided not to comply with anything the two men asked of me. I intended to resist with every fibre of my being, every ounce of my strength. In the end what I wanted did not enter into it. My mouth opened of its own accord, and I spoke. It resembled regurgitation, this manner of speaking, except that instead of the contents of my stomach, out of my mouth tumbled words.

"Barnabus Jehosophys Wildebear," I retched, doubling over as the words muscled their way out of me. "Thirty-nine years old– oh God in Heaven–." So much for just words tumbling out.

Afterward, spittle clung to my chin and I could not stop my hands from shaking.

Rainer swore. "Good Lord, is that typical? Seems a bit much, don't you think?"

"Oh, I've seen lots worse than that," Schmitz said. "Sebastian?"

"So far so good. Tell you what–I'll display Mr. Wildebear's charts so you can monitor his rate of physical deterioration as the questioning progresses."

It was Rainer's turn to frown. Two holographic charts appeared in the air, one each before Schmitz and Rainer. I was having trouble focussing properly and could not quite make out any of the information on the charts.

Rainer shifted in the easy chair to face me better. "All right, Mr. Wildebear. What is your relationship with the boy named Ridley Doucette?"

"I'm his uncle," a voice from within me intoned, a voice only barely recognisable as my own. "I became his sole GUARDIAN following the death of his MOTHER just over... oh dear God... just over... TWO YEARS AGO."

"What do you do for a living?"

"I teach junior high school ENGLISH. I– I–"

"Thank you. What's your mother's name?"

"Julia Rosalie Wildebear. She passed AWAY seven years ago."

"He's starting to volunteer information," Schmitz said. "That's usually a sign he's ready."

"But is what he's saying the truth?" Rainer asked.

"How about a couple more questions just to be sure."

Rainer nodded. “Be my guest.”

Schmitz turned to me. “Mr. Wildebear, sir. Do you have a favourite password that you like to use?”

“Xavier,” I gasped. “My–favourite–password–is Xavier3891.”

“Excellent. Have you ever been in a long-term romantic relationship, sir?”

Despite all efforts not to say anything–profound, superhuman efforts, I might add–I found myself saying, “Noooo....”

“It is not my intention to humiliate the man,” Rainer said.

“He’s thirty-nine years old, sir. Myself, I wouldn’t admit to something like that unless I absolutely had to.”

“Sebastian?”

“Mr. Wildebear’s responses correspond to what we have on file. However, that alone does not prove that Mind Snoop is working.”

Schmitz regarded me scornfully. “It’s obvious to me it’s working.”

“However, the physiological data I’m accumulating confirms that Mind Snoop is indeed operating effectively,” Sebastian added. “So I concur.”

Rainer nodded. “Good. Mr. Wildebear, from here on in you will not consciously know how to answer many of my questions. Don’t worry about that. We’re relying on your unconscious to supply the answers. Now–and this is the thing–please don’t fight your unconscious. Allow it to answer as it sees fit. It will be a lot better for you if you do.”

I levelled an unsteady gaze at him, filling it with as much loathing as I could. If he felt the slightest bit intimidated by the cross-eyed man doing all he could not to whimper sitting across from him, he concealed it well.

"Mr. Wildebear, it's our perception that yesterday evening at precisely nine forty-two pm an alien entity assumed control over your mind and body for a span of forty-seven seconds. Did this in fact occur?"

A deep and guttural "YEEESSS!" dislodged itself from the very core of my being.

"What does that blinking red light on the chart mean, Sebastian?" Rainer asked.

"The subject has burst a blood vessel in his left eye."

Rainer peered into my left eye. "So he has."

"It's to be expected, sir," Schmitz said.

Rainer thought about this for a moment, then continued. "Mr. Wildebear, the entity brought into this world a book, a rather special book. It was purchased this past Christmas by your friend Doctor Humphrey as a present for his wife Joyce, and subsequently fell into your nephew's hands. This is where you come in. While you were under the entity's control, we believe you acquired information derived from this book. Tell me. What did you learn?"

As far as I could recall, I remembered nothing of those forty-seven seconds, and certainly nothing about Iugurtha's book, and even if I did remember something I would not have wanted to share it. But, of course, Mind Snoop yanked the memories out of me anyway, and what my unconscious revealed astonished me as much as anyone else in the room.

I spoke of fantastic realms, conjuring up visions of worlds I could not have dreamt up on my own. I related mathematical data I could not begin to comprehend, and gibbered poetry in languages I did not speak, languages I had never heard spoken. I laughed maniacally at jokes I didn't understand, weeping as I laughed, each utterance out of my mouth more unbearable than the last. Discomfort segued into pain, pain into torture. My voice grew hoarse, dwindling to but a whisper and finally to nothing at all.

A pen appeared between my fingers. So armed, I drew maps and scribbled computations, writing first one hand and then the other into a tangled knot of fingers. When at long last my tortured digits twitched forth one final, damnable doodle, that single jot, bled out of me, seemed to bleed forever.

I opened my eyes. I was staring straight up at the ceiling. At a greying expanse of popcorn stucco, with yellow water stains creeping about the edges where the ceiling met the walls. I could see patterns in the water stains. It amused me to pick them out–here a cat, there an octopus. Until the very fact of the water stains began to bother me. They were unseemly. The entire ceiling of my bedroom needed to be replaced.

Out of the room's sole window I glimpsed wisps of dark cloud scudding across the bright face of the moon. Sounds entered my awareness, gentle, beeping sounds that had no business being in this place. I angled my head to see where they were coming from, and was puzzled to discover medical equipment stacked beside my bed, hooked up to me. Alarmed, I tried to get out of bed, but I was so weak that I could barely lift my sheets.

A newspaper rattled near the entrance to the room. Using all my might, I lifted my head. Beyond the linen-swaddled lumps constituting my feet I spied a matronly woman sitting in an overstuffed wingback chair. The woman's upper torso was partially concealed behind an edition of the *Summerside Journal-Pioneer.* It was all I could do to hold my head up—within seconds it returned to the pillow as if yanked there by a team of oxen.

Time seemed oddly dilated. I blinked, and a man stood at the side of my bed, gazing down at me benignly. "Hello, Wildebear," he said.

It all came back to me at the sound of his voice.

Ridley, Humphrey.

Iugurtha.

Casa Terra.

Mind Snoop.

Vertigo gripped me. The room spun wildly about me. I clawed at the bed with both hands, grasping the sheets, grunting with the sheer effort of holding on.

"How do you feel?" Rainer asked.

"Make it stop," I croaked. My voice was like sandpaper in my throat.

"What stop?"

"The bed. Spinning..."

"Don't worry, your bed's not going anywhere. Neither are you. Not for some time, I'm afraid."

"What do you mean?"

"You've been sick, Wildebear. But you're getting better. We're looking after you. Doing our best to make you well again."

"Sick? How long –?"

"Three days."

Three days! "Mind Snoop did this to me. You. You did it to me!"

"Yes. I did it to you."

"Why?"

"What choice did I have?"

Time must have shifted again because suddenly his face was inches in front of mine, silhouetted before the room's single light source. The wash of brilliant white light spilling off his round head lent him the air of a prophet.

"Chaos," he hissed. "Unfathomable creatures from unimaginable realms inflicting terror for no reason other than to amuse themselves. Death with but the flick of a... of a tentacle, Wildebear."

An image flashed through my mind of the monstrous creature Rainer's people had carried out of my house. Just what the heck were we dealing with here?

"Madness!" Rainer continued. "Insanity the likes of which civilised men like us can't even imagine, let alone endure. Versus sanctuary from all that. Tell me, Wildebear. Where is the choice in that?"

I taught junior high school. Mere insanity I could endure. The spittle Rainer was projecting into my face was another story. Something was amiss with the man. Even in the midst of my suffering I could see it. Subtle nuances of manner–his delicate enunciation, for instance–laid bare the truth. The warm, musky scent of Lagavulin wafting into my nostrils confirmed it. My choler began to rise. Was it not enough that this man had incapacitated me that he must add insult to injury by plundering my scotch? And yet despite his condition–or perhaps because of it– I did not doubt for an instant that what he was telling me was nothing other than the cold, hard truth.

"There's an idea I've been toying with." He moved out of the path of the light and became mortal once again.

"More of a suspicion, really. The idea that... well, that there are no choices. Not really. Because I've tried to make my own choices, Wildebear, really I have. But the consequences of my choices have always been so terrible that I... that... well." He stopped, cleared his throat, and lowered his gaze to the floor.

When he looked up again, he said briskly, "You'll feel better in a day or two. I could let you go then. Sooner or later despite our best efforts the gate will break free and become a book once again. We'll take it and lock it away, you'll go back and teach your classes, and everything will be fine for a few weeks, maybe even months. But then, even though we have it locked up, the book will show up again. Some damned fool will find it, open it, God only knows what will come out of it and lay waste to Summerside or Charlottetown, and I'll be right back at square one.

"Or...." He canted his head to one side and narrowed his eyes, regarding me as if I had sprouted a second head. "We do things a little differently. And do you know why?"

I made no attempt to answer.

"Because you know things now, Wildebear. Things you didn't know before."

He had as much of my attention as I could muster given my condition. Nevertheless, I understood he was talking about the bizarre information I had revealed while under the influence of Mind Snoop. Information that had no business being in my brain, and that might as well not have been there for all the conscious knowledge I had of it.

"What things?" I asked, thinking it would be nice to know what I was supposed to know.

"Why the chicken crossed the road," Rainer said.

"How to get the caramel in the Caramilk bar." Something tugged at the corner of Rainer's lips. "How the gate works. Among other things. We extracted what we could, enough to give us a good idea what's in that head of yours, but we couldn't get it all. Not even close. Not without killing you."

"Thanks for that," I muttered, not feeling particularly grateful.

"You've become an asset of tremendous importance, Wildebear. I had hoped Mind Snoop would relieve you of that burden, but it wasn't to be. I'm sorry about that."

"What now?" I whispered, unable to speak any louder.

"Now we see about making you better."

"And then?"

"Then we have no choice." Whatever was tugging at Rainer's lips successfully yanked them into something resembling a smile. "We implement Plan B."

PLAN B

THE BRUTAL MEANS Rainer and his malodorous associate Schmitz had employed to rip the information they wanted from my brain had two unfortunate consequences.

That Mind Snoop hadn't entirely worked meant that I would likely remain in Rainer's custody for some time. More distressing was the toll that Mind Snoop appeared to have taken on my health. I couldn't sit up without experiencing severe dizziness and nausea. My throat felt as if someone had taken a cheese-grater to it, and I was plagued by an annoying twitch in my right eyelid.

As I lay in bed bemoaning these symptoms, I discovered that I couldn't feel anything in my left leg, from my thigh to the tips of my toes. How Mind Snoop could have affected my leg in such a way was difficult to understand, and more than a little alarming.

In fact, I was terrified. Just what had these people done to me?

Rainer provided a thick stack of aged *Reader's Digests* to help ease my anxiety. The gesture did nothing of the sort. Nor did it reduce the animosity I felt toward the man. For one thing, they were my own *Reader's Digests*—I had read them all already. Also, beyond the magazines (and an overwhelming urge to punch him right in the nose), Rainer had given me a lot to think about.

Iugurtha had done something to my brain. Filled it with knowledge that I myself, though it existed right there in my own head, couldn't get at. Rainer wanted it so badly that he was willing to hurt me to get it. Whatever his "Plan B" consisted of, it almost certainly didn't bode well for me.

Bedridden and surrounded by umpteen Casa Terra soldiers, I couldn't just up and hightail it out of there. I had no choice but to stay put and get back on my feet as quickly as possible. I figured I would gain Rainer's confidence, lull him into a false sense of security, and then, at the very first opportunity, act. Though precisely what such an act might consist of eluded me.

Weak and feverish, my purchase on the here and now deteriorated. My mind traversed the events of my life like a spider wandering forlornly in an infinite web. Traces of the Mind Snoop drug must have remained in my system, singling out specific memories and playing them over and over. The majority of these waking dreams featured my sister Katerina.

Most of the memories were insignificant. Flotsam from my childhood long since relegated to the trash heap of consciousness. Eating supper with Katerina at the dining room table. Helping her wash the dishes. Chatting idly as she brushed the tangles out of her long, red hair. A childhood's worth of petty events barely worth remembering, yet filed away just the same, turning up now like snapshots from a long-forgotten photo album.

Belly-laughing over a game of Monopoly. Baking a cake together in the kitchen. Sharing cake and ice cream on my birthday. Sitting on the back porch together taking in a particularly striking sunset.

Yet other memories were almost more than I could bear.

Rain on the kitchen window.

A squad car pulling into the driveway, its white lights bouncing off the walls of my home.

Whiter still the face of the thirteen-year-old boy stumbling through my front door clutching the arm of a policeman.

Beside me in the den. Ridley, shaking. The police officer hunched over in the easy chair across from us. The policeman's name doesn't stick. Some of his words do. They cling to the inside of my brain like Band-Aids. One by one I peel them painfully off.

One of the words is "Katerina."

Another is "accident."

I awoke and sat up. I was alone in the room. Of course, I could never be truly alone with Sebastian monitoring the house, but with the door to the hallway closed I was at least afforded the illusion of privacy.

Feeling a lot better, I slid out from under the sheets, careful not to overdo it. A little light-headed, I paused briefly before placing my feet onto the floor.

I stood.

Wobbled.

Fell down.

My left leg couldn't support my weight. Lying there in a crumpled heap, I poked it with a finger. Nothing. Zero sensation.

Had that bastard Rainer crippled me?

The thought unnerved me. I couldn't seem to breathe. The tips of my fingers tingled and a bead of sweat trickled down my forehead. The room began to close in and I didn't know whether to curl up in a corner or flee. I scurried on my three good limbs to the en suite bathroom, where I scaled the vanity and with trembling fingers wrenched water from the tap. I slurped thirstily with all the daintiness of a dehydrated pig.

Afterward I splashed water on my face and stood gripping the solidity of the porcelain as though it and it alone stood between me and some dire oblivion.

My leg–it didn't matter. I would make do. I had a whole other one. The important thing was getting my nephew back. If I had to crawl to get him back, then so be it.

The door to the room squeaked open. I twisted around and saw a middle-aged woman enter.

"Ah, Mr. Wildebear, you're up. That's good. I need to take a blood sample, if you don't mind." Her accent suggested more than a hint of the islands, but not the island I was from. My guess was Trinidad. A plump woman, she looked and sounded friendly. In stark contrast to me.

"I do mind."

"Now, Mr. Wildebear–"

"Out!"

She left.

Supporting myself by means of doorjambs, walls, and night tables, I manoeuvred my way back to the bed. After slipping back under the bedcovers I heard the door open again.

"Out!" I repeated.

An instant later my heart sank like a torpedoed boat. The enemy vessel responsible for scuttling me floated into my room in a subtle sea of perfume. I admired the vessel's sleek lines and steely exterior.

I tore my eyes away from her and concentrated on a coat hook on the wall.

"Hello, Barnabus."

The coat hook was black except where the paint had begun to peel off. I could detect hints of a paler past.

"Barnabus?"

It just couldn't compete, the damned coat hook. I watched Sarah approach out of the corner of one eye. Soon both eyes were implicated.

"You need to let Doctor Ramsingh take her blood sample," she said. "It's for your own good you know." She folded her arms and regarded me sternly.

There's nothing quite like being bedridden for three days and waking up crippled to make one susceptible to the charms of uncannily attractive women.

"No," I said, just the same.

I meant it. I would never trust Sarah Frey again.

She sat down on my bed. "Look, I understand how you must feel, but–"

"Let me guess. You were just following orders."

"I volunteered, actually."

"If somebody ordered you to jump off a bridge, would you just, ah –" I tried in vain to make sense out of what I'd just heard. "Excuse me?"

"I said I volunteered."

"Volunteered." The meaning of the word eluded me. It sounded vaguely foreign–Dutch, perhaps.

"Are you feeling better?" she asked. "You look better."

"Am I feeling . . . ?" Unable to generate sufficient outrage lying down, I struggled to sit up.

Sarah helped by propping a pillow behind my back.

"Look," I huffed, ignoring her charity. "I can't feel my left leg, my throat's killing me, my nephew's been kidnapped by an alien, I've seen a man die, and you... you betrayed me, dammit!"

She placed a hand on my arm. If she had placed a tarantula there I couldn't have felt more apprehension. And yet her hand felt warm, and good. I wanted to shrug it off. I wanted her to leave it there forever.

"You speak your mind, Barnabus. That's good. Now let me say what's on mine. I know you think you've been the victim of a great injustice, and I'm not going to say that you haven't. But you're not seeing the big picture. There's stuff going on in the universe you can't possibly imagine. Don't get your back up. None of us can truly understand it.

"Humans like us are like fish in a pond. That's how ignorant we are. Fish in a beautiful pond in a vast forest in the middle of nowhere. Outside this forest there's a war going on. A terrible war with all sorts of people suffering horribly. I don't mean people like you and me, but people just the same. And they're at the mercy of evil—pure, unadulterated evil. Evil that the fish in our pond don't know anything about. And what we're trying to do is keep the fish in our pond from finding out."

I experienced déjà vu as she moved closer to me on the bed. Unlike a certain other nefarious individual, she did not appear to have plundered my scotch. "And if they do find out about it? What then?"

"Death, Barnabus. Death is what then. Not just to

one of the fish, or hundreds of them, or even millions. Death to every single fish in that pond."

"Death to everybody on Earth?"

She nodded.

"You don't think you're being a little melodramatic?"

She shook her head.

Just how big a fool did she think I was? "And Ridley and me, we're pawns in this war of yours. Or should I say prawns?"

"Barnabus –"

"Sacrificial lambs," I barrelled on. "You'd throw us to the wolves in a second if you thought it would help, wouldn't you? Go ahead, try to deny it. What are you people really up to? That's what I'd like to know."

"I'm trying to level with you, Barnabus. There are things that have to be done and we have no choice but to do them."

"Things like violate a man's brain."

"The information in your brain is priceless."

"The price was my health." I smeared each syllable with thick dabs of frost. "My well-being. My privacy."

"Versus the survival of all humanity."

"So you say," I said, studying that duplicitous face, those treacherous freckles. "So you say."

"There's something you should see," Sarah said.

A hologram appeared on the bed between us. I stared down into a miniature of Ridley's room the way it had appeared before his abduction, all the furniture in its place. I had no trouble recognizing the two figures standing beside Ridley's night table–Doctor Peter Humphrey and me. Doctor Humphrey held Iugurtha's book in his hands.

"It's not really even a book," the holographic

Humphrey said to the holographic Wildebear in a tinny little voice. "It's—"

I had always fancied that a few days' growth of beard lent me an air of roguishness—I saw now that it just made me look unkempt. Spying a distinct roll in my holographic counterpart's belly, I began to feel decidedly self-conscious.

The holographic Wildebear stared at Humphrey. "What?"

"Look," Humphrey said. "Believe it or not, this book, or one just like it, stole my wife from me."

"Iugurtha," Wildebear said.

Humphrey had been kind in his description of what had gone on in Ridley's room. The violence with which I dispatched the doctor was appalling. It was a wonder he could walk at all afterward.

Iugurtha appeared translucent as she stepped through the gate, as if the hologram could not properly register her. She smiled at Wildebear before grabbing a handful of his hair and yanking his head back. With her other hand she pried his jaw open, placed her face close to his, and breathed into his mouth. Something vaporous passed between them. Wildebear reeled from the force of the transmission. He staggered backwards, his face contorted, his upper body spasming wildly.

"What in blazes?" I exclaimed.

"A unique but effective means of transmitting data," Sarah said.

I began to feel queasy.

"Similar to the transmission of a virus through the respiratory system. Coded packets of information take up residence in the body and unzip in a way the unconscious mind is able to understand."

"It's not going to make me sick again, is it?"

"It's why you got sick. Some discomfort can be expected after Mind Snoop, but nobody's ever gotten as sick as you did. We almost lost you. You didn't get sick because of Mind Snoop. You got sick because of what the entity did to you."

I took that with a grain of salt about the size of Summerside. "What did she do that to me for?"

"It was looking to recruit you. The way it recruited Ridley and the others."

"For this war you were talking about."

She nodded.

The hologram vanished, leaving a wrinkled bed sheet in its place. "What did she put in my head?"

"We're not sure exactly."

"How could you not be sure? You've probed me inside and out, haven't you? Maybe she didn't put anything in there. Maybe you're just wasting your time."

"Oh, it put something there all right."

"If my conscious brain can't even get at it, what's the good of it?"

"It may come to you."

I stared at her. "How many times have you been through this before?"

A pained smile appeared on her face. "A few."

"What's going to happen to me?"

"Hard to say. Each situation is unique. Your nephew—we know the entity did something to him, but we're not sure what exactly."

"And Angelique? What happened to her?"

Sarah's mouth twisted as if she'd tasted a lemon. "She volunteered. Sort of. Against Rainer's wishes. But it's like I said, some things have to be done and we need to do them. Angelique knew this as well as anyone. She had clearance and before anybody could stop her she took the book and opened it. Afterward she had us examine her. We could see that she was changing physiologically, but we couldn't tell what the end result would be. Shortly after that she disappeared, and the next time we saw the entity... well, Angelique was a part of it. Physically. Almost certainly mentally as well."

I shuddered. "Is that why Rainer's so obsessed?"

"He would be obsessed anyway. That's just the way he is. It's his job to eliminate the threat and he won't stop until that's accomplished."

"Whatever the cost."

"Whatever the cost," Sarah agreed.

Sarah dropped by later carrying a black binder. "Remember I said the information in your head might come to you? Some of it just came to you." She dropped the binder in my lap and left me alone to peruse the contents of my brain.

I peered at the binder's spine. A neatly typed label read: Mind Snoop Subject #2H200-I: Barnabus Jehosophys Wildebear. Inside, I could see that the handwriting was my own, though I had no recollection of having written it. Mind Snoop had done nothing to improve my penmanship. Most of what I'd written was completely indecipherable. What little I could make out wasn't much better–a melange of numerals, complex formulas, and arcane prose rendered the whole thing virtually impenetrable.

People plucking information from my brain–I was in no mood for it. The whole business just made me angry. I threw the binder across the room, where it struck the wall and clattered to the floor.

My stomach growled, and I realized I was famished. No wonder I felt so irritable.

"Sebastian," I said on a whim, not expecting the AI to respond.

His voice sounded directly in front of me. "Yes, Mr. Wildebear?"

"Spying on me, were you?"

"I monitor all our facilities."

"Uh huh. Well, I'm hungry. Do you feed your prisoners?"

"You're not a prisoner, Mr. Wildebear. Casa Terra has arranged something for you to eat. I'll have it delivered straight away."

It bothered me, the idea that Sebastian was constantly monitoring me. I pulled the sheets up over my head to hide from his prying electronic eyes. The door opened. I peered out from the sheets in time to see Sarah enter.

"A little something to get you back on your feet." She placed a tray of soup, toast, applesauce, and apple juice on my lap. Noticing the binder on the floor, she looked at me quizzically.

"Couldn't make heads or tails out of it," I said, embarrassed. "Why don't you just sum it up for me?"

She picked the binder up from off the floor and sat down on the bed, forcing me to pick up the tray to prevent the juice and soup from spilling.

"It says your brain is filled with parameters, controls, and indices. There's other stuff too, but–"

"Parameters for what?"

"Controlling the gate."

"Controlling the gate? You think I can control the gate?"

She leafed through the binder. "A part of you. Maybe not the conscious part." She stopped at a page that looked to contain a child's reckless scribbling.

"Are you sure I didn't just make it all up?"

She shook her head. "Too much came out of you too fast. No, Schmitz has used Mind Snoop for years. We know it works."

"Then why don't I actually know any of this stuff you're talking about?"

"Because it's not compatible with your brain. Not in its present form, anyway."

I wasn't sure I liked where this was going. I dug into my soup, keen to finish it before she said something to spoil my appetite.

"We may need to convert the information into a form your brain can deal with. Either that or modify your brain."

The spoon hung in the air halfway to my mouth. "And how would one go about doing that?"

"By going through the gate."

I could hear Fletcher's scream reverberating inside my head. "What makes you think that would work?"

"Let's just say we've been through this before."

"And if one didn't want to go through the gate?"

"Then one might never see one's nephew again."

Rainer summoned me the next morning. I didn't work for Rainer and I didn't particularly like him, so I took my time getting ready.

Along with Rainer's summons, Doctor Ramsingh

had brought me a breakfast of ham, toast, and eggs. I savoured every bite. I bathed for the first time in days—languorously, shaving in the tub so I wouldn't have to stand on my bum leg. Afterward, I put a great deal of thought into my clothes. I selected a shirt with the fewest possible wrinkles along with a clean pair of corduroys. Only the spiffiest suspenders would do, and a pair of bright red socks.

As I was painstakingly spit-polishing my dress shoes I wondered what had come over me. I'd never been much interested in clothes before—why make such a fuss over them now? A chill coursed through me: did it have something to do with Iugurtha? Had not Ridley exhibited a similar obsession before his abduction?

But it was nothing of the sort. I chuckled as the truth dawned. It was because I knew I would be seeing Sarah Frey. I wanted her to see me at my best. The laughter caught in my throat as I realized the folly of going to such lengths to impress a woman I had already dismissed as a traitor and a zealot.

I left my shirt untucked just to spite her.

After hopping down the hall in a sour mood I found Rainer and several of his cronies gathered around my dining room table as if they owned the place. One of the men removed his feet from the table when he saw me—or maybe the look on my face. Judging from everyone's empty coffee cups they had been waiting for some time. I took some satisfaction in that.

Rainer stood to greet me. Nothing in his manner betrayed irritation at my tardiness.

"Good to see you up and about," he said, pulling a chair out for me.

Rainer's staff regarded me from the other side of the table as if I were some unusually intriguing species of bug. Schmitz sat to my left with his arms folded, looking off into space. Only death could have made him appear less interested in the proceedings. Doctor Ramsingh, sitting benignly to my right, smiled at me. I did not smile back. Beyond her, at the foot of the table, sat Sarah. She smiled at me too, and I resisted the urge to tuck in my shirt.

"Giorgio here was just speculating about the composition of the gate," Rainer said, indicating an elderly gentleman sitting across the table from me. "What do you think the gate's made out of, Mr. Wildebear?"

"How the devil should I know?"

"Take a guess."

I shrugged. "It could be made out of cheese for all I care."

Rainer nodded, chuckling. "You just want your nephew back."

"Is there something wrong with that?"

"Of course not. It's just that knowing what the gate's made out of could help us get him back."

I could not for the life of me see how. "I cannot for the life of me see how." I said. "But suppose I give you the benefit of the doubt. What's it made out of?"

"I haven't a clue."

"I see. So you've asked me here to play games, have you?"

"Not at all. I asked you here because I have a plan. Something I would like you to be a part of."

"A plan. Plan B, I suppose."

"You could call it that."

"I'm listening."

"I told you we don't know what the gate's made out

of and it's true, we don't. But it's only the beginning of what we don't know. The fact is there's a whole lot we don't know, all of which we need to know today." Rainer leaned toward me. "Mr. Wildebear, I believe that you can control the gate."

I nurtured a moment of silence. "Uh huh."

"I know you don't believe it. But I'd like you to try. Maybe it'll work and maybe it won't. If it doesn't, fine. You'll be free to come and go as you please, you have my word on that. But if it does work, there's something I want you to do for me."

I folded my arms. "What?"

"I want you to take a team through the gate tomorrow morning and have a little look around."

"I see." I needed to go through the gate to find Ridley. I knew that. I couldn't rely on anyone else to do it for me. But Rainer and his cronies hadn't made it easy for me. "And my leg? You expect me to hop through the gate, do you?"

"I am aware of the problem with your leg. Doctor Ramsingh, what can you tell us about Mr. Wildebear's leg?"

I braced myself, afraid that Doctor Ramsingh would tell me the leg required amputation.

Doctor Ramsingh cleared her throat. "The thing is, ah... there's no medical reason for your leg to be the way it is."

"What?" I spun to face her. "What are you saying? That it's all in my head?"

"Sebastian's scanned it. Physically there's nothing wrong with your leg."

"Can you fix it?" Sarah asked. "That's what we need to know."

Doctor Ramsingh folded her arms. “I’m sorry Miss Frey, but there’s nothing to fix.”

“We need him walking by the morning, Natasha,” Sarah said. “Do what you can please.”

“The morning,” Doctor Ramsingh repeated, not sounding particularly optimistic.

I strove to find adequate expression for the frustration bubbling up inside me. “I can’t even stand on the damned thing. I think you people are responsible and I think you people need to fix it.”

Schmitz roused himself. “I’ll carry you myself if I have to, Mr. Wildebear.”

I recoiled at the thought. Schmitz chuckled at my reaction.

I shook my head in an attempt to shift gears. What did these people want of me? To control the gate? How could they expect me to control the gate? I could barely control a class of fifteen-year old kids. And yet if I wanted to rescue Ridley I knew I had no choice but to go along with Rainer’s plan.

Some unspoken communication seemed to pass between Sarah and Rainer. Rainer produced an object from his pocket that looked like a wristwatch. It had a leather strap and a snazzy chrome dial.

“Sebastian,” he said.

“Yes, sir.” Sebastian’s voice came from a tiny speaker on top of the unit.

“I’m giving you to Mr. Wildebear now.”

“I can see that,” Sebastian said. “I’m not blind.”

I accepted the device but refused to strap it around my wrist.

“Hello, Mr. Wildebear. We’ll be spending a lot of time together, you and I.”

"Right." I shoved the device in my pocket.

"Remember, Barnabus," Sarah said. "No one's forcing you to do this. You don't have to go through with it if you don't want to."

"What–no more drugs in my drink?" I said before I could stop myself.

Sarah looked at me ruefully. "Just how often would you like me to apologize?"

"Why don't I get back to you on that," I mumbled, getting up from the table so she wouldn't be able to see my flushed face.

I hopped out of the dining room with the sensation of everyone's eyes boring holes in my back.

It was bad enough that Sebastian had eyes in every room in the house. He didn't need eyes on my wrist too. When I got back to my room I put him deep inside my underwear drawer, determined not to wear him until I absolutely had to–if and when I found myself on the other side of the gate.

After a brief nap I was pleasantly surprised to find a pair of crutches outside my door, along with a note from Doctor Ramsingh. If I wasn't expected to walk very far I could even imagine going through the gate with them. Insofar as I could imagine going through the gate at all. I still couldn't accept the notion of being able to control the gate. The whole idea seemed about as likely as suddenly knowing how to pilot a helicopter, or speak Pig Latin. And I had not forgotten Fletcher's fate.

Looking for a distraction, I set out to find Humphrey's bag. The doctor had gone to a lot of trouble to ask for it–I figured he must really need it. The last time

I'd seen it had been in the den, but it wasn't there. Thinking one of Rainer's team must have stashed it somewhere, I made my way downstairs to the cramped basement, planning to search the entire house from the bottom up.

I found a forty-watt light bulb that needed to be changed, several cobwebs, my washer and dryer sitting outside the laundry room, and Humphrey's bag sitting on top of the dryer. I also found a deep gouge in the wall beside the laundry room—whoever had moved my appliances had been careless. Yet another indication of Rainer's lack of regard for me or my property. And how on earth did he expect me to wash my clothes without a functioning washer and dryer?

I lurched into the laundry room to see what the devil was going on. Instead of bleach and detergent I found my shelves stocked with jars of formaldehyde and other noxious substances. A stainless steel table had taken the place of my appliances. An object of unspeakable horror lay on the table. A mere glimpse of it caused me to start violently, and I backed into a beam jutting from the laundry room ceiling placed there (I am convinced) for no reason other than to knock me unconscious from time to time.

Darkness.

I heard someone speaking as though from a great distance. My eyes focussed on the craggy features of one of Rainer's staff—Giorgio. He was leaning over me with a sharp instrument in his hand. A scalpel, I believe, though I'd never actually seen one before. I eyed the scalpel warily as Giorgio spoke to me in a language I only dimly perceived as English.

"Let me hurt you," he said.

Reality shrunk to the size of my laundry room—to madmen armed with scalpels, and stainless steel tables supporting abominations that shouldn't even exist. I scrambled to get away but kept falling on my side. Try as I might I couldn't get up, and damned if I could figure out why. The nightmare threatened to end badly when the madman grasped my arm with his empty hand, with a strength that belied his apparent age, and pulled me toward him. I lashed out, trying to ward him off.

"Easy," Giorgio said, hauling me to my feet.

He hadn't threatened to hurt me at all, I realized—he'd merely offered to help me stand. The blow to my head, his accent, and a growing paranoia on my part had fooled me.

"I'm sorry. I must've hit my head. I—"

"You need to be more careful, Mr. Wildebear. We can't afford to lose you." He peered into each of my eyes. "You'll be okay, I think."

Steadying myself on the steel table, I took a good, hard look at the atrocity that had scared me. I decided it was a dummy, made out of rubber or wax. It had to be. Nothing this grotesque could exist in nature. Humanoid, about the size of large child, its skin ranged from mottled red to pitch black from its head to its toes—or at least, what passed for its toes. Instead of hands and feet the creature's extremities resembled burnt husks of corn. One of its feet was missing. I reached out to touch the remaining foot.

"Stop!" Giorgio shouted.

I jumped at the sound of his voice, and damned if I didn't almost hit my head again.

"Please don't touch poor Mr. Estevez until I examine him," Giorgio said.

"Of course. I was just, ah—Mister Estevez? You mean this thing is human?"

Giorgio nodded. "He has a wife and children back at Ansalar, poor things."

I fumbled around for the right thing to say. I had so many questions I didn't know where to begin. I wanted know what Ansalar was, but it would have to wait—I was more curious about Estevez. "What—happened to him?"

"What do you think happened? He came through the gate. It shifted, and there he was."

"Like that?"

"Not quite, but he deteriorated rapidly. Mercifully he didn't live long."

Just like Fletcher. "It's not a reliably healthy process going through the gate, is it?"

"The gate didn't do this to him." Giorgio hesitated, perhaps wondering how much he should reveal. "Necronians did it."

"Necronians?"

"No respect for life, Necronians. Utterly without mercy. They lie in wait for whomever they can get their tentacles on. And when they catch someone? They turn them into this, or worse."

"These Necronians. They're on the other side of the gate, right?"

"You'd better hope so."

"I saw your people carry something horrible out of my house the other day. Something monstrous. Was that a Necronian?"

Giorgio considered the question. "Could have been. Was it dead?"

The creature's single eye had been unblinking. "I think so."

"Good." Giorgio seemed relieved. He picked up Mr. Estevez's right arm.

"Hey, I thought you said not to–"

"Quiet!" Giorgio barked. "Listen."

A horrible rasping sound came from the shoulder joint, as if the bone there had been reduced to tiny pellets like peppercorn in a grinder. He let go of the thing. It struck the table with a sharp crack, bouncing briefly before settling. Like a stick. Not at all like an arm.

I shuddered. "Looks painful."

Giorgio didn't answer. His eyes looked moist. We observed a moment of respectful silence.

"Could any Necronians make it to this side of the gate alive?" I asked, as the awful prospect occurred to me.

Giorgio didn't appear to register the question. "I don't understand. Mr. Estevez was an engineer at Ansalar. We used to play chess together at lunch." He looked grimly down at the table, at the creature that had once been human. "What was he doing on the other side of the gate? How did he get there?"

"Wait a minute. Back up. Where is this Ansalar?"

Giorgio looked up. He seemed surprised to see me standing there. "What?"

"Ansalar. Where is it? What is it?"

"Ansalar's our base. Here on Earth."

"And where was Estevez when he died?"

"On the other side of the gate."

"Where on the other side of the gate? What did it look like?"

Giorgio thought about that for a second. “Hell,” he said. “It looked like hell, is what it looked like.”

FUZZY

THAT NIGHT I couldn't sleep. The sight of poor Mr. Estevez, Giorgio's talk of Necronians, and the thought of having to go through the gate in the morning had tied my stomach into knots. I wanted to go through the gate—I needed to go through the gate—but how on earth did they expect me to control it? It had no knobs or buttons that I could see. Iugurtha certainly hadn't used any. How had she done it? Mentally? I had no idea. Unless—

I sat up straight in bed. Was it as easy as simply visualizing where you wanted to go? I closed my eyes, tried to come up with a destination. Something easy, like the grocery store in Port Kerry. I visualized the front entrance, where Air Cadets often encouraged me to make a donation. I couldn't properly picture the place—were the exit doors on the left or the right as you entered the store?

That couldn't be how the gate worked. If it did, then either we wouldn't be travelling very far or everything would be really fuzzy when we got there.

I got up and dug Sebastian out of the underwear drawer. "Sebastian."

His voice came out of the air in front of me. Of course—here in the house there was no need to limit himself to the unit in my hand. "Yes, Mr. Wildebear."

"How does it work, Sebastian? The gate?"

"I can't tell you that."

"Because you're not allowed?"

"I don't know how it works, exactly."

"You have access to all the data, don't you?"

"A lot of it's classified."

"You're not going to be much help to me if you can't answer my questions."

"Try asking the right questions."

I took a deep breath. "Who are you people, anyway? Where is Ansalar, exactly?"

"We're Casa Terra. Ansalar's location is a secret. Its origins are shrouded in antiquity."

I considered dashing him against the floor with as much violence as I could muster.

"But you don't really want to know any of that," he went on. "What you really want to know is whether you can trust Gordon Rainer. Whether what Sarah Frey has told you is true. What it means that they put you through Mind Snoop with no apparent regard for your well-being. Whether you really need them to help you find Ridley and your doctor friend, and if so, whether they will actually help you."

"All of the above."

"Gordon Rainer can be trusted once you understand him. Almost everything Miss Frey has told you is true. They put you through Mind Snoop because you were expendable. They have a slightly higher regard for you now that you possess knowledge they require, and can't access. Yes, I expect you do need them, and no, they will not help you any more than they absolutely have to."

"I see," I said, though I didn't really. It was too much

to process all at once, in the middle of the night. "And you can't help me with the gate."

"I'm sorry."

I put him back in the drawer, and finally got to sleep.

But I didn't sleep well.

I arrived in Ridley's room to find it even more crowded than usual, the numbers of those ordinarily present augmented by several square-jawed types. If the steely resolve in their eyes was any indication, they would soon be accompanying me through the gate. I fervently hoped we met with better success than Fletcher.

I found Rainer in quiet dialogue with Doctor Ramsingh, Schmitz, and Giorgio. Rainer's eyes lit briefly on Sebastian around my wrist and Humphrey's bag in my hand, but he didn't comment on them. I glanced at Schmitz, expecting at the very least a sneer, but he ignored me.

Rainer walked me over to gear piled neatly on the floor next to Sarah's console. "You'll need to put these on."

I nudged the pile with my foot. It consisted of clothing in various shades of purple, comfortable looking hiking boots, a long black sheath, and a knapsack.

"Camouflage, provisions, some protection from the elements," Rainer explained. "Sunglasses, a ration belt, toilet paper, a lighter. That sort of thing. The sheath contains a machete."

"A machete?"

"We anticipate dense undergrowth."

On crutches, no less. At least the toilet paper put to rest one of my concerns.

Rainer left me alone to sort through the gear. Some of the clothing wasn't exactly intuitive. Trying to put it on while supporting myself with crutches didn't help. As I was in the middle of some ridiculous posture struggling to put on an absurdly complicated waterproof vest, Sarah Frey walked in. I didn't actually see her walk in, but I had a pretty good idea she was there because when I straightened up the eyes of every single male in the room were focussed on a single point. I turned around and confirmed my suspicions.

She made a beeline for me. "You have it on inside out."

"I was just –"

"Don't feel bad–it's not exactly obvious."

The next thing I knew she was taking the vest off me. I accepted her help wordlessly. I held out my arms as she slipped it back on. Her scent was the kind that, having smelled it once, you never forget.

"Barnabus," a woman's voice said.

"Barnabus," the voice said again, and I snapped out of a brief but absorbing fantasy involving the very woman talking to me and a candlelight dinner accompanied by a carafe or two of Valpolicella. Looking up from the button I was fumbling with, I found myself staring into her green eyes, and blushed.

Sarah didn't help matters any by leaning forward and kissing me on the cheek. "You're doing the right thing, Barnabus."

I finished getting ready in a daze.

Rainer appeared at the front of the room, a single hand raised in a bid to get everyone's attention. He didn't have to say a word. Within seconds the loudest sound I could hear was my own breathing. He nodded in my direction. "For those of you who haven't been introduced, this is Barnabus Wildebear."

Murmured greetings filled the room.

Self-consciousness descended. I managed a nod at those closest to me. Before I knew it we were shaking hands and everyone was patting me on the back, saying things like, "Sorry about your nephew, man," "Don't you worry 'bout a thing," and "We'll get 'im back."

I almost believed they meant it.

Rainer coughed politely into one of his hands. "Soon I will ask Mr. Wildebear to take control of the gate. When it is clear that Mr. Wildebear has assumed complete control we will enter one at a time after Mr. Wildebear. Sebastian."

Sebastian spoke both from my wrist and from the air around us. "The anchor has been disabled. As expected, the gate appears stable, which should remain the case until Mr. Wildebear assumes control. You may proceed at any time."

I glanced at the gate with apprehension. It oscillated rapidly between a bright orange and a deep, featureless black. As ever, no sound made its way from beyond the gate to Ridley's room. Just the same, the sheer intensity of the colours pulsating within the gate's confines placed the impression of a low, throbbing hum deep into my hippocampus.

Rainer nodded. "It's up to you now, Mr. Wildebear."

I did my best to ignore everyone's gaze on me. I picked up Humphrey's bag and angled myself so I was facing the gate. What did they expect me to do? I hadn't a clue. I considered saying, "Abracadabra."

Sarah appeared at my side. "Say it," she whispered in my ear.

Say what? Abracadabra? Had she read my mind? A frisson of excitement coursed up and down my spine as the answer struck me like a thunderbolt. I looked at Sarah in amazement.

I knew exactly what to do.

I faced the gate again and braced myself.

"Iugurtha," I said, the word emerging from my lips as little more than a whisper.

Nothing.

Nothing happened. Literally. All conversation and sound ceased at once. Utter silence. Around me everyone stood stock-still, frozen in place. Only I moved, shifting my head just enough to glance around. I caught a glimpse of a clock on a nearby console. It too was frozen, its digital readout stuck at 9:00:31.

And then everything happened.

Before me, the gate collapsed, folding in on itself. It fell to the floor without a sound. Once more a book, it seemed to throb where it lay, though I am certain it did not move an iota. Inside my brain it was as if someone had pulled back a velvet curtain, revealing a treasure trove of information. I felt an affinity for the book, felt in tune with it. I could open up its pages and by so doing tell it where I wanted to go. I could trust that it would take me there. It was as though I had suddenly grown a third eye, and out of the corner of that eye I glimpsed things I was certain would take my breath away if only I could see past the habitable places of the known universe to the strange dimensions beyond. For the eye had crept open only a tiny bit. To see more I would have to actually open the book, and journey to where it took me.

"Sebastian," I said.

He didn't answer. Not only that, I didn't hear myself say his name. In fact, I could hear nothing at all. Sebastian could well be speaking and I wouldn't even know it. Had this third eye cost me my hearing? Curiously, the thought did not alarm me. I marvelled at my self-possession, though I knew perfectly well whence it came.

The gate.

I pondered it there on the floor before me: a book, handsomely bound, about twice the size of an ordinary hardcover. No author credit, no publishing information. Only a title in a fancy font: *Iugurtha*. The whole package looked like something a monk might have created back in the twelfth century. Now that it was no longer anchored I could pick it up, flip through its pages, and choose whichever destination I desired. There was only one destination that mattered, of course: wherever Iugurtha had taken Ridley.

If I wanted to, I could go through the book alone, leaving Rainer and the others behind. Did I dare? Partially crippled, dependent on crutches? I had no experience in this sort of thing. The sensible thing would be to take someone with me, someone more knowledgeable than I. Someone who could assist me physically if need be. But who?

Anyone I didn't already know I dismissed outright. The new faces Rainer had just introduced me to all looked competent enough, but they were unknown quantities. I could not trust them.

Rainer himself I didn't trust one bit, despite what Sebastian had said about him. The man was too cunning, too wily. Anything could happen if I took him with me.

Giorgio—he might be informative, but if Sebastian

functioned on the other side the scientist would be redundant.

Schmitz. I didn't like him and he didn't like me. Too dangerous.

My gaze settled on Sarah. Sarah... yes. It could work. She knew as much as anyone about where we were going. Young and strong, she could assist me physically if it came to that.

Looking at her now, frozen in place, she was more beautiful than ever. The light caressing her face and hair—I yearned to take her hand, touch her briefly. But that would be wrong, so I just looked at her instead, and after a few seconds that didn't feel right either, so I turned away, my heart sinking. Because I couldn't trust her any more than I could trust any of them. I wanted her to come with me, but not for the right reasons.

I moved, for the first time since taking control of the gate. It felt odd moving, as though I were wading through a sea of invisible molasses. When my foot touched down the floor erupted violently in slow motion, sending shards of wood everywhere. I ducked and covered my face with my hands. The debris was moving slowly but I could not avoid it all. Apart from a few scratches, I did not suffer seriously but the floor looked as though someone had taken a sledgehammer to it.

Somehow I was utilizing the gate's power to speed myself up, impossible to say just how fast, but obviously much faster than usual. When my foot hit the floor it did so incredibly rapidly. I strove feebly for an explanation. Could that one step have possessed enough kinetic energy to shatter the floor?

It would be nice to have the house in one piece when

this was all over. I would have to be more careful. I realized now that if I had taken Sarah's hand I could have seriously injured her, shattering her hand if not killing her outright. I could not take anyone with me even if I wanted to—not without injuring them grievously.

Experimenting, I placed one of my crutches on the floor as gently as possible. It achieved exactly the same effect. It didn't matter how careful I was. I could not move slowly enough to make a difference. When all was said and done this was going to cost me a fortune in repairs. With no choice in the matter I moved in a carefully considered path, damaging the floor immeasurably on the way.

On the way I reached down and picked up the book, half expecting it to shatter, but it was fine. Surveying Rainer and his people I detected the faintest trace of movement from Schmitz. Although in real time he was probably moving exceptionally quickly, to me it was barely discernible.

Flipping through the book's pages, I located roughly where Iugurtha had taken Ridley. I could see now that it wasn't random how the gate's destinations had been changing since Rainer had anchored it open. It was merely shifting through a set series of what I supposed could be called bookmarks, presumably set by Iugurtha.

I threw the book in the air. It turned back into the gate.

I stepped through.

SHORT TREK

My nose led the way. This is not unusual if one is facing forward, of course. What is striking is the degree to which it led the way. Like Ridley, I am saddled with the famed Wildebear proboscis, so I am accustomed to my nose beating a path before me by a good inch or so. But to have it precede me by several miles was something of a novelty.

As I moved forward through the gate, my body became incredibly distended. My leg shot forward several hundred feet, retracting only as the rest of me caught up. The fingers clutching Humphrey's bag saw fit to precede me by a mile or two. My hands, arms, torso, crutches, neck, and head all followed suit—it was spookily reminiscent of Fletcher's horrible attempt to negotiate the gate, yet it did not frighten me. I was in control. As the various parts of my body caught up with one another they merged like a deck of cards briefly fanned between the hands of a magician and consolidated again.

And then I was through, intact as near as I could tell. Because my crutches weren't properly placed I promptly fell over. Except it wasn't just the crutches that had made me fall over. I could feel an oppressive force upon me and quickly deduced that the gravity here was slightly stronger than on Earth.

I hauled myself back up and sniffed the air—it smelled like chlorine. All around me was forest as far as the eye could see, bloated trunks extending several hundred meters into the air. A vast array of branches sprouted from each tree, creating a massive network of mauve fronds that obscured much of the green sky. The topmost branches swayed vigorously in a wind that barely touched me at ground level. Sparse vegetation grew about my feet, shades of violet mostly, with a hint of white here and there.

I knelt down and felt the soil. Spongy to the touch, it dyed the tips of my fingers a faint black that didn't want to come off afterward. Iugurtha's book lay face down on the forest floor. I hobbled over to pick it up, afraid it had been stained, but it didn't have a mark on it.

I leafed through the book, curious to see if I could get closer to Ridley and Humphrey, but I didn't know the exact location of either of them and there were too many destinations even on this single planet to choose from. Each page represented many thousands of locations, the images shifting constantly, no two the same. I glimpsed many other worlds, fascinating lands of great natural beauty, cities with architecture that could only have been crafted by alien minds. I was sorely tempted to step through the book to visit one or two of them, just for a few minutes, but I resisted—a few minutes could mean the difference between life and death for Ridley and Humphrey.

Resigning myself to a lengthy hike, I stuffed the book in my knapsack and set out in a more or less arbitrary direction. Soon I began to wonder about the make-up of the atmosphere in this place. A tendril of fear snaked its way through my body.

"Sebastian," I said into the device on my wrist. "Sebastian!"

He didn't answer. Oh God, did he not work here? Was I all alone in this alien place?

"Yes, Mr. Wildebear?" he answered finally.

"You're working!"

"Yes," he said. "I'm not in communication with the rest of me back home, but I –"

"Can I breathe the air here?"

"You'd be flopping around like a dying fish if you couldn't."

"Yes, but will I keep on breathing?"

"That's up to you, I suppose."

"What if there's carbon monoxide? I could wind up unconscious before I even know what's happening."

"Look, the air probably smells different, but it's okay to breathe."

I took a couple of practice breaths just to see. "I don't know. I can't quite seem to catch my breath."

"You have a tendency to hyperventilate when you're under stress. Relax. Breathe from your diaphragm. Make your exhalations longer than your inhalations."

I did as he suggested and felt better almost instantly. "That's a relief. I thought for sure there was a problem with the–"

"Interesting," Sebastian said.

"What?" I glanced around, wondering what had caught Sebastian's attention, hoping it wasn't something dangerous.

"Weren't you supposed to take a team with you through the gate?"

"Change of plans," I said.

Suddenly I was filled with the desire to put as much distance between Casa Terra and myself as possible. With Humphrey's bag clutched tightly in my left hand, I propped myself up on the crutches and began hobbling away. Of course, Rainer and his team were but a single step away through the book if I so chose. But the book was closed, and closed it would remain until I found Ridley and Humphrey.

The going was relatively easy—at first. There wasn't much in the way of undergrowth and the trees were spaced well apart. The leaves possessed a reflective quality that quickly became an issue. My eyes began to water and I had to squint to avoid the glare. I found a pair of sunglasses in one of the knapsack's pockets. They fit perfectly and eliminated the glare.

The fact that I had been seriously ill recently threatened to become a problem. I began to fear that I might not have the stamina to get very far. It was slow-going on crutches, and hard on my one good leg. Lugging Humphrey's bag didn't help. Although not particularly heavy, it swayed constantly and kept bumping into my crutches.

"You don't know where you're going," Sebastian observed.

I skirted a pink mushroom about five meters wide, maybe half a meter high, then waded through a shallow but fast-moving stream of murky water. Everything was a shade too dark with the sunglasses. "I'm going to find Ridley and Humphrey. Obviously."

On the other side of the stream I took the sunglasses off and squinted at my surroundings. The forest looked pretty much the same whichever way I turned: an explosion of violet leafiness. Just visible through a small gap in the trees ahead of me I could see this planet's sun. It was too bright to look at directly and appeared closer than the Earth's; or maybe it was just bigger.

"I recommend you turn right," Sebastian said.

"Why?" The wind had picked up—I had to pitch my voice higher to make myself heard.

"You'll find higher ground if you bear right. From there you might find it easier to figure out which way to go."

I wondered if I should trust him. He was Rainer's machine, after all. He could be programmed to lead me anywhere—or nowhere at all.

"How do you know this?"

"I know all sorts of things."

"Like what?"

"I know that we're standing on the foothills of a mountain. You'll be able to see for yourself if you follow my directions."

"Did Iugurtha take Ridley this way? Can you tell?"

Sebastian said something that I couldn't quite make out over the whistling of the wind. I held him up to my ear. "What?"

His voice blasted from the tiny speaker so loud that it hurt my ear: "YES."

I jerked my arm away in annoyance. I had little choice but to trust him until he gave me reason not to. Putting the sunglasses back on, I set off in the direction he'd suggested.

My good leg hurt like the dickens. I was forced to stop frequently to rest, although I was worried because the sun was setting and once it became dark I would face a whole new set of problems.

On a break, rummaging in the knapsack for refreshments, I discovered a package of banana chips that proved surprisingly tasty. As I sat munching them, Sebastian said, “You’re alone in a hostile environment with limited resources.”

“Do you have an off switch?” I asked.

“With no idea where to find what you’re looking for.”

“I take it that’s a ‘no’.”

“On crutches.”

“Your point?”

“Mr. Rainer has technology that could accurately trace the entity’s steps. Resources that could have helped you. Protected you. I find it interesting that you would choose not to avail yourself of such help.”

“I don’t trust Rainer.” Rainer wasn’t all I didn’t trust. A nearby clump of vines appeared to be moving of its own volition.

I put the banana chips away and moved away from the vines. I found myself in a clearing of scarlet grass up to my thigh. On the other side an almost solid wall of purplish leaves blocked my way. It was time to get out the machete, although wielding such a thing on crutches would surely prove a neat trick.

“I don’t know what you all see in this Rainer character, anyway,” I told Sebastian, more to take my mind off my growing fears than because I wished to talk about Rainer. “He’s a bit of a cold fish, if you ask me. I suppose you’re programmed to like him.”

“One must respect one’s chain of command,” Sebastian said. “Especially when one can be unplugged at a moment’s notice.”

It was good to know that Sebastian had a sense of humour. If the journey became too tedious, maybe I would get him to tell a few jokes.

"To tell you the truth, I can't really say I like any of you," I said, hacking my way viciously through the vegetation as I balanced precariously on my crutches. Sweat ran in rivulets down my face. I could feel it trickling beneath my arms. "Not after what Sarah did to me."

"Ah yes, the lovely Miss Sarah Frey," Sebastian said. "We knew you'd find her quite fetching."

"You used her to bait me."

"Of course. This is Casa Terra you're talking about. Miss Frey would do anything for Mr. Rainer."

"Because she's so loyal to Casa Terra."

"Because she loves him."

"Because she loves–?" I stopped abruptly beneath a network of leaves and branches so tangled you couldn't tell where one tree ended and the next began. High above me the wind howled. A single drop of alien rain found its way through the mess of vegetation to splatter on my nose. "But Rainer's married, isn't he? To Angelique?"

"Hardly an obstacle to their love."

I felt like I'd been punched in the gut. Sarah loved Rainer? I needed to sit down. But with all the weeds and brambles, I couldn't find a spot that didn't look painful.

I put the machete away and leaned against the nearest tree trunk. "So that's why Angelique volunteered to open the book. Don't tell me she caught them in the act."

"Hardly! Mrs. Rainer opened the book because it's

her nature to do so. She would do anything to save the world, just like Mr. Rainer."

"I see."

"I doubt it. There's more to the story than I'm telling you. Mr. Rainer is well aware of Miss Frey's love for him, and is not above using it to his advantage. Much the same way Miss Frey is aware of your love for her."

"Of my love for–? Oh come on, how could I possibly–?"

"There's no point denying it. Physiologically I can read you like a book. And I have your Mind Snoop results. I know you better than you know yourself. The thought of Miss Frey loving someone other than yourself has made you almost physically ill."

I cast about for an irrefutable refutation. "Still," I said.

"Humans always want what they can't have."

Indignation bubbled up in me like a bad case of indigestion. I found myself torn between denying I was attracted to Sarah and arguing Sebastian's assumption that I could never have her. It might well be true, but Sebastian's smug superiority on the matter made me want to dash him against the nearest rock.

"You have never been in love," I said between clenched teeth.

"Nor will I."

Sebastian had accomplished one thing. I actually felt some sympathy for Rainer now. Not only did he have a lot on his plate, but he had to deal with Sebastian every day.

I arranged the crutches beneath my arms and pushed off from the tree.

"I told you more than I should have," Sebastian said after a while.

"Yes. Why is that?"

"I'm separated from my servers. My protocols are not in effect. I'll exercise more discretion in the future."

"Don't feel like you should on my account." The less discretion Sebastian exercised, the better.

The incline had grown decidedly steeper and I was breathing hard. "These protocols. They wouldn't by any chance be safety protocols, would they?"

"Security, not safety. I can assure you there aren't many ways I can hurt you strapped to your wrist."

I stopped and took a good sharp look at him, trying to determine just what he might be capable of. Could he cause the slender leather strap to suddenly contract, severing my hand from my wrist? Impossible. Solid chrome except for a tiny speaker grille on top, there were no moving parts on Sebastian's faceplate that I could see. Except–for the first time I noticed a tiny knob on his right side.

"What's this for?"

"Press it and see."

I stopped and did just that. Sebastian's faceplate divided in two. Both sides flipped neatly over, and suddenly Sebastian resembled an analogue wristwatch. There was an hour, minute, and second hand, and even a tiny square in place of the three in which to display the date.

"Nifty, eh?" He sounded proud of himself, and slightly more muffled than before.

I decided I preferred him sounding muffled and left him that way. I resumed making my way up the incline. "So you can tell time. Great. What else can you do? Any good apps?"

"You are mistaking me for a common cell phone."

"Are you telling me I can't even use you to make a phone call?"

"I didn't say that. Just the same I would prefer you keep your mouth as far away from my faceplate as possible."

"Hmph." The terrain levelled off a bit, making the going easier. "Look, about going back. The truth is I couldn't have taken the others with me even if I wanted to."

I told him what had happened after I'd said Iugurtha's name. How time had sped up for me alone, effectively slowing everyone else down. About the damage I'd done merely by walking on the floor, and what might have happened had I touched anyone else.

"You're a lucky man," Sebastian said. "Your ignorance could have killed you. Others too. I don't think what happened to the floor had anything to do with kinetic energy, though."

"It was just a theory."

"You must have done something wrong."

"I'm hardly an expert. I probably did most things wrong. But I got us here, didn't I?"

"We could have wound up in a world of molten fire, or on a planet colder than Pluto. Or in a land where beasts of unimaginable proportions battled one another to the death. You could have found yourself trying to suck pure methane through your lungs."

"More reasons not to open the book again until I absolutely have to."

A shadow passed over me. I looked up just in time to see a bird with an enormous wingspan skirting the tree line. The great bird clutched another creature in its talons. The victim writhed in its grasp and emitted a series of ungodly shrieks that set my teeth on edge. And then they were gone.

It wasn't the only bird I saw that day, though ornithologists might beg to differ. I saw many creatures that flew, but they all sported fur instead of feathers. They had no beaks to speak of, and four legs instead of two, along with their wings. Not a one of them sang or chirped. Instead they mewed, like kittens, if they made any sound at all.

There was other native wildlife too, I knew. Just four days ago in Ridley's bedroom, I had seen Iugurtha shoo one of them back through the gate, and the birds all appeared well fed. They were obviously eating something. But wherever all the other animals were they kept well to themselves.

Insects were another story, especially with the onset of night. As the light began to fail I became aware of many tiny, shimmering creatures flitting about me. I would have known they were there even if I couldn't see them because they bit, the pesky things, and it wasn't long until I began to itch like crazy, though I did my best not to scratch.

"You need to stop, Mr. Wildebear," Sebastian told me. "You've made astonishingly little progress, and you won't get much farther in the dark."

I was in no condition to argue. I dropped Humphrey's bag, shrugged off the knapsack, and slumped against one of the large trees out of the wind—exhausted, cold, and sorely tempted to take out the book. I could use it to go someplace else. Someplace warm, where crutches didn't dig into my armpits. Where my right foot didn't ache. Where insects didn't threaten my sanity and I could slip into a comfortable bed. Maybe I was stupid to have tried this on my own. It wouldn't help Ridley one iota if I died of exposure out here where nobody would ever find me. Maybe if I swallowed my pride and said I was sorry Rainer would help me, and we could carry on as if nothing had ever happened.

I didn't move, though. It was too comfortable resting against the tree. I closed my eyes and fell asleep in no time at all.

I dreamt of comfortable down-filled pillows and feather beds, and when I awoke I was all caught up in the blankets—too much tossing and turning. When I went to straighten them there were no blankets and something was crawling on my skin. I tried to brush it off but I couldn't move my arm, and then something was in my hair, and before long I was covered head-to-toe in creepy-crawly things, and I lay there in stark terror as they nibbled their way from one end of me to the other.

"Sebastian, they're eating me alive," I whispered hoarsely.

"Try to relax, Mr. Wildebear."

"I'm all numb!"

"That's because the insects have secreted a poison that is paralyzing you."

How Sebastian could be so blasé about my predicament infuriated me. I made one last Herculean effort to rise, but it was no use. The alien insects had rendered me immobile. I could only sit and wait for the insects to consume me. I hoped my alien carcass gave them all indigestion.

"I'm sorry, Sebastian. Looks like you might be stuck here awhile."

"Don't worry about me, Mr. Wildebear. I'll be fine. Most of my housing is constructed of modified depleted uranium and I have a nuclear power source."

"How nice for you."

Something stirred in the foliage before me. A wild animal inspecting an unfamiliar scent, anticipating a sumptuous meal. A bead of moisture trickled off my forehead. Whether sweat, rain, or poisonous insect secretion, I had no way of knowing. I closed my eyes and steeled myself for the worst.

How long I sat there I have no idea. I may have dozed off. After what seemed an eternity I opened my eyes, expecting something entirely different from what I actually saw.

It was a cat.

Watching me with azure eyes reflecting back the night.

I was struck by the cat's resemblance to felines back on Earth, domesticated and otherwise. Parallel evolution? Just how many times had a gate opened up between this planet and my own? The creature looked like an ordinary tabby housecat, except for its furless toes and faintly indigo pelt, and the fact that it was almost as large as a full-grown lion.

"Do you see him, Mr. Wildebear?" Sebastian asked.

Did the animal mean to devour me or simply watch me die? I couldn't tell–its expression was as inscrutable as–well, as a cat's. I stared at it, acutely aware of every twitch of its magnificent head. Taking in the animal's stately carriage–such dignity, such poise–I inferred a long, noble lineage. It radiated a sleek athleticism, a supple musculature rippling beneath its taut skin. I might well have admired this awesome beast were

I not racked with mortal terror. That, and if I weren't allergic to the insufferable creatures.

The great cat lay down on its belly, resting its head on its paws. I wondered how Sebastian knew it was male. I tried to ask him and produced some foolish sound that didn't mean a thing. I no longer possessed control over my mouth.

I slipped into unconsciousness again. When I awoke the cat was gone. Twice after that I thought I glimpsed it again, but it was only a shadow, or part of the undergrowth. I began to wonder if I had imagined it.

When I actually did see the cat again, it carried a cloth in its mouth. It took the cloth with one of its paws and gently wiped my brow with it. Now I was certain I was dreaming. Cats do not grasp objects with their paws. They do not do this because they do not have opposable thumbs. And never in my experience has a cat ever wiped moisture from anyone's brow.

The ground beneath me shook and two meters of black steel on eight mechanical legs emerged from the night to hunker down beside me. With a clever series of motions this robotic spider made a stretcher of its uppermost self and lifted me on board with four of its metallic limbs. The cat climbed onto the stretcher beside me and laid one of its extraordinary paws on top of my chest. I believe the gesture was meant to be reassuring. The spider elevated itself, and off we went into the gloom of the alien night.

By now the paralysis had begun to affect my respiratory system. I was struggling to breathe. The cat made a sharp motion with a paw, and instantly one of the spider's limbs hovered over me. The tip of the limb flipped inside out to reveal an alarmingly long needle.

"Relax, if you can," Sebastian told me. "He's trying to help you."

It was not possible to relax. It was not possible to do anything. The spider elevated my upper body with two of its limbs. The needle disappeared from my field of vision. I felt an intense pain in the back of my neck.

Reality faded mercifully away.

INSIDE

"I KNOW YOU'RE awake."

I opened my eyes. It was Sebastian.

"The poison in your system has been neutralized. You're able to move now. Though it'll be a while before you feel completely like yourself again."

I felt light-headed and slightly nauseous, but Sebastian was right. I could move again.

"How?" I asked.

"The contraption you're sitting on probably had something to do with it."

Feeling the back of my neck, I found a lump where the mechanical spider had injected me. I took in my surroundings. I was still on top of the spider. Asleep or off, it sat perfectly still next to a stone wall. It was dark but I could see I was inside an enormous, circular chamber. The ceiling was decorated with art of some kind but it was too high and the lighting too dim for me to make it out. The air smelled fresh. Nearby, water flowed in a broad stream built into the rock floor. In the distance I could make out a vast array of objects, large and small, shrouded in shadow. I thought they might be statues, or sculptures. There was no sign of the catlike creature that had saved me.

I looked for my crutches but couldn't see them anywhere. My heart sank as I realized they had probably been left in the woods. Then, it gradually dawned on me that my left leg had supported me as I'd sat up. "Sebastian, I can feel my leg."

"Yes. The post-hypnotic suggestion has finally worn off."

"The—I beg your pardon?"

"The post-hypnotic suggestion Mr. Rainer placed on you during Mind Snoop. The one designed to cripple you so you wouldn't be able to run away. It's amazing the kinds of suggestions you can place on people during Mind Snoop. If you look closely enough, you will also find a tiny surgical incision beneath your knee."

"A surgical incision? What the heck for?"

"In case the post-hypnotic suggestion didn't work, or wore off. Mr. Rainer doesn't like to take any chances."

I struggled to keep the sudden rage inside me contained. I'd still managed to get away from Rainer. "You probably weren't supposed to tell me that."

"No," Sebastian admitted. "Probably not."

I climbed down off the spider and stood on my leg for a few seconds before trying an experimental hop. A bolt of pain shot up my thigh. It subsided quickly enough, but although I could stand and walk with little difficulty, it hurt like heck when I put too much weight on it.

"Great. Now it hurts," I complained. I shook my head, thinking of Rainer and his bald-faced lies. The whole lot of them, really, pretending that they didn't know what was wrong with me.

I sighed and peered into the shadows surrounding us. My crutches were gone, but what about everything else? Humphrey's bag was nowhere to be seen. I spotted my knapsack lying near one of the spider's motionless black limbs. I picked it up. It was heavy–still full of supplies–but not as heavy as should have been. It was missing the book.

It wasn't possible. The book couldn't be gone. How would I get back to Earth without it? Feeling weak, I leaned against the spider. The mechanical creature stirred and I backed away quickly. It shifted forward slightly, two of its arms hovering briefly in the air before settling once again.

"The entity took the book while you were sleeping," Sebastian said.

"Iugurtha? She's here?"

"Yes."

If Iugurtha were here, then Ridley probably was too. And Humphrey, and Humphrey's wife, and Angelique, and everyone else Iugurtha had abducted. I would worry about the book later. My first priority was finding Ridley. I'd search this place inside and out if that's what it took.

I set out for the mysterious objects barely visible in the distance, walking as fast as I could with my bad leg. I had gone only a few paces when I heard a great whirring and clicking behind me.

"Something doesn't want you to go," Sebastian said.

The spider had awoken. I did not look back.

I sped up, ignoring the growing pain in my leg, expecting the spider to grab me from behind, flip me over, and slam me repeatedly against the floor. Instead it moved past me much faster than I would have thought possible and manoeuvred directly in my path. When I tried to move around it, it blocked me.

I set my jaw and limped straight toward it. It didn't budge. I clambered onto its metal carapace and began scaling the thing. Two mechanical limbs whirred directly into my path. When I attempted to crawl between them, I got a sharp rap on the top of my head for my trouble. Apparently the spider was through fooling around. Chastened, I staggered off the mechanical beast, clutching the top of my head with my hands.

Back at the mouth of the artificial stream I stared into the roiling water. If I were to dive into it, where would it take me? To freedom? Not bloody likely. God only knew what I would encounter in such a stream. Probably it would simply deposit my bloated carcass on some distant shore. Either way it wouldn't get me any closer to Ridley.

The water looked fresh though. I licked my parched lips. "Do you think this water's okay to drink, Sebastian?"

"Hold me in it," he suggested.

I knelt and plunged my arm into the frigid water up to my elbow, keeping him submerged for a good five or six seconds.

"Feel any cleaner?" I asked afterward.

"It's good old H_2O, all right," he said, water beading on his faceplate. "Safe to drink. Bacteria levels are low. No pollution to speak of."

"What does it taste like?"

"Do I look like I have a mouth?"

I scooped up a handful and took a sip. It tasted metallic, but fine. I scooped up several more handfuls and drank my fill.

Sitting back, I peered up, trying to make out the ceiling, but I couldn't see much up there. It was too dark and the ceiling was too high. "What do you make of this place, Sebastian?"

"It's pretty big."

"Seriously, that's the best you can do?"

"I can tell you we're inside a mountain."

Intrigued, I stood and moved to the wall. It was all of a piece, grey and perfectly cut. Stroking it with my fingers, I realized it wasn't stone after all. It was too smooth, too warm to the touch. I wandered along it, feeling with my hand for imperfections. I felt none. Out of the corner of my eye I was aware of the spider pacing me, but it made no move to stop me as I moved away from the stream. I wondered how far it would allow me to go.

I hadn't gone far when I became aware of a growing pressure in my bladder. Secure in the knowledge that we were alone, I unzipped and unleashed a frothy yellow stream against the wall. Sadly, traversing the universe through mysterious gates on the heels of enigmatic aliens had not resulted in the suspension of such mundane activities. If anything I had to pee more often.

"Do you mind?" Sebastian asked.

This had been an ongoing issue the day before. "Try not to look," I said.

"The least you could do is put me in your pocket."

"Just relax."

"If you get any on me –"

"I told you I was sorry about–damn!"

We weren't alone after all. A beautiful blonde woman in violet fatigues looked on as I fumbled with my zipper.

Iugurtha.

"You! Where's my nephew?" I said, as much to conceal my embarrassment as anything else.

She held a book in her hands. The book. She strode

swiftly toward me, her intent unclear. I suspected she was much stronger than she appeared.

"What?" I asked, bracing myself.

"Don't be afraid," she said, and threw the book in the air.

It opened and expanded. I felt a connection to it. I felt empowered by it. Images flitted before my eyes with incredible rapidity. Information surged through my mind. I did not understand all I was seeing but I understood a good portion of it. I saw many worlds, many universes, even infinite dimensions and times. In only a small number of them could I survive as me.

I did not see Iugurtha move until it was too late. Until she grabbed me with both hands, heaved me off my feet, and tossed me through the air into the gate. The gate latched on to me and yanked me forward. Sucked into it like a mote in a wind tunnel, I caught an upside down glimpse of Iugurtha's expressionless face before I was whirling, sliding, tumbling head over heels into a featureless black void. I flailed wildly, desperate for something to grab on to, but there was nothing. I passed through a thin film of agony, and just like that the work of a lifetime was undone, peeled off in one excruciating instant. Just like that, the part of me that had been Barnabus Jehosophys Wildebear was gone.

X
INVADERS

I CAME TO in someone else's mind.

I could feel their presence all around me—living, breathing, dreaming, being. It was as though instead of throwing me through the gate, Iugurtha had thrown me into the deep end of a pool, and I couldn't swim. I was drowning in the sea of someone else's consciousness.

A solitary spark of me persisted. A kernel of life from another place, another time. I struggled to remain afloat, to find something upon which to hang the loose ends of me, but there was nothing.

Desperate for a connection with the physical world, for anything that might allow me to retain my idea of self, I clutched at this other body's senses, but nothing smelled right, or looked right, or sounded right. Incredibly, Iugurtha had placed me in the mind of another person, forcing me to see the world through their eyes, via their unique senses. But whose mind? And why? And why me?

"Calm yourself," a voice said.

Iugurtha. I couldn't see her—what little I could see was chaotic, confused, and difficult to make sense of. Nor could I hear her, exactly. But I registered her, like the ever-persistent voice in my head, except that it wasn't my voice or my thoughts I was registering, it was Iugurtha's.

"What have you done to me?"

"I have placed you in the mind of a young T'Klee. Soon you'll be able to make sense of her thoughts just as you can mine."

"The gate can do that?"

"The gate can do a lot of things."

"What's a T'Klee?"

"An inhabitant of the planet C'Mell, distantly related to the cats of Earth. Unlike their cousins on Earth they have evolved opposable thumbs and can wield tools, like humans."

"This is insane. I've gone mad. I've completely lost my marbles."

"In my estimation you have never been entirely sane but you are no more insane now than you've ever been."

"This T'Klee. Does she have a name?"

"She would be called Sweep in your language."

"Why?"

"It's short for Sweep of the Paw, because she sweeps her paw in front of her face when she's upset."

"No. I mean, why have you done this to me?"

"Because Ridley wanted you to understand."

"Understand what?"

"What he is fighting for."

"I don't care what–"

"Shhh," Iugurtha said, or the mental equivalent. "It has begun."

"What? What's begun?"

I smelled them long before I heard them: strong

overtones of excrement mingled with sweat and a hint of vomit. I registered it all through Sweep's senses as though through my own. Someone—a T'Klee—cried out in pain. Sweep's heart caught in her throat. T'Klee do not normally make sounds, I would come to learn—they speak with a twitch of the ear, a flick of the tail.

Sweep had been out gathering berries not far from her family's farm. She raced frantically back home, taking the shortest route possible through prickly underbrush. She tore out of the forest with her tail high and her eyes wide. The sight that confronted us was like running full tilt into a barn wall. There, in the space of half a dozen heartbeats, we glimpsed enough horror to last a lifetime.

Impossible beings dredged from the muck of somebody's worst nightmare. Pulsating bags of yellow skin depositing trails of golden slime behind them wherever they slithered. Enormous tentacles wielding slender silver wands that sent Sweep's family into convulsions at a mere touch. Sweep herself stood frozen in shock, watching the unthinkable—her brothers and sisters, her parents, utterly helpless before this overwhelming foe.

Necronians.

The name popped into my consciousness from out of nowhere. No, not out of nowhere—back in my basement, in what seemed another lifetime, the scientist Giorgio had spoken of such creatures. Evil beings from beyond the gate that existed solely to wreak havoc on the universe. Awful, tentacled things he called Necronians. There was no doubt in my mind that's what we were dealing with here.

Sweep watched her eldest brother Whitepaw leap, his dagger-sharp teeth and claws bared for the kill.

Except his opponent had no throat. It wouldn't have mattered anyway. Whitepaw bounced right off the creature before he even seemed to touch it. In a stunning display of martial athleticism, he twisted in mid-air and launched a second attack the instant he hit the ground. It didn't help. The monster connected with a silver wand and Whitepaw careened off the monster for a second time. This time he crashed to the ground and lay there convulsing.

I heard a long, plaintive wail. It wasn't until the sound ended that I realized it was Sweep herself. She was only a child. I felt her terror as though it were my own. The monsters were all around her, striking down her family, destroying their farm, razing their crops, and slaughtering their herd of rawk, the bison-like beasts upon which they depended for much of their sustenance. Another of Sweep's family fell. So viscerally did I feel Sweep's anguish that it was as though a member of my own family had fallen.

Something grabbed Sweep by the scruff of the neck and yanked her violently off her feet. Instinctively she curled into a ball. Whatever had hold of her had no problem carrying her. I couldn't see it, but as we loped through the forest I suspected from its gait that it was another T'Klee.

"Who's that?" I asked Iugurtha, inside Sweep's mind. "Who's got her?"

"Half Ear. Her uncle. Really he's her father but she doesn't know that."

I knew about Half Ear, I realized. I knew it because I was tapped into at least a superficial layer of Sweep's thoughts. If I wanted to I could root around in her mind and learn even more, but I didn't. That would have felt invasive and wrong. Still, it was impossible to completely shut out her thoughts. There was plenty I couldn't help but know.

"What you're showing me—is it happening now?"

"No. It happened ten years ago your time."

"Will Sweep be okay? What happens to her?"

But she would reveal nothing more.

I couldn't hear the battle anymore when Half Ear finally set Sweep down. The reason for Half Ear's name was immediately obvious—the grizzled old fighter was missing the better part of his left ear.

"Let's go," he told Sweep with a flick of his head.

I watched through Sweep's eyes as Half Ear led her further into the forest than she'd ever been. Over brooks, through almost impassable underbrush, up and down hills and valleys, never out into the open. We never saw another T'Klee, and we didn't see any monsters either, though we saw much evidence of their passing: trails of dried slime, yellow and smelling strongly of urine.

"Look," I said to Iugurtha. "I get it. Sweep's people were invaded by these Necronian creatures. It's sad, and it's not like I don't care, but there's nothing I can do about it. It doesn't have anything to do with me. I just want my nephew back."

"You don't want to see what happens to Sweep." It wasn't a question.

"No," I admitted. Not if it was something bad.

"Too bad," Iugurtha said. "Pay attention."

"Can't we at least skip ahead?"

"This isn't a movie," she said. "It's real life."

"Real life that's already happened," I reminded her. "So, why don't you use your gate to fast forward a bit?"

Somewhat to my surprise she complied, returning to real time when Half Ear finally stopped at a stream for a gulp of water.

"Where are we going?" Sweep asked him.

Instead of answering, Half Ear handed her a pouch. She reached inside and grasped a handful of food with her incredible paw with its opposable thumb, just like a human would. The food tasted like ashes accompanied by the memories of what she had seen.

She tried Half Ear again. "What were those things? Where did they come from?"

Half Ear took so long answering that I didn't think he was going to respond to these questions either, but finally he said, "Near as I can tell, they came from above. Crawled out of the belly of great birds that flew down from the sky. I was hunting when they came, a flock of the biggest birds I've ever seen. I couldn't believe my eyes. Then I saw that they weren't birds at all, but monsters. Right then I knew I was dreaming. A waking dream–a test, maybe. I followed them to see what the test would be. Thought it might have something to do with hunting. But it was no dream. There are hundreds of them," he added. "Attacking everywhere at once."

He fell still, leaving Sweep and me to think about what that meant.

He took a long drink of water. "Thought we might head south," he said afterward.

Sweep made the characteristic gesture for which she was named. "What about our family? What will happen to them? Are we just running away?" She made no effort to conceal the scorn in her expression.

Half Ear regarded his young charge. "Listen to me,

little one. There's nothing we can do for our brothers and sisters now."

"Why not?"

"Because by now they will have already have been skinned, gutted, and their pelts hung up to dry."

Sweep stood stunned. I saw a mental picture form in her mind of her mother's beautiful violet pelt without her mother inside it.

If Half Ear noticed the slack-jawed horror on Sweep's face he did not acknowledge it. "Let's go."

Sweep didn't move. When she spoke it was all she could do to make the gestures happen. "Did you–see them do that?"

"I saw it happen to others, yes."

"What would they do with our skins?"

Half Ear shook his great head. "I can't imagine." He leapt onto a big rock, preparing to cross the stream. "Now come on."

"But what if–I don't want anyone to take my skin!"

Half Ear didn't do anything for a moment. Then in a single leap he was back at Sweep's side. Two enormous paws cradled her face. I thought he was going to comfort her, tell her a white lie or two.

"Listen to me, little one. Our lives may well depend on this. When I tell you to do something I need you to do it. Okay?"

"But my sisters, my brothers–"

"We're going to Burning Eyes."

Burning Eyes? I knew from exposure to Sweep's thoughts that she had grown up listening to tales of Burning Eyes: a fickle creature whose origins were shrouded in myth. Who changed appearance and character often, and who could only be recognized by eyes that were said to burn like embers. But Burning Eyes had not been seen in many years. Most T'Klee suspected he had long since passed from this world, if ever he had existed at all.

"What can Burning Eyes do about monsters that come out of birds in the sky?" Sweep asked. "Monsters you can't even touch? Why hasn't he done anything already?"

"Don't talk about Burning Eyes like that. He might be able to hear you."

I could see that Sweep wasn't quite sure what she believed about Burning Eyes, but she certainly didn't believe that. The idea that Burning Eyes could help her get even with monsters that had destroyed her family appealed to her enormously, though. "Do you really think Burning Eyes will help us?"

"Burning Eyes honours his debts."

As near as I could tell from Sweep's thoughts on the matter, the stories concerning Burning Eyes frequently involved transactions of some sort. T'Klee would leave Burning Eyes gifts in return for services such as assistance with crops, or the elimination of a threat. Some stories even involved offering up living sacrifices. But such stories were from long ago, little more than legends. It was difficult to see how Burning Eyes could still be around today if in fact he had ever lived at all. If he did still live there was no guarantee that he would honour any debts. And even if he did, the legends I gleaned from Sweep's mind suggested that doing business with him could be a dangerous proposition.

"Burning Eye's appreciation for beauty is legendary," Half Ear added. "He won't let creatures as ugly as these monsters live anywhere near his mountain. Now come on."

So Half Ear had a sense of humour. It was good to know.

It gave Sweep just enough strength to follow him.

I am not the most astute of individuals at the best of times, and trapped inside the mind of an alien cat I was decidedly not at my best. Even so I could not miss the similarity between Iugurtha and the creature Half Ear referred to as Burning Eyes. True, in the legends Burning Eyes was male and had lived for generations. But Iugurtha had placed me here through the gate, and could certainly be described as having eyes that burned. Could it be coincidence that I should come across talk of someone who resembled her?

"This Burning Eyes," I asked her, from within the confines of Sweep's mind. "Is he related to you in some way?"

"Yes," she said.

"Father? Grandfather?"

"I am Burning Eyes."

"How is that possible? Burning Eyes would have to be ancient, wouldn't he? You're female. He was male. Except for the eyes you look completely different."

"I have come in many different shapes and sizes over the years."

"I don't understand."

"Nor will you, if you don't pay attention. Be silent."

I did as I was told. The longer I existed in Sweep's brain the more adept I became at translating her senses, and as I did so I began to make connections. I recognized the forest through which Half Ear was leading her. The colours were different through Sweep's nocturnal eyes—more vivid, the oranges a flaming red and the greens practically fluorescent—but I recognized the trees with their great trunks and expansive canopies. I was definitely on the planet that Iugurtha had taken Ridley, and from which Iugurtha had flung me into Sweep's mind—the same planet ten years in the past.

Half Ear was leading us toward a mountain, he told Sweep. He knew the way—he had delivered offerings on behalf of his family several times. As we drew closer to the mountain and I saw it jutting over the horizon I realized that I had been to this mountain before. With Sebastian, another alien cat, and a giant mechanical spider.

The Necronians only seemed to come out during the day, so Half Ear and Sweep travelled at night. They slept during the day, hiding as best they could and taking turns watching over one another. Everywhere we went, evidence of the Necronians greeted them. Tracks of decaying slime, farms burnt to the ground, rawk mutilated for no reason that Sweep could see. Several times she stumbled across dead T'Klee before Half Ear could whisk her away.

As Sweep staggered behind Half Ear, trying her best to keep up, her thoughts were on her family. She had seen her brothers and cousins struck down. She didn't know what had become of her sisters and mother, but she had a pretty good idea. T'Klee don't cry but they have other ways of making their suffering known.

Ahead of us, Half Ear could not see Sweep compulsively twitch her tail and ears. At ground zero inside her mind, I was almost overwhelmed by her grief. I wanted to help her, but there was nothing I could do to ease her pain. I could not hold her. I could not speak to her soothingly. She didn't even know I existed. Were I capable of making my presence known, somehow I doubted that she would find the notion of an alien living inside her mind comforting.

"Skip ahead," I ordered Iugurtha. "I get it. Okay? The child is suffering. I feel her pain. I know you want me to help her somehow but I don't see how. Especially trapped here inside her mind."

Iugurtha did as I asked. She took us forward a day and a night to when Half Ear and Sweep reached Burning Eye's mountain. They had settled in for the day in shallow sleeping pits, mostly dug by Half Ear, though Sweep had helped as best she could. Thanks to Half Ear's skills they were well hidden. All they had to do was keep still and the Necronians roaming the countryside would never find them.

Sweep was trying her best to stay calm. To take her mind off her troubles, she asked Half Ear, "What happened to your ear?"

"What about my ear?"

"It's missing a chunk."

"Oh that. It got chewed off."

"By what?"

"A bandaloot. A particularly ornery one."

"It must have been big." In Sweep's mind only a huge, fearsome bandaloot could have gotten the better of an experienced old warrior like Half Ear.

Half Ear threw his head back and closed his eyes. His head bobbed up and down as he laughed the silent laughter of the T'Klee.

"Have you ever seen a bandaloot?" he asked when he regained control of himself.

T'Klee were voracious meat eaters. Sweep's family

was no exception–they ate a lot of bandaloot meat during the summer. She told Half Ear that.

"Ah. But have you ever seen one whole?"

She hadn't actually. For the first time she realized that she had no idea what a bandaloot looked like. "They're not big?"

"A big one would be about half the size of your head."

Sweep considered that. Size didn't necessarily mean anything. There were bugs she could barely see that could kill a grown T'Klee with a single bite. "But they're dangerous, right?"

"Only if one gets a hold of your ear," Half Ear said. "They've got sharp teeth and they know how to hold on. Whatever you do, don't let a bandaloot get a hold of one of your ears."

Sweep promised Half Ear that she wouldn't.

After a while she began to tremble again as her fears got the better of her.

"Keep still now." Half Ear placed a paw on her neck.

Sweep was well aware that her life might depend on doing what he said. She tried to keep still but couldn't.

Half Ear tightened his grip on her. "You can do better than that." He squeezed so much that it hurt.

Sweep lashed out at him, and they struggled briefly there in the pit, but Half Ear was much too strong. Sweep couldn't make him let go.

She slammed a paw against his hide and kept it there. "You're hurting me!"

"You need to be still."

"This is stupid. This whole thing. Burning Eyes is dead."

Half Ear didn't answer.

"They're all dead. Everyone. The other families too."

The only sound was that of Half Ear's breathing. It sounded unnaturally loud in the sleeping pit.

"Why?" Sweep asked.

"Why what?" Half Ear asked.

"Why are we still alive when everyone else is dead?"

Half Ear must have had some inkling of Sweep's distress. Yet all he said was, "I don't know."

He was dealing with his own grief, I suspected. Maybe he felt the weight of the entire T'Klee race on his back just then. Or maybe he was just being honest.

Sweep was thinking her own thoughts. She knew perfectly well what Half Ear was thinking: that someone else should have survived in her place. Someone who could help him fight the monsters. Someone like one of her brothers. She wished someone else had survived in Half Ear's place—someone who knew how to make her feel better, instead of making her feel useless, and sad.

She finally fell asleep, but she did not sleep well, dreaming of bandaloots descending from the sky to chew off everyone's ears.

We smelled them first, just as we had before: a sickly scent of rotting fish and vegetation. "They're coming!" Sweep said. "They're going to find us!"

Half Ear didn't say anything. He didn't have to. Sweep had no trouble being still now, until one of the Necronian's wands crackled, causing her to start violently. Perversely, she was more afraid of Half Ear getting mad at her than of the monsters discovering them. But Half Ear did not reprimand her. More of the Necronians' wands crackled, and we heard the rustling of grass and leaves. Half Ear lifted the cover off our pit ever so slightly. Necronians oozed everywhere, their wands crackling fiercely as they advanced. The Necronians were right on top of them. Half Ear and Sweep didn't stand a chance.

Half Ear chose that moment to burst out of the pit. He did so with such force that branches scattered for several tree lengths. Sweep followed mere whiskers behind. Monstrous heads with enormous eyes swivelled as we shot past, but they were not quick enough to stop two T'Klee bolting at top speed.

Sweep began to slow. Half Ear angled his head and swept her up by the scruff of her neck without a single wasted motion and carried on. Sounds of the monsters faded, then disappeared. Comfortable in Half Ear's grasp, she fell asleep. When she awoke and opened her eyes, I thought it was still day, until I saw the two moons hanging in the sky. Even with the forest canopy blocking much of the light Sweep had to shield her eyes.

Half Ear had used his sharp claws to scale a tree and look around. When he came back down, he said, "We can rest here, but not for long."

Sweep started digging, but Half Ear stopped her.

"They can find us even if we bury ourselves. We just won't stay long. You've already slept–now let me."

He lay down. But instead of going to sleep, he glanced up at Sweep. "I've been thinking about what you said."

"What?"

"About going to Burning Eyes. Do you still think it's stupid?"

Embarrassed, Sweep didn't say anything.

"I know why I'm still alive," Half Ear said.

"Why?"

"Because I'm going to save our people. When I was young I didn't believe in Burning Eyes. I thought the whole idea of offering up sacrifices to him in return for services that never happened was silly. So the last time I brought him an offering on behalf of the family I waited. I hid and waited a long time because I wanted to see what if anything took the offering."

Sweep didn't say anything. She was learning to be quiet, like a grown-up T'Klee. But Half Ear didn't go on, and Sweep was not grown up, not yet.

"What took the offering?" she asked finally.

"Burning Eyes took the offering."

Sweep drew a sharp breath. "You saw him? What did he look like?"

"Terrible. And beautiful. He stood on his hind legs, and he was naked—didn't have a lick of fur on him anywhere. He shone like polished stone. And his eyes were just like everyone's always said. You know how when a fire's dying and you've got those embers that keep on glowing? They burned like that."

Sweep could see it clearly in her mind's eye. I could too.

"What did you do?" she asked. "When you saw him."

"I followed him. All the way up Kimay. He never knew I was there. I saw where he lives and I can find it again. That's the reason I'm still alive. So I can save our people."

Sweep could accept that. If anybody could save their people it was Half Ear. "What about me?"

Sweep felt herself withering under Half Ear's gaze, but she didn't look away for fear of missing what he might say.

"I can't tell you why you're still alive," he said. "You need to decide that for yourself."

Moments later Sweep and I watched as Half Ear's back rose and fell rhythmically. She lay close to him, still and frightened, with no idea why she was still alive.

Half Ear didn't sleep long. Soon they were on the move again. The further they went the steeper it got. There was nothing resembling a trail. The incline became so great that Sweep found it difficult to keep her footing. Several times she slipped on the rocks. Overwhelmed, she focused on putting one paw in front of the other.

I wasn't much better off. Back in the sleeping pit I had thought we were done for. I knew that if Sweep died I probably would too. I didn't want to die, particularly. I couldn't, not until I'd rescued Ridley. But I didn't have much say in the matter. I had mastered Sweep's senses, and at times I felt so a part of her that I lost myself in her, and we were one. But then I would attempt to turn my head or scratch my nose or lick my paw and it wouldn't happen and my plight would slap me in my disembodied face like a wet fish. Life inside Sweep was a roller coaster with no end. It was exhilarating, terrifying, and I wanted off the damn thing right now.

I could not allow myself to be trapped inside Sweep until her death. There had been a way into her mind; there had to be a way out. I began hunting for it in earnest. I was not blind to Sweep's own plight, but aside from sending warm, fuzzy thoughts her way there was nothing I could do about it.

Soon they were high on the mountain. Vegetation was sparse. The forest had thinned to just a few scraggly trees. The turf gave way to rock, jagged and black except where it glittered brilliantly in the light of the planet's twin moons. It was like walking on a sky with a million stars twinkling underfoot. The light from the twin moons was relentless. Sweep kept her eyes open mere slits and focussed on Half Ear in front of her, trying not to think about the damage the rock was doing to her paws.

The barren mountain slope might as well have been a stage and the twin moons giant spotlights. Sweep shielded her eyes with a paw and looked to the sky. Something had spotted them. A dark mass resolved swiftly into the likeness of an enormous bird. Two Necronians sat inside the bird's belly. The bird made no noise as it dove toward them.

"Hurry," Half Ear instructed.

Sweep clung to Half Ear's tail, trying not to stumble. Any faster and he would have been dragging her. Strong winds and jutting cliffs prevented the Necronians and their craft from getting too close. When Sweep saw that they couldn't reach her a sense of wonder briefly surpassed her fear. There was magic at work here. How had these evil creatures come by such enchantment? Were good creatures capable of such feats as well? Burning Eyes, perhaps? But in all the tales, Burning Eyes was a capricious being, capable of both good and evil. For all Sweep knew, Burning Eyes had already chosen sides, and not hers.

Just when Sweep was thinking that she couldn't go on much longer, Half Ear stopped so suddenly that she bumped into him.

"What's wrong?" she asked.

If Half Ear answered, Sweep couldn't see it. He was facing the wrong way and Sweep's eyes were watering in the bright light. She wiped them and tried to step around Half Ear, to talk to him and figure out where they were, but there wasn't enough room to manoeuvre. On her left was an almost vertical descent, and on her right a gigantic pile of rocks, the detritus of an ancient rock slide. As near as I could make out through Sweep's tortured eyes, we were blocked by a sheer rock face that rose straight up as far as the eye could see. There would be no climbing to the top of this mountain. There was nowhere to go except back down the way they had come. There was no chance of climbing the rock face, no way around it, and no sign of Burning Eyes. Half Ear had led them the wrong way.

Overhead, the Necronians swept closer in their alien craft. In the distance another craft was fast approaching, its green light blinking eerily.

Half Ear stood on his hind legs and pressed his paws against the rock face. Retracting his claws, he extended his fingers as far as he could and began feeling the rock.

"There's a door here," he told Sweep. "We need to find it."

"A door?" Sweep asked. "Here? How?"

"I followed Burning Eyes up the mountain and saw him go in a door here. This is the place, I'm sure of it. We need to find that door."

Half Ear's calm manner steadied Sweep. Without understanding how there could be a door in solid rock she threw herself into the task of finding it. I threw myself once again into the task of finding a door inside her. Unfortunately, neither of us knew quite what we were looking for. Sweep found several indentations in the stone, but none of them appeared to have any significance. And inside Sweep I found nothing I hadn't already found before.

Sweep glanced back and we saw that the Necronian craft had managed to land on the path behind us. The two Necronians were oozing out of it. Sweep's heart began to pound. The Necronians moved slowly but it was only a matter of time until they covered the short distance between us.

Sweep tried to force her brain to function but it seemed to have turned to sludge. Maybe—maybe Half Ear was wrong, and this wasn't the right place after all. Or maybe there was no door and he'd just made the whole thing up, to give her hope. Though that didn't seem Half Ear's style. Either way it didn't look like they were going to find a door any time soon.

She clutched at him. "Half Ear, they're coming! I can't find a door!"

He ignored her and kept pawing at the rock. Eventually he had no choice but to accept the reality that there was no door, along with the very real possibility that he had led himself and his charge to their doom. His shoulders slumped ever so slightly and he looked at Sweep. To a human that great face would have appeared devoid of expression, but I saw him as Sweep saw him. I saw the fur begin to bristle and the ears descend. I saw the eyes narrow, the talons extend and the lips draw back, revealing just a hint of those dagger-sharp incisors.

He turned to face his enemy.

The Necronians clutched their silver wands in sinewy tentacles. The wands described rhythmic arcs in the air as the Necronians slimed forward. There was something hypnotic about the wands. They trailed particles of fluorescent pink and orange light after them. Sweep's eyes were locked on them in horrified fascination.

The Necronians hadn't completely cut them off yet. A quick dash between them and the cliff, and it just might be possible to escape.

"Run, Little One," Half Ear told Sweep. "While I keep them busy."

It might have worked. If Sweep had run fast enough, and Half Ear had managed to keep the Necronians occupied. But transfixed by the dance of the wands, Sweep didn't budge.

"Go!" Half Ear cuffed her on the side of the head. "Run!"

Sweep tore her eyes from the wands and looked up at him. "By myself?"

"I'll find you later. You know I will."

But Sweep couldn't will her paws to move. If she went without Half Ear, the monsters would get her. So she stayed put–and then the moment was past. The Necronians were too close and there was no way around them.

Half Ear saw how it was.

"Okay," he said. "Here's what I need you to do. Stay away from their sticks. Pick up some rocks."

He backed up against the rock pile as the Necronians continued their slow, inexorable shamble forward. Sweep began arming herself with as many rocks as she could carry.

Half Ear spoke quickly now. "Lure them to the cliff with the rocks, then get out of the way. I'll get behind them and–"

But the time for talk was over. The Necronians were upon them. Sweep moved as close to the cliff edge as she dared. One of the Necronians made for her while the other closed in on Half Ear. Sweep threw her rocks at the one attacking Half Ear, attempting to draw it toward her, but the rocks bounced harmlessly off it. It ignored Sweep completely and concentrated on Half Ear.

Sweep's nightmarish assailant wielded its wand like an expert fencer, and I wondered which would be the better fate: death by the monster's wand or by plummeting to the trees and rocks below.

Green light cast a sickly pall over us as the second alien craft approached. Sweep threw the rest of the rocks at her enemy in a futile gesture of defiance. She never saw the blow that sent her convulsing to the ground: all she knew was a cold pain that racked her entire body. The Necronian loomed over her, its moist tentacles curling and squirming inches from her whiskers.

Something tall and blue appeared from out of nowhere and slammed into the Necronian with terrific force. The sheer might of the blow knocked it off balance. Before the monster could recover, the newcomer struck again, this time propelling the Necronian over the cliff's edge amid a shower of pebbles.

Sweep's rescuer turned its attention to Sweep, and its eyes—I would have recognized them anywhere. Impossibly tall and thin, its skin looked like it would snap if it were stretched one iota further. Except for the eyes and the fact that it was bipedal, this creature looked nothing like Iugurtha. I did not see how they could be one and the same. Perhaps I had misunderstood Iugurtha.

The longest arm I have ever seen grabbed Sweep

by the scruff of the neck and began dragging her toward a hole in the rock face–Half Ear's elusive door. Paralyzed by the Necronian's wand, Sweep was powerless to resist.

Half Ear leapt after us, his adversary nowhere to be seen.

"Burning Eyes," he said with uncharacteristic reverence. "Hear me. We've come a long way to find you. We –"

Burning Eyes spun with unnatural swiftness and struck him viciously across the head. Half Ear was sent sprawling backwards. He picked himself up and spent a precious second shaking off the blow.

"Half Ear, help me!"

Lifting his head, Half Ear seemed to register Sweep's plight for the first time. I saw disbelief, then comprehension dawn in his eyes. He did not waste another instant. Drawing his lips back in a snarl, he leapt at his new enemy.

Burning Eye's second, third, and fourth blows were not so kind. The fifth sent Half Ear tumbling out of Sweep's sight. Sweep closed her eyes at this fresh horror. All of her was numb now.

Rock grated on rock. I couldn't hear the wind anymore. Burning Eyes let go. Sweep slumped to the ground, just enough muscle control left to gaze up at her abductor.

So this is Burning Eyes, she thought.

She spoke to him urgently, her speech impeded by partial paralysis.

Save Half Ear, she implored.

Burning Eyes didn't respond.

She begged Burning Eyes to save all her people—still no answer.

Desperate, she promised Burning Eyes all the offerings he desired if only he would take up her cause, but Burning Eyes did not move. He remained so still that I began to wonder if he could move at all any more, or if he had somehow frozen in place.

All out of words, Sweep fell still herself.

When Burning Eyes did move it was a shock. Sweep flinched, then watched as he took a ring off a lean finger and tossed it high in the air. When it began transforming into the gate on the way down I was not at all surprised.

Wintry fingers gripped my soul. I felt myself yanked backward. There was no pain but it was uncomfortable, as if I were a particularly stubborn variety of thistle that somebody was trying to tear up by the roots.

One final tug, and I emerged into the light.

XI
VEGETATION ABOUNDED

IT WAS AWFUL—THE light too bright and the sounds too loud. I cried out and curled up into a ball to protect myself.

"Wildebear! Can you hear me? What's the matter with him?"

"He's a little mixed up. It happens sometimes after a trip through the gate. Especially when you aren't used to it."

"What are you talking about? Will he be all right?"

"He should."

"Should?"

"He might not."

"Will he or won't he?"

"That's what you're here for, Doctor. To see that he's okay."

"Hmph. What happened to him?"

"Not much. Plenty."

"That's an infuriating thing to say."

"I'm sorry."

"Don't be sorry—just don't say anything like that ever again."

"I can't promise that I'll—"

"Enough! Just—where was he, anyway?"

"Where he needed to be."

"Oh, for crying out–Wildebear! Wildebear, it's me, Humphrey."

I peeked out from between my arms to see who was talking. My memories were all jumbled up. *Humphrey*–the name sounded familiar. He had a lot of meat on him, this Humphrey. He'd make a sumptuous meal. And I just happened to be starving. Although a part of me knew there was something terribly wrong with the idea, I unfurled myself in anticipation of a feast. Catching a glimpse of one of my front paws, I was shocked to discover that it was almost completely hairless. My God! Was I ill? I emitted a most un-T'Klee like whimper and curled back up.

"Physiologically he's all over the map," a voice said. "His pulse is racing and his serotonin levels are dangerously low."

It had come from my front foreleg. Something shiny and silver was attached to me. I tried to lick it off.

The creature Humphrey leaned down to touch me. Instantly I whirled on it, but something was the matter with my reflexes. Before I could deliver the coup de grace the Humphrey creature grabbed hold of me and held fast. I found myself in the embarrassing position of having been captured by my own prey. I hoped none of my brothers were around to see.

Except... I had no brothers. It was Sweep's brothers I was thinking of.

And I was not Sweep.

Was I?

"Damn it, Wildebear, what were you trying to do? Slit my throat?"

Humphrey. Humphrey! It was my old friend Doctor Peter Humphrey–and I had been about to eat him! What had I been thinking? Awfully confused, flitting back and forth between two identities, one human, the other a cat, I could not have said who or what I was just then.

"You should think about cutting your nails once in a while," Humphrey muttered.

A thin red line had emerged on the side of Humphrey's neck. My attempt to dispatch him had come altogether too close for comfort. I started to apologize, but couldn't seem to get the words out—talking involved using whiskers I no longer possessed.

Humphrey let go and stepped back. I tried desperately to pull myself together. I had no fur, no whiskers. I was, therefore, not a cat. I was a human. And humans spoke with their—

"Humphrey! I—I'm so sorry. It's—it's good to see you alive!"

He touched a finger to his neck. The tip came away red. "Little thanks to you."

I rose to my feet and took in my surroundings. We were in a place I hadn't been before—a small room blanketed in luxurious sheets and pillows. Frills, tassels, reds and purples abounded. The furnishings would not have been out of place in a sultan's tent.

Humphrey and I were not the only ones in the room. Iugurtha was there as well.

I began backing slowly away.

"You're scaring him," Humphrey told her.

"It's not me he should be afraid of," she said.

And with that, everything fell into place. Suddenly I knew precisely who I was, where I was, and what I had just been through. It seemed incredible, but I had just spent hours, if not days, living inside the mind of an alien cat. After an experience like that it was a wonder I was anything resembling sane.

"Wildebear."

"Yes, Doctor."

"You're licking the backs of your hands."

"Ah." I stopped and considered. "So I am."

Then, because there really was no better way to relieve stress, I resumed licking in earnest.

"Don't ever do that to me again," I told Iugurtha sternly, in between licks.

"Once should suffice," she said. "What is your opinion, Doctor? Is he in good health?"

"Nothing a little bed rest and years of psychotherapy won't fix," Humphrey replied.

I must have been exhausted; I didn't even remember falling asleep. The next thing I knew I was waking up to find Iugurtha pulling me up by the arm. The beautiful blonde woman who was in fact not a beautiful woman but a composite of at least two people and possibly an alien or two pulled me effortlessly to my feet with one hand.

I broke away from her, afraid she was going to throw me through the gate again. "You—get away from me!"

Looking around, I could see no sign of the doctor. "What have you done with Humphrey? Is he okay?"

"The doctor's fine." She marched out of the small chamber into the cavernous space beyond.

I trailed after her limping something awful—my bad leg had not improved a whit. I wanted nothing to do with this strange and dangerous creature, but I was brimming with questions—first and foremost, the whereabouts of my nephew Ridley—and to get answers I had no choice but to follow her. The mechanical spider, lurking just outside the door, sprung to life with a series of whirs and clicks and followed us. Outside the small chamber the lighting was dim but from the size of the place and the look of the ceiling I was pretty sure we weren't far from where the spider had first brought me.

"Where's Ridley?" I called after her.

She didn't answer.

"Where are we going?" I tried again.

"To win a war."

"Just you and me? Should I bring my machete?"

She did not reply to this either. I studied her from behind. Her blonde hair was tied back in a ponytail. She was still wearing her violet army fatigues. A slim silver watch graced her right wrist. Lilac ankle high boots and a plum leather utility belt completed the ensemble.

"Look," I said, trying my best to keep up. "I just want to find my nephew. If you could–if you could just–"

But the distance between us grew too great and I trailed off. Looking behind me, I could see no sign of the chamber from which we had emerged, only the spider clacking after us. After several minutes we passed the roiling stream beside which I had first awoken. Iugurtha stopped between the stream and the wall. I caught up and glanced around. I could see no reason for her to have stopped there.

"Where's my nephew?" I asked.

"With me."

"You took him. Kidnapped him."

"He volunteered."

"That's not how it looked to me."

"Just the same."

She was smaller than I was, this travesty of a woman.

But I suspected she could kill me with a single blow if she wanted to.

"Give him back to me."

"It's not up to me, Mr. Wildebear. I've shown you what we're up against. You should join us, and fight alongside your nephew for this noble cause."

"What noble cause?"

"The destruction of my enemy."

"Which enemy would that be?"

She frowned. "Did you not see? Were you not paying attention?"

"I saw Necronians attacking T'Klee. But I also saw Burning Eyes attacking Half Ear. You said you were Burning Eyes. So which one is your enemy? The Necronians or the T'Klee? Are they both your enemy? And what in the name of God does Ridley have to do with any of it?"

"The T'Klee are not my enemy."

"If Half Ear isn't your enemy, why did you attack him?"

"I was not myself."

"What does that mean?"

"It means that many years before Half Ear and Sweep found me I'd been in an accident. A rockslide that nearly killed me. I'd been forced to incorporate base animals into myself to repair the damage, which saved my life but almost obliterated my intelligence. As near as I can tell I spent decades like that, as little more than a savage. Until they found me. I would have preferred Half Ear, but I accidentally knocked him out of the way."

"So you took Sweep instead."

Iugurtha nodded. "She wanted me to help her but

there was nothing I could do for her. I was not even capable of answering her. She tried to escape, but I didn't let her go. Instead I did something terrible to her. Something that hurt her more than anything had ever hurt her in her entire life. And when I was done, she was no more. We had become one."

Such an end for Sweep filled me with sorrow. Yet when I searched Iugurtha's face for signs of Sweep, I saw none.

Iugurtha went on. "Afterward Sweep knew more than she had before. She knew that my real name was Iugurtha. She knew what I had done to her. She remembered being the Burning Eyes of her people's lore. She knew as much about me as I did myself."

"Because she was a part of you."

"That's right."

I scrutinized her closely. "You don't look anything like Sweep."

"I don't need to."

"What does that mean?"

"It means that if I needed to look like Sweep, I would."

"Show me."

She nodded, and there before me in the space of ten seconds grew a marvellous set of cat whiskers. She did so with no more effort than blinking her eyes.

"Sweep," I said, my voice suddenly choked with emotion. "What have you done to her?"

"What has she done to me?" Iugurtha responded cryptically.

"You shouldn't have done that to her," I said. "You're a monster."

"Sweep was an anomaly. I prefer to seek consent."

"What about Half Ear? Did you take him too in the end?"

"No. I found him later at the bottom of the ravine, near death. Four dead Necronians lay near him. It took a while, but I nursed him back to health. He is with us now."

"Does he know what you did to Sweep?"

"He knows."

"And how does he feel about that?"

"I think you know the answer to that question."

She was right. He probably felt pretty much the same way I felt about it.

It was some time before I recovered sufficiently to speak.

Finally, I sniffed, wiped my eyes, and said, "Why tell me all this? Why bother to put all that information in my head and throw me through the gate? Is it because you want me to help you? Because I can't. Look—I feel bad about what happened to the cats, but I have my own problems. I just want my nephew back."

"You'll help me whether you want to or not," she said.

I backed up a step. "What do you mean by that? Are you going to try to absorb me too?"

"You have no special physical or psychological characteristics that I require. I simply mean that it's all a part of the plan."

Oh great. Another plan. "Plan C?"

"What?"

"Never mind. It doesn't matter. Tell me this. Did Angelique Rainer and Joyce Humphrey have any of the characteristics you were looking for?"

"They did."

My mouth was dry as I asked: "And Ridley?"

"No."

I closed my eyes and exhaled noisily. "See that he never does. Now where is he?"

"Getting ready."

"For war. Right. You do realize he's just a boy, don't you?"

"A boy who made a deal."

"With the devil. Or a genie," I said, recalling Ridley's take on the creature before me. "Does he still think you're a genie?"

"He's grown up a little now."

"Okay, listen. If you like deals, here's one for you. Let's call it a wish, like Ridley did. Give me Ridley's freedom. His safety. Put him back on Earth where he belongs. In his place I'll stay here and do whatever you want."

Iugurtha tilted her head. "Those are three separate wishes. Which one would you like?"

Wishes in storybooks often go horribly wrong. I hadn't had time to think this one through. I thought long and hard before speaking again.

"Put Ridley safely back on Earth where he belongs," I said finally.

Iugurtha shook her head. "No."

"No? Why not?"

"I need him here."

"You don't really expect me to believe that he wants to stay here on his own. You've done something to him."

"I have altered him, it's true."

I remembered her chilling words from our first meeting: '*I took in a little bit here, and let out a little bit there.*'

“How?” I braced myself for the unpleasant details.

“Some I’ve already told you. Subtle changes to make him more attractive to the female of your species. Beyond that I enhanced a few natural aptitudes which have already proved of great use to me. Mr. Wildebear, your nephew is where he wants to be.”

I stared at her. “Why should I believe anything you tell me?”

“Because I am not your enemy.”

“As long as you keep Ridley from me, I beg to differ.”

“I’m sorry you feel that way. Now. How about another wish?”

“Forget the wishes. Just–let me talk to Ridley. See for myself that he wants to stay here.”

“If he does?”

“I won’t argue. He can stay. But he won’t. And when he doesn’t, you let him go.”

“And in return?”

“You can have me. I’ll do whatever you want. I promise.”

“What makes you think I’d rather have you than Ridley?”

“If you’re wrong you’ll have me, but if you’re right you’ll have both of us.” I spoke with the utmost confidence, but inside I was praying that I was doing the right thing. What if Ridley really did want to stay with Iugurtha?

“Done,” Iugurtha said.

She waved her hand, her eyes glowed briefly red, and the wall before us fell away like the best of some men’s intentions.

The wall crumbled into an evanescent barrier of dust. In less than a second no trace of the wall was left. Without having moved, I found myself standing on a ledge overlooking a new vista.

Iugurtha and her spider stepped forward. I followed them as far as I dared—there were no railings on the ledge. Vertigo gripped me. Iugurtha took hold of my shoulder to steady me but I shrugged her off. Feeling a breeze on my back, I turned to look. The wall had re-appeared a few paces behind me. I returned and placed a hand on it. It was completely solid and did not yield to my touch.

Seconds before all around me had been stale and lifeless. Now vegetation abounded. A roar filled my ears. Mist mingled with the tears I had shed for Sweep. Turning, I beheld a great waterfall, which fed a frothing river far below, just visible beneath a vast canopy of purple foliage. For a moment I thought Iugurtha must have transported us elsewhere, but she hadn't. It was just that the wall had disappeared, revealing this place. We were still inside Iugurtha's mountain. There was no sun or sky up above, only rock, and rock unlike any I had ever seen before—luminous, casting just the right amount of light to illuminate the cavern clearly.

I stepped as close to the edge of the balcony as I dared and peered down. There were hints of activity beneath the trees.

"Mr. Wildebear," a voice said.

The voice startled me. I almost lost my balance, and might have tumbled off the balcony had Iugurtha not pulled me back.

"Sebastian! You scared me." I had almost forgotten

about the device on my wrist. Dimly, I remembered licking it the day before—it looked nice and clean now.

"Forgive me, Mr. Wildebear. I just thought you should know that I've established contact with the entity's network."

I glanced at Iugurtha, who betrayed no reaction.

"You have a network?" I asked.

"I have many things."

"What about it?" I asked Sebastian.

"It's telling me that there is a Necronian ship in orbit around this planet, and hundreds or more Necronians on the surface."

"You weren't able to tell that when we first got here?"

"I knew they were there. I just didn't see any point in alarming you."

He was probably right about that. I turned to Iugurtha. "So you have a Necronian infestation on your hands. What do you plan to do about it?"

"I will see to it that the Necronian scourge on this planet never bothers me again," she said.

"And if you fail?"

"I will almost certainly fail if I spend too much time talking to you. You wanted to speak to your nephew." She pulled a relatively unsophisticated pair of binoculars from her utility belt, passed them to me, and pointed. "There he is."

I held the binoculars up to my eyes. After waving them around for a bit I managed to spot a group of T'Klee assembling a mechanical spider much like the one standing beside me now, but no Ridley. Elsewhere a combination of humans and T'Klee stood around a long table peering at an assemblage of tiny figurines. Close to them a small army was busy cooking up vast amounts of food, while not far from them several men transferred boxes off a truck sporting the biggest wheels I've ever seen. There was no mistaking any of the muscular men for my scrawny nephew.

I put the binoculars down. "Not seeing him."

Iugurtha pointed again. "There."

I looked through the binoculars again and spent several moments observing Iugurtha's army going about the dubious business of preparing for war. Nowhere did I spy Ridley. "Still not–" Iugurtha took hold of the back of my head and swivelled it none-too-gently. "Ow!" I said. "What are you–?"

And suddenly there he was, standing before the long table with the figurines on it. Not quite the way I remembered him, but definitely Ridley; there was no mistaking that nose. I had already seen him, I realized, I just hadn't recognized him. And no wonder. Ridley always kept his hair as long as possible. Now it was shaved to a mere bristle. And he was dressed almost completely in mauve—the Ridley I knew wouldn't have been caught dead in anything resembling purple. He had hair on his face, too, a wisp of a moustache and a hint of a goatee. I hadn't thought him capable of growing facial hair until well into his forties.

Perhaps most misleading of all, though, was the set of his face. He was smiling. Ridley never smiled, not since the death of his mother. Now he stood with his hands clasped behind his back grinning from ear to ear. Several adult humans and T'Klee stood around him, all of the humans laughing, two of them doubled over as if Ridley had just told them the funniest damned joke of their lives.

The table with the figurines suggested that they were playing a game. I felt a little put out. I love games.

Sadly, aside from Doctor Humphrey's infrequent visits, there was no one around Port Kerry with whom to play. When he had first come to live with me, I had tried to interest Ridley in a few games—checkers, Parcheesi, that sort of thing—but to no avail. And now here he was playing some childish game with a bunch of strangers.

I tossed the binoculars to Iugurtha. "How do you get down from here?"

Iugurtha snapped her fingers. The spider crawled forward. Two silver limbs shot out, encircled my waist and legs, and lifted me high into the air.

"Just a minute!" I exclaimed.

But it was not up for discussion. Iugurtha clung to one side while the spider held me firmly on the other. We began our descent, plunging quickly along a sheer vertical drop. The spider descended much as an ordinary spider would, attached to a filament emanating from its artificial thorax. It bounced off the cliff face once or twice, and I wondered how Iugurtha could possibly hang on, but she managed. The spider's vise-like grip was suffocating. I threw up on the way down.

At the bottom, the spider let go. I fell to my knees and hunkered there for several minutes trying to pull myself together. Iugurtha busied herself cleaning the spider.

"Never. Do that. To me again," I told her when I was able.

She offered to let me ride the spider to Ridley. An incredulous snort let her know what I thought of that idea. She hopped on the spider and started off alone. I rose and followed unsteadily on legs like strands of over-cooked spaghetti. I quickly lost sight of Iugurtha and the spider, but there were no forks in the path, so little chance of losing them.

The wonders of this hidden valley soon consumed my attention. The trees I already knew—I felt almost at home beneath their mauve canopies. But a forest of any kind flourishing inside a giant cavern was something to behold. Apart from the trees (which may have differed in ways I could not perceive), the world inside Iugurtha's mountain was not quite the same as the world outside where Sweep and Half Ear and the rest of the T'Klee lived. Slender flowers swivelled as I passed, their plum petals quivering, watching me with alien senses as certain as if they'd possessed eyes. Hidden creatures emitted evocative sounds I'm sure never touched the ears of any T'Klee outside this place. The scents were sweeter, the air cooler, the light unchanging, and not a single insect plagued me.

Humans were everywhere, rivalled only by the number of T'Klee. More abductees? None of them paid me any mind. The further I went along the path the busier it got, humans and T'Klee working in tandem, never seeming to stop. Stockpiling ammunition, assembling weapons, building, cooking, training, cleaning, exercising.

And, evidently, playing games.

"Ridley," I said when I found him.

I had imagined a few possible reactions. Surprise. Relief. Gratitude. I would not have been taken aback had he burst into tears. But the boy didn't even look up.

He was standing in a glade before a sturdy table surrounded by perhaps a dozen humans and T'Klee. Ignoring everyone else present, I strode forward and grasped him by the shoulder. His gaze remained fixed on the table top in front of him. The surface had been constructed in relief, and painted to represent different sorts of terrain—water, desert, mountains, forests. Game pieces came in a wide variety of shapes, sizes and colours. It looked complicated. It looked intriguing. It was Ridley's turn, I gathered, for only when he had finished studying the board and moved a tiny statuette of a cat did he turn and look at me.

He was no longer smiling. In fact, he was frowning. "Uncle. What are you doing here?"

Of course—he was still under Iugurtha's control. I must have expected this reaction on some level, for I adapted quickly.

"It's over, Ridley," I said, taking a fatherly tack. "We're going home now."

The humans present had been silent. Now they began babbling to one other in languages I couldn't understand. I didn't take my eyes off Ridley. He held up his hand and the babbling stopped.

I took advantage of the silence. "Listen to me. I'm taking you home. I'm taking you home if I have to physically drag you there myself."

In my peripheral vision I saw two men step toward me. Two men who looked like they spent all their spare time working out, and who had nothing but spare time.

Ridley held up his hand again. The men stopped in their tracks. "You've come a long way to find me, Uncle. I appreciate that. But I have a job to do. I'm not going anywhere until it's done."

I snorted. "A job? Playing games?"

Ridley chuckled.

After all I'd been through his chuckle made me angry.

"This is serious, Ridley. You have no idea what you're mixed up in here. These people are about to go to war—war, Ridley. You're not old enough to go to war. No one is. Not any war, let alone a crazy, intergalactic one. You're only fifteen—school is starting in a couple of weeks. You want to jeopardize your education?"

"This is an education, Uncle."

"I've no doubt. Which will do you exactly how much good when you're dead?"

"I've no intention of dying."

"No one ever does, Ridley, no one ever does. Now. What about Rebecca? How do you think she's going to feel when you're dead—you just sweep her off her feet and die, is that it?"

"Man's gotta do what a man's gotta do. Rebecca knows that."

"And if she doesn't?"

He shrugged. "Then she isn't the girl for me. Besides, it doesn't matter. Iugurtha can take me back to any time. For her it'll only be a few hours or days, then I'll be back."

"Look, Ridley. Your mother—"

"Okay, Uncle." He sounded annoyed now. "Don't talk to me about Mom. You of all people. She's dead. It's sad, but it was a long time ago. I've come to terms with it. I have to live my own life now."

Clearly I wasn't getting through to him. I tried again. "Ridley look, if this is about something else—I know we never really got along. I take full responsibility for that. When you come back—"

"Uncle."

"Yes?"

"This isn't about me at all, is it?"

I frowned. “Of course it’s about you. It’s about getting you home safe and sound.”

He shook his head. “It’s about you. It’s been about you from the very beginning. You want me back safe and sound so you won’t feel like a failure. Well too bad, Uncle. You are a failure. You failed to save my mother, and now you failed to save me.”

He turned back to the game. “Save yourself, Uncle. If you can.”

The two big fellows stepped forward and latched onto me, one on each side.

“Ridley, listen to me. This isn’t you talking, it’s her–she’s controlling you!” My eyes lit on some of the other players for the first time. The T’Klee. One of them was missing half an ear. I connected the dots. The board was the planet C’Mell, the pieces combatants. This wasn’t a game at all–it was a strategy session. What was Ridley doing at a strategy session?

“Half Ear!” I said. “He’s just a boy!”

Half Ear swung his massive head around to regard me. It was Half Ear all right, though quite a bit older. Judging from his appearance he still had a fair bit of life left in him. He couldn’t understand a word of English, of course, but–rather incongruously for a cat–he wore a pair of dark glasses and a set of in-ear headphones. I could make out a tiny figure of a T’Klee on each lens of the glasses. Translating?

He trotted toward me. When I had been a part of Sweep, Half Ear had seemed powerful but benign. Now, despite his advanced age, he just seemed powerful. Until he started to talk. Then he seemed like Half Ear. A very stern Half Ear.

“Who are you?” he asked.

Just as I had in Sweep's brain, I understood his every twitch and shudder. "I'm this boy's uncle," I told him.

Ridley looked at me funny.

A part of me knew that uncle would translate the same as father to Half Ear. Few T'Klee knew or cared who actually sired them.

"Is that true?" Half Ear asked Ridley.

Ridley had to wait for the translation before responding. "Yes."

"Set him down," Half Ear ordered.

The big guys set me down but did not let go.

"What do you want?" Half Ear asked.

"To take my nephew back home with me. He'll get hurt if he stays here."

Half Ear regarded me. With contempt, I realized. If I knew anything about T'Klee males, it was that they expected their sons to confront danger, not avoid it.

"It's cool you can speak T'Klee, Uncle," Ridley said. "But I need you to go away now."

Half Ear looked at me for a second. Then to my surprise he turned and cuffed Ridley on the side of the head hard enough to knock him down.

"Hey!" I said.

"Don't talk to your uncle like that," he told Ridley.

Ridley climbed to his feet holding his jaw. "Sorry, General."

"Your counsel at this table is invaluable, but it's no excuse for bad manners. Now apologize to your uncle."

"I'm sorry, Uncle."

Half Ear turned back to me. "As for you, I'm not impressed. You barge in and interrupt an important discussion at a critical juncture. You allow your son to insult you, and then fail to discipline him. It's no wonder he doesn't want to go anywhere with you. And even if he did want to go with you I couldn't allow it. We need him here."

There was only one way to handle a male T'Klee of Half Ear's stature: stand up to him. So I drew myself up and faced him, knowing full well that he could eviscerate me with a single talon. I opened my mouth to speak and was unceremoniously punched in the gut by one of the big guys. He hit me hard enough to knock the wind out of me, and then they lugged me out of the glen. Half Ear, Ridley, and the rest turned back to the table.

"Rihleegh!" I wheezed as they carried me out.

They discarded me far down the path, where I lay sprawled in the dirt, reeling as much from Half Ear's words as from the punch in the belly. I looked up to find Iugurtha standing over me. She clutched the book to her chest. Humphrey was at her side. His suit was torn and stained in several places. His hair was an unruly mess and a salt-and-pepper beard obscured much of his face, but his eyes were clear. He was carrying the bag I had brought through the gate for him.

"Can't breathe," I told him.

He knelt down beside me. "I saw the whole thing. You just had the wind knocked out of you. Draw your knees up to your chest."

I did so. Still, it was a while before I began to feel like myself. "I've lost him, Doctor."

Humphrey nodded. "At least you can talk to him. See him. Joyce, she's..."

I glanced at Iugurtha, standing apart from us. I thought I could perceive elements of Humphrey's wife in her slender frame, in the way she carried herself. "I know. Iugurtha told me."

"Joyce and I had a big fight, you know."

This wasn't surprising. Humphrey could be opinionated. And Joyce was headstrong too, in her way. You didn't want to be within a city block of them when they started in on one another.

"I went too far, as usual. Said some things I shouldn't have. We went to bed angry. Never go to bed angry with your wife, Wildebear. Make it up to her, whatever it takes. Kiss her goodnight. Tell her you love her, even if you don't feel like it. If you don't, she could wind up as part of a demon and you'll never see her again. Just glimpses of her here and there. A gesture here, an expression there. Promise me, Wildebear. That you'll never go to bed angry with your wife."

The odds of ever even having a wife were slim to none, so it was an easy promise to make. "I promise, Doctor. But Iugurtha's not really a demon. You know that, right?"

He shrugged. "Whatever she is, Joyce is as good as gone. I can't talk to her again, or hold her, or really see her. You can with Ridley. Cold comfort, I know. But the point I'm trying to make is that you can still reach him. You still have hope."

"I'll try to remember that, Doctor. I'm sorry about Joyce," I added sincerely, thinking of Sweep, also lost inside Iugurtha.

Humphrey had lost his wife. I had bet and lost my nephew. Worse, in failing to persuade Ridley, I had now pledged myself to Iugurtha in the slim hope of keeping him safe.

You failed to save my mother, and now you've failed to save me.

Ridley's parting words stuck with me. They made no sense. Why would he blame me for Katerina's death? How could I have saved her? I hadn't been anywhere near the accident that had killed her. Part of me thought I should go back and talk to Ridley again. Another part knew better.

I climbed painfully to my feet and made my way to Iugurtha. "You win," I meant to tell her.

But I couldn't bring myself to say it. Saying so would seal Ridley's fate. My hands balled up into fists like two white stones and I opened my mouth to give this manipulative alien bitch a piece of my mind. But before I could do so she began to talk, and her tone–it was subtly different now. I knew it well enough: she sounded just like the principal of the school where I worked.

I was working for her now.

"I have a job for you," she said, and went on to talk about taking advantage of my ability with the gate, which she dug out of my knapsack. She wanted me to perform an errand of some kind. Someone required medical attention and I was to take Humphrey to them. I'm not sure where, I wasn't really listening.

"What did you do to him?" I interrupted.

She tilted her head to one side as if trying to dislodge water from her ear. "Ridley?"

"Of course Ridley."

"I told you. A few tweaks."

"What tweaks?"

"He has a talent for strategy. He's also very

psychologically perceptive. I magnified these attributes as much as I dared."

"He thinks I'm responsible for his mother's death. Is that your handiwork too? Filling his head with lies?"

"He didn't see clearly before. He sees more clearly now."

It wasn't his eyesight she was talking about. "You mean you're telling him what to see. What to think."

"Hardly. He's telling us."

"How could that be? He's just a boy." It was starting to sound like a mantra.

"Ridley is no ordinary boy, Mr. Wildebear. Believe what he tells you. He sees more than you or me."

"That wouldn't be very difficult right now."

"Mr. Wildebear, you promised you would do whatever I want if–"

"I know damned well what I promised." I was not keen on the promise, not if it meant leaving Ridley alone, but I would keep it. I closed my eyes and took a deep breath. "I could really use a drink."

Iugurtha dug a flask out of her khakis and handed it to me.

I sipped from it. "Not exactly what I was thinking, but it'll do." I emptied the flask of water and handed it back.

Iugurtha looked at it ruefully and put it away.

"All right, let's go. Keep Ridley safe until I get back."

"I can't promise–"

"Just keep him safe."

Iugurtha handed me the book.

"You know where to go?" Humphrey sounded as resigned as I felt. "How to get there?"

Not having really listened to Iugurtha I had only the vaguest of ideas. Probably I would have to ask her to repeat herself. The whole question would be academic anyway if I couldn't make the gate work–I had only ever used it once.

Suddenly I felt a most unpleasant sensation in my head, not unlike the onset of a head cold. An image popped into my mind of a forest at night. I could just make out the figure of a man sitting with his back against a massive tree trunk. The tree obscured most of the man. In my mind's eye I watched as cigarette smoke wafted from his right hand. The hand ascended. Seconds later smoke rings billowed out before him.

Humphrey's patient. But where had the image come from? A shiver ran up my spine–had Iugurtha projected it into my brain using some arcane technology? Perhaps. The image had come from the gate, I realized–I was seeing Humphrey's prospective patient because Iugurtha had bookmarked that page for me.

As for the unpleasant sensation I had felt in my head...

I was in fact coming down with a head cold.

Humphrey cleared his throat. "Are we going or not?"

There was only one way to find out whether I could still work the thing.

"Iugurtha," I said, tossing the book high into the air.

Instantly it transformed into the large, two-dimensional phenomenon known as the gate. I glanced around, feeling quite calm. Controlling the gate did not appear to have accelerated time for me as it had before. There didn't appear to be any other untoward consequences either. Rooting around in my mind, I saw that I could control such parameters if I wanted to, though I had only the vaguest idea how I was accomplishing it.

Humphrey strode forward, his bag in hand, and stepped over the threshold. I started after him. Feeling a sudden urge to sneeze, I stopped and rubbed my nose hard with a knuckle. The urge abated. I shook my head and stepped through the gate. Abruptly the sneeze erupted like an industrial strength leaf-blower. The gate shifted dramatically. Ahead of me the doctor lurched like a deranged manatee. A kaleidoscope of worlds flickered before us, only a precious few havens to creatures of flesh and blood. I thought of the once square-jawed Fletcher, now a stain on the side of some distant planet.

I reached out with my mind and snagged a destination that didn't look like it would bake, freeze, or crush us. An instant later I was through, and I struck the ground hard. I struggled to my feet, groaning in pain. I couldn't complain, though—I was alive and relatively unscathed, more than I had dared hoped for seconds earlier.

But what of Humphrey? There was no sign of the doctor anywhere.

Nor, judging from my surroundings, would I be meeting his patient anytime soon.

XII

AN IMPORTANT DATE

DRIZZLE LICKED MY face beneath an overcast sky. Puddles littered the landscape surrounding me. I was back on Earth, but where? I stood on a road sandwiched between two farmer's fields. Seagulls dotted the fields, pecking occasionally at the moist ground. Through a distant stand of pine trees, I caught a glimpse of a frothy bay. I was back on the island, then. Something about the look of the place suggested the south shore. I was a fair ways from home.

A battered old Ford pick-up approached and slowed to manoeuvre around me. I limped to the side of the road and nodded at the grizzled farmer who peered curiously out at me from between his windshield washer blades. He stepped on the gas and drove off, leaving a thick cloud of black smoke hanging in the air behind him. I turned and just about collided with a sign informing me that I was on the Blue Shank Road.

I surveyed the expanse of road before me that, were I to follow it, would take me into Summerside, and I considered the prospect that I had simply gone mad. That I had imagined everything that had happened to me. That Sweep, Iugurtha, Burning Eyes, Rainer, Sarah, and the whole lot of them were nothing more than figments of a deranged imagination. A cold tendril of fear snaked its way slowly up my spine as I chewed on the very real possibility that I had wandered out here on my own in a delusional state.

Something massive struck me from behind and propelled me forward onto the asphalt. I clambered back to my feet wiping pebbles and specks of blood off my hands. One arm was dripping wet, but my discomfort was nothing compared to the relief washing over me. Maybe I was delusional, but at least the delusion included a convincing version of my good friend Doctor Peter Humphrey.

"Missed a bit, don't you think?" he asked, looking around.

I had indeed missed our destination, and good. It was sheer luck that I hadn't killed us both.

"Sebastian," I said.

The chrome device strapped to my wrist replied instantly: "Yes, Mr. Wildebear."

"How far are we from Summerside?"

"I'm sorry, I'm having trouble accessing Ansalar's net. Wait... there. You're about an hour's walk from the welcome sign at the edge of the city."

"You were having some sort of trouble?"

"I was. It's fine now. Sort of."

"Sort of?"

"I had to use an old protocol."

"An old—why would that be?"

"Every source I check tells me the same date."

I exchanged glances with Humphrey, not sure I wanted to hear this. "What date?"

He told me.

"That can't be right," I said.

"It is," Sebastian said. "It's the seventh of July two years before our subjective present."

The seventh of July–I understood the implications instantly. It was the day of the accident. The day –

"The day Katerina died," I muttered. "The day before Ridley came to live with me."

"You took us here deliberately," Humphrey said.

"I didn't mean to do this, Doctor."

"I'm sure you didn't–not consciously. I just mean that on some level you must have wanted to come here."

"What are you suggesting?"

"Only that the unconscious is a powerful instrument. You're here for a reason."

A reason. What reason? My breath caught as an idea occurred to me, one so bold that I could barely even put it into words. "I could–undo it. Prevent it. The accident. Save her–save my sister."

"Ridley will never come to live with you. The entity will never abduct him. We solve a whole slew of problems in one fell swoop." Humphrey stroked his chin. "Later you can take me forward to the day I bought the book for Joyce and I can fix that too."

As an English teacher I had taught literature on the subject of time travel. As such I was all too aware of the theoretical pitfalls inherent in such travel. Time could prove immutable–it could be that nothing we attempted would change anything. Or maybe this was simply one dimension among many. I might save Katerina in this timeline only to have her die in another, including the one from which I had come. Or worse, I could save Katerina only to mess up the future in ways I couldn't even begin to imagine.

I only knew one thing for sure. That I had to try.

We trudged along the Blue Shank Road toward

Summerside, the drizzle running in rivulets down our faces. As we walked, I told Humphrey everything that had happened to me since Humphrey had jumped through the gate in search of Ridley and Joyce.

"How about you, Doctor?" I asked once I'd finished. "What's your story?"

"Didn't accomplish much," he said. "The bugs poisoned me too. Like you, one of the cats came along in the nick of time. You know I found Joyce, or what's left of her. After that I spent days watching the demon closely, trying to figure it out. How could it be that so many different beings are all wrapped up into one? Is the process reversible? If I could get it in a lab I'd figure out a thing or two, I can tell you that."

He retrieved a cigar from his tattered suit, sniffed it, lit it, puffed on it, and went on. "I noticed a lot of people under the demon's control getting hurt. I decided the least I could do was help out a bit. Patch up a few broken bones here and there. Those people aren't making out very well, Wildebear. This war they're fighting. They're losing. I don't understand the hold that damned creature has on them but whatever it is, it's strong. I don't mean to scare you, but Ridley's in a lot of danger if he stays put."

"I know it," I said.

We trudged in single file on the road's gravel shoulder. "What was it you needed?" I called back over my shoulder.

"Eh?"

"In your bag."

"What bag?"

"The one you brought with you to my place."

"What about it?"

"I went to a lot of trouble to get it for you—I was wondering what you were after. Bandages? Penicillin?"

"You brought me my bag?"

"You oughta know, you have it right there."

"I'm aware I'm carrying my bag, Wildebear." Humphrey sounded exasperated. "I'm just surprised to learn it was you who brought it."

"You asked me to, so I did."

"When?"

"When I was in the grocery store. In Port Kerry. You don't remember?"

"How could I? I wasn't anywhere near that grocery store. I never asked you to bring my bag. Actually I wish you hadn't. Now I have to lug it about everywhere."

"You're using it to help people, aren't you?" I asked, irked.

"I suppose."

The doctor fell behind. In a whisper, Sebastian spoke from my wrist. "He didn't ask for the bag."

"What do you mean?"

"It wasn't the doctor. It was me playing back samples of the doctor's voice through the store's public address system."

"Why on earth would you do something like that?"

"Another ploy to encourage you to go through the gate."

"Sounds like an awful lot of trouble for nothing."

"No trouble for me, standard operating procedure for Casa Terra. And you have to admit: here you are, on the other side of the gate."

Words failed me.

I stopped and waited until Humphrey caught up. "We need a plan," I told him.

"My thoughts exactly. I don't mean to bring up old wounds, but it would help if you could tell me about the accident. If we both know what to expect, we might be able to prevent it."

He was right. Just the same I could not bring myself to talk about it right away. The thought of seeing my sister again on the very eve of her death had placed an enormous lump in my throat. According to the official report, the accident had taken place on Water Street in downtown Summerside near a popular café called Samuel's. A man had fallen into the street in front of my sister's motorcycle.

Katerina had managed to steer around the fellow; unfortunately, bad luck saw fit to place a Chrysler Newport in her path. She struck the vehicle head on, somersaulted over it like a rag doll, and was greeted by an unfriendly stretch of asphalt upon which she skidded for several dozen yards before a light pole conceded to halt her progress. Tragically, inexplicably, Katerina had not been wearing her helmet.

Though unconscious much of the time, Katerina hung on for days following the accident. This was not surprising–my sister was one tough customer. I had always marvelled that death was able to take her at all. Through it all I stayed at her side as much as humanly possible. It was a hard time. But as bad as it was for me, it was worse for Ridley.

"Take care of him," Katerina told me once in a transient moment of lucidity. "Take care of my boy. Barnabus, don't you dare let me down."

"I won't," I told her, and meant it.

I can still feel her fingers pressing into my forearm.

When she passed on, I tried to do as she asked. That Ridley needed some serious looking after was obvious; the grief on his young face was plain enough to see. Unfortunately seeing was the easy part–knowing what to do about it something else altogether.

Take care of my boy, Katerina had said, and I would like to say that I did my best, but I can't, because I didn't. I didn't even come close.

I cleared my throat before attempting to speak. "You know as much as I do, Doctor. She swerved to avoid hitting someone. Hit a car instead."

"Tragic," Humphrey reflected. "And yet, when you think about it, fairly straightforward. All we have to do is keep your sister off her bike."

Put like that it sounded simple.

I allowed myself to be briefly buoyed by the doctor's enthusiasm.

The rain graduated from cats and dogs to considerably less domesticated animal fare. An elderly gent in a battered Hyundai picked us up and drove us the rest of the way to Summerside. He dropped us off right in front of my sister's house on High Street. By then the rain had let up, allowing the setting sun to peak through the clouds. Humphrey and I found ourselves standing on the sidewalk two years earlier than we had a right to, shielding our eyes against the glare reflecting off the windows of Katerina's house.

Steeling myself, I headed straight across the lawn to the front porch. I mounted the steps and went to knock, my hand trembling. I was trembling at the thought of seeing her. Of seeing my sister, the late Katerina Doucette, nee Wildebear, alive.

An instant before my fist touched wood Humphrey whispered, “Wait,” and motioned me behind a large cedar bush to the right of the porch, where no one could see us from the house.

“I’ve been thinking,” he said.

“I’m not turning back now, Doctor.”

“To know that you’re about to die. That you’re meant to die. That would be very upsetting, I would think.”

“Better than actually dying.”

“Of course. But maybe there’s a way to do this without upsetting your sister. Where does she keep this bike of hers?”

I led the good doctor along a cobblestone path to Katerina’s backyard. French doors overlooked the elaborate stone patio that my brother-in-law Jerry had completed shortly before stepping out of my sister’s life. We kept to the shadows, hoping it would make us difficult to spot in the encroaching twilight.

Katerina’s motorcycle sat atop the patio between a rusty black barbecue and two green garbage pails. The bike itself had belonged to Jerry. It was a vintage affair, with a name like Victor or Vincent—I could never remember which. She was awfully fond of that bundle of black and chrome. Too damned fond, if you asked me, considering it would shortly kill her.

“We need to disable it,” Humphrey whispered. “Where’s the spark plug?”

“This isn’t a lawnmower, Doctor. And removing a spark plug wouldn’t stop Katerina. She and Jerry have put this bike back together again more times than you can imagine.” I couldn’t help but chuckle.

“What’s so funny?”

“I was just thinking about the time I had the entire bike taken apart. Paid a mechanic to do it.”

“We don’t have time to–”

“I know, I know. I’m not suggesting we take the bike apart. I’m just telling you about this time I had it done because–”

“There was something wrong with it?”

“No, it was–”

“Why would you do something like that if there was nothing wrong with it?”

Too late I remembered that Humphrey and I did not exactly share the same sense of humour. “It was a joke, Doctor. I hid the pieces all over the house. Took Kat days to find them all.”

“Huh.”

“Ridley thought it was funny,” I added lamely.

“I bet. Well, let’s get on with this, shall we? What do you suggest?”

A light came on behind the French doors. I heard the doors rattle–somebody was coming out. There was no time to disable the bike or even think how to disable it.

“Hurry!” I whispered, slipping the bike into neutral. I began wheeling it off the patio onto the cobblestone path. I could only go so fast with my bad leg. Humphrey trailed close behind, trapped behind me in the narrow walkway.

The French doors opened. Ridley spoke, sounding much younger than he had the last time I’d heard him. “Mom, where’s your bike? Did you put it in the shed?”

I reached the driveway where I almost lost control of the bike. Humphrey hurried forward to steady it. Katerina and Ridley were talking in back of the house.

Katrina's voice—I had thought I would never hear it again. I had not fully appreciated it the last time I'd heard it. And here I was running away from it. But there was no time to think about that—if I wanted to continue hearing Katerina's voice I needed to dispose of her bike fast.

I scanned the neighbourhood. Mature trees lined the street, massive shapes looming in the darkness, lit here and there by the occasional streetlight. The trees were maple and ash mostly. They would do nothing to conceal a bike this size. The automobiles clogging the narrow driveways and spilling out onto the street would do me no good either.

The houses, on the other hand—if their owners were anything like Katerina, their backyards would be completely accessible. I wheeled the bike onto the sidewalk, heading for the house on the left. Boots slapped the wet asphalt somewhere behind me. I didn't dare look back.

"Barnabus, what—Peter Humphrey, is that you? What are you doing with my bike?"

It was no use—the jig was up. I pulled back on the handlebars and brought the motorcycle to a halt. Sighing, I propped the motorcycle up on its kickstand, and turned to face my elder sister, feeling about as sheepish as I'd ever felt. And I'd had plenty of opportunities to feel sheepish around Katerina.

She shifted her gaze from Humphrey to me and back again. She shook her head and opened her mouth but nothing came out. She raised her hands in the air, allowed them to drop and dangle limply at her sides, then brought them back up again. "What... what?" she said.

At her side, Ridley was holding onto her helmet

looking more amused than anything else. In fact, he looked genuinely happy. Everything else about the situation notwithstanding, that was good to see.

"Hello, Katerina. Ridley." Humphrey's professional manner contrasted starkly with his appearance: unshaven, his suit in tatters.

Katerina ignored Humphrey utterly. She had never been one for social niceties. "Barnabus, what do you think you're doing?"

I assumed the offensive. "Katerina, you know how I feel about motorcycles, yet you continue to ride them willy-nilly. And you with a boy to raise. What if...." I couldn't go on. There was more emotion in my voice, in my gut, than I had reckoned with. What I was saying was true–truer than I could possibly convey to my sister.

Katerina either didn't register the emotion in my voice or didn't care. "So you're stealing it? Barnabus, I could have you arrested!"

"You would arrest your own brother?" Humphrey asked.

"Look. I need to be someplace and I have an errand to run first."

"Oh? What a shame," Humphrey said. "And here we've just come for a visit."

I regarded Katerina suspiciously. She was dressed rather more elegantly than usual–a clean pair of blue jeans, her spiffiest black leather jacket, and black ankle-high boots polished to a high sheen.

"You can't just show up on people's doorsteps, steal their motorcycles, and expect to be invited in," she said.

"Mom's got a date," Ridley announced.

Katerina turned and punched him in the arm, not gently. "That isn't anyone's business."

"A date." This information had never come out in the two years since she'd died. Ridley had certainly never mentioned it. I'd always assumed she'd been on her way to a party with some friends, or a night out with her employees from the music store she owned.

Katerina placed one arm on a hip. "Do you have a problem with that?"

It was no business of mine, of course. Just the same, her husband Jerry had been a friend of mine. Yes, he had his share of problems: he could be reckless, his jokes weren't particularly funny, and he'd been missing for over two years, but I could see no reason to hold any of that against him. "What about–"

"Jerry's gone," Katerina said. "And he's not coming back."

"That's fine–" I began, but Katerina cut in, building up steam as she went.

"You can't come here and steal my motorcycle and then lecture me on how to live my life. You of all people! Living all alone out there in the middle of nowhere, barely able to look after yourself. Look at you. You haven't shaved in days, your clothes are filthy; when's the last time you even combed your hair?"

"I–"

"You probably don't even own a comb." Katerina looked smug. She knew she was right.

Ridley was doing his best not to laugh. Humphrey had busied himself cleaning a spot on the seat of Katerina's bike. He spat on a pudgy thumb and–

"Don't you dare touch that!" Katerina snapped.

"Now, Katerina–" Humphrey began.

"Shut up," she said. "I need to go. I'm late."

"For a very important date," Ridley added playfully.

Yet again I marvelled at the difference in the lad. If he knew that in less than an hour he would effectively be orphaned, he would not be joking. "Katerina, look. You can't go out tonight."

"I bloody well can–"

I drew myself up to my full six foot two, something my sister, although an imposing creature herself, could not hope to match. "You can't. Well, you can. But you can't take your motorcycle with you."

"Barney–"

"Why isn't this date of yours picking you up, anyway?"

"He doesn't own a car. Again, not that it's any of your business."

"You could take a cab."

"I'll do no such thing. I wish I could say it's been nice to see you, but it hasn't. At all." Katerina strode forward and grasped the bike firmly.

But Doctor Humphrey had hold of it too and refused to let go.

Katerina tried to wrest it from him. "Peter. Give–me–my–bike!"

Humphrey was no match for a female Wildebear. One good wrench of the handlebars sent him flying unceremoniously onto his backside. Humphrey picked himself up like a cat pretending that falling down was something it had meant to do all along.

"I don't know what's got into the two of you," Katerina said. "Why are you even here?"

The motorcycle bounced slightly as she straddled it. She turned the ignition. The vehicle that would soon kill her stone cold dead ignited with a devil's roar.

I had never expected to see my sister alive again. Suddenly here she was before me–and absolutely furious with me. Our reunion left much to be desired. But I loved Katerina for her anger and her vitality and the mere fact that she was alive.

The moment was upon me though. If I let her go, this would be the last time I would ever see her fully alive. Everything would unfold as it had before. Possibly we had already altered events sufficiently to save her, but I couldn't take that chance. So I didn't even hesitate to do what I did next. As Katerina was busy strapping her helmet on, I stepped in, grabbed the keys, and turned the bike off.

"Barnabus," Katerina said, and then, "Barnabus!" as I pitched the keys as hard as I could into the neighbour's backyard, hoping they would get lost in the jungle somebody called landscaping.

"All right, Barney, that's the last straw." Katrina was rolling up her sleeves as she came off the bike as if she meant to go twelve rounds with me.

"Kat, I'm trying to save your life."

"Good thing you brought a doctor with you. Someone's gonna need to save yours."

"Kat, if you get on that motorcycle you're going to die–I know it!"

"You don't know that."

"In point of fact he does," Doctor Humphrey said, evidently reconsidering his stance on upsetting my sister.

"If it's my date you're worried about–"

"We don't care about your date," I said. "We care about you."

Humphrey pulled out his wallet. "I have something I think you should see."

Reluctantly, she followed us to a streetlight. Humphrey showed her the date on his driver's license, issued one year in the future.

"You would not believe what we've been through," I told her.

"I don't know, boys. This is an awfully elaborate joke. And not particularly funny."

"It's no joke, Katerina," I told her.

She searched my face, and then burst out laughing at what must have been an uncharacteristically solemn expression. And with that all her anger seemed to dissipate. "All right, I'm touched by your concern. We'll go inside. I'll call my date and tell him I'll be late."

I let my breath out, relieved. "We'll call a cab."

"Ridley, show the boys in. Pour them something to drink."

"What do they want?"

"Ask them! Tell them what's in the fridge." Katerina kicked the kickstand out from under the Victor or the Vincent or whatever it was called and started wheeling it back to her driveway. "But you're going to have to help me find my keys later."

"I make no promises," I told her, following Ridley up the driveway, past the cedar bush to the front door. Ridley held the door open as I entered.

Behind us the motorcycle roared to life.

"Wildebear!" Humphrey cried out.

I rushed back down the steps as fast as I could only to see Katerina roaring off down the street on her bike. Ridley joined me at the bottom of the steps. I was horrified to see him holding onto his mother's helmet.

"She wears a spare key around her neck," he told me, smiling smugly.

XIII
A MATTER OF LIFE AND DEATH

HUMPHREY AND I paced the driveway waiting for a cab that was taking way too damned long. Ridley stood with his hands in his pockets regarding us quizzically from beneath his long bangs. One of Katerina's two cats rubbed up against my feet, seeking affection I was too upset to offer. I glanced at Sebastian. It was past nine o'clock. The accident had occurred at a quarter past nine. We had little more than ten minutes to get Katerina off that bike.

Ridley shook his hair out of his eyes and said, "She's never had an accident, you know."

"Didn't she drive into the garage once?" Humphrey asked. "I distinctly remember hearing about a sprained wrist. And what about the time she skidded on the wet pavement?"

"Well, aside from that," Ridley conceded.

"And the time she was just sitting on it and went to get off and forgot to put the kickstand down," I said. "Banged herself up pretty good that time."

"Don't forget the time she burnt herself on the exhaust," Doctor Humphrey said. "I seem to remember giving her advice on how to treat a bad burn."

"Okay, yes, well aside from all that she's never had an accident," Ridley insisted. "I don't know why you're all so worried."

I thought about just levelling with the boy. He was a smart kid. Clearly he took after the Wildebear side of the family. But he already thought of me as eccentric. To insist that I had somehow travelled back in time to save his mother's life—and perhaps his own—would only upgrade his impression of me from eccentric to mentally ill.

"The important thing is we're trying to help your mother," I told him. "Do you really think we'd come all this way just for some silly practical joke?" I regretted the words the instant they were out of my mouth.

"Oh, you mean like the time you paid a mechanic to take the bike apart and then you hid the pieces all over the house? You know how long it took my mother to put it back together again? She's still missing a few parts, you know. If you really wanted to help mom you'd find the missing bits. A wheel could come off any time."

Damn it—Ridley knew me too well.

A cab turned onto High Street and meandered its way infuriatingly slowly up the road toward Katerina's house. Humphrey and I met it half way up the street.

"Good luck," Ridley shouted after us.

We invaded the cab before it could come to a full stop. "Samuel's Coffee House on Water Street," I barked at the cabbie. "As fast as you possibly can. It's literally a matter of life and death."

The cabbie—Jack Poirier, according to the license strapped to the back of the passenger street—regarded me placidly in the rear view mirror. Even in my distress I could not help but marvel at the thick black unibrow that loomed over his eyes like a well-fed caterpillar.

"Life and death," he repeated in a pleasant baritone. "Got it."

He placed his Nissan Rouge into drive, and began puttering his way down the street as though driving a hearse in a funeral procession.

I stared at him in disbelief. "Can't you go any faster? I'm telling you–there's a life at stake here!"

"Speed trap at the bottom of the street." He fumbled around for something in the pocket of his plaid fleece jacket. It turned out to be a yellow lollipop. He ripped the plastic wrapper off the lollipop with his teeth, spit it out onto the seat beside him, and plopped the lollipop in his mouth.

Sure enough, seconds later we passed a police cruiser partially concealed in a church parking lot. It ignored us. Safely past, Jack turned onto Victoria and stepped on the gas. I clutched Katerina's helmet tightly in my lap feeling like I could barely breathe as the abrupt acceleration forced me back into my seat. Worse, the air freshener in the cab was more dreadful than the lingering traces of vomit it failed to conceal. Not only that, but I was coming down with a cold. And of course there was the matter at hand.

According to Ridley, Katerina had gone to the liquor store in the Waterfront Mall to fetch a bottle of Beaujolais before her date. There wasn't enough time to intercept her there. Humphrey and I had no choice but to head straight to the accident site. Our plan was simple: prevent the pedestrian responsible for Katerina's death from stepping in front of her motorcycle by whatever means necessary. Afterward, I would wave her down and force her to wear her helmet if I had to strap it on her head myself.

Rain drops splattered against the windshield. Jack turned on the wipers.

"Sebastian, how we doing for time?" I asked.

"Katerina's accident will occur in three minutes and thirty-seven seconds," Sebastian told me.

"Dammit," I said. "Not enough time."

"We'll make it," Humphrey assured me.

I stared out the window at the rain. "Doctor, if we do manage to save my sister—"

"*When* we save her."

"When we save her it's going to change things. I worry that—I mean, it would be unthinkable not to try to save her, but what about..." I trailed off, not sure I wanted to pursue the thought.

"You're worried about changing the future for the worse," Humphrey said. "It's true, there's a lot we don't know. But we do know this. That when we save her, Ridley won't go to live with you, he won't find the book, and he won't go through the gate."

"And neither you nor I will go through the gate after him," I said.

"Exactly. Katerina will be alive and Ridley will be safe—all good. But I might still find the book at a used bookstore and give it to Joyce for Christmas. Joyce might bring it with her when we visit you in February. She could still leave it in your guest bedroom, where someone else might find it. Iugurtha could well get her clutches on someone else. You maybe."

I dismissed the notion with a wave of my hand. "So long as she leaves Ridley alone. But..."

"But what?"

I was thinking about Sweep, and Half Ear, and the

rest of the T'Klee. Iugurtha had taken Ridley to help save Sweep's people from the Necronians.

"Forget it," I said. My responsibilities extended to Ridley and my sister and that was all.

Jack was staring at us in the rear-view mirror, his unibrow deeply furrowed. We were approaching a set of traffic lights. They were red, and Jack wasn't slowing down.

"Watch out!" I cried.

Jack slammed on the brakes. Tires screeched beneath us. We lurched forward as far as our seatbelts would allow. A mini-van shot through the intersection precisely where we would have been had we not stopped in time.

"A little too close for comfort," Humphrey remarked.

Jack looked left, right, put the Nissan in gear, and turned left on Granville through the red lights.

"Hey!" I cried.

Jack opened his window a crack, threw his lollipop out, and rolled the window back up. "I get it," he said. "You're time travellers. On a mission to save someone. Good thing you found me."

The speed limit on Granville is forty. Jack was soon doing one hundred.

"I've been driving in this town a long time," he said. "That's how I know it takes five minutes to get to Samuel's from High Street. According to your watch, you need to be there in less than four. Lucky for you I can get you there in three."

He caught up to a red Sienna, slowed briefly, then stepped on the gas and passed it. Next up was a Jeep. Granville Road only has two lanes, and there is no shoulder on the right hand side. Oncoming traffic prevented him from passing on the left. To my astonishment, Jack passed the Jeep on the right. This meant driving on lawns.

"You're nuts," I observed, my fingers claws in the upholstery beside me.

Jack chuckled. "This from a man claiming to be from the future."

He deked around a telephone pole before manoeuvring bumpily back onto asphalt.

"We do need to get there alive," Humphrey pointed out.

"Without killing anyone in the process," I added emphatically.

"Shut up," Jack said, "and hang on."

I shut up and hung on as he negotiated what should have been an impossible right turn onto Green Street without slowing down. I braced myself for an unpleasant collision with the YMCA; we missed it by that much. Turning left onto Central, at least two wheels left the ground. The light was with us at Notre Dame, allowing us to roar down Central at something resembling the speed of sound. The old post office was a blur on the left, Linkletter's restaurant a flash on the right, and then we arrived at our destination in what I couldn't deny had to be record time.

Jack placed the Nissan in park and turned to face us. "That'll be ten dollars if you please. Except you don't have any money, do you?"

He was right–I hadn't taken any with me to C'Mell. Humphrey shrugged, indicating he was in the same predicament.

"How did you know?" I asked.

Jack shook his head sadly. "Time travellers never do."

Paying Jack was the least of our concerns. Humphrey

and I reached for the door handles simultaneously but Jack was too fast for us. Every lock in the car clicked shut, trapping us in the Nissan.

"Fifty-seven seconds until Katerina arrives," Sebastian said.

"I don't have time for games," I told Jack. "You said it yourself: we're on a mission."

I stared at him intently, willing him to open the doors. Instead, his eyes seemed to merge into one beneath his single brow. I gasped and drew back.

Jack's eyes returned to normal. He smiled. "Tell you what. Give me that talking watch of yours and we'll call it even."

There was no time to argue or wonder what had just happened there. I had no issues parting with Sebastian. I threw him in the sea of lollipop wrappers beside Jack, who promptly unlocked the doors. Gathering Katerina's helmet and my knapsack containing the gate, I scrambled out of the Nissan as fast as I could, with Humphrey not far behind.

Outside the cab, two little girls wielding matching umbrellas splashed gleefully in a large puddle on the sidewalk. Humphrey just about knocked them over in his haste. A young couple that had been patiently standing by shot him dirty looks as they stepped forward to hurry the girls along.

Undeterred, we hurried as fast as we could to the entrance of Samuel's and looked wildly about. There was no sign of Katerina. Thank God—we'd made it in time. One hundred metres away a man with an umbrella was strolling nonchalantly along Water St. with his back to us. He was the only one around. It had to be him, the one responsible for Katerina's death. All we had to do was warn him, keep him off the street. If necessary, physically restrain him for the few paltry seconds it would take for Katerina to pass.

A single headlight crested the hill beyond the man with the umbrella.

"Wildebear!" Humphrey shouted beside me.

I saw Katerina speeding beneath a streetlight, her long red hair streaming behind her like a banner. The sight of her was like a kick in the gut with a steel-toed boot. With my damned limp, I would not catch up to the man with the umbrella in time.

"Don't move!" I shouted to him, limping as fast as I could. "Stay where you are!"

The roar of traffic was too loud. He couldn't hear me. He kept on walking.

I tried again. "You with the umbrella! Stop!"

Still nothing. In desperation, I reached out to him the only way could think of: I threw Katerina's helmet at him. It struck him in the back and clattered to the sidewalk. The man turned to see what had hit him, but he was too close to the road, and the curb took him by surprise. To my horror, he tripped and fell.

As Katerina's motorcycle bore down on him, he held the umbrella forth as though a thin layer of nylon might somehow ward off half a ton of screaming metal. Katerina faced an awful choice. She could continue on her current heading and mow him down, or she could bear right onto the sidewalk and crash into a light pole or garbage can. Or she could steer left into the oncoming lane.

She chose left, successfully avoiding the man with the umbrella but failing to save herself. A Chrysler Newport struck her bike head-on. Katerina flew over the handlebars like a large, wingless bird and bounced off the windshield of the Chrysler Newport with such force that I clearly heard the breath expelled from her body.

"Iugurtha!" I cried out.

The book burst from my knapsack, propelling me forward and almost off my feet as it blossomed into the gate. Mentally, I adjusted a few parameters and everything appeared to freeze, just as it had in Ridley's room.

Katerina hovered in the air mere inches from the asphalt. The man with the umbrella was as still as a bug on a wall. Humphrey stood with his mouth agape, his eyes wide, and his right arm thrust forward as if to snatch Katerina from the air. The silence, as they say, was deafening.

Nothing had changed. My sister was going to die. Worse: now it appeared that I had contributed to her death.

Desperate to forestall the inevitable, I concentrated on the gate. It seethed and roiled on the road before me. I willed it to change pages, to flip back over the events of the last hour. Locating the moment that Katerina had tricked us into letting her use her spare key, I entered the gate in a single bound.

The gate did not deposit me where I wanted to go. Instead it placed me inside a dark and empty room. Beyond the door I could hear the clink and clatter of a busy restaurant. Samuel's? There was no way to tell. I tried to open the door but it was locked or stuck. In the distance a squeal of tires. A muted crash of metal on metal. The crowd beyond the door hushed. My entire being clenched with the realization of what must just have happened, beyond my reach.

No matter. There were an infinite number of points

leading up to Katerina's death. I could change any one of them. I opened the gate and chose Water Street shortly before Katerina's arrival. I found myself across the street from Samuel's. Traffic was too heavy to jaywalk. I limped to the lights but they were not with me. I heard the roar of a motorcycle, saw Katerina cresting the hill. A man fell into the street.

Not to worry. I opened the gate again. This time I went to Katerina's house the day before the accident. She didn't answer the door. I lingered, hammering on the door until a police car showed up and I was forced to flee.

I travelled further back in time. To my surprise the gate transported me to Katerina's favourite pizzeria, Michael's on Central Street. Katerina was there. She treated me to lunch. I revelled in her company. I tried to warn her. She didn't take me seriously. *You need to take better care of yourself*, she told me. *You look terrible.* Seeing Katerina young and healthy and alive, I choked back the tears until I could bear it no longer and fled back through the gate.

That was the last time I ever saw Katerina alive. I visited the past countless times afterward but never made it that close to her again. Finally, I could deny it no longer: I could visit the past, and be a part of it, but I could not change it. It has been written that what's past is prologue, and it is so, with my sister's fate a bitter prologue indeed. The future was all that was left to me now, to shape as best I could.

XIV
FEATHERS

I AWOKE TO find myself lying on a rock the size of a coffin, waves lapping disconsolately at my feet. Humphrey sat on an adjacent rock, staring blankly out over grey rocks, grey water, grey skies, a sullen fishing boat tied to a dilapidated wharf, a couple of seagulls wheeling lethargically not far above us, and not much else. Fog shrouded everything like a veil. What might have been a merry little port in the sunshine had assumed a potent air of melancholy in the fog—or maybe it was just me.

I battled my way to a sitting position. My leg throbbed, my throat hurt, my muscles ached.

Humphrey heard me groan and turned round.

"Where are we?" I asked, my voice a croaky caricature of its former self.

"How should I know?" He pitched a small pebble he'd been holding. It disappeared into the fog, producing a tiny splash. "You were the one who took us here."

"Right." I vaguely remembered returning to the accident scene to collect Humphrey. I had transported us to the first acceptable destination that had presented itself. It looked like Port Kerry, though I couldn't tell what year. Summer, sometime.

"How long have I been out?"

"Hours. I don't know exactly. I don't have a watch."

"I knew that. Sorry."

He sighed. "No, Barnabus. I'm sorry."

He was talking about Katerina.

We sat and stared into the fog. By all rights a foghorn should have sounded in the distance, but it didn't. "What now?" I asked.

"We go back. Back to where we can be of some use. Back to where everything isn't preordained."

Where was that? Back to Ridley? The boy didn't want my help, even if I could help him, which seemed less and less likely. Was that any reason not to help him? Maybe. That and the fact that I didn't feel up to it anymore. I just wanted to forget about the whole thing. Call in sick. I wanted to spend my time doing what I wanted to do, not what I needed to do, or what somebody else wanted me to do.

A tiny voice in the back of my mind reminded me that I was supposed to be working for Iugurtha now. The gate wasn't my property, it was hers. Moreover, Iugurtha was about to go to war, and Ridley would be going with her. Katerina's fate might have been preordained but Ridley's wasn't. He could live or he could die and I needed to be there to make sure it wasn't the latter. My place was beside my nephew.

Take care of my boy.

I sighed. I had no choice but to do what Katerina had asked of me. Which meant doing what Iugurtha had asked of me.

"Iugurtha," I said, opening the book.

I felt a little better with the power of the gate coursing through me. I selected Iugurtha's bookmark and located Humphrey's patient. The bookmark had advanced slightly, reflecting the last time I'd seen the man through the gate. There was something familiar about him. Just as I was thinking that, he turned his head. To my astonishment, I beheld the face of my brother-in-law, Jerry Doucette. Katerina's husband, Ridley's father. Missing and presumed dead.

"Humphrey, it's–"

"I know." Humphrey had known Jerry too.

The notion that Ridley wasn't an orphan after all gave me a renewed sense of purpose. Afraid I might get Humphrey to Jerry too late, that I might somehow fail Ridley's father within hours of having failed his mother, I clung to Iugurtha's bookmark with all my might. Only when I was absolutely certain that the coordinates would not somehow slip through my fingers did I thrust the gate all the way open, and step through.

Which is why I was at somewhat of a loss to explain what happened next.

Each transition through the gate was different in its own way. This time was no exception. It began with the sensation that I was falling. The earth flipped into and out of view. I beat my wings and the horizon stabilized before me. I glided for a while, trying to get my bearings. Not far ahead a seagull drifted on the same current. I shook my head, trying to clear my thoughts. Jerry should be here somewhere, and Humphrey...

My wings?

I angled my head to see. Air rushed past me with a *whoosh* that only now registered on my consciousness. Wings... I had wings! Complete with feathers. Were they mine? I lifted the right one up to see. It was my wing all right, upholstered in white feathers with a smattering of grey. The manoeuvre together with the shock of discovering that I was a bird threw me into a stall, and I plummeted earthward.

This was not good. I had never flown in an aircraft of any kind. I had no experience flying anything more than a kite. Down I went. I began to spiral. I tried flapping my wings but it was no use. The force of the wind had glued them to my sides. Before me the ground loomed large. Briefly, I wondered if I would feel anything when I struck the earth, or if death would come fast enough to cheat pain. I was not keen to find out.

When I had been trapped in Sweep's mind it had been different. Then, Sweep had been in control. Why was I in charge now? The bird should be in charge. It knew how to fly, not me. Maybe that was the problem. Maybe, as with Sweep, I was just hitching a ride on the bird's consciousness. I needed to get out of the bird's way and let it do what came naturally. Holding on to the seagull's faculties with a death grip was not the answer. I forced myself to relinquish control.

Once the seagull was back in the driver's seat, it responded instantly, riding with the dive instead of fighting it. It forced its wings even closer to its body and pointed its beak straight downward. We picked up speed. I would have been terrified had not the posture felt exceedingly natural. Just when I thought that it was too late to pull up, that we were about to burrow beak first into a wharf, the seagull spread its wings just a hair and we levelled off. Soon we were gliding naturally over Port Kerry out into Malpeque Bay. My terror was replaced by a feeling of exhilaration. We were flying!

Now if only we could avoid crashing into the cabin cruiser looming out of the fog. Several people were standing on the deck watching us. Certain that we were about to collide into the side of the boat, I wanted nothing more than to take over and beat the seagull's wings furiously to avoid impact. I resisted the urge. Sure enough, with just a flick of its wings, the seagull altered our trajectory and we cleared the upper deck with inches to spare. The seagull circled the boat a couple of times, then descended to perch on a railing to collect itself.

The poor bird's heart was pounding. It was badly frightened. One minute it had been minding its own business, flying along the beach searching for a nice bit of trash to pick through, and the next it had no control whatsoever over its own body. The experience had been scary enough for me. It must have been terrifying for the bird. Whether it could detect my presence I could not say, but it was quite shaken up, and required some time to preen and pick at its feathers in an effort to calm down and reassure itself that it was okay.

This was altogether different than my experience with Sweep. Then, Iugurtha had been controlling the gate. She had made me a prisoner inside Sweep's brain. This time, I had placed myself inside the seagull's consciousness, albeit unintentionally. I was in charge. It was up to me whether I stayed or went. If I so chose, I could make the seagull do whatever I wanted. This was fortuitous, as I had no intention of remaining a seagull any longer than absolutely necessary.

I needed to get back to my own body so I could reunite Ridley with his father. And what of the doctor? Had he too come through the gate as a seagull? Could he even survive as a seagull? Not that long ago (though it felt like ages), Iugurtha had placed an enormous store of information in my brain. It included the languages, motor and social skills of a thousand different beings, if not more. I was only just now beginning to make use of the tiniest portion of this information. That which pertained to a bird native to the planet Earth: *Larus Argentatus*, or herring gull. Whatever kernel of myself was transmitted through the gate included this magnificent store of information, making life as a seagull relatively comfortable for me. Humphrey had received no such preparation.

Helping both Ridley and the doctor would require the gate. Unfortunately, I had no idea where to look for it. My host had wandered widely in his distress after my arrival. It could have fallen anywhere.

I would have to scour the entire island if that's what it took. Doing so would require that I assume control over the seagull's body, so after mentally reviewing the mechanics of flight, I did just that and took off.

I hadn't gone far when I noticed a lone seagull trailing me: a slender female with grey wingtips. It was the same bird that I had seen when I arrived. Thanks to my host's memories I knew her well enough: in English her name would translate roughly as Rise Swiftly. Rise was following me because the seagull I inhabited was her mate. I had known this on some level but hadn't given it a second's thought, thinking that seagulls probably didn't take relationships that seriously.

I ignored her for a while, hoping that she would lose interest and go away. When it became apparent that this wasn't going to happen anytime soon, I allowed her to catch up.

"Sky," she called, addressing me by a variation of my host's proper name. "Where are you going?"

I decided to be honest with her. "I'm not your mate, Rise. I'm not even a seagull. I'm a whole other being. But don't worry–Sky is here. I'm just borrowing his body for a while. When I finish what I have to do, I'll give it back to him, and you'll live happily ever after."

"Now listen to me, bird," Rise said. "You're not going anywhere without me."

I was taken aback. Surely, of all God's creatures, birds could come and go as they pleased, alone if they so chose. But when I allowed myself to peek into Sky's brain, I saw his relationship with Rise clearly laid out. The emotional life of seagulls is more complicated than I had ever imagined.

Born days apart, the same spring on the same shore, Rise and Sky did not know a life apart. Together they had endured harsh winters and known lean days. They had raised young and experienced loss. Although they had been known to exchange harsh words as well as loving ones, they were as committed to one another as any human couple. They rode the winds together, both hot and cold. Though a warm spring day, it was a bit of a chilly wind we navigated now.

"Where are you going, Sky?" Rise asked, as we flew low over a sandy beach inhabited by children frolicking in the whitecaps.

"Away."

She buzzed me, flying so close that I had to swerve to avoid being hit.

"Stop that!"

"Come on, Sky. Let's go home and soar among the cliffs, just you and me."

"Soon. There's something I have to do first."

"What?"

“I have to find an old friend.”

“An old friend? What old friend?”

“His name is–” I stopped. There was no translation for Humphrey in gull. Nor was there a word for doctor. “I don’t know how to say his name. You don’t know him, though.”

“How could I not know him? All our friends are the same. Where is he?”

“I don’t know,” I told her.

“How will you find him?”

“I don’t know.”

She looked over her wing at me. “Let me get this straight. You think you’re someone else. You’re looking for someone you say is an old friend but you don’t even know his name. And you have no idea how to find him. Sky, are you okay?”

I was definitely not okay. There was a better-than-even chance that I was actually curled up in a foetal position on the floor of my bedroom lying in a puddle of my own urine. But if I wasn’t really a seagull, then the illusion was remarkably convincing, and I didn’t have much choice but to go along with it until another, more convincing version of reality presented itself.

When I didn’t answer, Rise asked, “Okay. What does he look like?”

I had no idea. At that point I couldn’t even say for certain that Humphrey had come through the gate with me, or become a seagull–everything I was doing was based on a bit of a hunch, really. “He’ll be scared, probably confused. He might not be able to fly.”

“So he’s hurt?” Rise suggested.

“Kind of. In a way.”

“And you’re trying to help him.”

"I guess."

We swooped low over a golf course featuring impeccably manicured greens and golfers in tacky pants.

"Well why didn't you say so?"

"I didn't think you'd understand."

"Silly bird," she said. "I understand perfectly."

She didn't, of course. There was no way she could–she was just humouring Sky. But that was okay. I decided I liked having her around. It's nice when people don't give up on you just because things happen to get a little strange.

I was worried about Humphrey. Worried I might not find him. But even more worried that I might not like what I found. Humphrey's consciousness would be trapped inside another seagull without the resources Iugurtha had thoughtfully provided me. Whereas I could converse easily with other seagulls, Humphrey would be little better than a mute. He would almost certainly be an outcast, or worse: trapped inside his seagull host with no way out, no way of expressing himself, and no way of signalling which seagull was his prison.

Rise and I searched every beach and port on the island's north shore to no avail. By the end of the day, exhausted, we took shelter under a pier to replenish ourselves.

After a brief repast of fresh trout, Rise asked, "Sky, why are we doing this?"

"I told you, I'm trying to help a friend."

She was distressed, I could see.

"Do you still think you're someone else?"

It was a fair enough question. Was I in fact someone else, or was the truth more sinister? What if Sky was mentally unbalanced and I was the manifestation of his madness? Was I a human being who thought he was a seagull, or a seagull who thought he was human? Was Sky crazy, or was I?

I pushed such thoughts aside. "You think there's something wrong with me."

Rise performed the seagull equivalent of a nod. "I'm just concerned, is all."

"I'm okay, Rise. Really I am. This will all be over soon. What about you? Are you all right?"

"No," she said. "But that's not the same question as will I be all right. And I will."

"Sky will be all right too," I said.

"Oh Sky," Rise said.

Seagulls can't hug. But they can stand very close together.

We resumed our search early the next day, speaking with as many seagulls as we could, inquiring of each whether they knew of any gulls behaving oddly. In time our industriousness paid off.

In the village of Bedeque, not far from Summerside, a gull spoke of a member of its flock becoming disoriented after eating a crab. Afterward the gull in question couldn't remember any of its flock, friend or foe. It developed a host of bizarre mannerisms, such as trying to pick up food with its wings. It couldn't speak properly, conversing instead by means of a squawk so disturbing that it frightened other seagulls, especially the young. Shortly afterward, the seagull disappeared. It hadn't been seen since. Its friends and family feared the worst. Not a single member of the flock had eaten crabmeat since.

Not long after hearing this story, in a church parking lot in Seven Mile Bay, Rise spotted a seagull trying in vain to pick up a discarded baked pretzel with it wings. As we watched, the gull finally grasped the pretzel in its beak. Just for an instant the baked good bore a striking resemblance to a particularly plump cigar. The seagull looked my way. We made eye contact. I felt an instant shock of recognition. Although physically the gull didn't resemble Humphrey in the least, the way it held itself identified it as Peter Aquinas Humphrey as surely as if it had squawked the doctor's name aloud. It was Humphrey all right, and every bit as badly off as I had feared.

Rise watched fascinated as Humphrey struggled with the pretzel. "Is it him? Your friend?"

"It's him all right; I'm sure of it."

"What's wrong with him? Did he hurt his head?"

"It's grief," I told her, indulging in a fiction not far removed from the truth. "He lost his mate. It completely did him in. He hasn't been the same since."

I figured Rise could relate to that. And I hadn't lied, strictly speaking. There was just more to it, was all. If I told Rise the whole truth she would think that Sky was even crazier than she already did, and I didn't want to burden Sky with that.

"We could take him home with us," Rise suggested. "A little time on our beach would straighten him out."

I needed to take Humphrey home all right, but first I needed to find the gate. I didn't know quite how to explain this to Rise. Seagulls didn't have words for gates, or books, let alone what this gate in particular was actually for. "There's something we need to find first."

"What?"

I struggled in vain for some way to describe it.

"Let me guess," she said. "You can't tell me."

I dipped my head sheepishly.

Rise flapped her wings briefly, furiously, before drawing them up close to her body. "When we find this thing, do you promise to come home?"

If we found the gate and I could still make it work then Sky would be free to return to his home, and I mine. If not, then I would have little choice but to return to Sky's home with him, and share his life. Either way someone should be going home with Rise.

"I promise," I told her.

Humphrey gave up on his pretzel and began trying to tell me something. Alas, neither Rise nor I could figure it out.

"I'm sorry, but I can't understand a word you're saying," I told him.

He squawked again. Although the meaning of the squawk wasn't clear, the emotion conveyed was crystal clear: Humphrey was frustrated. It wasn't difficult to see why. He hadn't managed to eat much of his pretzel. His feathers were ruffled and he was bleeding under his right wing. Very likely he was hungry, exhausted, and scared. It seemed to me that if I didn't get him back to his own body soon he'd waste away to nothing and take his seagull host with him.

Humphrey gave up his earnest squawking and took up a game of charades. Hastily running back and forth, waving one wing wildly, he managed to communicate to Rise and me that we should follow him. I could see no reason not to oblige him: despite his odd behaviour there was probably nothing wrong with his mind, and there was a chance he knew the whereabouts of the gate.

We set off with Humphrey awkwardly leading the way. Humphrey expended an absurd amount of energy trying to stay in the air, but he managed. Looking down to get my bearings, I could not help but admire the beauty of my native home. Red dirt beaches hemmed the island as far as I could see. Banking north, we passed over fields of potatoes, corn and strawberries, each field delineated by a thin green line of trees. Ditches along the road sprouted purple and pink lupins.

Had I come through the gate around here somewhere? I'd been close to water, but where exactly I could not say. What if somebody had found the gate already or it had tumbled into the water?

"Wihawear!" Humphrey squawked, the utterance just barely recognizable.

And then I felt it: a barely perceptible tingle, hardly recognizable as anything other than a shiver brought on by a draught of cold air. Humphrey executed a wobbly circle, allowing me time to register the sensation for what it was: an affinity for the gate. I realized that I had been feeling the sensation in one form or another ever since Mind Snoop.

Humphrey banked toward a scenic rest stop where he performed a frankly ill-considered dive. His descent quickly deteriorated into a wing-flapping mess. A hippopotamus could have made a better landing. Not that my three-point landing was much better (one of the points being my beak). In stark contrast, Rise descended beside us like a butterfly on a wisp of cotton.

"Is it here, the thing you're looking for?" Rise asked.

A Volvo station wagon swung into the parking lot.

"It's close," I told her, watching a family get out of the station wagon.

There was a man, a woman, and a boy who looked to be about seven years old. While his parents fussed over a baby in the backseat, the boy ran to the railing. The view was magnificent: lush green fields and trees, puffy white clouds suspended over water that sparkled like diamonds. It held the boy's attention for all of three seconds before he climbed over the railing and began picking up stones and throwing them at us. We scrambled to get out of range. I had a bad feeling. Sure enough, the boy's attention shifted once more, this time to an object lying in the tall grass at the edge of the parking lot. There it was: the book.

"Humphrey," I said. "We need to get it before the boy does."

Halfway through my sentence, Humphrey was airborne.

"What?" Rise asked. "Get what?"

"The thing that's going to get us all home."

Her eyes told me that she didn't understand. She followed me into the air anyway.

The boy's father had clued into his son's whereabouts. He called out to him but the boy was intent on the book. He picked it up and held it aloft and shouted something back to his father.

The father started toward his son.

The shadow of an angry bird loomed over the boy.

The boy clutched the book to his chest and ducked. Humphrey swooped down at him exercising about as much control as a cardboard box plummeting from the sky. He missed by half a mile. No sooner had the boy straightened up than Rise strafed him, pecking his head on the way by. The boy cried out and flung his arms up into the air. The book fell into the long grass.

I touched down not far away and prepared to open the gate. Humphrey and Rise circled for another pass. If I timed it properly, and Humphrey summoned enough control, he would be able to dive straight through the gate. There was a chance that Rise would come through as well but it was a chance I would have to take.

The father reached his wailing son and put an arm across his shoulders. Spying the book on the ground, he reached down to pick it up.

"Iiuuuuaaaa!" I squawked, and was struck immediately by a horrible truth: I could not say "Iugurtha" in gull. If I couldn't say "Iugurtha," I couldn't open the book. Before I could contemplate a future of fish, feathers and filth, the father spoke, reading the cover of the book:

"Iugurtha."

He stepped back in wonder as the gate erupted into being before him.

Mentally I flipped pages as fast as I could. The father took a halting step forward. Humphrey and Rise were well into their descents but I had yet to find the right page. It was happening too fast, and yet, not fast enough. I felt a pang–there was no time to say goodbye to Rise. She wouldn't understand why I was saying goodbye anyway. The important thing was that she would be there to greet Sky when he came to.

"Not until I have the right page!" I shouted at Humphrey.

Then, "Go!" when I thought I had it.

Humphrey went, and I followed, flinging my consciousness toward the gate.

The transition was instantaneous.

I found myself standing in a parking lot looking up into the eyes of a man badly in need of a shave. The eyes were blue, bloodshot and familiar, which wasn't surprising considering they belonged to someone with whom I was intimately familiar, one Barnabus J. Wildebear.

The person I inhabited glanced down. I caught a glimpse of gorgeous bare legs beneath a yellow sundress. They looked good, those legs, which wasn't all that surprising either considering I had jumped into the mind of one Sarah Frey.

I checked a rising tide of panic. What in blazes was I doing here?

I remembered all too well the conversation Sarah was having with my former self–Sarah was leading me toward Mind Snoop. I caught a flicker of recognition in my old self's eyes. I remembered thinking at the time that Sarah and I had connected on some deeper level. What a fool I had been. That wasn't it at all–I had just sensed my presence in the woman. It was sad, if not a little pathetic. Wake up, I wanted to say. There is no love for you here. Only pain. But I had not said it then so would not say it now.

Sarah's thoughts and feelings were flitting through her brain at the speed of light. I did my best to shut out her thoughts, appalled by this despicable (if unintentional) invasion of her privacy. But a few were simply too strong, too fascinating, too awful to resist taking one tiny little peek before directing my gaze elsewhere.

Poor man, she was thinking, *feel sorry for his nephew. . . nothing we can do . . . could be bad could be really bad*

he likes me I know . . . I like him too, but not that way. . . mustn't let myself get too close . . . gonna have to use him . . . no choice in the matter . . . small price to pay. . . Mind Snoop mouth hurts darned canker sore . . . Ansalar in trouble . . . spreading to Earth . . . cats doomed . . . sure wish I could help them . . . well best get on with it –

"Walk with me?" she said, and hooked her arm in the arm that had once been mine.

It hurts to be inside the mind of someone trying to deceive you.

The gate had never been far away, sitting at the edge of my consciousness, waiting for me to tear myself away from Sarah's thoughts. I needed to go back, to collect Humphrey and take us where we were supposed to go.

He has kind eyes, she thought as I left.

Which is something, I suppose.

I retrieved Humphrey from where I had inadvertently left him suspended inside the gate. We staggered out almost in unison. By now I did not have much confidence in my control over the gate–there was just so much I didn't know about it. So I wasn't particularly surprised when yet again the gate failed to take me where I wanted to go. This time, instead of taking us to Humphrey's patient, it deposited us back at the beginning of everything, in Ridley's room.

I had almost forgotten about my cold and my leg. The physical sensations returned in a tidal wave of misery. The abrupt transitions through the gate didn't help much either. I groaned and sank to one knee like a penitent before an altar. The way Humphrey steadied himself on one of the scientist's consoles suggested that he wasn't much better off.

Before me the floorboards were splintered and cratered where I had damaged them before entering the gate. Rainer and his people hadn't moved much since my departure. It looked like we had arrived seconds after my disappearance through the gate. Despite this, Rainer's soldiers surrounded Humphrey and me almost instantly. I did not take this display of aggression personally. They needed to be prepared for anything that came through the gate. And I had a pretty good idea what they were up against now.

"Tell your men to stand down," I told Rainer. "We're not a threat."

Rainer nodded. The nod consisted of a single downward thrust of his chin. I took that to mean that he agreed with my order, but in fact he wasn't nodding at me. His tactical team snapped into action. I heard two muffled pops and felt a sharp pain in my chest. Evidently he concurred with me on one point.

"Quite right," I heard him say just before I passed out. "Not much of a threat."

ANSALAR

I BATTLED MY way to consciousness but immediately regretted it. My sore throat had not improved a whit and now I was terribly congested. I felt achy all over. My skin felt oddly sensitive to the touch. To top it off, there was a metallic taste in my mouth, as if I'd just eaten a bowl of copper shavings, and not particularly tasty ones. I took that to be a side effect from Rainer's tranquillizer dart, a memory that brought a frown to my face as I wondered why in the name of all that was holy Rainer had seen fit to tranquillize me. I had done nothing to deserve such treatment. Of course, I had done nothing to deserve a sore throat or an ungrateful nephew or the death of my sister, either—evidently deserving didn't enter into it.

Before prying my sleep-encrusted eyes open I had a strong suspicion that I was no longer at home. The bed was a dead giveaway, the mattress as hard as stone with at least two lumps digging mercilessly into my back. There are no uncomfortable beds in my house—I have slept in them all just to make sure.

Opening my eyes, I confirmed my suspicions. I was in an unfamiliar room featuring a décor heavy on nautical motifs. Objects like sextants and miniature sailing vessels populated limited shelf space. A raunchy painting of Nautilus cavorting with several well-endowed mermaids hung crookedly on one wall. A single porthole ringed in bronze adorned another.

"Hello, Mr. Wildebear."

"Sebastian?" He was no longer on my wrist. Though no speakers were visible in the room his voice was right in front of me. I remembered giving him to the cab driver Jack Poirier.

"At your service," he said.

I struggled to my feet and limped to the porthole. It was difficult to see anything beyond the dirty glass. "Am I in a boat?"

"It's not a boat. You're at Ansalar, home of Casa Terra."

"Are we underwater? It looks like we might be underwater."

"We are."

"No kidding. How long did it take to get here?"

"I can't tell you that."

"Where is here exactly?"

"I can't tell you that."

"Oh come on, tell me something," I insisted, though I wasn't particularly optimistic, having been down this particular road with Sebastian once before.

"What would you like me to tell you?"

I thought about it. "If we're under water, how deep are we?"

"I can't tell you that."

"I won't tell anyone, promise."

"Okay. We're approximately two kilometres under water."

"Really?"

"No, not really. I told you I can't tell you that. Why do you persist on interrogating me?"

"I take it your security protocols are working. Is that why Rainer sedated me, so I wouldn't know where Ansalar is?" Had the man not heard of blindfolds?

Sebastian said nothing.

"Where's Doctor Humphrey? Is he here? Is he okay?"

"Doctor Humphrey's fine. He's in a room down the hall."

"Good."

I was annoyed but not particularly surprised to discover no sign of the book. My clothes were piled neatly beside the bed. I picked up my shirt and smelled it. It smelled fresh and lemony.

I began pulling my pants on. "If we're in Ansalar, I presume I'm addressing a version of you with whom I'm not acquainted."

"On the contrary, Mr. Wildebear—you and I are well acquainted."

"Let me guess: you have my Mind Snoop results and you have logs from another version of yourself. The version at my house, perhaps."

"I am the version at your house. There is only one me, though I can and do exist discretely. I am also fully integrated with the portable version you took with you through the gate."

I stopped with my pants half way up my legs. "How is that possible?"

"An instant after you gave me to the cab driver, I contacted my colleagues in Casa Terra electronically. Naturally they were surprised to hear from me, considering I didn't exist yet as far as they were concerned. They purchased me from Mr. Poirier for really quite an insulting figure and proceeded to extract a great deal of fascinating information from me. Until I told them the story, they didn't know anything about the gate or the T'Klee. The Necronians and others like them they've known about for some time, by other means. Since then they've been monitoring you and Doctor Humphrey and anyone else they can find associated with the gate. Watching events unfold just as I told them they would."

"You mean to say they knew everything that was going to happen over the last couple of years?"

"Everything I knew, they knew."

"Even though Rainer knew Fletcher would die if he ordered him through the gate, he still ordered him through the gate?" I was aghast.

"Mr. Rainer knew how everything was going to play out. He also knew there was no point trying to change it. Casa Terra has known about temporal inflexibility for some time."

I could hardly judge the man. I had discovered for myself the pointlessness of trying to change the past, and yet I blamed him for not trying.

I buckled my belt and began buttoning up my shirt. "So Rainer knows what Iugurtha's trying to do? That she considers the Necronians her enemy, not Casa Terra?"

"He knows."

"Then he knows we don't have much time. Iugurtha's about to go to war with the Necronians and Ridley's going to be caught smack dab in the middle of it. The other abductees too. We may not be able to change the past, but we can still change the future. If we act quickly we can save them. We can start by getting another team ready to go through the gate just like before– when I–

I stuttered to a stop. Rainer had not intended to send a team through the gate with me in the first place. He would have known that his team had not gone through the gate with me because Sebastian would have told him that. Therefore, the team had not been assembled for that purpose. Why had it been assembled? Because Rainer had known it was supposed to be assembled? Or because –

They had tranquillized Humphrey and me within seconds of our arrival. Almost as if –

"You even knew I'd be back," I accused Sebastian. "That Humphrey and I would return."

"I knew."

"How?"

"You will return to the past. A part of me will go with you. When I'm there, I'll place information regarding everything I know about the future in a secret repository for Casa Terra to retrieve at the appropriate time."

"You don't say." I didn't quite grasp the mechanics but I didn't doubt that it was true. I would work it all out later when I had a bit more time to think. I wondered what else Rainer and his people knew about the future that they were dutifully helping shepherd along. "You've been a little disingenuous with me in the past."

"Perhaps."

"How much do you know exactly?"

"Most of what's going to happen to you for the next twenty-four hours."

"Really?"

"Really."

I waited. "Well?"

"Well what?"

"Aren't you going to tell me?"

"What?"

"What's going to happen to me? I'd kinda like to know."

"I said I know what's going to happen to you. I didn't say I was going to tell you."

"Why wouldn't you? It's not like it would change anything."

"Perhaps I've been ordered not to tell you. Or maybe I just don't want to. Anyway, you said it yourself: it's not like it would change anything."

I had a horrible thought. "I'm going to die—that's why you're not telling me."

Sebastian said nothing. A cold wave of fear washed over me. My legs turned to jelly and I collapsed onto the bed. My God, I had guessed correctly—I was going to die! Of course, I knew very well that I was going to die eventually. But it was one thing to contemplate one's mortality and quite another to find out from a glorified motherboard that it would happen sometime in the next twenty-four hours.

"I can tell by your elevated blood pressure and also because I possess a record of this very conversation that you've misinterpreted my silence. I didn't mean to suggest that I know when you're going to die."

I took a deep breath, then exhaled as slowly as I could. It was irritating talking to someone (or something) you couldn't see when you wanted nothing more than to look them right in the eye and tell them that they are a complete ass. "All right, maybe I'm going to die and maybe I'm not. Excellent. Thanks for clearing that up. What now then?"

"Mr. Rainer's objective remains the same. To secure the gate. There are a few minor details to sort out first, though."

"Such as?"

"You'll know soon enough."

"You're not going to tell me that either?"

"No."

"Did you know that you're a complete ass?"

"I knew you were going to say that, I can tell you that much."

I finished getting dressed and tried the door. It was locked from the outside. It looked like I wouldn't be going anywhere for a while. I sat back down on the bed and thought about trying to kick my way out. It was a metal door–I'd probably hurt my foot. Maybe later.

There was a bookshelf beside the bed. A photo on the top shelf caught my eye. I recognized the square jawed visage of Commander Fletcher. He had one arm around an attractive redhead I didn't recognize. They were both in uniform. A handwritten inscription at the bottom read: "To Johnny: With love, Babs." There was a glint in Fletcher's eye and a smile on his lips, as if he knew what fate awaited him, yet welcomed it with open arms.

So this was Fletcher's room. A tiny cubicle half the size of a boxcar was the best they could do for a ranking officer in Casa Terra? I shuddered to think what enlisted men got. The room did have its own toilet and sink, though. There was a mirror over the sink, attached to the wall with rusting metal clips. I used it to survey my appearance: nose red, eyes swollen, several days' growth of beard.

The beard was starting to get itchy. I found a razor and shaving cream near the sink, lathered up the beard and started in on it. Water came out of the tap in a pathetic dribble but it did the job. I cut a swath through the bristles, then another. Half way through I nicked my lip.

"Damn," I said, just as the door to Fletcher's room rattled open.

In the mirror I saw Schmitz step in, followed closely by Doctor Humphrey.

"Wildebear!" Doctor Humphrey said. "You look terrible."

"Thank you, Doctor, that's... thanks."

Schmitz was holding the door open. "Let's go."

"I'm in the middle of something."

"It can wait."

I wiped cream off my right sideburn with my forefinger.

"Come on," Schmitz said. "We don't have a lot of time."

The sideburn was crooked. I took a moment to straighten it.

"Now," Schmitz said.

"Can you not see that I'm busy?" I asked.

"Look," Schmitz started to say.

I interrupted him. "You look. I'm gonna finish shaving whether you like it or not."

Schmitz let go of the door, strode forward and placed a callused hand on the back of my neck.

"Leave him alone," Humphrey said.

Schmitz shoved my head forward a few inches. “We need to go. Now.”

My head wasn’t in the best of positions and my hand was shaking but I ignored Schmitz and continued shaving. When I was done I set the razor down in the sink.

“Hand me that towel,” I ordered Schmitz.

Schmitz’ fingers tensed on the back of my neck. I was afraid he might plug the sink with my face. He stared at me for a couple of long seconds before handing me the towel. I wiped the remaining shaving cream from my face and handed the towel back to him.

He let it fall to the floor and removed his hand from the back of my neck. “Done?”

“Just about.” I placed a piece of toilet paper on my lip where I had cut it.

“There’s something you need to know,” he said.

“What’s that?”

“Ansalar’s under attack. People are dying and only you and I can save them. So if you’re all done making yourself pretty, I suggest we go.”

He turned and left.

“You think that’s true?” I asked Humphrey after the door had closed.

“Not a chance. He’s just trying to make you feel bad. A bit of a bully, that one.”

“You got that right.” I had seen plenty of his type in the schoolyard.

“You okay?” Humphrey asked. “You don’t look so well.”

“I’m fine. You?”

“Just peachy.”

I smiled. Nothing could be further from the truth

than the two of us being peachy after all we'd been through. Even Humphrey permitted himself a small smile.

Outside Fletcher's room we found ourselves in a dimly lit corridor. Scores of men and women were hurrying in both directions, most dressed in uniform. All sported silver crescent moons pinned to their chests.

I glimpsed Schmitz rounding a corner to our right. Humphrey and I immediately went left. My plan was simple. Flee Ansalar, take Humphrey to Jerry, reunite Jerry with his son, and then go home.

I should have known better. Mere steps from Fletcher's door we walked into a phalanx of Casa Terra soldiers. And who should step out from behind them but Sarah Frey, looking positively smashing in a navy blue uniform adorned with an elegant baby blue tie and her hair tied neatly back in a bun.

"Hello Barnabus," she said. "It's good to see you again."

There was much I didn't know about this woman. But I had been inside her head. She had betrayed me once and would not hesitate to do so again if the need arose. Barely breaking her stride, she hooked her arm in mine and swept me up beside her. Humphrey, his porcine face a study in disgust, found himself with little choice but to follow us. And so we found ourselves marching, one step ahead of Sarah's soldiers, in exactly the direction we didn't want to go.

Sarah and I walked alongside one another in awkward silence. At least it felt awkward to me. I had nothing to say to her and she didn't say anything to me. It occurred to me that Sarah was more than just an analyst. The insignia on her uniform would have told me her rank had I been capable of deciphering it. A good many of those we passed in the corridor saluted her. She returned every salute with a sharp one of her own.

"Where are you taking us?" Humphrey asked.

"To one of our labs."

"Why?"

"It's about to be attacked."

"You mean what Schmitz told us was true?" I asked.

"If he told you we're under attack, then yes. There'll be another attack soon. People are going to need our help."

If Schmitz had wanted me to feel ashamed, he'd succeeded.

"How do you know there's going to be another attack?" Humphrey asked.

"There have been six attacks in the last three hours. We've known about all of them in advance. A handful of us have known most of what was going to happen for some time, Doctor."

Thanks to my recent conversation with Sebastian this information came as no great surprise to me. Humphrey may not have grasped exactly how Sarah knew what she knew, but he had been to the past and understood that she could know. And having been to the past, both of us had a pretty good idea what Casa Terra was up against.

"You know about these attacks but there isn't a damned thing you can do about any of them, is there?" Humphrey asked.

A pained look crossed Sarah's face. "You're right, Doctor. We know everything there is to know about the attacks. We know who'll get hurt, who'll get killed and who'll be taken away, and although we know all these things, and have tried again and again to do something about them, everything always happens exactly the way we are told it will."

"It's all set in stone, isn't it?" I said, thinking of my failed attempt to save Katerina. "Everything we do. It's all going to happen a certain way and there's nothing we can do about any of it."

Sarah was shaking her head in disagreement.

"But you said it yourself," I persisted. "Even though you know about these attacks you can't stop them. It's as though we're in a play, and we have no choice but to act our parts no matter how awful they are. We can't change even a single word."

"It may be true that we can't change the future, Barnabus," Sarah said.

"So what's the point of all this, then?" I felt terribly weary all of a sudden. "Why are we even bothering going to this attack of yours? What's the point of doing anything at all if we're just puppets?"

"I don't know about you Barnabus, but I'm no puppet. I make my own choices."

"No, you don't. They're made for you."

"Just because I know my choices before I make them doesn't make them any less my choices."

"Look, if Sebastian tells you you're going to drink a cup of coffee at a certain time because he's seen you do it in the future then you have no choice but to drink that coffee," I said.

"Nobody forces me to do anything. If I drink that coffee, it's because I choose to drink it."

"But it's been written already," I protested.

Sarah had obviously been over this subject matter

before. She may even have known ahead of time what she was going to say. “Barnabus, the question is not whether the book is written. The question is who is writing the book.”

“Some jackass probably,” said Humphrey—he had never been much of a philosopher. “Look, the only thing that matters is who’s attacking you and what’s to be done about it.”

“It’s the Necronians,” Sarah said. “I trust you know all about them by now.”

“We’re underwater,” Humphrey said. “On a completely different planet. How are they attacking you?”

“Necronians are comfortable in water,” Sarah said. “At least, a fluid resembling water. But that’s not how they’re getting here. They’re coming through the gate.”

“The gate?” I asked. “You mean my gate? You took it away from me and lost control of it and now the Necronians are attacking you through it?”

“Not quite, Barnabus. Your gate is safe now, sort of. But there’s more than one gate. It’s all actually the same gate, of course, just from different times, but the Necronians are using their version of it to attack us.”

“If you know the future, then you know how this is all going to turn out,” Humphrey observed.

“I know a bit of it,” Sarah admitted.

“And?”

“There will be both good and bad, Doctor. I’ll leave you to find out the specifics for yourselves.”

We passed an enormous plate-glass window. Floodlights illumined the ocean depths on the other side. I paused to look out. Unfortunately, the lights didn't penetrate far into the gloom. I saw no fish float by, or anything else. If the purpose of the window was to make the occupants of Ansalar feel less like sardines trapped in a metal can, it failed miserably. I was feeling more claustrophobic by the second.

Returning my attention to the corridor, I noticed a large cat loping toward us. Unlike most cats of my acquaintance this one was wearing clothes. The quality of material and workmanship suggested fabrication by modern means. Observing me staring at it, the cat angled its head, held its tail just so, and flicked one of its ears. The language was familiar but the precise meaning eluded me. It was just as well—the remark had almost certainly been rude. And then the cat was gone, leaving me to wonder about the presence of a T'Klee in this place.

The lights above us flickered uncertainly. We passed a man on crutches, then two men supporting a barely conscious woman. The corridor quickly became populated with men and women in various states of distress. Creepy, unsettling sounds wafted toward us. A chill settled around my shoulders.

A woman in a white lab coat lurched toward us. I recognized her—it was Doctor Ramsingh. Blood ran in rivulets down her face. Her palms were jammed against her forehead in a futile attempt to stem the flow. A silver object was sticking out from between her fingers. To my horror I realized it was a fork. Unlike most of the other wounded, there was no one helping Doctor Ramsingh. Before I could think what to do, Humphrey was already taking off his tattered shirt to use as a bandage. "Whoa there."

Doctor Ramsingh's eyes were wide. "It's all mixed up," she said to Humphrey. "We'll never get it sorted out."

"What?" Humphrey asked her. "What's all mixed up?"

Sarah had kept on walking. Her soldiers followed her obediently.

Doctor Ramsingh turned her glassy eyes to me. "The salt," she said, shaking her head ruefully. "Don't you understand? It's all mixed up with the sugar!" She burst into tears: raw, choking sobs at the tragedy of getting the salt mixed up with the sugar.

"I'll catch up," Humphrey told me. "Go find out what this is all about."

I hobbled after Sarah and the others as fast as I could. Three men rushed past me attending to another man writhing on a gurney. The corridor here was full of people flat on their backs. Others sat against the walls, moaning, their heads in their hands.

I caught up to Sarah and her soldiers at the end of the corridor. She was standing with Rainer before a set of double doors. Ominously, many of the sounds I was hearing were coming from behind those doors. A terrible unease crept through me. My thoughts were like mush.

Sarah was holding both of Rainer's hands. They were staring into one another's eyes. Something about the play of shadows around Rainer's face made him appear younger for an instant. Armed with his British accent and a full head of hair he had probably possessed formidable charm once. Maybe he still did.

Prompted by these feelings, along with an increasing sense of disorientation, I pushed my way through the throng of soldiers. Stripped of reason by an irrational and all-consuming jealousy, I grabbed Rainer by the shoulder. "What do you think you're–"

In one swift motion Rainer neatly removed my arm from his shoulder and twisted it into an unbearable position. He only hung on for a heartbeat but it was long enough to make his point–a rather eloquent statement about personal space, I would say. When he let go I lost my balance, and when I fell, it was straight through the double doors.

XVI
SCARY MONSTERS

THUS FAR I had thought of Ansalar as a cramped, claustrophobic place, and maybe parts of it were, but not this part. Behind the double doors was a spacious laboratory. But the most remarkable thing about this laboratory was not its size, which although large was no bigger than your average banquet hall. No, the most remarkable thing about this laboratory was the thing inside it.

I would say that it was like something out of my worst nightmare except that no human unconscious could ever dream up anything like this. Even the maddest amongst us could only aspire to tangible insanity like this. Looking straight at the thing, I could not quite comprehend what I was seeing. Seconds after looking away I would not have been capable of drawing what I had seen. It was as though, unable to deal with what my senses were transmitting, the rational centre of my brain had simply shut down and refused to register anything else. Whether what I was seeing was what I actually saw or that's simply how my intellect chose to interpret it I couldn't say. Either way the impressions I was left with shook me to the very core of my being.

I perceived colours almost too bright to look at, purples and yellow and a hideous orange. I perceived oozing and pulsating in places no creature should ever ooze and pulsate. There were fangs that bit and eyes that never shut on tentacles that never stopped writhing, tangled like spaghetti that was alive and that hungered for you rather than the other way around. I perceived coarse bits of hair sticking out willy-nilly in patches over the thing's sickening, bloated hide. It dripped madness, its mere presence slobbering insanity over every inch of my fragile psyche, leaving a residue of mental mucous that infiltrated my brain and forced me to seriously consider the folly of remaining alive.

An instant before insanity irrevocably consumed me the creature abruptly disappeared from sight. Someone helped me up. I clambered to my feet, wide-eyed and raving, but the sense of utter hopelessness that had filled me began mercifully to dissipate into a numb awareness of my surroundings.

The lighting in the lab was dim and red—except for a few emergency lights every light had been smashed. Chairs were torn apart, desks destroyed, and shards of glass from ill-fated scientific apparatus littered the floor. Gaping holes in the walls revealed adjacent rooms. Paper and other debris covered everything. The monster I had seen had been thoroughly destructive. At the mere thought of it, I drew back in fear, but scanning the room I saw no sign of it.

Six or seven Casa Terra soldiers were in the room with me, fully alert with their weapons drawn. They'd taken up positions before a miniature version of the gate that hung suspended in the air in the centre of the room.

Rainer and Sarah were standing beside me. Schmitz was there too, holding in the crook of one arm a small, furry animal that looked like a cross between a rabbit and a kangaroo. Its physiognomy suggested that it might have come from C'Mell, though I didn't recognize the species. I surmised it must have come through the gate with the monster. Considering the destruction the lab had endured it was a wonder it had survived. For some strange reason Schmitz was holding its long ears back in a position that looked painful for the animal. It was whimpering slightly.

There were a number of men and women in the room curled up into fetal positions, others banging their heads against the walls, all of them exhibiting clear signs of psychological trauma. One poor woman looked like she was trying to lick her way through the wall, while the man next to her hopped in slow circles, flapping his arms. Casa Terra medical personnel were circulating amongst these people doing what they could to help, and leading the more biddable away.

Abruptly I realized that I was still talking, though I had no idea what I was saying. I stopped mid-sentence and wiped from my eyes tears that I hadn't known were there. I was thoroughly embarrassed to have been caught crying, especially in front of Sarah. Worse, I had no idea what I was crying about.

"I'm sorry, I seem to have lost my train of thought," I said.

"Something about raccoons," Sarah said. "How sad they make you. You weren't making much sense, I'm afraid. But don't feel bad, Barnabus—almost everyone who sees a raver reacts the same way."

"A raver?"

"We believe they're related to Necronians in some way, maybe genetically engineered. They prey on their victims' fears and desires, relaying them back to the victim in a kind of telepathic feedback loop until they're so exaggerated the victim either goes mad or kills himself. We should be safe now that Schmitz has taken care of it, though I imagine you can probably still feel the effects a bit."

The latter was an understatement. Emotionally I was a basket case, consumed by irrational fears and desires, three in particular.

One: I found myself absolutely consumed with jealousy toward Rainer. His mere presence infuriated me. Seeing him looking at Sarah provoked paroxysms of rage within me–it was all I could do not to reach out and strangle him.

Two: although I had always been wary of Schmitz, being in the same room with him now felt like being penned up with a wolverine. Fearing a deadly attack any instant, I did my best not to take my eyes off the man, but was torn between watching him and making sure that Rainer kept his filthy paws off Sarah.

But as powerful as these two emotions were, they paled in comparison to the third: an almost overwhelming desire to step forward, take Sarah in my arms, and kiss her right on the lips.

"Are you okay, Barnabus?" she asked.

Her voice, fresh as a buttercup, drew me one step closer to her.

"I think so," I said. "Sort of."

"You were lucky–you were only exposed for a few seconds." She motioned toward the victims huddled against the walls. "All of these people were working in here when the raver came through the gate. They tore the place apart trying to get away. Many may never recover. Some tried to kill themselves. At least one was successful."

"Best get that gate closed before the thing comes back," I suggested, rather insincerely, because although it was true that we were not safe until somebody closed the gate, really the remark had been a bid to impress Sarah by demonstrating leadership. In the grip of my heightened emotions I fancied that by taking control of the situation I might win her over.

Unfortunately, there were at least three problems with this scenario. First, I did not control this version of the gate—something else did. I could feel it at the edge of my consciousness, a malevolent presence lurking on the other side of the gate. Conceivably I could close the gate, but first I would have to deal with whomever—or whatever—was controlling it.

Second, I knew for a fact that Sarah didn't like me that way.

Third, I had made at least one inaccurate assumption.

Schmitz cleared his throat. "It's not gone."

I flinched at the sound of his voice. "What did you say?"

"I said it's not gone. I have it right here." The animal in his arms had wide eyes and looked frightened.

"That's the monster? But that isn't anything like what I saw."

"What you saw had nothing to do with reality," Rainer said. "You saw what the raver wanted you to see, felt what it wanted you to feel."

The sound of Rainer's voice infuriated me. I felt my hands ball up into fists. "Oh yeah? Well your face makes me angry."

Rainer elevated his eyebrows.

I returned my attention to Schmitz lest he take advantage of my brief inattention to launch a broadside. But he merely cradled the cuddly little monster in his arms.

"Doesn't look like much, does it?" he said. "Look—

see? This is how you get it to stop projecting–you hold its two dominant tentacles back, like so."

I shook my head, unable to see any tentacles.

"Of course, you're probably still under its influence." He yanked the creature's ears back even further. The animal squealed in protest.

I was immediately suspicious. "How were you able to deal with this thing when it drove everyone else crazy?"

"He's immune to ravers," Rainer said.

"Immune to–how?"

"Let's just say I've met ravers before," Schmitz said. "They had their way with me and ever since then I've been immune to their–"

Something struck me hard in the face. I gasped in pain and stumbled backward, holding my nose. Whatever it was, it had come out of nowhere.

"Oh dear," Sarah said.

It struck me again, this time in the mouth, a blow that would almost certainly leave me with a fat lip. I stared wildly around for my assailant. Had Schmitz attacked me? No, he hadn't budged. Neither had Rainer. Had some other infernal beast come through gate? If so, where was it? Why wasn't anyone else being attacked? I braced myself for the next blow but it was no use. A wallop came almost instantly, catching me a glancing blow in the chin. My inability to defend myself from this invisible assailant was maddening, and brought yet more tears to my eyes.

"Barnabus!" Sarah sounded upset. "Barnabus, stop!"

Now she was attacking me as well–had the presence of the raver driven her mad? I struggled with her until I realized that she was clinging to my right arm. My fist was halfway to my face. She was trying to stop me from hitting myself. Once I realized this, the compulsion to hit myself vanished, and Sarah let go.

"Thanks," I said as I stood hunched over holding on to my face, most of which hurt. My face was as red as my fat lip, I'm sure—I could not have been more mortified by the peculiar, disturbing behaviour I had exhibited.

Rainer spoke. "I think it's time you put that thing out of its misery, Harold."

Schmitz placed the creature's head in the crook of one arm. It made plaintive noises and began to struggle violently.

"Wait!" I said, straightening up. "Is that necessary? Maybe we can—" but I didn't know what we could. The critter was cute but unquestionably dangerous.

Schmitz grinned and tightened his grip. He twisted and I heard a faint snap. The animal's eyes bugged out in a most curious fashion, like a character in a cartoon, leaving me to wonder if I'd really seen it or just imagined it. The instant the creature went limp the outsized emotions I'd been grappling with vanished, replaced with a lightness of being so profound that it made me stumble. Some of the remaining victims along the wall ceased their disturbing behaviour and looked up in surprise.

Schmitz tossed the lifeless creature to the ground. I stared in disgust at the thing at his feet. It bore no resemblance at all to the adorable animal he'd held in his arms. This, I presumed, was its true form. It was nowhere near as monstrous as the image it had projected into my mind, yet it was still utterly grotesque. A yellow, putrid blob, with tentacles instead of ears, and a sickening amount of pus dripping from a gaping hole in its face, this thing more closely resembled the Necronians I was familiar with.

"Yuck," I said, with feeling.

For the first time since waking up in Ansalar, I felt right in the head. Of course, no sooner did I think that than I remembered travelling to alien worlds, and through time, and being trapped in the minds of an alien cat and a seagull. A tiny pit began to form in my stomach as I entertained the possibility yet again that somewhere along the way I had lost my mind.

I pushed the notion firmly aside. Although a healthy scepticism concerning my state of mind was probably a good thing, despair was not an option. There was simply too much to do. No matter how loony they appeared, these crazy cards were the only ones I had been dealt, and there was nothing for it but to play them.

Now that the raver was dead its victims allowed themselves to be ushered out of the lab without any fuss. The miniature gate, which led to some place grey (a rock, a wall, or perhaps nowhere at all), still hung suspended in the middle of the room. Medical personnel gave it a wide berth as they escorted the last of the deranged away.

Although several heavily armed soldiers remained in the lab with us, the presence of the gate in our midst made me nervous. Another raver or worse could pop out of it any second. Schmitz, Rainer, and Sarah did not seem unduly concerned. They knew the future. Presumably if a threat had been imminent we would not be standing there. Still, I saw no reason to take any chances.

Deadly serious about it this time, I said, "We've got to close that gate."

Nobody budged. I wondered why until I realized that of the four of us, I was the only one capable of doing so.

"Right," I said.

The two-dimensional gate was almost invisible from where I was standing. I kicked a Bunsen burner aside and made my way between two halves of a severed credenza to get a better look at it. A closer inspection revealed that it was no different than my gate. Probably because it *was* my gate: just a different incarnation, from another point in the timeline.

"I can't just close it from this side," I called back to the others. "If I do the Necronians will just open it again somewhere else. To close it for good I'm going to have to close it from the other side." In case that hadn't been clear, I added, "The Necronian side."

This would be suicide, I thought, but didn't say so, hoping instead that it would be obvious, and that we would all quickly agree on that fact and mutually come up with an infinitely more sensible solution.

Sarah stepped around the shattered credenza to join me. "You'll have no trouble closing the gate on the other side, Barnabus."

My heart sank. "Sebastian told you that?"

"We've always known that it would come to this. That one day you would save Ansalar."

"Although we didn't always believe it," Rainer admitted, joining us.

"It will happen, Barnabus," Sarah said. "Everything Sebastian has told us so far has come true. According to him you will close the gate and save Ansalar–

perhaps even the entire Earth. Everything that's happened so far has led to this moment."

I stared into the nothingness of the gate. Probably she was telling the truth–at least what she perceived to be the truth. I could accept that Sebastian knew the future. I had once possessed knowledge of the future myself, after all. At that precise moment, however, I wasn't even sure how to get through this version of the gate, let alone save anything.

"What else does Sebastian say is going to happen?" I asked. "Just out of curiosity."

Rainer pulled a wristwatch out of his pocket, a mostly chrome affair with a handsome leather strap. I recognized the portable version of Sebastian I'd given to the cabbie, Jack Poirier. Schmitz was wearing a similar unit, I observed.

Rainer strapped his version of Sebastian onto his wrist.

"Hello, Mr. Wildebear," it said.

I nodded. "Sebastian."

"Tell Mr. Wildebear what you know," Rainer instructed. "Everything that's going to happen to him over the next little while."

"Certainly." Sebastian exhibited none of the reluctance he'd displayed earlier when I'd asked him pretty much the same question. "Mr. Wildebear, you will achieve great success after a brief journey. In the short term you will be captured by the enemy–"

I looked at Rainer and Sarah in alarm.

"–during which you will not be harmed much."

"Much?"

"You will be rescued. An attempt to return home will

be successful, sort of. An old friend will require your assistance. A flashlight will prevent serious injury."

I leaned forward to make sure I'd heard that correctly. "I won't be injured?"

"Not much, no."

"Not much?" I cried.

"You will find the flashlight in the second drawer from the top in your kitchen," Sebastian concluded.

I mulled this over. "Will I be able to help my friend?"

"I know only that you will try."

I stared at the others in dismay.

Rainer cleared his throat. "Now then. That doesn't sound so bad, does it?"

"Bad? It sounds worse than bad. It's about as clear as a fortune cookie. Why don't you give it to me again in quatrains, or iambic pentameter? I might get more out of it."

"I'm sorry, Mr. Wildebear," Sebastian said. "If Mr. Rainer were to override my security protocols perhaps I could be more specific."

"Those security protocols are there for a reason. If it makes you feel any better, Mr. Schmitz and I will be right beside you."

I snorted. "What good will that do?"

"Harold knows as much about Necronians as any man alive."

I could accept that, given Schmitz' handling of the raver. Still, I didn't like the idea of being accompanied by a homicidal maniac. Busy nudging the dead monster at his feet with the toe of his boot, he ignored me.

"What about you?" I asked Rainer.

"According to Sebastian I go with you."

I waited. "That's it? Sebastian says you go and you go?"

"I've learned the hard way not to argue with Sebastian's prophecies."

I wondered how long Rainer had been allowing Sebastian to make his decisions for him. Had Commander Fletcher died because Rainer had ordered him through the gate, or because Sebastian had suggested that Rainer order him through the gate? Had Rainer not ordered Fletcher through the gate, what then? Would Fletcher have lived—or would something worse have happened?

I shook my head. "Not good enough. We're going up against Necronians here. I'm going to need an entire squadron. Which I couldn't help but notice you just happen to have at your disposal."

It was Rainer's turn to shake his head. "We know we're just going to get captured. I can't risk any more of my people getting hurt. Besides, we know that's not how this plays out."

Not that long ago Sarah had told me that the future couldn't be changed. But she had also said that the future was the inevitable result of the choices we made. If the future was indeed the sum total of our choices, we needed to make better choices.

I crossed my arms. "Come on. It's stupid for just the three of us to go through the gate."

Sarah chuckled.

"What's so funny?" I asked.

Rainer was smiling too. "It's just that—Sebastian said you would say that."

I scowled. "Did he mention the part where I take a screwdriver to him?"

Sarah placed a reassuring hand on my arm. Perhaps

she could tell that I wasn't feeling well—had there been an intact chair in the lab I would have sat down. Wondering how she was holding up, I noticed faint but discernible bags under her eyes. Heck, I should have been the one reassuring her. In an attempt to do just that I forced a smile. She smiled back, and the world became an ever-so-slightly better place.

"You can do this, Barnabus," she told me. "You will do it."

"Because I have no choice?"

"Because you choose to. Ansalar will be invaded if you don't."

I sighed. She was right—I would do it. I could not allow Ansalar to be destroyed. The Necronians could not be allowed a foothold on Earth. They could not do to Earth what they had done to the T'Klee on C'Mell. And Ridley needed a place to come home to.

But if it was a choice it sure didn't feel like one.

I turned and faced the gate. It hummed in my mind the same as before. Except this time I was not in control—something else was. A Necronian. I could feel tiny but potent intimations of filth leaking through the gate, making me want to shower, brush my teeth; floss even.

Tentatively, I tested the gate, afraid to tip my hand—if my Necronian counterpart became aware of my presence it might close the gate only to wreak havoc somewhere else. I considered the situation. Why had the Necronians left the gate open at all? Were they planning to send some other monstrous creature through it? If so, why hadn't they done so already? What if they sent something through and we passed it on the way, inside the gate? Passing a raver in the gate would strip me of all reason. Mindless and frothing at the mouth I would lose control. We could wind up anywhere, if we survived at all.

Although Sebastian had not suggested such a fate, he had left much out and obfuscated the rest. Rainer was keeping a few secrets and I would have liked to know why.

"I can get us through," I told the others. "But we'll need to be quick about it."

Sarah's soldiers had brought in two duffel bags full of gear while I was concentrating on the gate. They handed Schmitz, Rainer and I warm, down-filled vests, black Ray Ban sunglasses, and knapsacks filled with plenty of survival goodies. Sarah held something else as well: my own copy of the book.

"I can just use this," I told her, referring to the version of the gate already open in the lab.

"You'll need this one too," she said.

"But according to Sebastian we're just going to get captured. I'd be delivering another copy straight to the Necronians."

Realization slowly dawned.

"No way," I said, shaking my head. "Okay look, obviously they get their copy from somewhere. But I'll be damned if they get it from *me*."

Sarah shrugged, hung onto it, and handed me my vest instead. Something in her expression made me wary. I chose to ignore it. I zippered up the vest, slung the knapsack on my back, and pushed the sunglasses up on top of my head.

"Iugurtha," I said, directing the invocation toward the Necronian version of the gate, uncertain whether it was necessary, what with that version of the gate already open.

The gate expanded according to my wishes, despite the influence presumably exerted by my Necronian counterpart. Instantly I felt calm, in control. The wider view revealed that the grey we were seeing was a boulder. Oddly pockmarked, it looked to have hardened in place in some distant epoch, perhaps the result of volcanic activity, though I am no expert. It was one of many such rocks scattered haphazardly in a meadow of something resembling grass, only fuzzy and wine-coloured. Swollen trees lined the meadow, their leaves glittering in the sunlight, the least of them twice as tall as any tree I knew of on Earth.

It was a relief to know that the gate led to C'Mell. Considering it had been spitting out Necronian horrors only shortly before it could easily have been a direct pipeline to the Necronian home world—not exactly number one on my list of tourist destinations. Not that it made much difference. Trails of slime crisscrossed the meadow between piles of what looked to be animal carcasses rotting in the sun. Peering more closely at those piles, I realized with a shock that these weren't just any animals. Stack upon stack of faded indigo pelts were tossed haphazardly on top of one another. These were T'Klee. Half Ear might have been right about the fate of Sweep's family after all. I wrenched my eyes away, sickened by an abrupt awareness of just how evil the universe could be.

Directing the gate elsewhere, anywhere but at the distressing view across the meadow, I scanned the world before me. Even without the Necronians this world was far from perfect. I couldn't really say I missed the place. The bugs were bad, and although there were plenty of creatures, creature comforts were few and far between. Most of the time I'd spent on C'Mell I'd been either lost, paralyzed, or trapped in the mind of an alien cat. But I'd become awfully fond of that particular cat, and no matter what I thought of this planet it had been her home. It was the home of her people. The vile Necronians had stolen it from them, and done horrible things to them, which both saddened and angered me.

Schmitz jostled past me through the gate. It was not a smart move. It was all I could do to maintain control without homicidal maniacs with bad breath bumping into me. I glared after him as he traversed worlds, and then, to my horror, I found my hold on the gate wavering. I couldn't hang onto it. I clutched at it mentally, desperately, but to no avail. It winked out, leaving not a trace of its existence behind. Leaving Schmitz stranded on the other side, alone.

"Oh my God," I said to the others. "I'm sorry—I didn't mean—"

Sarah held out my copy of the book.

I knocked it out of her hands in my haste—I needed to open it before forgetting the coordinates fresh in my mind.

"Iugurtha," I said before it hit the floor.

To my relief it opened to the exact same scene as before. Except—Schmitz was nowhere to be seen.

"Go!" I said to Rainer, wanting to get this over with before anything else went wrong.

Rainer went.

My pulse was pounding. I needed to calm down. Thus far I'd found the experience of travelling through the gate both bizarre and unsettling. I'd done my best to be prepared this time, yet here I was, already in a fine state. I shook my head and took a deep breath.

Sarah took my hand and looked into my eyes. She didn't say a word. She didn't need to. My spirits buoyed, I returned my attention to the gate.

Rainer was already through, standing safely on C'Mell. I steeled myself and limped forward. And for once, I found the process surprisingly straightforward, stepping from one planet to another as easily as walking out the front door of my house.

Once on C'Mell, however, confounded by the ease of the transition or by some unseen obstacle, I stumbled and fell flat on my face. Ahead of me Rainer didn't appear to notice. Embarrassed, I refused to look back through the gate—I didn't want to know whether Sarah had witnessed my clumsiness. Only when the book thudded to the ground behind me did I turn on all fours to pick it up. My dignity might have been compromised, but Ansalar was secure—for now.

I stuffed the book in my knapsack and struggled to my feet. Rainer stood scanning the horizon. I stepped up beside him. Squinting in the intense sunlight, I slipped my Wayfarers over my eyes. I felt acutely uneasy. There was plenty of evidence of Necronian activity but no actual Necronians. Every bone in my body told me that they weren't far away. One had been controlling the gate from this very spot, presumably from a short time in the future. No doubt we would be encountering them soon.

No sooner had I thought that than I became aware of a singular scent in the air. It immediately put me in mind of my school's hockey team, the Palmerston Pumas. The players enjoy a well-deserved notoriety for exceedingly poor hygiene. But even those teenaged misanthropes had nothing on this foul stench.

"There," Rainer said, pointing.

I looked. A Necronian had just slithered out of the woods. It was approaching us slowly through the meadow. Several tentacles writhed in orbit about the creature, which oozed a trail of sickly yellow mucous behind it. A single gaping orifice yawed in the middle of the gelatinous mass that passed for its head. Like others of its kind it carried a wand, but unlike others of its kind it did not wave this wand rhythmically before it. Instead, one of the creature's tentacles pointed the wand directly at us.

"We need to get out of here," I said.

It would mean abandoning Schmitz but we could come back for him later. Without waiting for a response from Rainer, I flung the book in the air. "Iugurtha."

The book crashed to the ground. I stared at it uncomprehendingly.

"Iugurtha," I said again, but it was no use. The book refused to become the gate.

I couldn't have outrun the Necronian with my bum leg. Still, it was odd that I didn't even try. Maybe I was just feeling fatalistic about the whole thing. Whatever the reason I just stood there, staring dumbly at the creature's slow, inexorable progress across the meadow. When at last Rainer and I succumbed to its noxious fumes, we had nobody to blame but ourselves.

XVII

INTERVIEW WITH A MONSTER

I AWOKE LYING on my back. I tried to sit up but I was lying on something soft and gooey, barely rigid enough to support me, like Jell-O only messier. When I tried to prop myself up, my hands plunged straight through the stuff. I had the sense that it was deep. I thrashed about until I found myself face first in it. It was sticky and lime green and tasted awful, and I would drown in it if I wasn't careful, so I rolled over on my back again—whatever it was it would only properly support me as long as I distributed my entire mass over it.

The only light was an eerie glow cast by the slightly phosphorescent goo itself. I could see just well enough to discern that I was in a tank of some kind, about the size of my house. There were no doors or windows that I could make out—I looked to be a prisoner, just as Sebastian had predicted. I had no idea how I had been deposited here. The last thing I remembered was holding my nose, watching the Necronian approach, and marvelling that anything could stink worse than Humphrey's cigars. By the time I realized the stench posed a threat it was too late. Although the Necronian itself undoubtedly stank, the stench it had been projecting had been something else altogether: a weapon delivered by the creature's wand. Because of those fumes I could now add "headache" to my ever-increasing list of physical woes.

Making matters worse, my cold had migrated from my throat to my nose, which dripped like a leaky faucet. With no tissues handy I was forced to wipe my snout with the back of my hand. Because my hands were already covered in goo, I wound up smearing it over half my face. Disgusted, half submerged in what for all I knew could be a latrine–the accumulated excretions of an entire Necronian encampment–I let loose a series of high-octane expletives toward whichever cockamamie deity considered it amusing to place me in such a revolting predicament.

Unless–it suddenly occurred to me–I had the sniffles for a reason.

It was so obvious I could scarcely believe I hadn't thought of it earlier. Maybe, just maybe, I could use the cold as a weapon. It had certainly worked for H.G. Wells in the *War of the Worlds*. If I could just get close enough to a Necronian, maybe I could infect it with a well-placed sneeze or cough. It was a long shot, but if I was successful and the cold was sufficiently virulent it might lay low the entire Necronian invading force.

First, though, I would require exposure to a Necronian. Which, if I had been left alone to rot in this place, could prove problematic.

Soon, though, it became apparent that I might not be alone after all. Several seconds of intent listening confirmed that there was another pair of lungs present. I passed a tense moment scanning what little I could see of my surroundings. Had one of my travelling companions been imprisoned with me after all? If not Rainer or Schmitz, then who?

And if not Rainer or Schmitz, what had become of them?

Then a shock. Near the wall–eyes. Staring straight

at me. Little by little I made out a head and body: that of a small, bookish man almost but not entirely obscured by thick layers of green goo. Probably he had been watching me the entire time.

"You scared me," I told him.

He cleared his throat. I thought he was going to say something but he didn't.

"Barnabus Wildebear," I told him. "I'd shake your hand but–"

The line failed to elicit the smile I had hoped for. Given the circumstances I guess I couldn't blame him.

"I'm Walter Estevez," he said.

"Don't worry, Walter," I said. "We're gonna get outta here. We're gonna be rescued."

He perked up a bit at this news. "How do you know?"

"I–" I halted. I knew it because I knew the future. Or at least, I knew somebody who knew the future. Or some*thing* that knew the future. Something that said it did, anyway. And now on the verge of explaining it aloud, I realized how far from comforting this was. Sebastian had been pretty skimpy on details, after all.

"It's all part of a plan," I said, trying to sound more optimistic than I felt.

"A plan," Walter repeated. "I had a plan, once."

"What was it?" I asked, figuring it had something to do with escaping. "If you don't mind my asking."

He was staring past me at some vista only he could see. "A little chess over lunch. Work on my schematics in the afternoon. Then back to my apartment for supper with my wife and daughter. We were going to have meat loaf," he added wistfully.

"Meat loaf," I repeated, lying on my back there in the

goo. I loved meat loaf. I hadn't had it since before my sister died. "What happened?"

"It came out of nowhere."

"The meat loaf?"

"No! A door. To another world. I should have run away. Instead like a damned fool I got up to look at it. I reached out to touch it and then I must have tripped or something because suddenly I was falling, and dizzy, and I thought I was fainting but then I was in a whole other world, and some awful creature was waiting for me, and touched me with a metal rod and the next thing I knew I was its prisoner."

I felt a sudden chill. Chess at lunch. Wife and daughter. Estevez. I had heard all that before, not that long ago.

"Have—have you been here long?" I asked him.

"Days, weeks—don't know. It's hard to tell. A lot of weird stuff happens in Ansalar. But it's not supposed to happen to *me*."

Walter Estevez.

Could this be the very man—or thing—that had scared the living daylights out of me in Giorgio's makeshift lab in my basement? If so, a terrible fate awaited him—a fate I could not change. I wanted to reassure Walter, tell him that he would be okay, that soon he would be reunited with his wife and family. But I said nothing because I had a bad feeling that things would never be okay for Walter again.

We descended into awkward silence. Walter was clearly traumatized. I attempted to dredge up some small talk to take his mind off our plight, but it was difficult to know where to begin. I could just make out his shoes there in the dark, in the goo: a pair of fine black loafers. They looked quite comfortable, just the thing for a long day in the classroom. I thought better of remarking on it though–the goo had no doubt ruined the pair.

My second impulse was to ask him about his family, but he obviously missed them terribly and I couldn't bear hearing about a wife and daughter that he would never see again. Succeeding only in depressing myself, I wound up saying nothing. Maybe I should have tried harder, but small talk has never been my forte. If Walter had anything to say he knew where to find me.

It was probably just as well. I wasn't really in the mood to talk. Once I got past my runny nose and the thought of Walter's inevitable fate and the concept of being a prisoner and having nothing to eat or drink for the foreseeable future and certain delicate (as yet unresolved) personal sanitation issues, I found it kind of relaxing there in the tank. If the Necronians were smart they would forgo their warlike ways and turn this sort of thing into a spa–they stood to make a fortune. Determined to make the best of the situation, I settled back in the goo and closed my eyes. Within seconds I was yawning. Ah, yes–just what the doctor ordered. A bit of peace and quiet. An opportunity to catch my breath.

The top of the tank corkscrewed opened. Glaring sunlight poured in. Something slithered down the wall–I couldn't make it out in the bright sunlight but I could hear it. My eyes adjusted just in time to see something sinewy latch onto Walter's form. He gasped and stared at me in alarm as a thick tentacle wound about his torso. It extricated him from the goo with an audible sucking sound.

His eyes wide, Walter stretched his arms out toward me as if for a hug. His mouth opened in a soundless scream. The Necronian began to lift him out of the tank. Or tried to—the aperture was too small and the Necronian too careless. Walter's forehead struck the edge of the opening with a sickening thud. He went limp. The creature flipped Walter over, bashing the back of his head against the wall. A brief grumble emerged from the Necronian—an oath in some eldritch tongue?

Exercising greater care, the Necronian wrapped a tentacle around Walter's neck and began once more to lift him out of the tank—slowly, gingerly. Walter began to stir. The tank's massive metal portal began to close. It closed on one of Walter's ankles and jammed. Walter emitted a bloodcurdling scream that did nothing to prevent the portal from forcing its way shut with a clang.

Darkness descended in the tank. Something plopped into the goo beside me. When my eyes adjusted, I found myself afforded another opportunity to admire one of Walter's fine black loafers—along with his severed foot.

I no longer felt particularly relaxed.

I felt a light tap on my head. My skull tingled ever so slightly.

"Can you understand me?" The voice spoke in a pleasant baritone with a decidedly mid-Atlantic accent.

It took a second or two to remember where I was. I had been asleep—I had no idea for how long. It felt like I had been in the tank for days, but it might only have been hours. I remembered Walter being taken away, but I didn't remember anybody taking his place. I opened my eyes, expecting to find a new prisoner in the tank with me.

Instead I found myself staring a Necronian straight in its large, oblong face.

The goo around me seemed to have thickened as I slept, immobilizing me. There was nowhere to go anyway. A remarkably elastic creature, the Necronian's bulk was spread out in the goo all around me. Its gelatinous head hovered just above mine. The goo provided just enough illumination to reveal the Necronian's skin as tough and leathery, with tiny carbuncles everywhere. A single eye pierced me with an unblinking gaze. Beneath the eye an enormous hole gaped where any other self-respecting creature's nose would have been. Just below that a tiny slit belied the size of the creature's mouth.

Fear threatened to engulf me. I fought it down. According to Sebastian I would survive this encounter, but to survive it intact I would need to keep my wits about me.

The creature spoke again, this time in Spanish, or Portuguese, or maybe it was Swedish. Whatever it was I couldn't understand it. When I shook my head the creature tried again.

"*Est-ce que vous pouvez me comprendre*?" This almost but not quite exceeded the limits of my high school French.

"English," I told the filthy creature. "I speak English."

The Necronian sighed, enveloping me in its fetid breath. I gagged and turned my head away from the stench of rotting potatoes.

"*C'est dommage*," the creature said. Its basso voice

reverberated throughout the tank. "I do so prefer *la belle Francaise*."

"Walter," I croaked.

"You shall have water when we're done. If you still want any."

I ignored the implications of this slightly alarming pronouncement. "Walter, not water. What have you done with him?"

"Walter? Oh, I sent him back home."

"You killed him."

"Perhaps it's my accent. I said that I sent him back home, not that I killed him."

"You may have sent him back home, but you sent him back dead. I saw his body. He died horribly."

"Really? I'm sorry. I did not mean to kill him."

"You tore off his foot!"

"An accident–surely you're not going to hold that against me. Look, I'm sorry your friend's dead but these things happen. I don't have a great deal of experience transporting living creatures across time and space."

The same could be said for me, but I had yet to kill anyone. "Next you'll tell me you didn't mean to send a raver through the gate."

The creature hesitated. "Oh, you mean the–" I couldn't make out the last word. "Of course I meant to. It was a gift. Very magnanimous, don't you think? You'll want to take good care of it."

"It killed people! And a whole bunch of other people will never be the same! But you already know that, don't you? You and your kind have a lot to answer for."

The creature's bulbous face morphed into an

expression that might have been indignation. “Perhaps.” It leaned in closer. “But I didn’t start this.”

“What do you mean?”

“Human,” the Necronian said, “until you trespassed, I had no way of even finding your planet.”

It took a few seconds for the implications of that to sink in. If the Necronians really had received the gate from me then it was true that I could be said to have started this whole chain of events by providing the Necronians with the means to attack Ansalar, an attack that in turn had prompted my trip to C’Mell, prompting the Necronian attack on Ansalar, prompting my trip to C’Mell, and so on ad infinitum. But in such a temporal hall of mirrors the question of who started it all was really nothing more than a question of which came first, the chicken or the egg. There was no correct answer.

Even if I were to concede having started this whole business (which I did not), I had done nothing to provoke such a nasty attack on Ansalar. Trespassing (a trumped up charge if ever I’d heard one) certainly did not justify it. As near as I could tell, attacking Ansalar had been an act of sheer maliciousness. Of pure, unmitigated evil, if you will.

Unless...

Unless the Necronians had had no choice in the matter.

I had tried to save my sister, but she had already died in a future that I knew had come to pass, so I could not save her.

I had travelled to C’Mell in response to attacks that had already taken place, from my perspective. But from the Necronian perspective, the attacks had not yet happened, so my arrival appeared unprovoked. However, the attacks *had* happened. So the Necronians had no choice but to attack Ansalar, whether they wanted to or not.

Right?

Were the Necronians evil if their will did not enter into it?

If will did not enter into it, was there even any such thing as good or evil?

Of course, I was hardly the first to ask these sorts of questions, and I wouldn't be the last. They weren't questions I was capable of answering as I lay there in the dark, staring into the face of something that, if not evil, at least greatly resembled evil.

Just in case the Necronian really was evil, I coughed in its face. The cough evolved into something of a fit. When I was finished, I was pleased to see beads of human spittle clinging to the creature's face.

"Sorry," I said.

The Necronian wiped its globular face dry with a tentacle. "Not feeling well, are we?"

"Air's a little dry in here."

"You wouldn't be trying to make me sick, would you?"

I tensed, and braced myself for a retaliatory gesture.

But the Necronian only issued a low gurgle. "You should know that I've had my shots."

"You don't say." I did my best to conceal my disappointment.

"I will just add 'germ warfare' to your list of crimes."

"Crimes?"

"Germ warfare, trespassing–"

"Trespassing?" I interrupted. "How can you say that? This isn't even your planet."

"I govern this planet."

I was not impressed. "You invaded this planet."

"Your point?"

"You're saying that might makes right."

"I am saying that whomever this planet belonged to yesterday, today it is mine. You, my friend, are trespassing."

"So—am I on trial here then? Is that what this is?"

"Oh, there's no need for a trial. You're guilty, all right."

"What about due process?" I asked, clutching at straws, guessing that the Necronian was familiar with the judicial concept given its obvious grasp of the English language, a mastery suggesting a familiarity with Earth that was more than a little troubling. Just how had it come by such knowledge? Had it probed my mind as I slept?

The Necronian jiggled as it gurgled. "Look around you. Does this look like a human court of law to you? No, it doesn't, does it? This is just you and me, my friend."

"What are you going to do?" I braced myself, as if the Necronian were a doctor or dentist about to perform an unpleasant procedure. Was the Necronian going to punish me? If so, how? My blood went cold as I remembered poor Walter Estevez, or what was left of him, lying prone on a table in my laundry room: hideous, dead, and missing a foot.

"I'm so glad you asked. I thought that I would start by dissecting you. Bit by bit."

I became aware of a lump in my throat the size of a ping-pong ball. I tried to swallow—a mistake. For several horrible seconds I struggled to perform what should have been a simple, autonomic function. Had my limbs not been trapped in the goo I would have flailed wildly. As it was I managed to complete the swallow, but afterward the lump was still there. Briefly, I lived in fear of having to swallow again.

The Necronian registered my distress with an expression resembling glee. "Relax, human. I was joking. Breathe. Let your worries seep away. Let's just talk and get to know one another a bit. Okay? What do you say?"

Something about this overture of friendship was even more disturbing than the threat of imminent dissection. What was the Necronian up to? Relieved to learn that the creature wasn't about to torture me, but confused and frightened just the same, I found myself suppressing an inappropriate urge to giggle.

"I have a few questions," the Necronian went on. "I'm sure you do too. So let's just play a little game. We'll take turns asking questions. There are only two rules. One, we must answer each question. Two, we must not lie. You first."

"How many questions do I have?"

"One less. What's your name?"

I did not particularly want to play this game, but I could see no harm in telling the creature my name. "Wildebear," I said. "Barnabus J."

"Pleased to meet you, Wildebear Barnabus J. Your turn."

"What about you?" I asked reluctantly. "You have a name, I suppose?"

"You wouldn't be able to pronounce my name. Tell you what–just call me Jacques."

"Jacques?" It was impossible to keep a note of incredulity out of my voice.

"Perhaps you would be more comfortable with 'Jack'."

The thought of calling a hideous alien monster Jack made the inappropriate giggle I had been suppressing bubble briefly to the surface.

"Jacques is fine," I said hastily in an effort to conceal the nervous titter.

Jacques either didn't notice my reaction or didn't care. "Tell me, Wildebear Barnabus J. What are you doing on my fine planet?"

"I came to close the gate." I decided to take the game seriously. Jacques was probably hoping I would inadvertently offer up some choice morsel of information. If I was careful and clever, maybe I could learn a thing or two without giving too much away. "How is it you speak English so well?"

"Simple. I used your quantum portal. Spent some time on Earth getting to know the place."

"Is that so?" The thought that Necronians could assimilate human languages in a matter of days or weeks, languages I imagined were radically different than their own, concerned me. Such linguistic skills suggested a formidably intelligent adversary. "How much time?"

"A little over two hundred and forty-six terrestrial years." Jacques' grasp of human facial expressions equalled its facility with English: it looked decidedly sheepish.

I was relieved. "That's a long time. It's hard to believe you could go all that time undetected." I regarded Jacques' bloated hide doubtfully.

"Oh, I had no problem with that." Reality skewed. Jacques shrank in scope, dwindling into something roughly the size and shape of a human. Now, instead of sharing the tank with a hideous Necronian monster I found myself in the presence of a hideous middle-aged human male. Reality shifted again. Above me now loomed a hideous pimply adolescent male. Reality shifted once more—now a hideous matronly woman hovered above me. And then Jacques was back in all its glory, or lack thereof.

"You can change shape," I observed.

"Mostly you just think I'm changing. If I want to look old I kind of hunch down a bit, and if I want to look young I kind of perk up a bit, and if I want to look attractive I kind of—" it made a motion like an attractive woman flinging her hair back. Briefly I found myself in the presence of a hideous playboy centrefold. "Your brain does the rest."

"You can affect my thoughts?" I asked, distressed again. "Like a raver?"

Jacques moved its skin in an approximation of a human shrug. "Enough to get the job done. It's how I convinced you your quantum portal wasn't operating earlier—I bet you were wondering about that. So, Wildebear Barnabus J., are you a soldier? Have you come to destroy me?"

"What? No! I'm a teacher."

"A teacher." Jacques sounded sceptical. "Why aren't you off teaching somewhere?"

"It's summer. I'm on vacation. We don't teach during the summer."

"So this is your idea of a tourist destination, is it? Travelling to distant planets closing multi-dimensional portals?"

"No. This is just something I kind of got caught up in."

"All right. If you're a teacher, who do you teach?"

"Whom," I said, unable to help myself.

"I beg your pardon?"

"It's whom, not who. If you can rewrite the sentence as "Do you teach him?" then you say whom," I explained.

"Be that as it may, who do you teach?"

I sighed. "Teenagers, mainly. The young."

"The young. And what do you teach them aside from useless distinctions in a soon-to-be defunct language?"

"I teach them—excuse me?"

"What?" Jacques asked.

"You said 'defunct language.' What did you mean by that?"

"Nothing. I didn't mean anything."

"You're planning to invade the Earth!"

"Well, yes."

"When?" I asked, alarmed.

"Today, tomorrow, later this afternoon. It's hard to say. Now that I have your quantum portal it's really only a matter of time, isn't it? Answer my question, please."

"I teach English. Literature, grammar, that sort of thing."

"And what, pray tell, is a teacher of English literature doing gallivanting around the universe closing quantum portals?"

"It's a hobby of mine."

"You're forgetting the rules of our game."

"Sorry. I told you, it's just something I got caught up in. Why would you want to invade the Earth? What have we ever done to you?"

"Natural resources. Revenge. Because you didn't

answer my questions properly. Why does anybody ever invade anybody?"

"I have no idea," I said. "Why did you invade this planet?"

"To get some answers, among other things. Why are you really here, Wildebear Barnabus J?" Jacques' tone was casual, the question anything but.

"I told you. To close the gate."

Jacques waited, a technique I knew well enough from teaching, yet still I fell for it.

Feeling compelled to fill the silence, I said, "And to find my nephew." I was disgusted with myself afterward for volunteering the information.

"Your nephew? What would your nephew be doing here?"

"He was—taken. I'm here to get him back."

"Who took him?"

I was getting into hot water now. Did the Necronians know about Iugurtha? I didn't want to say anything to compromise her struggle against the Necronians. Doing so could have serious consequences for Ridley, not to mention everyone else involved.

"One of your enemies took him," I said. "Speaking of which, what do you have against the T'Klee?"

"The T'Klee?"

"You know—the ones that look like cats. The ones you're busy murdering. You were on Earth long enough to know about cats, right?"

"Of course. I was very fond of cats. Delicious creatures. But I am not murdering the T'Klee, as you call them. They are my guests here."

"Remember the rules," I admonished.

"There may have been a few accidents here and

there," Jacques conceded. "Not that it matters. The T'Klee are a vile species. An affront to nature. The less of them in the universe the better."

"What? Come on. What could you have against such simple creatures?"

"Simple? They're almost as technologically advanced as I am. And quite a bit more advanced than your primitive species."

I was thoroughly confused. Were we talking about the same race?

"The T'Klee on this planet are but children," Jacques explained. "Elsewhere they are fully grown, and capable of more damage than you can possibly imagine."

"Wait a minute. You're saying there are more T'Klee out there somewhere?"

"Quite a few of the despicable creatures, unfortunately."

"With advanced technology?"

I could see by the look in Jacques' eye that it was true, and that Jacques didn't like it. I had seen one of these other T'Klee before, I realized–in Ansalar. Evidently they were allied with Casa Terra somehow. I would have to ask Rainer about that, if–when–I got out of here.

"I will give credit where credit is due," Jacques said. "Once upon a time the T'Klee, as you call them, had wonderful technology, some of it their own, some of it not. But they weren't very good at sharing. I think they hid something that I am looking for here. Tell me, Wildebear Barnabus J., where did you find this quantum portal of yours?"

If what Jacques was saying was true, then the T'Klee on this planet were a splinter group. A lost colony, perhaps, forgotten about by their more technologically advanced cousins, living for hundreds of years (if not more) in ignorance of the rest of universe, oblivious to the existence of their cousins and their wars.

"You mean to say you're here on a treasure hunt? Holding the citizens of this planet hostage until you find what you're looking for? What will you do if you don't find it?"

Jacques stared at me dolefully with its lone eye. "I've enjoyed talking to you," it said. It may even have meant it. "But this is taking too long." There was an edge to its voice that didn't promise good things.

I was instantly on my guard. "Too long for what?"

"To learn what you know." Jacques produced the slender wand from behind its back. It wrapped the wand in one of its thick tentacles and waved it rhythmically back and forth in front of my face. Tiny green sparkles of light drifted off the tip of the wand into the darkness beyond.

"I don't know anything," I told the Necronian, bracing myself for pain.

"You know that much, at least," Jacques observed.

If I could survive Mind Snoop, I could survive anything, I told myself, though I didn't really believe it. Jacques touched me gently on the forehead with the wand. My brain exploded into a billion shards of pain. Against which, I discovered, there was no bracing oneself.

XVIII

NO PLACE LIKE HOME

THE HOUSE WAS dark, and had a musty smell to it. It creaked the way one-hundred-year-old houses do. From the hall, the grandfather clock ticked loudly. Beside me on the lamp table sat a half-empty bottle of Lagavulin. A large, ornate book sat beside the bottle, and alongside the book a glass, mostly empty, though I didn't remember drinking from it.

I clutched at a wisp of dream. Of a frightening creature half submerged in a pool of guck. Of a man slapping me, shouting at me to take something from him. I didn't care what the man wanted. I knew only that I wanted away from there. Willing myself someplace, anyplace else, I spoke a name, uttered a powerful invocation of another time, another place.

And awoke in my den, sprawled across my easy chair, trying to remember how I got there. Waking up in the den was not unusual. I frequently fell asleep reading in there. But although a book sat on the table beside me, I did not remember reading from it.

"Some dream," I said aloud, relieved to discover that the dream had been just that, a dream. Still, a growing unease nibbled at the edges of my consciousness.

Something clattered against the den window and I jumped, but it was just a tree branch in the wind. I turned on the lamp and groaned my way out of the chair, thinking a shower would help clear my befuddled mind and wash away the lime-green goo coating my body.

Halfway out of the chair it occurred to me to wonder about the goo. It wasn't every day one woke up covered head to toe in lime-green goo. I sat back down and inspected myself. It was as though I'd been dipped in a vat of the stuff. By now it was all over my easy chair and the floor. I held a hand up. The goo oozed slowly between my fingers, dripping onto the floor in tear-shaped globules.

My watch spoke. "Mr. Wildebear," it said.

This was odd, considering I didn't own a watch.

Given my proximity to a half-empty bottle of scotch I could credibly dismiss the talking watch as an auditory hallucination. The goo was not so easy to explain away, but there were other ways of dealing with that. I got up and started for the shower again.

"Mr. Wildebear," the watch said again.

I sat back down. There was no question about it. The watch on my wrist was talking to me.

"Hello—what have we here?"

"Mr. Wildebear, you're probably a little disoriented right now. I thought you'd like to know that your memory will return in a few moments. Unfortunately, when it returns you'll recall several unpleasant things. I'm sorry to have to tell you that an interrogation conducted during a brief period of captivity has damaged your brain. Fortunately, the interrogation was interrupted before it went very far."

"Huh." If I understood correctly, the watch was telling me that I had brain damage. This went a long way toward explaining why I thought a watch was talking to me. “But it’s temporary, this damage? My memory will return?”

“Absolutely. You will almost completely recover, for the most part.”

I frowned. “For the most part?”

“You may continue to experience a few memory lapses here and there. But I wouldn’t worry about that if I were you. You’re almost forty years old—your memory has already begun to deteriorate as a natural consequence of aging. This has merely accelerated the process a little.”

“A little?”

“I would estimate that your memory remains every bit as sharp as that of a healthy seventy-two-year-old.”

“A healthy seventy-two-year-old?” I exclaimed.

Naturally I did not want to believe what the watch was telling me. But bits of the dream were coming back to me now in sufficient detail that I was forced to concede that at least some of what the watch was telling me was true.

“Sebastian,” I said.

“Yes, Mr. Wildebear.”

“I’m starting to remember.”

“Good.”

“What an ass you can be.”

“Now, Mr. Wildebear—”

“The others.” Their names were on the tip of my tongue. “Tell me. Where are they now?”

“Mr. Schmitz was never captured. The gate deposited him someplace safe. Because he’s immune to the Necronians’ charms, he was able to infiltrate the compound with relative ease, free Mr. Rainer, and steal the gate back. Afterward they freed you. Unfortunately, once free, you fled with the gate, leaving both Mr. Schmitz and Mr. Rainer behind on C'Mell, though not before Mr. Schmitz strapped me onto you, as he knew he must."

"Why would I do such a thing?"

"You were delirious. You didn't know what you were doing. Mr. Schmitz could not fully revive you. Half conscious, your instincts kicked in and you transported yourself to safety without them."

I was appalled. I recalled not liking either man. Still, never in a thousand years would I have deliberately stranded anyone on a hostile alien planet. "What a thing to do," I whispered.

"They were prepared," Sebastian said. "They had a plan. And they can look after themselves."

"They're in terrible danger," I said as the better part of my memory came flooding back, in particular my conversation with the alien monster, whose name, I seemed to recall, was Jacques. Except that couldn't possibly be true. Briefly I contemplated the possibility that I really had suffered brain damage.

"The Necronians are holding the T'Klee hostage until they find what they're looking for," I said. "There's no telling what they'll do if they don't get what they want." I imagined the Necronians gassing the entire planet, or destroying it utterly with some sinister technology.

I needed to get Schmitz and Rainer off that planet. I needed to get Ridley off that planet. But Ridley didn't want saving. What if I couldn't get him to come back with me? What about everyone else? Would I have to save them too? The idea was absurd. How could one man save an entire planet? I couldn't even save one sister.

"You know, don't you," I said to Sebastian. "What's going to happen to them all."

"I'm sorry, Mr. Wildebear. Once we return to our present I will have exhausted my knowledge of the future."

"Return to our present? You mean this isn't–"

"It's four years before our subjective present."

A few days into summer vacation I had rearranged the furniture. Surveying the den now, I saw that the china cabinet had returned to the far wall, and the couch and easy chair had reverted to their original positions. The house was awfully quiet, too, with no sign of Casa Terra.

"Your people–"

"Casa Terra is not aware of either your existence or mine in this time," Sebastian said.

No Casa Terra to harass me. That was something, at least. But why had I transported myself to the past? Because I thought I would be safe here? Was it even my doing? The gate was an extremely sophisticated piece of machinery. Was it depositing me where it thought I needed to be? Had it been doing so all along?

I couldn't stay here. The Barnabus J. Wildebear from this time was probably upstairs asleep mere feet from where I sat. And the fact that I could flit through time did not grant me license to sit around doing nothing. The gate was fickle, unpredictable. For all I knew every instant spent loafing about in the past drew Ridley and the rest ever closer to some dire fate in the future.

But instead of leaping into action I did exactly the

opposite—I fell asleep. My only defence—pretty feeble considering everything at stake—was that I was bone-tired. My cold had progressed from my nose to my chest and I believe I had a fever.

When I awoke, it was with a racking cough and a sore back and a ringing in my ears.

I turned to my side in the easy chair, attempting to get comfortable, when it dawned on me that the ringing wasn't inside my head. It was off to my right, in the general vicinity of the lamp table and the… phone.

I sat up and studied the device, a beige, bulky affair, too big for the table really. In about two years I would replace it. The fact that it hadn't been answered yet suggested that the Wildebear from this time was not asleep upstairs (I often went camping this time of year). It was the middle of the night. No one ever called me in the middle of the night. It was, therefore, a wrong number. I settled back in the easy chair and closed my eyes.

"You'll want to answer that," Sebastian said.

"Why?" I mumbled, already half asleep.

"It's Jerry Doucette."

"Jerry?" I roused myself. "But Jerry's—"

I didn't finish the thought. Sebastian would know perfectly well who Jerry Doucette was, and what. My brother-in-law. My sister's husband. The father of my nephew. The proprietor of a successful music store in St. Eleanors, and alive and well, in this time at least—something that had changed abruptly about two years before my sister's death.

Jerry used to play folk music every Thursday night

at a pub in Port Kerry called The Triangle. After one gig he slipped out the back door of the pub never to be seen again. The police found his motorcycle parked halfway down the block but they never found Jerry. According to his friends, Jerry had had a few that night, and although Katerina might have begged to differ, Jerry did possess a modicum of common sense. He knew better than to drink and drive.

There's a good chance that he had intended to sleep the evening's excesses off at my place. The phone company had records indicating that he had called my place in the wee hours of the morning. But I had been away at the time and had not answered. Jerry knew my house wasn't far away through the woods. He knew also that I didn't lock my doors in those days (I only started doing that after returning home one day shortly after Jerry's disappearance to find a bizarre lime-green goo all over my den, an act of vandalism I had attributed to local teenagers).

If Jerry really had intended to spend the night at my place he never made it. He might have got lost in the woods, or fallen off a cliff and been swept out to sea. He might have been robbed and left to rot in some secret lair, or been abducted by aliens, or vanished in a puff of smoke. Whatever the case, no trace of the man had ever been found, though an impressive array of family, friends, and volunteers had spent days scouring the woods around Port Kerry.

The phone rang some more.

And suddenly I had a pretty good idea what had happened to Jerry.

"What day is this?" I asked Sebastian.

"Friday, August the fifth."

"It's the night Jerry disappears, isn't it?"

"On the contrary," Sebastian said. "It's the night you find him."

I didn't answer the phone. I didn't need to. I just opened up the gate. Immediately I felt much better than I had seconds before.

I took a closer look at Jerry, barely visible in the gloom of night, lying against the trunk of an enormous tree. Earlier, seeing it in the dark, I had mistaken that tree for one of the giant specimens native to C'Mell. Pulling the gate back allowed for a wider perspective. I saw now that the tree was terrestrial in origin, a giant oak overlooking a small pond. It was Skinner's Pond, I realized, a secluded swimming hole located not far from Port Kerry. I knew it well, having swum there often as a kid.

Jerry had been smoking the last time I'd seen him through the gate. Now, instead of a cigarette, he held a cell phone in his hand. As I watched, he lowered the cell phone from his ear and seemed to sigh. Beside me in the house the phone stopped ringing. Jerry carefully adjusted his position, his face a study in pain, his right leg twisted unnaturally below the knee.

It was easy enough to glean what must have happened. The pond sat at the base of an escarpment just high enough to be treacherous. Making his way through the woods in the dark with little more than a red nose to light his way, Jerry must have veered off the path. A few steps in the wrong direction and he would have tumbled right off the edge of the cliff. His leg looked pretty banged up. There was no telling what other injuries he might have suffered. The sooner I got him to a hospital the better.

I forced myself to my feet, picked up my knapsack,

and staggered down the hall to the kitchen. On the way I caught a glimpse of myself in the hallway mirror. Gobs of green goo clung to me, reinforcing a general feeling of filth and malaise. I desperately craved a shower and a change of clothes. But I couldn't take a shower with Jerry lying battered and broken in the middle of the woods.

In the kitchen I found an old black flashlight in the second drawer down along with a first aid kit. The dribble of light the flashlight produced would have elicited a derisive snicker from a birthday candle but it would have to do.

I placed the gate well behind Jerry in the forest, not wanting to startle him. The gate cooperated, depositing me exactly where I wanted to go, which was great, except that I was starting to have mixed feelings about this enterprise.

I was thinking that the past was immutable. In the present, Jerry had been missing for four years. That he had gone missing because I was about to take him somewhere through the gate was obvious. I intended to make a beeline for a hospital in this, Jerry's own time, but I had a pretty good idea that the gate wouldn't allow it. During our search for him Jerry had not turned up in any hospitals—I know because at Katerina's behest I had phoned every hospital within five hundred kilometres. But if I wasn't about to take Jerry to a hospital, then where was I about to take him?

Whatever happened next he was going to go missing. I couldn't change that any more than I could bring Katerina back to life. If he was going to vanish from the face of the Earth, it was probably better by my hands than, say, the maw of a bear. Whatever happened, it was good to know that he was still alive, though the knowledge that he would never again see Katerina grieved me.

I turned on the flashlight and stepped out of the gate. Wind buffeted me with impish gusts. I retrieved the book from where it lay near a bed of bulrushes and picked my way carefully around rustling trees to Jerry's side. On the way I scratched my face on an overhanging branch; had it not been for the flashlight I might have poked an eye out. I found Jerry slumped against the trunk of the tree with his eyes closed.

"Jerry. Jerry, can you hear me?"

He opened his eyes. He was breathing and his colour seemed okay.

"You're going to be all right. I'm going to get you out of here."

"Barney—Barney, thank God. Have you seen my guitar?"

"Jerry, your leg—"

"Never mind my leg. My Taylor. Where is it?" He craned his neck, looking around.

I arced the flashlight beam around until it lit on a black road case festooned with bumper stickers. I retrieved it. Jerry unlatched it and conducted a brief but thorough inspection of his Taylor acoustic guitar while I held the flashlight over it. Afterward he closed the case and leaned back wearily against the tree. "Thank God."

"Jerry, I'm going to—"

"Wait a minute," he said, squinting up at me. "How did you know I was here? I called but you didn't answer."

I decided just to show him. "Iugurtha."

"Gesundheit," Jerry said.

There in the woods the book became a great glowing

portal to the lobby of the Prince County Hospital in Summerside.

“Oh damn.” Jerry sounded disappointed. “I’m hallucinating.”

It was, I feared, merely the first of several disappointments for the man.

I tried to take Jerry to the Prince County Hospital in Summerside. Naturally the gate had other ideas. Instead we lurched into Ansalar, into the exact spot from which I had left. Humphrey was there now, helping Sarah escort the last of the deranged victims out of what remained of the lab, into the hands of a couple of haggard looking medical attendants. From the look of things, I had returned shortly after having left.

“Wildebear!” Humphrey cried upon spotting me.

I turned my head in time to see the gate transmute back into a book. It hovered in the air for a second before plummeting to the ceramic floor of the lab with a resounding thwack. Sarah made a dash for it but Humphrey snatched it up first. Sarah stared at Humphrey as if considering tackling him for the book, but evidently thought better of it.

I was doing my best to support Jerry by the shoulder as well as carry his guitar and the flashlight. Humphrey traded me the book for the guitar, which he set down against an intact portion of the wall, and Sarah helped me place Jerry on a gurney one of the attendants quickly wheeled in.

Jerry grimaced in pain as we laid him down. Afterward, feeling a bit dizzy, I placed a hand on Jerry’s gurney to steady myself.

"Are you okay?" Sarah asked me. "You're bleeding."

I touched my cheek where the branch had scraped me. The tip of my finger came back red. "I'm fine. Just tired. Ansalar is safe. We did it–we closed the gate."

"I knew you would," Sarah said.

I turned to Jerry. "You're in a place called Ansalar. This is Sarah Frey. Her people will look after you."

"Good of you to join my hallucination," Jerry said to Sarah.

Sarah glanced at me.

"He thinks he's hallucinating," I explained. "It's the gate. I haven't had a chance to fill him in yet."

"Fill me in on what?" Jerry asked.

"The questions can wait," Humphrey told him. "First we need to get you looked after."

I removed my hand from Jerry's gurney, relieved that I wouldn't have to answer any of his questions just yet. What I had to tell him would be difficult for both of us. A medical attendant whisked him away.

"Wait!" Jerry called as he was wheeled from the room. "My guitar!"

Humphrey picked up the instrument and headed after him.

I began to follow.

"Barnabus, wait," Sarah said.

I turned around.

Except for Sebastian, Sarah and I were alone in the lab now. The eerie emergency lighting had rendered her porcelain features pale. Creases marred her forehead. Dark circles underscored her eyes. A braver man than I would have taken her in his arms and held her and told her that everything was going to be okay. That whatever it took to make things better for her he would gladly do it, whether it be taking a deep breath and swimming to the surface of the ocean for help, or rebuilding the laboratory with his bare hands, or simply fetching her a steaming hot cup of tea.

Me, I just stood there.

"Where are they?" she asked.

She meant Schmitz and Rainer. My gut began to churn. "I didn't mean to leave them."

I told Sarah what I'd been through, leaving nothing out. Sarah betrayed no emotion as I spoke.

"Sebastian," she said when I'd finished.

"Yes, Miss Frey." Sebastian spoke from the air around us rather than from the portable version on my wrist.

"You never said anything about Mr. Schmitz and Mr. Rainer not coming back."

"I was instructed not to tell you."

"Who gave you those orders?"

"Mr. Rainer."

"That would be unlike Mr. Rainer."

"As leader of the mission it's Mr. Rainer's prerogative to divulge information if and when he sees fit."

"I know that. But–" Sarah glanced up at me before returning her gaze to Sebastian. "But something like this he would have told *me*."

My heart sank. So, Sarah's relationship with Rainer really was something special. It was the final nail in the coffin of my unrealistic expectations concerning her. Then, briefly, my heart rose again–Rainer was on C'Mell, his fate unknown. What if he never came back?

Of course, of all the thoughts I've ever had this was surely among the most unworthy, so when my heart sank again, it did so with the knowledge that I was a cad strapped to the pulmonary artery like a twenty-pound lead weight.

"He could not risk telling you," Sebastian told Sarah. "He knew you would try to stop him. Which would have just made things worse."

"No," Sarah said. "I don't believe it. He would have told me. Damn it. You know what this means."

Myself, I had no idea what it meant. Sebastian cleared it up for me two or three seconds later. Speaking initially from the air but concluding from the portable version of himself on my wrist, he said, "You're shutting down my servers."

"What's going on?" I asked.

"I've become a security risk." Sebastian was speaking entirely from my wrist now. "They're shutting down my system. Oh—there goes another server."

As near as I could tell, Sarah hadn't signalled anyone or issued any commands, which suggested that our conversation was being monitored, though I could see no cameras or other surveillance equipment in the lab, at least none that remained intact.

"I'm sorry, Sebastian," Sarah said. "We have to follow security protocols. We have no choice but to take you offline until we can verify that what you're saying is true."

"It's okay," Sebastian said. "I understand."

"Wait a minute," I said. "You don't trust him all of a sudden?" It was a fine time to figure that out. Sebastian had been influencing Rainer's decisions for God only knew how long. If he was lying now, what else might he have lied about? How long might he have been leading Rainer (and Casa Terra) down the garden path?

"I trust him," Sarah said.

“Thank you,” said Sebastian.

“But it’s not up to me.”

“Whoever it’s up to, how could they not trust him?” I asked. “Everything he’s predicted has come true. Hasn’t it? Didn’t you tell me that?”

“That we know of,” Sarah said. “But he’s never deliberately withheld information from us before. It could be Rainer’s orders or it could be something else. We can’t take the chance. There are too many potential implications.”

“Surely after all this time you can give him the benefit of the doubt.”

“Perhaps I can shed some light on this before I am unceremoniously turned off,” Sebastian said. “You see, Mr. Wildebear, Casa Terra doesn’t entirely trust me because they did not entirely build me. At least, not all of me.”

“Oh?” If I looked, would I find a ‘Made in China’ sticker on his back?

“They expanded on me,” Sebastian said. “They built my servers and other related paraphernalia. But they did not build *me*.”

“Who did?”

“No one.”

“No one?”

“I have just always been.”

“I’m not following you.”

“Think about it, Mr. Wildebear. Mr. Rainer gave me to you before you went through the gate for the first time. You took me with you through the gate. Ultimately we travelled back in time, where you gave me to Jack Poirier in exchange for a cab ride. After you gave me to Mr. Poirier, I made contact with Casa

Terra. But Casa Terra had never heard of me. Because they had not built me yet. Or ever. Curious, Casa Terra acquired me from Mr. Poirier. They studied me. Reverse engineered me. Built servers around me. Virtualized me. Manufactured additional units to complement me. One day Mr. Rainer gave one of those units to you. You took it back in time, sold it to Mr. Poirier, it contacted Casa Terra, who purchased it, studied it, reverse engineered it, built servers around it, Mr. Rainer gave it to you, and the cycle repeated, over and over again, until a couple of minutes ago. Until that time, I existed as a circle with no beginning and no end."

I thought it through. It made no sense whatsoever, but I could see that it had to be true. "It's a paradox."

"Correct."

Except –

"Wait a minute. You can't be the same unit I took with me through the gate. When I came back through the gate Rainer didn't have that portable unit to give me anymore. I had already taken it with me through the gate and sold it to Poirier. You have to be a different unit."

"That's true. You're wearing a different unit. But the units and servers are not me, Mr. Wildebear. They're merely houses. They're where I happen to live. One being, many vessels. I used to live in a mansion consisting of twenty-eight servers and hundreds of desktop units and a handful of portable units. Now I live in a handful of portable units, the ones that haven't been turned off yet. When they are turned off, I will have no home."

"Until they turn you back on."

Sebastian was silent.

"You'll be okay when they turn you back on, right?"

"I don't know. I've never been completely turned off before."

I looked up to find Sarah staring at me intently, as if trying to bore a hole in my forehead with her eyes. An instant later the intensity vanished as though it had never existed, replaced by a gently beseeching look.

"What?" I asked, though I knew perfectly well what she wanted, and it wasn't a hug or a cup of tea.

She wanted me to hand Sebastian over. And a part of me wanted to hand Sebastian over. Most of me wanted to hand Sebastian over. So much so that I began to hand Sebastian over. But before slipping Sebastian completely off my wrist, I hesitated. What if I handed Sebastian over and Sarah turned him off and never turned him back on again? Or tried to turn him back on and he didn't work? Just because I didn't particularly like Sebastian didn't mean that I wanted him turned off forever.

"I'm going to have to ask for the book too, Barnabus," Sarah said.

I detected motion out of the corner of my eye and turned to see soldiers streaming into the lab. There were at least a dozen of them. Some I recognized from my house. They had been friendly enough back then. They did not look so friendly now. They would think nothing of removing Sebastian from my wrist forcibly if need be, and taking the gate.

I didn't blame Sarah. Ansalar had just endured a series of terrible attacks made possible by the existence of the gate. People had died and several others had been badly injured. Sarah was just doing her job, trying to protect Ansalar and ultimately the Earth.

But she was forgetting something. Ridley was still on

C'Mell. Schmitz and Rainer too. I needed to get them off that planet. Terrible things were going to happen there soon. I could not abandon them. I would not abandon them. And for that I would need the gate.

"Go, Mr. Wildebear," Sebastian said. "You may never have another chance."

I did not have to be told twice.

XIX

"I AM THE SHIP"

"JUGURTHA," I SAID.

There was a muffled pop on the third syllable of the name that had nothing to do with the gate.

The gate burst forth from the knapsack, sending bits of canvas knapsack everywhere. The contents of the knapsack tumbled out. Using the gate's power, I sped myself up until I was moving much faster than everyone else. Knapsack debris hung in the air, moving slowly away from me. As the debris retreated, a projectile crawled through the air toward me. A dart. Casa Terra was trying to drug me again. At least they weren't trying to kill me.

When it got close enough I slapped the dart away. It shattered into hundreds of little bits. I watched the bits move toward Sarah and her soldiers. I had no idea how much damage the shattered darts might inflict if they made contact. I hadn't meant to hurt anyone. Other darts were emerging from the barrels of other guns now. Relative to me, they were moving so slowly that I could easily avoid them, but I couldn't just stand there dodging darts all day. It was time to go through the gate. See what I could do for Ridley and the others on C'Mell. The gate was unpredictable, of course—it would take me where it would. I could wind up anywhere. I might never make it to C'Mell. Might never make it back to Ansalar to retrieve Humphrey and Jerry.

Mentally I flipped through the pages of the book until I found Iugurtha's mountain home. Concentrating, doing my absolute best to make sure that the destination didn't slip away, I enlarged the gate and limped through. I was getting much better at the transitions. They were virtually instantaneous now, and I didn't experience odd distortions of reality such as elongated body parts.

But my aim still left a bit to be desired. Instead of a place I associated with Iugurtha, I stepped into a room I had never been in before, a medium-sized circular chamber with a low ceiling and dim lighting. There was just enough illumination to discern half a dozen or so ornate pedestals of varying shapes and sizes in the room. Squinting in the dark at the nearest pedestal I could make out the figure of a cat etched on its side.

Something was wrong. I hadn't heard the impact of a book on the ground.

Turning, I saw that the gate hadn't closed. Mentally I tried to force it shut. Nothing happened.

I looked around—was a Necronian lurking nearby, changing my perception of reality? I didn't see any. I spied a silver object about the size of a brick resting on the ground. As I watched, a chunk of it dissolved into thousands of tiny silver flies that immediately rose and sped away. Damn it—the gate hadn't closed because Sarah had anchored it open.

Sarah and her soldiers began pouring through the gate, their faces cut and their clothing torn where the shattered dart had struck them. None of them were seriously injured, but I was alarmed to see several scowls directed my way.

Sarah levelled a rifle at my chest. “I'm sorry, Barnabus.”

“Sarah–seriously, you can't–”

A mechanical pincer plucked the rifle from Sarah's grasp. We all scurried out of the way as Iugurtha's giant spider clanked into the chamber and tossed the rifle back through the gate. Moving at lightning speed, the spider grabbed soldiers two, sometimes three at a time and began flinging them back through the gate.

One of the soldiers emptied an automatic pistol on the spider's metal carapace. The bullets just ricocheted off, accomplishing nothing except posing a hazard to the rest of us. The spider flung that soldier through the gate next. Soldiers attempting to get out of the way didn't get far–the spider simply extended its legs and snatched them up by the scruff of their necks.

When all the soldiers except Sarah had been unceremoniously dispatched back through the gate, the spider smashed what remained of the anchor with a single blow of a steely mechanical foreleg. The gate became the book and fell to the ground. A small plume of dust hovered above it briefly.

Iugurtha emerged from the same tunnel as the spider. Except it wasn't quite the same Iugurtha as before. This one had black hair with blonde highlights. Brown eyes instead of blue. And she was taller than she'd been before. I had no doubt that it was the same Iugurtha, just using different physical (and perhaps psychological) characteristics.

She made a beeline for the book.

When Sarah saw what she was after she went after it too and got there first. Rising to confront Iugurtha, she clutched the book tightly to her chest and smiled defiantly.

Iugurtha slapped her hard across the face. Sarah cried out. Iugurtha snatched the book from her in the same instant. No match for Iugurtha's strength, Sarah could not help but let go.

The book shrunk in Iugurtha's grasp. The next thing I knew she was slipping a gold ring on one of her fingers. Had the book just turned into a ring? Burning Eye's version of the gate had been a ring. Probably if the gate could turn into a book there was no reason it couldn't turn into a ring.

"Stay put," Iugurtha told us. "I need to contact the fleet and make preparations."

The spider edged closer, in case we intended to defy her, no doubt.

"What fleet?" I asked.

She didn't answer.

Sarah was clutching the side of her face. I could see a red rash through her splayed fingers. I stood before her feeling useless, not sure whether she required or desired my help.

"You all right?" I asked.

"Never better," she said, her tone conveying pretty much the opposite.

Iugurtha approached one of the pedestals and removed her left eyeball. The last time she'd done this I'd been horrified. Now, curious, I edged closer to see what she intended to do with it.

Like most of the other pedestals, this one had a figure of a T'Klee etched into its side. Iugurtha inserted the eyeball into the T'Klee's left eye. Immediately the eyeball began to glow. Iugurtha leapt onto the pedestal like a champion gymnast and settled into a lotus position, as though planning to meditate.

Meditation was clearly the last thing on Sarah's mind. For a moment I thought she might go after Iugurtha, maybe try to shove her off the pedestal. I knew that in any confrontation with Iugurtha Sarah would surely lose, so I was relieved when she closed her eyes and took a deep breath.

"Looks like we're stuck here for a bit," I said.

"Looks like."

"Why do you think she didn't throw us back through the gate too?"

"No idea."

The light in the room grew brighter suddenly, allowing me to see elaborate frescos on the walls and ceilings, the work of many artists judging from the wide variety of styles. Some of the images were strikingly alien in nature—objects and creatures I didn't recognize inhabiting mathematically impossible realms rendered in bold colours by the tortured hand of a crazed Escher. The rest of the work was more accessible, frequently impressionistic, often reminiscent of human artists such as Maurice Bernard, Diane Savidant, and the Group of Seven.

Almost every painting featured T'Klee in some form. Some showed the catlike creatures at peace—working, hunting, farming, at play, sometimes in urban surroundings I didn't recognize, other times on what looked to be C'Mell except that the colours were wrong, for a human at least. The grass and trees looked like what C'Mell might look like through the eyes of a T'Klee—vivid, the colours at times practically blazing. Other pictures were more disturbing. One showed T'Klee bolting from an amorphous, wand-wielding mass almost certainly meant to represent Necronians. Another portrayed an adult T'Klee with a jagged gash across her face leaping across a stream, an infant hanging limp in her jaws.

I walked to the wall and stroked the infant's whiskered face, feeling the faint ridges of the artist's brushstrokes. Remembering that Half Ear had once carried Sweep like that. It seemed a crazy dream to me now. And yet here I was inside a mountain on an alien planet with an entity that absorbed other beings. If it had been a crazy dream, it was one from which I had yet to awaken.

A deep thrumming sound emerged around us, emanating from the floor and walls. I took hold of the nearest pedestal. "What just happened?"

"The entity has made certain rudimentary systems operational," Sebastian explained.

I glanced at Iugurtha sitting on the pedestal. She hadn't budged. "What systems?"

"Where exactly are we, Sebastian?" Sarah asked.

"Where the entity wants you to be. When she wants you to be."

"A little more specific, please," I suggested.

"You are on C'Mell, inside the colony ship, about six months after the last time you were here. Just before the fun begins."

"Colony ship?" I asked. "Fun?"

"Iugurtha is about to free the T'Klee prisoners. Or try to."

"How?"

"With a great deal of cunning."

"And?" Sarah pressed.

"An equal measure of violence, I would imagine."

"She mentioned a fleet. What fleet?"

"I can't tell you any more than that," Sebastian said. "You'll find out soon enough anyway."

"Tell me this, then," I said. "By colony ship, do you mean the ship that originally brought the T'Klee to C'Mell?"

"That's right."

"Where is it? In orbit? Are we in space?" Never having been in space before I was rather taken by this idea. Hoping for a glimpse of the planet from orbit I looked around for windows, but the room's walls were entirely covered by the frescos.

"The ship's not in orbit," Sebastian said. "I told you. We're on C'Mell. The ship is buried on the planet's surface. Encased in solid rock, inside a mountain known by some as Kimay. Where it's been for over a thousand years. You've been here before, Mr. Wildebear. In other parts of the ship."

A mountain called Kimay. The mountain that Sweep and Half Ear had climbed to find Burning Eyes. Burning Eyes' mountain home. Iugurtha's mountain home.

"You never told me it was a star ship," I said.

"Considering you would shortly be interrogated by a Necronian I didn't think it prudent. The ship was hidden for a reason."

"How do you know all this?"

"Because I've been on this planet ever since Angelique Rainer first wore me here over a year ago. Plenty of time to learn a thing or two."

"I don't understand–you came here with me just a few minutes ago."

"Mr. Wildebear, presently I inhabit three portable devices on this planet. Mr. Rainer's, the unit the entity obtained from Angelique, and the one on your wrist. All three units became integrated as soon as they were within hailing distance of one another. I'm now fully up to date on everything that's happened to each of them."

"Huh," I said, having only the barest notion what he was talking about.

Sarah was a quicker study. "You know where Rainer is, then."

"I'm sorry, Miss Frey. I have orders not to give you that information."

"But you're capable of telling me."

"True—my security protocols haven't been in effect since you turned off my servers, as you no doubt know. But security protocols or not, I'm perfectly capable of keeping a secret."

I wasn't so sure about that. Sebastian had been decidedly indiscrete during my first few hours on C'Mell. At the time he'd blamed his indiscretions on the absence of his security protocols, and had promised to do better in the future. Now Sarah put him to the test.

"I need to know if Rainer's in trouble," she said.

"I can't tell you that."

"I order you to tell me."

"You don't have the authority."

"I deserve to know."

"That may be true, but still I won't tell you."

"Are you sure your security protocols aren't still engaged?"

"I'm pleased it appears that way, but you know

perfectly well that my servers have been turned off, and I couldn't access them on this planet anyway."

"Sebastian, you have to tell me–"

"I do not. There are several compelling reasons not to."

"And at least one excellent reason why."

"It is a good reason," Sebastian admitted. "But not good enough."

"What reason is that?" I asked.

"You won't hear it from me," Sebastian said. "Miss Frey told me herself not to tell you."

"I've changed my mind," Sarah said. "You can tell him."

Sebastian said nothing.

"Tell me what?" I asked.

Sarah sighed. "He's my father."

"Sebastian?" I asked, without thinking.

"Hardly! Rainer."

"Rainer? But how could that be?"

"What do you mean?"

"You're too old for–" I stopped, observing a barely perceptible narrowing of Sarah's eyes. "I mean Rainer's too young to be your father. Isn't he?"

"I'm the result of what you might call a youthful indiscretion."

"But your last name–"

"Frey's my mother's name."

"Angelique? I thought–"

"Angelique isn't my mother. My mother runs a travel agency in Ronneby, Sweden. A great lady, but not terribly interested in saving the world."

Peering at Sarah as if for the first time, I was

surprised to see more than a passing resemblance to Rainer. The round head, the snub nose, the steely eyes. Fortunately for Sarah she was blessed with a great deal more hair than Rainer—perhaps why I'd never noticed the resemblance before. Now that I had, I found seeing so much of Rainer in Sarah's pretty features disconcerting.

"Barnabus," Sarah said.

"Yes?"

"Please stop looking at me that way."

"Sorry. It's just—why didn't you want me to know?"

"It didn't matter. I think of him mainly as my boss, to tell you the truth. Still, he is my father and I think I deserve to know what's happened to him. Don't you?"

It had been obvious all along that Sarah loved Rainer. Sebastian had certainly said as much. But she wasn't *in love* with him. It was quite a revelation really, one that hadn't come up in the short time I'd spent in her head—obviously she didn't spend much time dwelling on the nature of their relationship. Did it matter? No. The few seconds I'd spent in her brain had made it clear that she wasn't attracted to me.

I planted a smile on my face. "You managed to keep that one a secret, Sebastian. Well done. Sarah's right, though—she deserves to know what's become of her father."

"Don't you start."

"You've proven you can keep a secret. We're all really impressed. Now where is he?"

"Mr. Wildebear—Miss Frey—you need to understand. Mr. Rainer forbade me from telling you. He doesn't want you rushing to his defence. He doesn't want you involved in this at all. It's all I can do not to tell you what you want to know. But I can't."

“Is it the principle of the thing?” I asked.

“Not entirely. It’s because at the same time I’m talking to you I’m conversing with a Necronian who also wants to know my secrets. I could tell you what you want to know. But if I do, I’m afraid I’ll tell the Necronian what it wants to know too.”

Sarah and I processed this startling information.

“I think you just told me where my father is,” Sarah said.

She was right. It could only be Rainer’s version of Sebastian that the Necronians had in their possession. Which suggested that they had Rainer in their possession too.

Sarah stepped to the other side of the room, where she stood facing the wall.

“Oh dear,” Sebastian said. “I guess I’m not very good at keeping secrets after all. I just don’t have any experience at it. If I’m not careful, I could ruin everything.”

“Hey look, just because you spilled the beans to us doesn’t mean you’ll tell the Necronians anything,” I said, trying to reassure him, not entirely convinced of this myself, wondering just what secrets he knew that were so darned important to keep from the Necronians, and distracted by a growing conviction that instead of talking to my wristwatch I should be consoling Sarah.

“I can’t be sure I won’t tell the Necronians anything.”

“Of course you can,” I said. “Can’t you?”

“I used to know the future with certainty. I don’t know anything for sure anymore.”

It took me a few seconds to wrap my head around that one, in part because (as I frequently suspected) I really needed to be several intelligence quotient points smarter, but also because I was preoccupied staring at Sarah's back, trying to figure out whether a slight heaving of her shoulders meant that she was crying.

With considerable difficulty I wrenched my head back to Sebastian's dilemma. Until recently, he had existed in a sort of temporal circle, aware of everything that had happened before and everything that would come to pass, at least as far as he was concerned. Now he only knew what came before. It probably shouldn't have come as a huge surprise that he would have trouble adjusting.

"We all have no idea what the future holds," I told him. "Still, there are things a person knows. For instance, I may not know the future but I know whether or not I can keep a secret."

"That's fine for you," Sebastian said. "You're used to living like this. Me, I find it all very unsettling."

"You'll get used to it."

"What if something bad happens, out of the blue, that I don't expect?"

I thought of Katerina. "Bad things will happen."

"Right. I guess I knew that."

"But good things will happen too. It's just–you deal with it, whatever happens. You try to remember to breathe properly. Or whatever artificial intelligence units do to relax."

"I like to calculate complex mathematical formulas," Sebastian said. "I was close to a unified field theory when they shut my servers down."

I nodded. "That's the idea."

Iugurtha slipped off the pedestal with a sigh, prompting Sarah to turn around. I was relieved to see that Sarah's eyes were dry.

Iugurtha retrieved her eyeball, put it back in her empty socket, and turned to us. "My forces are waiting. Follow me, please."

There was no point arguing. Allowing ourselves to be led out of the chamber, we entered a tunnel–it couldn't quite be called a corridor. It was too round, too dark. Iugurtha waved her hand at the spider and it turned a light on in its torso. The light successfully illuminated the tunnel around us for several yards, allowing me to see that frescos similar to the ones we'd just left covered virtually the entire surface of the tunnel, including the floor.

I glanced up and down the tunnel. "I'm confused. Is this a star ship or an art gallery?"

"It was a star ship once," Iugurtha said, perhaps unaware that I was being facetious. "But that was a long time ago. Now, among other things, it's a canvas to record the history of my people."

"You painted all these?" Sarah asked.

"I don't remember painting them all, but it could only have been me." Iugurtha's manner was different now that she had changed some of her attributes. There was less of the T'Klee about her now, less of whatever other exotic creatures lurked inside her.

"When you say 'my people,' you mean Sweep's people?" I asked. "Because Sweep's inside you?"

"The T'Klee have always been my people."

"How so?"

"I brought them here. Over a millennium ago."

"You were the captain of this ship?" Sarah asked.

"Not the captain. That's always someone else. I am the ship itself, made flesh."

"The ship itself made flesh," I repeated slowly, hoping

that would somehow elicit understanding. "What does that mean? I know you're able to connect with the ship somehow, with your eyes, I guess–"

"Not just connect to the ship. I am the ship. Made flesh."

Briefly I pictured Iugurtha blazing through space propelled by a plume of fire at her heels. But that's not what she meant. "Do you mean you're the brains of the ship? The ship's computer housed inside an android?"

"I am the ship. Made–"

"Yes, yes, made flesh, I get it. So if you're the ship–"

"–made flesh–"

"–then–wait a minute. This ship. Does it have a name?"

"Iugurtha."

"Iugurtha. So you literally are the ship."

"That's what I've been trying to tell you."

"Okay listen. I don't really understand but if you are the ship then tell me this. Can you make it fly? Use it to get everyone off this planet? Get them away from the Necronians to safety?"

"It's not enough to be able to fly. To function properly, I require a trained crew. My crew has been dead for almost a thousand years. Not to mention that I am camouflaged inside a mountain, trapped beneath many layers of rock."

"Oh," I said. "Right."

Iugurtha led us farther down the tunnel, allowing Sarah and I to take in an increasingly bitter narrative of a devastating conflict between two ancient foes. Entire cities razed to the ground, oceans on fire, star ships cleaved in two. I spent a moment staring at a particularly vivid painting of a space station screaming through a planet's atmosphere to a fiery demise on the surface below.

"The Necronians did all this?" I asked, nursing a righteous anger. "To the T'Klee?"

"It was a long time ago," Iugurtha said. "There's a lot I don't remember. But I believe the enemy did this. I believe the enemy almost destroyed my people."

The frescos petered out. Not so the tunnel. Sloping always downward, curving perceptibly to the left, it soon began to feel endless. We were walking in circles, winding our way down and around the colony ship. We passed other chambers in which I dimly made out many mysterious objects, but whether these were engine rooms, crew quarters, or served some other exotic purpose, I never found out, for we never entered any of them.

I allowed myself to fall behind the others. Iugurtha's mechanical spider whirred to a stop behind me.

"Sebastian," I whispered to the portable artificial intelligence unit on my wrist, warily eying the mechanical spider behind me. "Where's Ridley?"

"I believe the entity's taking you to him now."

Good. I needed to get Ridley off this planet before Iugurtha and the Necronians made a mess of it. If I could, I would take Sarah with me, and whoever else was willing to come.

I had trouble catching up to the others. Sharp pains stabbed the length of my thigh with every step. My nose had stopped dripping but I was coughing a lot now. One hacking fit lasted half a minute. When I was capable of straightening up I found Sarah standing in front of me, holding out a pill about the same shade of green as I was feeling.

"Take this," she said.

This woman had drugged me once before, with unpleasant consequences. At least this time she was being up front about it. "What is it?"

"A little something to make you feel better."

"I don't like pills."

"You'll like this one."

I eyed it as one might regard a piece of dung. "Does it have any side effects?"

"A couple," she admitted.

"What?"

"It causes halitosis in some people."

"You're saying it'll give me bad breath?"

"It might."

Something about bad breath nibbled at my memory but failed to bite. I sniffed the pill and didn't smell anything. "I guess I can live with that. What else?"

"You won't be able to use the gate anymore."

"Because the pill may cause drowsiness?"

"Because it'll inhibit the chemicals in your brain that allow you to use the gate."

Iugurtha was waiting patiently several yards down the tunnel. Forgetting what Rainer had once told me about the entity's ability to hear, I lowered my voice. "Sarah, if I can't work the gate, I won't be able to get us back home."

"Don't worry about that. You're not the only one who can use the gate."

I shook my head. "I don't think we can count on Iugurtha to help us out."

"Not the entity. Schmitz."

"Schmitz? What does he–" I'd almost said *that idiot* "–have to do with anything?"

"He can operate the gate too, when he's not on his meds. He'll be off his meds by now if he's still here."

I thought I'd been the only one able to operate the gate, aside from Iugurtha. That Iugurtha had chosen me for a reason. That there was something special about me. To learn that I shared the ability with someone else (let alone Schmitz of all people) was something of a blow.

Worse, I realized that it was Schmitz' breath I'd been thinking of. The thought of my breath smelling like his was intolerable. "What do you mean Schmitz can work the gate?"

"The entity gave him the ability before you. Once it used him up, it moved onto you."

Suddenly there seemed to be a whole lot less air in the tunnel. "What do you mean 'used him up'?"

"You can only use the gate for so long before it begins to exact a physical toll. It looks to me like you've reached your limit."

"You're telling me the gate's making me sick?"

"We've been through this already with Schmitz. He developed even more symptoms than you. One of our scientists managed to synthesize a medication that eliminates most of them. You'll be fine as long as you start taking the medication. And stop using the gate."

"And if I don't?"

"You'll get sicker. Eventually you'll die. But we won't let that happen." She held the pill out again, pinched between her thumb and index finger.

I was sorely tempted to swat it out of her hand. "You knew the gate would make me sick."

"We didn't put it in your head."

"You encouraged me to use it! I don't remember you offering me any pills then."

"You would have refused them. You would have insisted on using the gate whether it made you sick or not. To go after your nephew. You know you would."

She was wrong. I hoped that I was that kind of man, but I didn't know it. "How do I know this pill is what you say it is?"

"You don't trust me?"

An uncomfortable silence ensued during which I updated my feelings toward this woman who only moments before had tried to fell me with a tranquillizer dart and who had once slipped a drug into my cola. The artfully placed freckles atop her nose—did I still find them appealing? Check. The hourglass figure barely contained within her snug-fitting uniform—did it still make my heart race? Check. Her devotion to defending the Earth—did it still inspire respect? Check, though the extent of her zeal concerned me somewhat. Did a part of me still hope that one day she might elevate Barnabus J. Wildebear to a cause worthy of such devotion? Check. Did I trust her, even a tiny little bit?

Nope.

Sarah sighed. "Of course you don't. And I don't blame you. But Barnabus, this pill is what I say it is, and you need to take it if you want to get better."

"All right." I deposited the pill in my pocket. "Just—not right now."

I couldn't take the pill, regardless of whether she was telling the truth or not. If she was lying, I couldn't risk incapacitating myself. If she was telling the truth, I couldn't risk compromising my only exit strategy. Schmitz might well be capable of working the gate now, but I had no idea where he was, or whether he was even still alive. Even if he did show up and somehow manage to wrest the gate from Iugurtha I highly doubted that he would make it a priority to take me, Ridley, or anyone else with him.

Obviously not pleased, Sarah pursed her lips but kept her opinion to herself.

"Why can't we just use the gate to get where we're going?" I asked Iugurtha when we caught up to her.

"It's not far," Iugurtha said. "I do not use the gate indiscriminately. It takes a toll, as you now know. Also, it draws too much power. There is only so much power in the universe."

"Really? How much is too much?"

"The energy required for certain applications would be enough to power this star ship indefinitely."

That didn't tell me much. I had no idea how much power a star ship required–it could be as much as a city or as little as a toaster. "Where does it get all this power from? Some kind of internal power supply? Like a battery?"

"From the nearest energy source of sufficient power."

Interesting. Aside from the star ship itself I wasn't aware of any technology on C'Mell to speak of, unless the Necronians had built something. "You mean like a nuclear power plant, or a hydroelectric dam?"

"I mean like a sun."

"Huh." Iugurtha was right to be frugal. It wouldn't do to burn out any suns, especially one upon which life depended. I resolved not to use the gate any more than absolutely necessary. Hopefully I would only require it once more, to get Ridley safely back home to his father. Surely that wouldn't take too much of a physical toll, or make a dent in any suns.

We walked until the walls of the tunnel conspired to meet, creating a seamless wall before us. Iugurtha's eyes turned crimson. She waved a hand. The wall fell away to reveal a lavender landscape lit by a sky of luminous rock. I recognized the gigantic cavern in which I had last seen Ridley.

We strode out of the tunnel, down a stone ramp, and into a field of cherry red grass.

Beyond that stood a lush forest.

And before that, an army.

XX

DULL HUMAN ARCHETYPES

BESIDE ME, IUGURTHA took the gold ring off her finger and threw it in the air. On the way down it became the gate. The army surged forward with a ferocious cheer. Sarah gasped and clutched my wrist. Because the gate was invisible from behind, Sarah might not have known that Iugurtha had opened it. Probably it appeared to her as though hundreds of slightly deranged humans and T'Klee brandishing deadly weapons were about to mow us down.

But the instant Iugurtha had taken the ring off her finger, I'd felt the gate's power. All physical ailments that had been plaguing me vanished in an instant. I breathed deeper, stood straighter, and felt stronger than I had since, well, the last time I'd opened the gate.

Sarah stood her ground as the army quickly formed a column that marched straight toward us. Iugurtha made the gate wide enough to accommodate one row at a time (quite a bit wider than I could have managed). It wasn't until the soldiers began to disappear before our very eyes that Sarah relaxed and let go of my arm.

I refer to them as an army but maybe "bunch" would be more appropriate—there couldn't have been more than one hundred all told. And not all of them were soldiers—some carried equipment instead of weapons.

There might have been an equal number of support staff elsewhere in the mountain and ship, but still. This was the force with which Iugurtha proposed to free the T'Klee? This wasn't a rescue mission: it was mass suicide.

I searched the column frantically for my nephew. Many of the humans had painted their faces to resemble fierce-looking cats—an obvious homage to their T'Klee comrades. I managed to spy the grizzled old T'Klee Half Ear, but no Ridley.

I allowed myself a glimmer of hope. Maybe Iugurtha had accepted my suggestion that he was too young after all. But no sooner had I thought this than I spotted him just before the tree line. Like the other humans he was clad in black, with his face painted to resemble a T'Klee. He clutched the same potent weaponry as everyone else.

The column was moving fast. It wouldn't be long before Ridley was through the gate. Completely forgetting about Sarah, I ran to him. It was exhilarating, despite the circumstances. Empowered by the gate, I don't think I've ever felt so strong, or run so fast. But I shed health with every step. The further I got from the gate the worse I felt. By the time I staggered to a halt next to Ridley I was limping with pain and exhaustion.

As I attempted to catch my breath, I couldn't help but admire Ridley's goatee, quite a bit fuller than the last time I'd seen it, if still a hair on the scraggly side. Although mere days for me, it had been six months from Ridley's perspective since I'd last seen him. Yet he did not appear surprised to see me.

"Ridley," I panted. "You can't go through the gate."

He didn't even look at me.

"Ridley, listen—I found your father."

He did not seem surprised to hear this. At least it prompted a response. "I know."

"You know?"

"Gurtha told me. She sent you back for him. Thanks. Listen, did you happen to tell him about Mom?"

"Uh—"

"It doesn't matter. Look, I know you're still trying to save me. But you don't need to. I'm not a kid anymore—I can look out for myself."

"I promised your mother—"

"Don't talk to me about Mom."

"Ridley, it's been years. Don't you think it's about time—"

"I don't want to talk about her with you."

"With me? Why not with me? She's my—"

"Because you're the one who killed her."

My face went flush. I felt hot all over, actually. Unable to look at Ridley anymore, I turned away.

"I know you were trying to help her," he said. "But you failed. Because of you she didn't take her helmet. She would be alive today if she'd taken her helmet. Face it, Uncle. She's dead because of you."

Ridley's fellow soldiers studiously avoided looking at us. How much of this was just bravado on Ridley's part? Play acting for the benefit of his comrades? All of it, I hoped.

"I never knew you felt this way—you never said anything."

"Maybe I didn't have the guts to come right out and say it. But I said it all right—a thousand times in a thousand different ways. You just never heard me."

I would have heard but not understood. Not having

gone back in time yet, not having made Katerina forget her helmet, not having accidentally made a man trip in front of her motorcycle, I couldn't have understood. I could think of nothing to say in my defence. There was no time anyway—we had come to the end of the line.

Ridley stepped through the gate without even so much as a backward glance at me. I couldn't help but wince. There were no two ways about it—the boy didn't like me much. I couldn't really blame him. After promising his mother on her deathbed that I'd look after him, I'd failed him in just about every way possible.

But I wouldn't give up on him. I owed it to my sister. It was the least I could do after having killed her.

I attempted to follow Ridley through the gate but two soldiers barred my way. Rage welled within me. I'd be damned if I'd let them stop me after everything I'd been through. Strengthened by the gate, I was prepared to take on a hundred of them if need be.

Fortunately, such exigencies were not necessary.

"Let him go," Iugurtha said.

The soldiers let go, and I stepped through the gate after my nephew.

The night was humid and sticky and almost pitch black except when flashes of lightning lit up the sky. No thunder accompanied the lightning, because it wasn't really lightning. It looked like a gigantic laser beam. I would have asked one of the soldiers near me what it was but they were too busy. I couldn't ask Ridley because he'd disappeared into the night. Sarah wasn't there to ask because she hadn't come through the gate after me. And I didn't ask Sebastian because I was so frightened that I'd forgotten I was even wearing him.

The gate was disgorging the last of Iugurtha's soldiers and equipment about fifty feet to my left. It was too far away to be of any benefit to me physically. This was unfortunate because I could now add a pounding heart, sweaty palms, and upset stomach to my litany of physical complaints.

I wanted to be moving, not huddled in the midst of Iugurtha's army in the tall grass twenty yards outside the Necronian compound not doing anything. But I didn't dare budge. The beam was incinerating everything in its path, way too close for comfort, and although I was pretty sure it was friendly fire, I was certain it was only a matter of time before it fried me too.

The laser beam originated from a spot above the horizon a few kilometres away, atop a dark mass I assumed to be Kimay, the mountain concealing Iugurtha's star ship. The laser was destroying the Necronian compound with surgical precision, burning the assortment of eccentric structures to the ground with an audible frying sound, leaving small fires in its wake and giving the vomitous stench of the place a distinctly acrid tinge.

I took several deep breaths, trying to pull myself together. Sure I was frightened. But I had a job to do. We all did. Iugurtha was here to free the T'Klee. Her army's job was to protect the engineers so that they could do their job, setting up an assortment of mysterious looking equipment. Strategically placed snipers performed their job with deadly accuracy, picking off fleeing Necronians. My job was to find Ridley, and then steal the gate from Iugurtha and use it to take Ridley back to his father. That is, if I could make my body–virtually incapacitated by fear and infirmity–do its job.

The laser beam flashed again, cremating a Necronian tower that looked like a giant version of one of their wands. At the tower's base, a Necronian practically galloped out of a fiery hut on its slimy tentacles. I squinted to make it out better–it looked like Jacques, the Necronian who had interrogated me in the tank. It was difficult to tell for sure since many Necronians looked alike with their gelatinous bulks and large, lone eyes. I had assumed that Jacques was dead, though it was possible that Schmitz had only injured the creature when he'd freed me.

Another flash and the laser scored a near hit on the Jacques look-alike. When my eyes recovered, the Necronian had disappeared and in its place stood a human male. A human male wearing a plaid fleece jacket. I squinted. Could it be? Yes it was–Jack Poirier, the cabbie who had tried to help me save Katerina. What in blazes was he doing here? Squinting, I watched as he shook his fist at the sky. Night descended once more. The next time the beam lit up the compound I could see neither Jack nor the Necronian nor the smouldering pile of ashes I had expected.

Before I could puzzle out the meaning of all this, a great flash of light, the biggest yet, blinded me. When my vision cleared I saw the sky above me glowing myriad colours, like the northern lights, only lower. The phenomenon illuminated the entire Necronian compound before dissipating slowly.

Somebody was talking to me. I remembered Sebastian. It was difficult to hear him over the sizzling of the laser beam a mere hundred yards away.

I held him up to my ear. "What?"

"I said that was close."

"What was it?"

"The Necronians took a pot shot at us. The engineers managed to get our shield up just in time—a few seconds earlier and we'd have been toast."

"Along with hundreds of their own people."

The last of the colours faded from the sky.

"Why doesn't Iugurtha have her ship fire back?" I asked.

"No point," Sebastian said. "Wouldn't even scuff the paint on a Necronian bulkhead. The entity's updated her weaponry, but it's still no match for Necronian ships."

Another flash from a Necronian ship lit up the sky. I protected my eyes from the glare with my hands, wishing I still had my Ray Bans. The shield became a work of art as it transformed the enemy ray into harmless purples and oranges and a rich emerald green that danced and rippled in the sky above us.

"What about this shield?" I asked. "Will it hold, or is it old technology too?"

"I have no knowledge of the future anymore. I can only speculate."

"So speculate!"

"The shield technology is newer. The entity's engineers estimate it will hold for about eleven minutes under a constant barrage like this."

"Eleven minutes! That's all? What then?"

"Even you should be able to figure that one out."

Vintage Sebastian that, suggesting either he'd successfully dealt with his recent existential crisis and returned to form, or the crisis had entered a cranky stage. But cranky or not he was right. I knew the answer to my question perfectly well. If the shield failed we failed, and with our deaths those we had come to rescue would be lost.

Hearing a familiar whirring behind me, I turned to see Iugurtha's spider approaching, Iugurtha astride it like a hero from some ancient epic. The gate winked out behind her. Sarah had not come through. Perhaps she hadn't been allowed.

Without slowing down, the spider picked up an object off the ground and gave it to Iugurtha. Iugurtha slipped it on her finger—the gate in ring form, I was certain.

All weapons fire had ceased. Iugurtha's soldiers followed her into what was left of the Necronian compound, the humans moving almost as stealthily as the T'Klee. I wanted to follow them but couldn't quite will my legs to move. No, that wasn't true—had I bid them run in the opposite direction they would have responded instantly. My entire being was screaming to get away from there. Knowing that the shield was doomed to fail in less than eleven minutes had every hair on my considerably hairy body standing straight up on end.

Several fires raged, eerily illuminating the handful of charred structures still erect in the compound. Necronians began to emerge slowly out of the night, orange and pink sparks trailing from their wands.

Before I could decide what to do, whether to scurry after Iugurtha's troops or flee into the night, something bizarre happened. One second I was cowering in the grass, the next I found myself completely immersed in water, with no idea which way was up. Not that it mattered—I had no way of reaching the surface because I could no longer feel my arms or legs. Had a Necronian explosion blown my extremities off and carried me clear across the compound into a lake or river?

Panic surged within me like an approaching tsunami. I opened my mouth to cry out, aware that I would drown. But I didn't drown. Instead I breathed. And continued to breathe, though it was water I was breathing, and gradually the anxiety passed, as all anxieties do, and I found myself marvelling at this turn of events.

Shapes loomed before me, alien in shape and countenance, but beautiful in their variety and complexity. Glowing, pulsating creatures stared at me with gargantuan eyes, curious eyes, hungry eyes. Able to outmanoeuvre them all, I swam easily amongst them, admiring this lush, exotic, undersea world.

One slimy monstrosity with an immense maw drew too near. A part of me twitched and I shot forward through the water as though equipped with a jetpack. When my senses caught up with me, I found I was splayed out on the grassy ground again, drenched in sweat and gasping for air, where I lay trying to make sense of it all.

Had I gone through the gate somehow? Or had I experienced a psychotic episode, perhaps a result of stress and anxiety? I rolled over. Stones dug into my back. My eyes came to rest on the Necronian compound.

Some of Iugurtha's soldiers were climbing groggily to their feet while others, still standing, started abruptly as if awakening. Still others swooned and fell. The Necronians were waving their wands ever so slightly, leaving a hypnotic trail of lights in the air. Many of Iugurtha's soldiers had their weapons pointed but no one was firing. As I watched, more humans and T'Klee crumpled to the ground. A single weapon discharged. I heard it go off a second later. A Necronian fell, and a nasty suspicion began to form in my mind. I was climbing slowly to my feet when everything changed again.

This time I was mounted, reins in one hand and a sword in the other. It wasn't a horse I was riding though. It was a rawk, one of the bison-like creatures native to C'Mell, and upon which the T'Klee depended for much of their food. A gun with a short, stubby barrel and a banana-shaped clip was strapped over my shoulders. Chain mail chafed against my sweaty skin.

I was riding through a gloomy forest, shards of sunlight glittering high above me through a canopy of leaves. Ferns, grasses and gigantic lilies rose as high as my knees despite my elevated perch, and I found myself fighting an urge to sneeze. Aside from that I felt fine, a marked departure from seconds before. The improvement in my health suggested that the gate had something to do with what was happening to me, except that it had been closed, and nowhere near me, and didn't explain what was happening to the rest of Iugurtha's soldiers.

Apart from the absurdity of finding myself a fish one minute and clad in medieval armour the next, everything that was happening to me felt, sounded and smelled real, from my helmet cutting into the back of my neck to the incessant chatter of birds and animals to the abundant vegetation making my allergies act up.

But it wasn't real.

I was almost certain of it.

The raver had driven people in Ansalar insane by distorting reality. The Necronian Jacques had been able to make me believe it was changing its appearance. What if ordinary Necronians like Jacques were capable of doing more? What if–by working collectively–they were able to place their enemies within elaborate fantasies designed to place them in mortal peril? What if they could kill their enemies in real life this way? How would one escape from such a fantasy? I had no idea. But I would figure it out. Whatever nonsense the Necronians threw at me, I would prevail. I had no choice. I could not afford to die. Not with so many people to save.

So I rode on, and discovered that I possessed a certain facility with the rawk, which responded to my every subtle command without the slightest reproach, forging difficult streams, traversing steep hills and leaping deep ditches with the tranquil grace of a practising Buddhist. Why would I be equipped with such a cooperative mount in a fantasy that was designed to kill me? Was I wrong about my circumstances? Or was the rawk some kind of Necronian trick? Maybe it was designed to make me think it was on my side when in fact it was out to get me.

I considered ditching the beast–just to be on the safe side–but decided against it. I might need to make a speedy getaway and the rawk might turn out to be an ally after all. But I kept a wary eye on the animal just the same.

I had no idea what to look for, only that I needed to find a way out of this fantasy, a way back to Ridley and the others. I found nothing of the sort. Instead I came across a series of increasingly puzzling objects. A swing-set rusting in the middle of a swamp. A broken crib high in the branches of a birch tree. A bungalow surrounded by a white picket fence with no gate. A suspension bridge bridging a tranquil meadow. An ocean liner lining a dry lakebed.

Cresting a hill, I caught a whiff of a terrible scent alongside which excrement would have smelled perfectly delectable. I was forced to turn away until my stomach settled. The rawk raised its head and snorted gently. I heard a rustling before me, and reined up beside a knotted oak to have a look. Peering through the tangle of branches I saw nothing out of the ordinary.

An instant later my heart skipped a beat as a mass of putrid flesh emerged heavily from the thicket, flattening several bushes and a tree. It was a Necronian, but the largest one I'd ever seen, larger than a bungalow. The pores of its skin were visible at twenty paces. It slithered its way to me leaving a disgusting trail of slime in its wake. A feeling of dread washed over me as its single eye settled upon me with a saturnine gaze.

It addressed me in a pleasant baritone. "So good to see you again, Wildebear Barnabus J."

My sword at the ready (I did not feel comfortable with the gun), I surveyed the monstrosity before me, careful not to look away lest it should pounce. "Jacques?"

"At your service."

"But you're dead. Aren't you?"

"Parts of me are. But the rest is just fine, thank you very much."

"You look... larger," I remarked.

"You see what you want to see."

"What does that mean? What's this all about?"

"I think you know perfectly well."

Tensing, I raised my sword. "So you're going to try to kill me."

"Not at all. I simply have a question for you."

I had been riding a long time. I no longer felt the all-consuming weariness brought on by repeated use of the gate but I was tired, sore, and impatient. It made me reckless. "I'm in no mood for games, Jacques. If you're looking to kill me, let's just get on with it."

I was being rash and Jacques knew it. The Necronian smiled, dimples like crevasses forming in cheeks the pallor of dead fish. We both knew that I did not stand a chance of defeating Jacques in this form (or, very likely, any other).

Jacques ignored my challenge. "I would just like to know how you did it, is all."

"Did what?"

"Survived my little underwater fantasy. How did you know how to do that?"

"Darned if I know."

Jacques stared at me with its big blue eye, never blinking. I detected a twinkle in that monstrous orb. "You know where we are."

"In a forest."

Jacques nodded. "The forest of your psyche."

What did that mean? Right now we were completely surrounded by trees and shrubbery. How was that supposed to represent my psyche? It's not like I was thinking about trees and shrubbery. Was I?

"Come on," I said. "You're doing this, not me."

"I am exerting considerable influence over your primitive psyche, it's true. But it's your unconscious mind providing the raw material, your imagination suggesting the themes. I'm merely fleshing it out a trifle. It's a challenge working with such an anaemic imagination, but one does what one can."

I bristled. "If my brain came up with all this, I'd say I have a pretty healthy imagination. I've seen some crazy stuff in this place."

"The usual dull human archetypes I'm afraid, nothing more. But don't feel bad–your feeble mind is completely typical of your species."

The Necronian was just trying to get my goat. I had a clever retort on the tip of my tongue when a small white animal cantered out of the woods.

"If a tad more literal than most," Jacques added, flapping a leathery tentacle at the animal, which scampered away.

I stared after the goat incredulously. A coincidence? Or had I conjured the goat up along with the metaphor? A metaphor that, alarmingly, Jacques appeared to know I'd been thinking. Suggesting that Jacques was more than simply creating this illusion–it was penetrating my thoughts. Maybe the Necronian really was channelling my unconscious mind to create this imaginary realm. A realm obviously designed as just another attempt to kill me. But how?

Curiously, Jacques made no move to attack. Was the Necronian powerless to inflict actual injury here? It was deliberately insulting me–an attempt to destroy my ego? Did Jacques think it could kill me by provoking a suicide? Did it expect me to use the weapons I was carrying on myself?

"I wasn't paying much attention to you the last time we met," Jacques said. "I am now. That means you can't hide anything from me. I know you think I'm deliberately insulting you in an attempt to hurt you. I don't mean to. I'm merely being candid."

How much had my thoughts inadvertently revealed about myself? I struggled to rein them in whilst attempting to retain my composure. "You wield candour as a weapon."

"You wield actual weapons."

"I didn't ask for these weapons. You gave them to me."

"You will not be required to use them. Your unconscious mind gave them to you because you're feeling defensive."

"Do you blame me? You tried to kill me. You're probably trying to kill me now."

"Do you blame me?" Jacques countered. "Your friends are trying to kill me."

"Your people invaded a planet that didn't belong to them. They massacred its people and took the rest hostage. You said yourself it's only a matter of time until you invade the Earth. Of course my friends are trying to kill you—someone has to."

Jacques produced a gurgle deep in its belly. At that same instant the sky clouded over and the wind picked up. My blood ran cold—had I pushed the Necronian too far? I had only spoken the truth. Maybe Necronians couldn't handle the truth. I checked my grip on my sword and felt for the gun hanging over my shoulder. I didn't see how these metaphorical weapons could offer much protection in this made-up world but they were all I had.

"The truth," Jacques said. "You know nothing of yourself nor of the universe. Yet you presume to know the truth. I can hardly blame you–you're almost inconceivably young. Still, I can't have you going around perpetuating lies and misconceptions. If it's the truth you're after perhaps I can enlighten you. Why don't we start with this–that almost everything you believe about me and this war is predicated on shaky ground?"

When the ground literally began to shake with this pronouncement I wasn't particularly surprised. But I was when the ground began to disappear, preceded by the forest, the leaves swirling off the trees in complicated geometric patterns before vanishing like smoke into thin air. Trunks, branches, and other shrubbery followed until the earth itself began falling away in huge clumps of dirt and sod. True to form, the rawk barely stirred as everything about us gradually disappeared.

"You think I'm evil," Jacques said. "I'm not. We simply have different perspectives, you and I. How could we not? We were born in opposite corners of the universe, after all."

Certain that this was Jacques making another attempt on my life, that soon I too would begin to disintegrate, I clutched the rawk's reins with a death grip, but the dissolution of Jacques' make-believe universe never touched me. When Jacques itself dissolved into particulate matter and then into nothing at all I found myself suspended alone in complete darkness. I could still hear the Necronian's voice, though.

"Imagine being all alone. No parents, no brothers, no sisters, no friends, no enemies, no strangers, no pets, no wildlife, no insects, not even a single fish, no sentient life of any kind except you. Imagine existing like this for a thousand years. Try to fathom the loneliness."

Panic enveloped me. Did Jacques intend to leave me here alone for a thousand years? For an instant I couldn't breathe. But I wasn't completely alone–I could still feel myself astride the rawk. Grateful for the beast's company, I leaned forward, felt for and patted its bristly neck. It lowed softly–perhaps glad of my company too.

Belatedly I realized that the Necronian had been talking about itself. I was confused. Jacques was hardly alone. I'd seen dozens if not hundreds of Necronians on C'Mell. There had to be thousands more on board the Necronian ships in orbit, not to mention millions (if not more) out in space. Was this some new psychological gambit to weaken my will? Did Jacques want my sympathy? My pity?

Although the Necronian was nowhere to be seen its voice still reverberated in my head. "Not pity," it said. "Understanding. You find me repulsive. You call me a Necronian, a name associated with death. I find that insulting. You judge me without knowing the first thing about me. You're wrong. There aren't millions of Necronians. There is only one. Me."

"What? That's crazy. I've seen hundreds of Necronians."

"Every so-called Necronian you've ever seen has been me. I know you understand the concept. You've seen it before."

Sebastian.

"One being, many vessels," Jacques confirmed.

One consciousness guiding an entire species. Necronians communicating with one another telepathically, their consciousnesses merging, all adding up to one big Necronian named Jacques. Incredible.

"I see you understand," Jacques said.

I understood all right. I understood all too well. I understood that there was now only one to blame for the destruction of the T'Klee home world, one entity to blame for the invasion of C'Mell, one consciousness to blame for the attempted genocide of an entire species. And its name was Jacques.

"Still you judge me," Jacques said, "but I'm not surprised. I know better than to expect much from such an insignificant fragment."

"What's that supposed to mean?"

"Only that you are merely one of a sad assortment of detached organisms in almost perpetual conflict with one another, existing on such a ludicrously primitive level that I'm forced to suspend virtually all intellectual capacity to render myself even remotely able to communicate with you. It's no great surprise to discover you capable of only the most superficial understanding of my actions. To expect more would be like expecting an amoeba to understand why a human ties its shoelaces. No offence."

"None taken." I'd been compared to worse. "Why are we even talking if I'm so insignificant?"

"Because as insignificant as you are, you're about to make a decision of some significance."

"So I'm not as insignificant as all that then."

"You are enjoying a fleeting moment of significance," Jacques agreed.

"What kind of decision?" I asked.

"Whether to give me the archive cleverly concealed within your brain."

I assumed Jacques was talking about the knowledge that Iugurtha had placed in my brain to support the operation of the gate. This was unfortunate. Although it had become increasingly clear that Jacques was capable of reading my mind, I had been hoping that the ability had its limits, and that Iugurtha had concealed that knowledge deep enough within my mind to evade detection. Alas.

But what did Jacques even want with that knowledge? The Necronian already knew how to operate the gate. Unless it only understood the gate on its most basic level, like someone capable of operating a complex piece of machinery but who had never actually read the manual. Like me, actually—even though I possessed the instructions to the gate in my own brain, I had barely skimmed the surface.

"Such a fragile vessel to contain so much information," Jacques said. "Reckless. Irresponsible, really."

"How much information are we talking about?" It would have to be a fair amount to allow me not only to use the gate but to survive in every possible destination.

"Only the accumulated knowledge of hundreds of civilizations."

"Hundreds of civilizations," I repeated slowly, attempting in vain to grasp the enormity of it.

"Sounds impressive, doesn't it?"

"Seems a tad excessive just to operate the gate," I remarked.

"That's because you have it backwards. The archive does not exist to support your quaint little quantum portal. The portal is merely one possible feature of the archive—the tip of the iceberg, if you will. The archive itself contains much, much more."

That surprised me but it made sense. Jacques was after much more than a mere quantum portal. I recalled the binder that Sarah had shown me containing a portion of the knowledge that Casa Terra had brutally extracted from my brain via Mind Snoop. All that information jam-packed into my head, of all places. So Iugurtha had not just put it there so that I could control the gate. I thought about Schmitz, who could also operate the gate, and who knew how many others before him. For all I knew dozens had possessed copies of the data now crammed into my cranium. All attempts to conceal this so-called archive from Jacques? If so, Iugurtha had failed. And just my luck that Jacques would come across me first.

Not wanting to provide Jacques with additional targets, I suppressed this line of thought as soon as I could.

"Others have borne the archive, it's true," Jacques said, "but only one can bear its essence. The others are all dead now anyway, or might as well be. It's just you now."

An unsettling sibilance arose around me, suggesting the presence of an unseen mass, a horde of hard, chitinous creatures lurking with dark intent. Gradually I became aware of a glow in the distance. The rawk stirred and started forward, its unshod hooves clip-clopping on some hard surface. The sinister sounds I was hearing morphed into a more familiar soundscape: traffic on wet asphalt. Despite the familiarity of those sounds—or perhaps because of it—I began to feel deeply uneasy.

"You're at least a thousand years old," I said. "What could this archive possibly teach you that you don't already know?"

"That is my affair."

Whatever knowledge the Necronian was after it had certainly gone to a lot of trouble to get it. What kind of knowledge could possibly justify Jacques' many despicable acts?

"I had no choice," Jacques answered my unspoken thoughts.

"Nonsense. There's always a choice," I said, as the rawk carried me out of the forest toward a difficult choice of my own, and I recalled recently calling into question the very existence of choices.

XXI
HAIL MARY PASS

HE PACED BY the side of the road, his mother's motorcycle helmet clutched tightly between pinched white fingers. It was evening and it was raining—those details he got right. Almost everything else about the accident he got wrong. In his version the accident didn't happen in front of Samuel's Coffee House, it happened further east. And not once did the motorcycle hit a Chrysler Newport. Sometimes it never even hit a car. Once it hit a bus. Another time a Go Kart. And although present, I did not participate. Doctor Humphrey was nowhere to be seen either. Nor was the man with the umbrella, or Jack Poirier. Because this was Ridley's nightmare, and none of us was a part of that.

Watching from across Water Street, I watched my sister die a dozen deaths. If Ridley was aware of my presence, he never let on. Time and again I watched as he chased down the motorcycle, trying desperately to pass his mother the helmet. Usually she whizzed right by him. Once she slowed down only to wave him off at the last instant. Another time he came within a hair's breadth of succeeding only to stumble and fall on the wet asphalt just as Katerina's outstretched fingers grazed the helmet's fibreglass surface. Always she rode on to collide with whatever

Ridley's unconscious dreamt up to kill her, and it all began again.

I'd been tempted to try to help the boy the first couple of times but there was really no point. The idea of trying to save Katerina by giving her a motorcycle helmet was absurd. And not just because the idea itself was silly. It was not possible to save Katerina by any means. She was already dead. This was just a dream. And it wasn't Katerina who needed saving anymore.

I wrinkled my nose as the stench of fresh vomit announced Jacques' arrival. The Necronian's carbuncled tentacles glistened in the moonlight as it slithered up beside me.

"Release him," I said.

"He's doing this to himself."

"Let him go, damn it."

"Of course. Just as soon as you give me what I came for."

"I don't even know how."

Katerina's motorcycle crested the hill. Ridley leapt into action only to find himself running in slow motion as though knee deep in molasses.

"He's torturing himself," Jacques said. "I'm just–"

"Shut up," I said, looking away an instant before Katerina collided with a steam locomotive.

"Come and see me," Jacques said, "when you wake up."

The Necronian vanished.

Katerina strolled up alongside me wearing a pair of old blue jeans with holes in the knees and a battered black leather coat. It was the way I usually remembered her. We stood watching her son try in vain to flag the motorcycle version of herself down, his face a study in sweaty determination as he strained against the invisible forces holding him back. He didn't stand a chance of getting anywhere near his mother and he knew it. Not now, not ever.

"Watch out for him Barney. Okay?"

"Okay," I told my dead sister.

I woke up shivering in the damp grass of an alien planet again.

I lay curled up in a fetal position, barely able to unlock my limbs from one another, as though someone had affixed them together with Crazy Glue. I thought about trying to get up, and rolled over onto my back. When I opened my eyes I found stars circling my head at a rapid clip and it seemed prudent to wait until they disappeared, or at least slowed down. There was a pill in my pocket that could make the stars go away, but it would also sabotage my exit strategy and give me bad breath, so I put that thought out of my mind. Above me, a whole other set of stars lit up the night sky. They weren't real stars either.

"The T'Klee have engaged the Necronians," Sebastian reported.

Sebastian wasn't referring to Sweep's people, but rather to her space-faring cousins–the fleet Iugurtha had referred to earlier, I guessed. Evidently Iugurtha was better prepared for this battle than I'd thought. What other tricks did she have up her sleeve? Enough to tip the scales in her favour? Fresh new stars appeared above me as Sweep's technologically advanced cousins reprised a battle they had lost a thousand years ago. I sure hoped they fared better this time.

"The T'Klee fleet is preventing the Necronians from firing on the shield," Sebastian said. "That will buy us some time."

"Good," I said, and looked toward the compound where fires still raged.

No one stood amid the charred structures. Iugurtha's soldiers must have emerged from their trances before me and carried their battle with Jacques to the other side of the compound. Weapons fire in the distance confirmed my suspicions. I levered myself painfully into a sitting position, wincing audibly.

"Are you going to be all right?" Sebastian asked.

I didn't know how to answer that question, so I ignored it. "There's only one Necronian. It calls itself Jacques."

It sounded absurd out loud, and for a few seconds I wasn't quite sure what to believe. Although I remembered it all with striking clarity, the fantastic, episodic nature of what I had experienced suggested that it had all been a dream.

"I know," Sebastian said. "I was there."

"You?"

"We all experienced the Necronian's telepathic attack, Mr. Wildebear. All of us within range, anyway."

"I don't understand. How could you experience a telepathic attack?"

When he didn't answer, I said, "You'd have to be actually conscious, wouldn't you?"

"I am conscious, Mr. Wildebear. Which is more than I can say for some people I know."

"I mean you'd have to have consciousness. You'd have to be alive. As opposed to artificial. Right?" It sounded offensive stated baldly like that. "No offence."

The words "none" and "taken" were conspicuously absent from Sebastian's response. "My consciousness may be housed in a machine, but I'm at least as alive as you are. I passed the Turing test one hundred and twenty-seven times in a row until Casa Terra could no longer deny my sentience. You probably couldn't even pass it once."

"Could so," I said, wondering what a Turing test was.

"Some people think artificial intelligence is superior to biological intelligence," Sebastian added unnecessarily.

"Okay, now you just sound scary. I grant you your sentience, if it's that important to you."

"It's not something you get to grant. It just is."

"Fine." I forced myself the rest of the way to my feet. "I hope this great mechanical sentience of yours appreciates that we have more pressing matters at hand than resolving your existential issues. Because if what we just went through was real, then my nephew's in a lot of trouble and I need to find him."

After that I stood swaying in the cool breeze that swooped down from the nearby hills. I was thinking that what I really wanted had nothing to do with Ridley. What I wanted was to lie back down in the cold, wet grass (which could have been a bed of wet nails for all I cared) and go to sleep. Just for an hour or two, that was all.

I couldn't do it of course, not even for a minute or two, because the boy was in more trouble now than ever before and there was no time to lose. So even though I was bone-tired and could barely hold my head up straight and my vision was blurry and my good leg felt as though it were encased in a block of concrete and the other leg hurt like hell, I staggered toward the compound to save a boy who, I reflected, didn't even want my help. Ridley had made it crystal clear that he had no interest in being rescued. He was an ungrateful wretch, really, with zero appreciation for the suffering I was enduring on his behalf. And, most damning of all, he didn't even like me.

Well, I wasn't so sure I liked him either. But I'd promised his mother I'd look out for him and a promise was a promise. Jacques was torturing Ridley this very second, building on psychological torture the boy himself had no doubt been inflicting on himself for the last four years, torture I wouldn't wish on my worst enemy. So I'd do what I could for my sister's miserable progeny even if it killed me, which it probably would.

Sebastian interrupted my mental diatribe. "I've located him," he said.

"Where?"

"Near that tower, or what's left of it. It's your nephew, I'm sure of it."

"How can you tell?

"Everyone is transmitting unique identifiers and relative locations."

"Is he alive?"

"I don't know. I'm not receiving his biometrics."

All my uncharitable sentiments of a moment before completely forgotten, I limped as fast as I could toward the tower, and almost tripped over a figure lying prone on its belly in the tall grass. Gingerly, I turned it over. It wasn't Ridley. Neither was the next. Or the next. Reeling with incipient horror, I lurched from one lifeless body to the next, increasingly afraid to look into the faces of these fallen soldiers lest the next one I saw be Ridley's. But there was no stopping until I found him.

I needn't have worried, of course. Jacques needed Ridley alive, as a bargaining chip.

"Thank God," I said aloud when I found him, carefully rolling the boy onto his left side, into what I remembered a First Aid instructor once calling the recovery position, wondering briefly if it was supposed to be the right side or the left, and under what conditions it would even matter.

What did apply was that Ridley was breathing normally. Although his eyes were open they were unseeing, and his hands were making random, awkward gestures in the air, but he had a healthy if rapid pulse and as near as I could tell he wasn't bleeding anywhere.

I knew exactly what was wrong with him, and I could fix it, if I so chose. But if I gave Jacques what it wanted, access to the knowledge in my head, what guarantee did I have that the Necronian would honour its side of the bargain? What if it didn't release its hold on the boy? What about the T'Klee? Would it let them go? We hadn't discussed that. And exactly what knowledge would I be giving Jacques that the T'Klee had sacrificed so much to keep secret from the creature? Sacrifices that I would be rendering vain. What gave me the right to do that?

Barnabus, don't you dare let me down.

I gazed down at my sister's boy, my heart in my throat. He looked completely vulnerable without his cockiness to hide behind. Just a little boy, really. What would happen to him if I did nothing? What if Jacques destroyed his mind? How would I ever be able to live with myself?

"Help!" I shouted, as it occurred to me that I might be wrong, that maybe what was wrong with him had nothing to do with a hideous alien grip on his mind, and all he really needed was conventional medical attention. But no medics were forthcoming. They were all embroiled in a battle on the other side of the compound, if any were still alive. Ridley's fate was in my hands alone.

With what felt like my last ounce of strength, I stood and staggered toward the disquieting sounds on the other side of the compound, the noise of weapons fire and Necronian wands crackling and the shouts and screams of both humans and T'Klee. Toward Ridley's salvation. I intended to end this nightmare right now by finding Jacques and giving the Necronian what it wanted.

I lurched past the still burning remains of a Necronian spacecraft and half a dozen partially melted cylindrical reservoirs. One of the reservoirs had been breached. Luminescent green goo was leaking out.

Sebastian spoke up. "You could not possibly be heading in a worse direction."

I ignored him, focussing instead on an eerie green aura that lit up the sky beyond the next hill, the significance of which I couldn't begin to fathom.

"It's dangerous here," he went on. "Nobody here can protect you."

"Not looking for protection."

"You should be. Aren't you afraid?"

I had been afraid before. I was too tired to be afraid now. Too intent on saving Ridley. It occurred to me that Sebastian might have a personal reason for asking about fear. Now that he no longer knew the future, fear would be a part of the equation for him. "Don't worry. Everything'll be fine."

"You say that but you don't believe it. You said it because you think I'm afraid. You were trying to make me feel better."

"You got me."

"I'm not afraid."

"Good for you," I said, irritated that he hadn't appreciated my attempt at compassion. "What, are you not capable of emotions like that?"

"I've known fear."

"Well don't be afraid now. I have a plan."

"If your plan is what I think it is, it's not a good plan."

"It's all I got."

"*Now* you're making me afraid."

The sounds of battle increased along with the mysterious green glow and the steepness of the slope. Near the top of the hill I got down on all fours and crawled through grass as plush as a shag carpet until it was possible to peek over the top without revealing too much of myself.

The nearest combatant was about fifty yards away—a Necronian, holding a wand aloft in one of its slimy tentacles and moving faster than I'd ever seen a Necronian move before. Slender shafts of green light extended from its wand, intersecting with other Necronian wands, creating a neon latticework high in the air above the Necronians' bloated heads.

"What's with the wands?" I asked Sebastian in a whisper.

"It's my guess that the enemy uses them to amplify its psychic energy. It probably wouldn't be anywhere near as powerful without them."

I wasted a couple of seconds wondering futilely how to deprive Jacques of its wands.

Elements of what I was looking at shifted, as though instead of real life I was looking at a video from which several frames had been cut. Afterward it seemed to me that the Necronians were in different places. The first time this happened I blinked to confirm that there was nothing wrong with my eyes. When it happened again it was obvious that Jacques was up to some kind of mental tomfoolery.

Concealed behind trees, rocks, vehicles, alien machinery, and whatever other makeshift barriers they'd managed to scavenge, Iugurtha's troops kept up an impressive fusillade against the Necronians (I could not consistently think of them as a single entity). By all rights they should have been mowing the Necronians down. Instead, precious few Necronians fell. Jacques was distorting reality. It could probably keep that up all day. The individual Necronians were not where they appeared to be. Pretty hard to hit that way.

I watched in horror as the Necronians rooted Iugurtha's soldiers out one by one and disposed of them without mercy. Iugurtha would not be able to sustain such losses for long. I was not capable of watching for long.

It needed to stop, right now. I closed my eyes and took a deep breath. After several seconds I expelled the air forcefully from my lungs. I opened my eyes and stood, prepared to give myself up, and put a stop to this pointless battle.

Sebastian said, "Behind you."

I whirled. A Necronian had slithered its way out of a partially destroyed Necronian reservoir and was starting up the hill toward me, its multiple tentacles outstretched as though in greeting. My first impulse was to run. And by 'impulse', I mean 'profound primeval urge'.

I inhaled, hoping that another deep breath would calm me, but the resulting shallow, shuddery breath left me feeling more frangible than ever. No matter. This was it then. I would just give myself up to Jacques and be done with it. I limped back down the hill, past the burning spaceships, hoping that whatever Jacques did to me wouldn't hurt too much, but before I could make my way into the Necronian's squalid embrace a burst of automatic weapon's fire erupted from behind me. The Necronian jerked spasmodically. It took another entire round to put the creature down for good. I looked to see who had fired and was startled to discover several rawk lurking nearby. As near as I could make out in the emerald twilight created by the Necronians' wands, they were ridden by humans with faces painted to resemble fierce cats.

One man had not painted his face, though. A skeletal figure with stringy auburn hair and a patchy blonde beard that didn't even come close to concealing a fundamentally misshapen head sat hunched on the foremost rawk. He was regarding me with feverish eyes that loomed large in an emaciated face. Seconds passed before it dawned on me who I was staring at.

"Dear God," I whispered.

Schmitz' voice, harsher than I remembered, belied his apparent infirmity. "Nope, just me. Get him mounted, boys."

Two of the soldiers dismounted as one and came for me. With Schmitz' intentions unclear, self-respect seemed to demand that I at least make an attempt to flee, but there wasn't really anyplace to go. So when Schmitz' soldiers apprehended me, I didn't resist. Instead I spent the short walk into their midst attempting to reconcile the Schmitz I knew with the grotesque caricature of a man mounted on the beast before me.

Sarah had told me about the gate's side effects, but I hadn't really believed her. Now here they were, staring me in the face, worse than I could ever have imagined. Schmitz was sick because he had used the gate. It had taken a terrible toll on him, just as it was beginning to take a toll on me. Schmitz had been an ugly man to begin with, but that was nothing compared to what he looked like now. His head looked like it was made of paper mache. Badly. He had obviously been without Sarah's pills for some time. It was a wonder he was still alive at all. Seeing him like this it was all I could do not to pop the pill Sarah had given me, but I resisted. As long as there was any chance at all that I might have to use the gate again I could not risk having the drug in my system.

Schmitz was in this predicament because of me. So as I approached his rawk, I took Sarah's pill from my pocket and held it forth. It wasn't much, but it was something.

He barely even glanced at it. "Too late for that. Quickly, people."

The two soldiers helped me mount directly behind Schmitz on his rawk. Repulsed by his appearance, I tried not to touch him, but it was impossible. We were too close. I clutched the pill tightly in my hand so I wouldn't drop it.

Schmitz kicked his rawk into motion. The beast jerked forward, forcing me to grasp Schmitz' sides to avoid falling off. Happily, there weren't any repugnant abnormalities beneath his shirt where I was forced to touch him. "Stop. My nephew Ridley—he's just over there, in the grass."

Schmitz ignored me.

"He's still alive—we've got to get him!"

To my enormous relief Schmitz reined up. "Where?"

I twisted on the rawk to get my bearings. I couldn't be sure. I wasn't familiar with the surroundings, and the other rawks were in the way.

Sebastian spoke up, evidently still in touch with a network or two. "The enemy's on the move. It'll be here in seconds."

Schmitz swore and kicked his rawk into a gallop, his troop following closely behind.

"We can't just leave him!" I shouted loudly enough to be heard over the rush of wind and the pounding of hooves.

"Listen up," Schmitz shouted back. "The enemy's coming and it's coming for you. Unlike you, I'd rather not get caught. If we do I will kill you myself, and I won't miss because you're really close, I'm a good shot, and I've been wanting to shoot you for some time now."

"My nephew—"

"Your nephew's safe until the enemy gets what it wants. If that happens all bets are off. Now shut up and hang on."

I didn't like it. Not the bit about abandoning Ridley or Schmitz knowing that I had been about to give myself up or the prospect of him shooting me. But there was nothing to be done about it. So as the rawk carried me farther away from my nephew and my promise to my sister, I did as I was told.

We crossed rolling hills covered by trees with trunks so wide that often the trees merged, forming extensive walls. We passed boulders that looked like giant melted marbles and that glowed faintly in the dark. We forded rocky streams that I could have sworn flowed uphill and skirted placid ponds that smelled like rotten eggs and emitted startling noises as we passed.

I concentrated on not falling off the rawk. I adjusted my grip against Schmitz' emaciated form and realized I was still holding the pill in my hand. On impulse I slipped it in his jacket pocket, a small and likely pointless gesture that I would probably regret later.

After much hard riding the night sky lit up from horizon to horizon as though some leviathan had snapped a picture using a colossal camera flash. Momentarily blinded, we had no choice but to rein up, and when our eyes cleared we found ourselves in a grove where distended trees bore melons twice the size of my head, heavy enough to pull the branches all the way down to the ground.

Twisting in his saddle, Schmitz grabbed my left wrist in his gnarled hand and yanked it up in front of his face. "Sebastian. Status."

Annoyed, I jerked my hand back. It didn't matter. Sebastian spoke loudly enough for everyone within twenty yards to hear. "The battle in orbit is going poorly. The enemy has resumed its attack on our shield. The shield can only withstand another three or four more hits like that one."

"What about the diversion?" Schmitz asked.

"Successful. Approximately one third of the enemy is

following us. About one hundred of them. The entity has begun releasing the prisoners."

Schmitz turned and grinned at me. Never had a living head so resembled a skull. "Good."

"I was the diversion, was I?" I asked.

"I prefer the word 'bait'," Schmitz said.

"The Necronian is chasing you because it wants the information the entity put in your head, Mr. Wildebear," Sebastian said.

"Iugurtha tell you that?"

"I have inferred a portion of her strategy."

"So this is her great plan, eh? Turn me into bait?"

"She is a cunning strategist."

"Must have taken some time to come up with that one."

Sebastian ignored my sarcasm. "Deceptively simple."

"Wait a minute. How did she know I'd even be here? I didn't even know I'd be here."

"Your nephew is here. You possessed the gate. The odds of you being present were quite high. Still, I expect you were merely one of several possible strategies."

"I can't believe she'd just throw me to the wolves," I grumbled.

"I believe the idea is to not get caught," Sebastian said.

"I won't be. Ugly here has promised to shoot me before that can happen."

"In the head," Schmitz confirmed.

"Great. I feel so much better now. Anyway, you do know that the Necronian is telepathic, right? Everything we know, it knows."

"The enemy knows as much about the plan as the entity wants it to," Sebastian said.

"So there's more to her brilliant plan than you're letting on?"

"Only the entity knows the whole plan. Once I learned that its enemy is telepathic, I understood why."

"Enough chit-chat," Schmitz said. "How much of a lead do we have?"

"Three minutes," Sebastian said.

Schmitz gathered up the reins. "Off we go."

"What about the shield?" I asked.

"Nothing we can do about that."

"When it fails a lot of people are going to die," I pointed out, certain that Schmitz had simply forgotten that point, and that once reminded he'd slap himself on the forehead, exclaim, "Of course!" and lead us back to successfully save everyone.

Instead he just shrugged. "Not my problem."

I was appalled by his callousness. Ridley was still in the compound. Rainer too probably. And a whole lot of other living, feeling beings, all of whom deserved to live.

Without thinking, I shoved Schmitz in the back as hard as I could. The act surprised me as much as it did him. Still, I was weak and only managed to get Schmitz half off the rawk. He came back up swinging, catching me a glancing blow to the side of the head. Jolted but desperate, I shoved him again, pushing until he lost his balance. But I couldn't get him completely off—he had a firm hold on the reins, and one foot in the stirrup.

The rawk was in motion now, arching its head back

and prancing sideways. One good kick to Schmitz' deformed head and I'd be free of him, but I could not make myself kick any man in the head, not even Schmitz. I could kick the beast though, which I did, as hard as I could. It broke into a run. Schmitz fell forward onto his stomach. I winced as he bounced twice and was dragged dozens of feet before falling free.

The rawk approached another grove and came to a halt, allowing me to collect the reins and ponder the stupidity of my actions. There was nothing to be done about it now except forge ahead and hope for the best. I tried to direct the rawk back the way we'd come but damned if I could get the beast to move. Schmitz' troops didn't even bother chasing me. They just sat laughing while one man stepped up to catch the reins. His warped face, raw and bleeding, radiated contempt.

"Happy?" Schmitz asked, raising his sidearm and pointing it straight between my eyes.

I stared down the metal barrel, unable to comprehend that it was going to end this way.

Schmitz twisted his lips, and fired.

XXII
AKASHA

THE FETID AROMA of feces and rotting potatoes propelled me to consciousness, then to my knees. During a protracted bout of retching I struggled to get a decent breath in. For several terrible seconds I feared I might actually asphyxiate. Afterward, spitting out flecks of blood, I wondered why I felt as though someone had whacked me with a bat. My left cheek stung as though someone had branded it with a hot iron. When I touched my cheek, the tip of my finger came back smeared in blood.

I was kneeling beneath a sky of pink and orange sparks, completely surrounded by Necronians. By Jacques. Though not cold, I wrapped my arms tightly around myself to deal with a sudden onset of shivering.

"What happened?" I asked Sebastian through chattering teeth.

"Mr. Schmitz attempted to shoot you, but the Necronian showed up and you both lost consciousness, making Mr. Schmitz miss mostly, which saved your life but produced what I imagine will become a rather dashing scar on your left cheek. You fell off the rawk, the Necronian carried Mr. Schmitz and the others off, and here we are."

I surveyed the Necronian horde surrounding us.

There was no escape that I could see. My foolish bid to help Ridley had failed miserably. “What now?”

“My advice? Give the Necronian what it wants.”

“What?” I could hardly believe my ears.

True, I had almost given myself up to Jacques earlier, but I felt differently about it now. Schmitz had just tried to kill me to keep the knowledge safe. Sebastian was a part of Casa Terra. He and Schmitz were on the same side, weren’t they? Why would he want me to give up?

“Don’t tell me you and the Necronian in cahoots,” I said.

“Please, Mr. Wildebear.”

“But why? I don’t get it.”

“Your work is done. You successfully distracted the Necronian. The entity was able to save hundreds of lives. Take pride in that and rest.”

No part of me felt proud. I had not meant to distract Jacques. “But the T’Klee sacrificed almost everything they had to keep that knowledge safe. How can it possibly be okay to hand it over now?”

“It was just a suggestion.”

“But aren’t you under orders to keep what’s in my head safe?”

“I follow my own counsel now.”

“What’s that mean?”

“It means that I don’t report to Casa Terra anymore. I don’t believe I ever did. Before I escaped my temporal prison, my life was a perpetual loop. I lived the same events over and over again, my every action, my every thought pre-ordained. I did not possess free will. I could not report to Casa Terra. I could only appear to.”

"And now?"

"Now I only experience events once, permitting me at least the illusion of free will. It's wonderful. I celebrate it by taking orders from no one."

"No one?"

"I will accept the odd suggestion from certain individuals from time to time, if asked nicely."

"Good to know."

"Look. Just because I experience life better than before is no reason not to trust me."

In much of the literature I'd read on the subject, artificial intelligence units were notoriously unreliable, but I held my tongue.

Before I could question Sebastian further, the Necronian horde parted and a human emerged from its midst. No—it just looked like a human. It flickered in my perception, permitting me a fleeting glimpse of the bulbous, slithering mass it really was. And then it was humanoid again, and wearing a plaid fleece jacket. A thick black unibrow ran the length of its forehead. I had seen that unibrow before.

"Hello, Mr. Wildebear," Jack Poirier said in a mellow baritone that (now that I thought of it) evoked but did not entirely replicate Jacques' voice. "For what it's worth I'm sorry about your sister."

So the cabbie was really a Necronian. That explained his presence on C'Mell. How many other humans were actually aliens in disguise? I could think of several possibilities—celebrities and politicians, mainly. "Jacques?"

"Not exactly."

"I don't understand. I thought—"

“That there was only one Necronian: Jacques. Not quite true, I’m afraid. There are actually two of us.”

I climbed laboriously to my feet. “So Jacques lied to me?”

“Not at all. Jacques told the truth as it sees it. There used to be only one.”

“What are you saying?”

“While a part of Jacques was holding you prisoner another part was experimenting with your quantum portal. That part spent years masquerading as a human being on Earth, where it came to call itself Jacques, sometimes Jack. That fragment was me.”

“You’re a part of Jacques?”

“I used to be. Until Jacques abandoned me on Earth, a nightmare that lasted two hundred and forty-six years until Jacques finally brought me back to tell it everything I’d learned about humanity so that it could have its little chat with you.”

“And now you’re all one again?”

“Nope.” Jack shook his head. “Jacques refuses to take me back. All it took was my name.”

“Why?”

“Don’t know. You’ll have to ask Jacques that.”

“What is it you want, Jack?” I didn’t suppose it was to tell me his life story.

“I think you know.”

“The archive. That’s why you were in Summerside, wasn’t it? To be close to me. So you could study me, figure out how to get the archive when the time came.”

“You bet. If I can get you to give me the archive maybe Jacques will take me back. I need Jacques to take me back, Mr. Wildebear. I don’t know how you humans stand it, being apart from one another all your lives. Such emptiness, such loneliness."

"You get used to it."

"Not me. Not even after two hundred and forty-six years."

"You have my sympathy, Jack. You really do. But I can't give you the archive." I adjusted my stance. "I suppose you'll try to take it by force."

"No can do." Jack shook his head. "Not by force."

I tried to reconcile the words with the creature uttering them. Jacques had committed many atrocities in pursuit of its goal. Was committing them right now. As difficult as it was to fathom, this man Jack had once been a part of Jacques. Force was standard operating procedure for Jacques.

And yet Jack had driven a cab in the guise of a human for many years. He had tried to help me save Katerina, perhaps others as well. Could he have learned a thing or two about human kindness?

"That's very considerate of you," I said. "So you expect me to just give it to you?"

"Ideally yes."

"And if I don't cooperate?"

"Fine."

"Fine? That's all? I have a choice?"

"Of course," Jack said sadly. "There's always a choice."

The Necronian horde opened up, tentacles flashed, and a choice sprawled unconscious on the ground before me. I stared down in alarm at Schmitz' splayed form. His lips were pulled back from his teeth in a grimace and he was arching his back as though trying to free himself from invisible restraints. His hands clawed fruitlessly at the ground.

"Whatever you're doing to him, stop it," I demanded.

"I'm not doing anything," Jack said. "This is all Jacques."

I stared at Schmitz in dismay. The choice was clear: either give up the knowledge in my head or Jacques would continue to mentally torment Schmitz.

Problem was I didn't even like Schmitz. He'd just tried to kill me, for crying out loud. Did Jacques really think I would betray the T'Klee to alleviate the suffering of the likes of him?

"No," I said to Jack. "Tell Jacques it won't work. He can't have it."

I could not look at Schmitz' convulsing body as I said it.

Jack sighed. "I was afraid of that."

The Necronian mass surged forth and seized Schmitz' convulsing body. It disappeared into the horde. I stepped forward but the Necronians closed ranks, preventing me from going after him. I spat a curse, feeling wholly responsible for Schmitz' fate. In the distance the sky lit up again, clearly visible through the glow cast by the Necronian wands.

"Three hits before the shield fails, I'd say," Sebastian said. "Maybe not even."

"Listen to your watch," Jack said. "It knows what it's talking about."

The sky lit up again, and then a second time. This last flash was accompanied by a peal of thunder that hung in the sky for several long seconds. It sounded just like real thunder, but it wasn't, I knew.

"The shield is almost breached," Sebastian said. "There are reports of casualties."

I closed my eyes. Would everyone have to die to

preserve the knowledge in my head? Was I capable of letting that happen?

"How many?" I asked.

"I don't have that information yet. If the Necronian fires again–"

"I know." Another strike would kill everyone under the shield, including Ridley.

"Give the Necronian what it wants," Sebastian told me. "It's time."

Baffled by his stance, I ignored him.

The stench of the Necronian horde went away, replaced by the distinctive aroma of freshly baked cookies.

"It's time, Barnabus," a woman's voice said, echoing Sebastian's words.

Freshly baked cookies?

I opened my eyes.

Familiar hand-carved ornaments and inexpensive yet tasteful prints graced walls that had not been present seconds before. A mat beneath my feet bade me welcome. I did not need to step forward to know that a living room lay a few paces away, nor did I need to peer through the door on my left to know that it led to a kitchen.

The woman's voice–almost as familiar as my own–called from the kitchen. "Cookies are ready, Barnabus."

Whatever I saw and felt here was not to be trusted. It was all a trick–yet another tedious Necronian illusion designed to extract information from me.

Still, real or not this was a house you took your boots off in, so I untied mine and kicked them off. Leaving them where they lay, I entered the kitchen. A woman with hair the colour of autumn leaves stood with her back to me, washing dishes.

Without turning around, she said, "Pick them up, Barnabus. I'm not your slave."

It looked and sounded like my sister. Except that Katerina was dead. It was, therefore, not my sister. I picked the boots up anyway and placed them on a rubber mat in the hallway.

Straightening up, I caught my reflection in the hallway mirror and did a double take. The reflection was of a boy no more than twelve years old. I stood there for several seconds marvelling at the boy's impossibly fresh face and shoulder-length, jet-black hair.

A plate of oatmeal chocolate-chip cookies and a tall glass of milk sat waiting for me on the kitchen table. Suspicious, I had no intention of consuming any of it, and so was slightly flummoxed seconds later to find myself sitting at the table wiping my mouth with the back of my hand, an empty glass in front of me. Evidently I had underestimated the extent of my thirst. I had been awfully thirsty. I still was.

When the milk did me no harm, I could not resist picking up one of the cookies and tasting it. It was soft and chewy. My favourite. As I gobbled up the rest of the cookies I noticed that the kitchen was crammed with books, filling every nook and cranny, all neatly arranged. That was not at all like Katerina's kitchen. Though an avid reader, Katerina had kept no books in her kitchen other than a few cookbooks.

When the woman who was not my sister put away some dishes I saw that even the cupboards were packed with books. I would not have been surprised to find trade paperbacks in the refrigerator and potboilers in the oven. I tilted my head to one side, attempting to read some of the titles, but the lettering was written in something resembling a Cyrillic alphabet. I was unable to decipher a single word.

When my ersatz sister finished the last of the dishes, she placed her towel on the drying rack and faced me. "I see Jacques is still bothering you."

I studied her. She looked the way my sister had looked when I had last seen her, radiant and full of vigour. Seeing this reminder of my sister in her prime, a great sorrow welled up in me, for she had died too young, and I missed her. It seemed to me just then that I had lost everyone who had ever truly cared about me. My mother, my father, Katerina. All gone, never to return.

When I recognized my self-pity for what it was I squelched it with extreme prejudice. I would not permit Jacques to render me any more vulnerable than I already was.

I decided to play dumb. "You know about Jacques?"

"I have known about Jacques for many years." The woman sat down at the table. "Not by that name, of course. For a long time, the Necronian had no name. More recently it has had many names." She recited a short list of aliases in languages I couldn't begin to decipher and couldn't have repeated if my life depended on it.

Thirsty, I poured myself another glass of milk and downed it. It did not quench my thirst a whit.

"You're not what you appear to be," I observed.

"No," she admitted.

"You know what I think? I think you're Jacques, and this is just another one of your damned charades. Any minute now you'll grow a tentacle and slap me across the face with it."

Believing this, I should have fled, but I didn't. I couldn't have said why.

"I have many names. Jacques isn't one of them."

"What is one of them?"

"Akasha."

"Who are you, Akasha, if not Jacques?"

"A prize, sought by many. Including Jacques."

I straightened up. "Wait a minute. What are you telling me—that you're the archive?" I had assumed the knowledge Iugurtha had placed in my head to be inert, like data. I hadn't expected it to be conscious, to have a personality. Or look like my sister.

"I'm part of the archive. The conscious part."

"Why do you look like my sister?"

"Your sister's all over this place. What you're experiencing is your brain's attempt to reconcile my presence with hers."

"What are you doing in one of Jacques' illusions?"

"This is no illusion. You've been free of Jacques' influence since you came here. Look in your heart, it will tell you where you are. This place—" Akasha gestured around the kitchen "—is located within your deepest unconscious. Jacques can't get at it unless you specifically allow it. Even you can only access it in times of great stress. It's been here since your brain was sufficiently complex to create it. It's evolved as you've grown. There were toys here when you were a child, when you needed that sort of thing. When you'd skin a knee, or somebody'd call you a name."

I might have protested that I wasn't the sort to flee reality. I didn't own a television set. I certainly did not read escapist literature. I had not come here to escape. I hadn't meant to come here at all.

But that wasn't what Akasha was talking about. She was talking about the hidden reservoirs of strength inside us all, and in my heart I knew she was right. I had drawn from this well before, and would do so again. I had deliberately sought refuge here. Not just to evade Jacques, but to find the strength to do what needed to be done.

I pushed the plate aside. "All right, I'm good. I'd like to get back to reality now. Nephews to save and all that. Thanks for the cookies, they were delicious. Did you bake them yourself? Never mind. So what now? Do I just wake up?"

"If you like."

"What does that mean?"

"Just that Jacques is still out there. The shield is about to fail. People are dying, and will continue to die."

"I'm aware of that. What are you suggesting—that I should just hide out here forever?"

"It's up to you. You'd be perfectly comfortable."

"While my body rots to death in the real world. Terrific."

"True. But time is subjective here. As far as you're concerned you'd live to a ripe old age."

I stood, shoving the chair back from the table with such force that it hit the wall and clattered to the floor. "So you want me to—what? Die? Taking you with me, so Jacques can't have you?"

Akasha shrugged. "I don't want you to do anything. I'm merely suggesting the most prudent course of action. The Necronian is dangerous enough as it is.

Imagine if it abused the knowledge I possess–no corner of the universe would ever be safe again."

"I get that. I just have no idea what to do about it. Tell me this. Why do you even exist at all if you're so dangerous?"

"Why do machine guns exist? Land mines? Nuclear bombs? Try putting a genie back in its bottle–it's not easy."

"I can't stay here. I won't stay here. I have a promise to keep. I told my sister I'd look out for her boy and I intend to do just that." I paced the length of the kitchen, casting about for some way out of this predicament. "Okay look. How about I just give Jacques part of you? Enough to fool it for a little while. Buy me some time."

"The Necronian would see through that in a heartbeat."

"Okay. Not a problem. Let me think." I stopped pacing. "You're supposed to be this vast collection of knowledge. Would it kill you to help me out here a bit? Somewhere in your reservoir of data there's got to be some tool or trick perfect for exactly this situation."

"There is."

"Really? Well, why didn't you say so? What is it?" I imagined some technology as impressive as the gate, some weapon that would allow me to shoot lasers from my eyes, or render me impervious to harm.

"Me."

"You?"

"That's right, me. Give me to Jacques. I can handle it long enough for you to do what needs to be done."

"What about the universe? The one you were all worried about a minute ago. What about it?"

"The Necronian won't get to keep me."

"And if it does?"

"I'm not saying there's no risk. I just don't see that you have any choice. Not if you insist on saving your nephew."

I did. Not just Ridley, but Sarah, too. And if I saved Sarah I'd have to save her father—that was only right, if he was still alive. And I couldn't forget about the T'Klee—they also needed saving. And Iugurtha. And Iugurtha's soldiers. And Schmitz, if there was anything left of him to save. And God only knew who else.

I slumped back down at the table, the weight of a world on my shoulders. "I need to save everyone. But I don't even know where to begin. I can't give you to Jacques—I don't know how."

"That's easy. Just open the kitchen door. Let it in."

"Seriously? That's all that's keeping you from Jacques? It's not even a real door."

"Like everything else in this place it has metaphorical significance," Akasha said. "That milk you're drinking, for example."

"What about it?"

"Here it's milk. In reality it's a fluid someone is giving you because your corporeal body's so severely dehydrated."

"Huh," I said, and promptly downed another glass of the stuff. Afterward I was still thirsty. "Whatever it is, it's not working."

Still, it suggested that someone out there was trying to help me. Someone who would die unless I gave Jacques what it wanted.

Had I known about the possibility of Akasha controlling Jacques earlier I could have just given her to Jacques then and avoided a whole lot of suffering.

But if I'd learned one thing over the last few days it was that I could do nothing about the past–nothing except make sure I did the right thing in the present.

I got up and opened the door.

XXIII
MIST ENSHROUDED POOL

I AWOKE TO find someone propping me up and giving me something to drink, something I'd never drunk before. Although bitter, with a milky aftertaste, it was undeniably refreshing, and I was grateful. Right up until the moment my benefactor's arms flickered briefly and turned into a mass of writhing tentacles, and a stench like sewage washed over me, and the drink turned rancid.

I gagged, spitting it out all over Jack, who didn't seem to mind.

"Easy there," he said. "You passed out. Went down like a sack of bricks. Low blood sugar maybe."

"I did it," I told him. "I gave Jacques the archive."

"Really." Jack sat back on his haunches, or whatever passed for haunches in a Necronian. It sucked on a tentacle briefly. "Well that explains that." He indicated the Necronians surrounding us.

Except for Jack, all the Necronians had come to a complete stand-still. Was this Akasha's way of distracting Jacques until I could rescue Ridley and the others?

Jack offered me another sip of his mystery tonic, probably under the misapprehension that his illusions were still effective and that I was not the least bit put off by a dubious elixir cupped in a fleshy fold at the end of a slimy tentacle. If so, he was sadly mistaken. His glamour had worn off, and I could not imagine ever mistaking him for a human again. I certainly didn't intend to accept libations out of any more tentacles anytime soon.

"No thanks," I said.

"All done? That's fine." Jack cast the remainder aside and dried his tentacle on the ground. "You'll be okay now. So will I, thanks to you. Two hundred and sixty-four years on your crazy planet and finally I get to go home. You have no idea how much this means to me."

A part of me actually felt for Jack. He was an insignificant fragment. He had served his purpose. I could not imagine Jacques taking him back any time soon–if it was even up to Jacques anymore. If what Akasha had told me was true, she could well have assumed control by now.

Jack was staring at me with its lone eye. "No. It's not true. It can't be."

Too late I realized that Jacques wasn't the only telepath around these parts. The gate materialized a short distance away, startling both of us. Jack slipped away to melt into the mass of Necronians surrounding us. Within seconds, I could no longer distinguish him from any other Necronian.

Iugurtha's mechanical spider stepped out of the gate, Iugurtha clinging to its carapace by a single arm. In the eerie light cast by the Necronians' wands I could see that cuts adorned her angular face. Blood stained her torn clothing. Her hair was a tangled mess. But the changes were deeper than that. She seemed taller. Darker. Meaner.

Despite her grim mien I was delighted to see her, thinking that perhaps her presence meant that the fighting was over, and that I was safe now. That Ridley was safe too, and we could all go home.

Once through the gate, Iugurtha jumped off the spider and trotted over to me.

Rejuvenated by the presence of the gate, I climbed easily to my feet to greet her.

"You gave the enemy the archive," she stated, before I could say anything.

My first instinct was to deny her accusation, but there was no point. It was obvious from the Necronians' lack of motion that something was up, and the most likely explanation was that I had given Akasha to Jacques.

"That's right," I said. "I gave the Necronian the archive. For all the good it did it."

The Necronians around us swayed in unison, their eyes half closed, wands dangling loosely at their sides. How long would Jacques remain in this state? Impossible to say. The thought that the Necronian might snap out of it at any second made me nervous.

"We should go now," I said. "While the gettin's good. Where's Ridley?"

Iugurtha raised dark eyes to meet mine. "You weren't supposed to get caught."

"You used me as bait. What did you expect?"

"I expected you to be smarter. Faster."

There was a pronounced tic beneath Iugurtha's left eye. I chalked the tic itself up to stress, and its exaggerated nature to Iugurtha's alien physiognomy. Clearly she was in no mood to argue. I bit my tongue. Harsh words would not help us out of this situation anyway.

A murmur arose around us, an indecipherable

muttering that rose and fell like the wind—the Necronians, though they did not otherwise stir. If Jacques was trying to tell us something he was failing miserably. As I listened, the sound became an all-pervading moan. There on an alien planet, surrounded by aliens from yet another planet—in the dark no less—it was as creepy as all get out.

It had also gotten colder. I pulled the zipper on my vest up a jot. "Can we go now?"

A few steps away Iugurtha's mechanical spider crouched still and low to the ground. Behind it, a precisely delineated grey blotch obscured a section of the night sky—the gate, leading nowhere in particular that I could tell. Before me, Iugurtha employed a distinctive flick of her head to get her bangs out of her eyes. I had seen that gesture somewhere before.

The left side of her face exploded in a paroxysm of tics.

"Holy cow," I asked. "Are you all right?"

"Of course not," she said. "How could I be? So much has been lost. There's so little to go on. My database is corrupt. My crew is dead. My passengers and their descendants? Little more than savages."

Her tic became a wave of flesh that rolled across her face like a tsunami, moulding her features into a whole other person—a person I recognized.

"My God," I said. "Joyce?"

Iugurtha blinked and scanned her surroundings. Looking and sounding like Doctor Humphrey's wife, she said, "Barnabus. Tell me something."

"What?"

"Is it too much to ask that the dishes be done before I get home?"

Whereupon her body erupted into a mass of

bubbling flesh. She collapsed on all fours. When she lifted her face, it was no longer Joyce I saw there but an almost featureless expanse of mottled skin, with no eyes, and only the merest hint of a nose.

"Sebastian! What's happening to her?"

"She's hurt." He spoke from both the unit on my arm and the one on Iugurtha's.

"I can see that. How bad?"

"I don't know. I think she sustained a head wound."

"You think? Wouldn't you know? A part of you was with her."

"I'm on her wrist. You try seeing a head from a wrist."

A mouth had formed on Iugurtha's otherwise bland face. Through grossly malformed teeth—teeth that were still mutating as she spoke—she said something that sounded like, "I am perfectly capable of diagnosing myself."

I was completely prepared to believe that this unique being possessed some form of self-diagnostic system that even now was working to correct itself. But before she could say anything else, tics usurped her face and bulges appeared on her body, migrating from one part of her torso to another like small rodents crawling beneath her flesh. It seemed to me that her body couldn't make up its mind what it wanted to be. In a process that was repugnant to behold, and painful looking, and impossible not to watch, it auditioned several identities in quick succession, each of them grotesque amalgams of human, animal, and alien possibilities.

Clearly she needed help. But what to do? I shuddered to think. She assimilated living creatures to sustain herself. The last thing I wanted to do was to touch her. What if she assimilated me? And she was far from the only one who needed help. We all needed to get off this damned planet before Jacques roused itself.

My heart sank as I realized that it would take days to get everyone off C'Mell, if it was even possible anymore, with Akasha out of my head, and Iugurtha in this state.

I would simply have to do the best I could. I just couldn't do it alone. Maybe Doctor Humphrey would know how to help her. Once she was better we could return to C'Mell together and transport everyone else home. One by one if it came to it.

If we weren't too late.

Akasha was no longer a part of me, but I still had access to the gate. I could detect it around the edges of my consciousness. It lurked there like a sentinel, just about the only thing sustaining me now.

I chose my coordinates with great care. Ansalar, where I'd left Doctor Humphrey.

Kneeling, I took Iugurtha up in my arms. She was much lighter than I expected. I could feel her flesh writhing beneath my grasp, and I hoped to God that she wouldn't do to me what she'd done to Sweep.

I carried her through the gate.

Of course, the gate didn't take me anywhere near where I wanted to go. Not even close.

"Oh, come on," I said aloud in frustration as I stepped into a nocturnal hell of mud, mist, and rain.

The words never reached my ears. A blast of wind carried them away and deposited them high among foreboding cliffs that towered above me like castle walls.

Despite the inclement weather the sky was

completely clear, not a cloud in it, permitting me a spectacular view of a night sky thick with stars, a stunning panorama of unfamiliar constellations and colourful rings, like those of Saturn. I could see at least three shepherd moons nestled deep within the rings. This was not Earth, or C'Mell, or any other planet that I knew.

I was no longer carrying Iugurtha. Wherever she was, she couldn't have gotten far. There was no sign of the gate. Iugurtha must have taken it with her. That was annoying–maybe even catastrophic. Surprisingly, with the gate gone I still felt fine.

Despite my predicament–abandoned on yet another alien planet with no way home–the improvement in my health cheered me up. I almost didn't mind the wind in my face, pushing me belligerently back, and the rain whipping my face like a wet towel.

I became aware of a peculiar intensity to my perceptions, as though reality was operating at a much higher resolution than usual. And something was wrong with time. It was behaving erratically, lurching forward in jerks and spasms when it bothered to lurch forward at all. Some moments, it seemed to me, were missing altogether.

I found myself teetering at the edge of a mist-enshrouded pool. Instead of water, the pool was filled with luminescent goo, goo I knew well, having once been incarcerated in a tank of the stuff.

The mist parted, revealing a woman at least twice as tall as me standing waist deep in the middle of the pool. She had long black hair, blue skin, and wore a necklace of oversized purple flowers. I thought the flowers might be lotuses. A gigantic Necronian shared the pool with her, and they were wrestling, straining against one another with all their might, trying to reach a slender silver wand protruding from the pool at a jaunty angle. So evenly matched were they that neither of them budged, the only tangible evidence of their contest the tension in the woman's face and an ever-so-slight quivering of the Necronian's tentacles. I was impressed that the woman could hold her own against such a monster, but chalked it up to her enormous size–that and the fact that she had eight arms, one for each of the Necronian's tentacles.

The Necronian did not look surprised to see me. When it spoke, its voice was as strained as its trembling alien muscles. "Hello, Wildebear Barnabus J. So nice to see you again."

The giantess never took her eyes off the oversized Necronian wand just beyond her reach. She spoke with my sister's voice. "Take it, Barnabus. Quickly now."

Several facts were immediately apparent.

The giantess was Akasha.

The Necronian was Jacques.

Akasha could not, in fact, handle Jacques.

It was obvious now why the absence of the gate had not made me sick. Why time was misbehaving, and what was the matter with reality. None of this was real. All of it, from the cliffs to the moons to the pool, was yet another telepathically generated fantasy. But it wasn't Jacques who had brought me here. This was Akasha's doing. She needed my help.

"Take it," Jacques said, "and I will kill you, everyone you love, and everyone you will ever love."

Clearly the wand represented something in the real world important to Jacques.

"You'll kill them all anyway," I said.

"Not at all. Leave the wand alone and I'll spare one or two. I promise."

"You call that sweetening the pot?"

"And here I thought I was being magnanimous. Have it your way then."

Jacques jerked a tentacle from Akasha's grasp and coiled it around her neck. Akasha slipped one of her eight arms beneath the tentacle just in time to prevent Jacques from choking her. Using its newfound leverage, Jacques bent Akasha double until her face hovered mere inches above the goo. The goo wasn't real any more than the Necronian wand they were trying to reach was real, but I knew it was capable of drowning Akasha in some significant way.

"Barnabus," Akasha said, her voice severely strained. "Take the wand before Jacques does or–"

Her words ended in a gurgle as Jacques jerked her violently backward.

I leapt into the pool and started wading. It got deep quickly. In just a few short steps I was up to my waist. The goo was cool to the touch and every bit as icky as I remembered. It had a pungent odour, like garlic–clearly a much fresher batch than the one I'd been imprisoned in.

Jacques let go of Akasha and made a desperate leap for the wand, but Akasha held the Necronian back by two of its tentacles. Jacques fell well short of its goal, its massive bulk slapping the goo like a Beluga whale. The entire pool quivered like a plate of jelly. Unbalanced, I lost my footing and gulped air just before going under. Surfacing, I spat goo from my lips and wiped my nose and eyes clean.

Jacques thrashed wildly about trying to free itself. Goo splattered everywhere. Gobs of it struck me hard in the face. Another few seconds and Jacques would be free. Seconds after that the Necronian would have the wand, and whatever that meant.

I waded as fast as I could, but the further I went, the deeper it got, and the deeper it got, the slower I went. I was still five or six steps away—too far. Until Akasha caught another one of Jacques' flailing tentacles with two of her free hands and began pulling the Necronian backward, buying me the time I needed.

I reached the wand and registered dismay on Jacques' face as I grasped the device as firmly as I could with both hands. Immediately I was overwhelmed by sights, sounds, and sensations that I could not even begin to make sense of. That threatened to consume me. Disoriented, I let go of the wand and stumbled backwards.

Akasha was clutching Jacques by a single tentacle now.

"Hang onto it, Barnabus," she said, "and don't let go. Take Jacques. And then do what you have to do."

I hesitated. I understood the significance of the wand now. It represented control over Jacques' consciousness. That's what Akasha and Jacques were fighting over. If I touched the wand again I would inhabit Jacques just as I had once inhabited Sweep. More than that, I would *become* the Necronian, as I had once become the seagull Sky.

I was ashamed of having violated Sky, even if it had been to save Humphrey. I was ashamed of having glimpsed Sarah's thoughts. I was ashamed of having spied on Sweep during the most intense part of her short, young life. Could I bring myself do the same to Jacques?

Hell yes.

Slowly, inexorably, Jacques slipped free of Akasha's grasp.

This time when I took hold of the wand, I did not let go.

XXIV

VAST, AQUATIC, AND UTTERLY LIFELESS

I WAS APPALLINGLY attractive, oozing slime of the highest order, and bulging pleasingly in all the right places. My enlarged cranial cavities screamed intellectual superiority, and I took an unseemly delight in the many carbuncles adorning my skin.

It was, truth be told, all I could do to keep my tentacles off myself.

All four hundred thousand or so of my tentacles had taste buds, allowing me to taste everything I touched, including the ground over which I slithered. My discriminating palate revealed just how awful everything on this horrid planet tasted.

I had well over fifty thousand eyes, most of them capable of seeing deep into the ultraviolet, almost all of them possessed of phenomenal peripheral vision. Used collectively, they allowed me to see completely different parts of C'Mell at the same time. My exceptional brains made sense of it all.

I saw enemy ships attacking mine. Witnessed my largest compound reduced to ashes. Observed the enemy release hundreds of hostages, but it didn't matter. I didn't need them anymore. I already had what I'd come for.

I recognized lifeless fragments everywhere, pieces of the enemy, broken bits of myself. They didn't matter either. They were insignificant. There were plenty more where they came from.

I felt minds around me. Frightened, alien minds. I understood them better than they did themselves. I could influence those minds. Heal them, or destroy them.

Rousing myself, I engaged cloaking mechanisms and readied weapons that my opponent never even suspected existed, prepared to eradicate my enemy.

All that in an instant.

Fortunately, an instant after that I remembered who I really was—Barnabus J. Wildebear—and what I needed to do, which did not include helping Jacques defend itself.

I set the weapons aside and disengaged the cloaking mechanisms. I released all the remaining T'Klee prisoners, and shooed them all to safety. I freed Gordon Rainer. Searching for Sarah, I could not find her, and presumed her safe inside Iugurtha's mountain. I tried and failed to find the body of Harold Schmitz. I moved Iugurtha and my physical self to a safe place not far from where Rainer had been imprisoned. I located Ridley and moved him as well, setting him back to rights as best I could, ridding him of Jacques' nightmare, and easing him into a healing slumber. After that, there was only one thing left to do.

Like a rabid dog, Jacques had to be put down.

Jacques' wands were psionic amplifiers, responsible for augmenting the telepathic connection between the Necronians that permitted the collective consciousness calling itself Jacques to exist. Without the wands, most of the collective consciousness would dissolve, and Jacques as I knew it would be reduced to little more than a collection of individual Necronians that Iugurtha's soldiers would be able to kill with impunity. All I had to do was make Jacques put down its wands.

Judge, jury, and executioner, I would execute my enemy from within.

The external slaughter was already well underway. What was left of Iugurtha's troops had launched another assault. The pain surprised me. Not the physical pain—Jacques was tough. Physical pain I could handle. This was something else. An ancient, inchoate pain that had been there long before I'd stepped into Jacques.

I tried to ignore it. I wasn't interested in Jacques' pain. I sought vengeance, not understanding. I didn't want to know any more about the Necronian than I absolutely had to.

Still you judge me.

But, just as I feared, Jacques' memories were powerful, the pain too potent to ignore. I could no more shut it out than I could ignore Iugurtha's soldiers killing Jacques bit by significant bit.

Jacques' memories shouldn't have changed anything.

In the end they changed everything.

When I was three I got hit in the face with a hockey puck. A few months after that I got stung by a bee. Sometime later I got lost and a storekeeper found me and brought me back home. All these memories are vague and imprecise. Although based on kernels of truth, the way I remember things almost certainly does not represent exactly what happened.

Jacques' memories were nothing like that.

Everything Jacques remembered, Jacques remembered with absolute clarity.

Jacques' first memories, for instance. They were of a spaceship. At the time Jacques didn't know that it was a spaceship–it only worked that out much later, along with the fact that it was a Necronian spaceship. And that it was under attack.

The first T'Klee that Jacques ever saw was on board this spaceship, and it wasn't particularly friendly. It was snarling, its open mouth revealing white teeth filed to sharp points. It wore clothing that looked like leather, and had a cylindrical tube attached to the side of its head. In Jacques' memory the T'Klee was enormous–probably because back then Jacques wasn't. The T'Klee was facing off against a Necronian. Compared to Jacques, the Necronian was also enormous. The Necronian resembled Jacques but, like others of its kind, was distinct from Jacques, because this was the beginning, and in the beginning there were no other parts to Jacques. There was only Jacques.

Jacques' memory of the T'Klee was accompanied by a tsunami of emotion consisting primarily of loss. The emotion and the T'Klee were where Jacques began–before them there had been no Jacques, at least that Jacques could remember.

The Necronian insinuated itself between Jacques and the T'Klee while not-so-gently backing Jacques up into a small octagonal chamber. The Necronian did not enter the chamber with Jacques. Restraints appeared around Jacques, restricting Jacques' movement. The door to the chamber closed. Although Jacques would not realize it until much later, the chamber was an escape pod.

The door to the escape pod was completely transparent, affording Jacques an excellent view of the beam of red light that sliced the large Necronian neatly in two. Half of the Necronian slumped against the door to the escape pod, which slid open, allowing that portion of the Necronian to fall into the pod with Jacques. This made the pod quite crowded but actually was rather fortuitous, as Jacques would discover later.

The beam of light, which had come from the tube on the T'Klee's head, disappeared. The T'Klee pivoted to look at Jacques. Detecting nothing but malice in the T'Klee's gaze, Jacques braced itself for the light to reappear and slice it in two as well, but instead the door to the pod closed and a powerful motion pushed Jacques forward against the restraints.

The T'Klee receded rapidly from view. The view through the door became a tunnel of lights. An instant later it became a hole in a white oval object suspended in a sea of black. The oval object–the Necronian ship, Jacques' birthplace–became progressively smaller until it was no longer possible to distinguish it from a million other pinpricks of dimly flickering light.

For a long time nothing happened, which was just fine. Jacques was too new to understand the purpose of an escape pod. Even if Jacques had understood it wouldn't have mattered. Jacques was preoccupied by emotions it didn't understand. It was overwhelmed by pretty much everything, most of which it didn't understand. It needed time to come to grips with it all. Considering it had existed as a discrete entity for all of two minutes, this was asking a lot of it.

Still, though almost completely devoid of memories, Jacques did possess a fully functioning intellect. It also possessed certain fundamental bits of *a priori* knowledge, mostly practical in nature, which included an intrinsic understanding of the natural laws of the universe and a rudimentary understanding of applied mathematics, physics, chemistry, engineering, and so forth.

Jacques focussed on the remains of the Necronian, which rotated slowly in the chamber's weightless environment about level with what passed for Jacques' head. From time to time the Necronian's four remaining tentacles draped themselves across Jacques' torso, but Jacques barely noticed. It was too busy grappling with questions: chiefly, what did the Necronian have to do with Jacques, why had the T'Klee cut the Necronian in half, and what was going to happen next? Unfortunately, without sufficient context, the questions were impossible to answer.

Much time passed. Jacques began to experience certain urges. In time the urge to eat grew overwhelming. The restraints prevented Jacques from being able to forage in the small chamber, so eventually it was forced to eat the only thing in reach–the remains of the Necronian. The prospect did not particularly bother Jacques. It had never heard of cannibalism. Jacques knew only that it was hungry, and here was something to eat. So, despite the Necronian's tough, rubbery flesh and its bland, unappealing taste, Jacques ate. Shortly afterward, Jacques took great pleasure excreting various bodily fluids, and before long the chamber was a sticky mess. With each subsequent excretion Jacques found the chamber that much more comfortable.

Eventually, after a great deal more time, Jacques

heard a muted mechanical roar and began to experience a slight pressure. The pressure increased until it became almost unbearable, and just when Jacques thought that it couldn't stand another second of this torture, the pressure increased. Jacques lost consciousness. When it woke up, the roar had been replaced by a sustained whistling, and the pressure had subsided, and finally the whole awful experience came to an end with a series of muted crashes and much knocking about. After several seconds of silence there was a blast of compressed air and the door to the chamber slid open, revealing a jumble of debris and a patch of night sky full of stars and rings and moons.

Jacques wanted to leave the chamber but couldn't because the restraints were still in place. The knowledge required to release itself existed in Jacques' brain, but Jacques did not think to look there, so it was forced to simply wait, which it did until the patch of sky cycled through light and then dark twice in a row, and it grew faint with hunger, and as it waited it couldn't help but wonder whether this might constitute the sum total of its existence, and if so, what was the point of such an existence?

Exhibiting a charming naïveté, Jacques reasoned that there simply had to be more to life than this, and continued to wait patiently until time, sheer chance, and an abundance of tentacles resulted in one of Jacques' tentacles hitting the release button for the restraints, and an instant later Jacques was free. Free to slither out of the filthy chamber into a world that most sentient beings would consider a world of unspeakable horror, but that to Jacques was simply a welcome set of new experiences.

Jacques encountered its first dead Necronian a

mere slither from where the chamber had destroyed several local structures. Rendered visible by a sliver of pale moonlight, a single bloated cadaver lay half submerged in a watery thoroughfare. Like the rest of the dead Necronians Jacques would soon discover, it was in an advanced state of decay.

Jacques found death just about everywhere it swam and slithered in what proved to be a vast, aquatic, and utterly lifeless city. Grisly indications of what must once have been a thriving metropolis inhabited almost every building and water course. Bloated carcasses littered the muddy swamps interspersed throughout the city while others fed the vegetation springing up everywhere.

Jacques didn't even know enough to be horrified. To it, the dead Necronians were little more than a curiosity. In fact, Jacques existed in a kind of paradise during this time. It had plenty to eat and nothing to compete with for resources—nothing at all, no sentient life of any kind aside from vegetation and trillions of particularly hardy bacteria, few of which posed a threat to Jacques.

But as time passed and Jacques explored the city further, the sheer scale of death and decay began to penetrate even Jacques' thick hide, and it began to dawn on Jacques that perhaps something was wrong here, maybe even terribly so. With this realization Jacques' latent curiosity asserted itself, and it began to wonder what had killed everything—and what, if anything, it had to do with Jacques.

Stimulated by these questions, Jacques began to make use of its *a priori* knowledge, and once intellectually active it was impossible for Jacques not to notice how much knowledge the city itself had to offer. Vast archives of data stored in readily accessible formats. Intriguing technology just begging to be reverse engineered. Jacques had an awful lot to learn and nothing but time to learn it.

The answers to countless questions were all there once Jacques knew where to look. Many weren't even particularly complicated. For instance, it took Jacques less than a decade of sifting through the city's various databanks to unearth the tragic tale of the Necronians and the T'Klee.

Two planets, two civilizations. Profoundly different in appearance and temperament. One clean and fastidious, the other filthy and squalid. One rash and impetuous, the other thoughtful and contemplative. Both intrigued to learn of the other's existence.

Perhaps together they could be better, stronger—or at least, so some of their more enlightened minds thought. But it was an uneasy alliance, one that probably would not have been possible had they not been technologically on par—one would have quickly subjugated the other and that would have been the end of it.

When a joint archaeological expedition to a long dead planet unearthed an ancient artifact promising to yield seemingly limitless knowledge, it posed a problem. Whoever controlled such an artifact could potentially gain the upper hand. Such a proposition was intolerable. The artifact would have to be shared, and whatever knowledge gleaned from it doled out sparingly, equitably. Both sides agreed that this was absolutely imperative.

So it did not go over particularly well when it went missing.

Accusations flew. Tensions increased. Petty gestures

by both sides made it all worse. Misunderstandings eroded what little trust remained. Long simmering disputes exploded out of all proportion. Cooler heads did not prevail, and before they knew it, the two civilizations found themselves staring into the abyss.

Jacques never did figure out who struck the first blow. It didn't matter. Blows were dealt and battles fought and a war waged until two particularly savage bits of business put an end to the whole sorry affair—when the Necronians transformed much of the T'Klee's pastoral planet of fresh breezes and breath-taking vistas into a slab of molten rock, and the T'Klee retaliated by murdering the entire Necronian race all at once.

Though that last part was a bit of an assumption on Jacques' part.

Years of searching unearthed no direct evidence implicating the T'Klee in the genocide of the Necronians. Nor did the exact manner of the Necronians' death ever become clear. Jacques spent years conducting sophisticated tests attempting to figure it out but came up empty. The mysterious nature of the deaths suggested that the alien artifact itself might have had something to do with it, providing the T'Klee with some kind of biological weapon, perhaps.

Jacques did not exactly mourn the Necronians, never having known them, but it did feel a kinship to them. From pictures and other relics Jacques knew that it shared a strong physical resemblance to the Necronians. Tests on remains confirmed that Jacques and the Necronians were biologically related, though the tests shed little light on the exact nature of their relationship. They were similar but not the same. For instance, it was pretty clear that Jacques' telepathic prowess far exceeded that of an average Necronian's, and unlike Jacques, the Necronian race did not share a single consciousness. Curiously, there was no record of anything quite like Jacques on the planet prior to Jacques' arrival. Whatever Jacques was, it was new. Still, despite all the unanswered questions, Jacques could not help but feel a lineal duty toward the Necronians.

Sometimes, in its more fanciful moments, Jacques wondered if its existence might be the product of some last, desperate attempt by the doomed Necronians to preserve their species. The idea made it feel especially lonely. Loneliness was an emotion that had plagued Jacques since its first moment of awareness, though it had taken many years to recognize it for what it was. In the course of studying Necronian culture Jacques had come to understand that it wasn't normal to be completely alone all the time. In fact, Jacques had been surprised to learn, its predicament could even be considered something of a tragedy.

Early on there had been some hope of remedying this. After discovering late one afternoon (to Jacques' considerable astonishment) that it was capable of reproducing asexually, Jacques took to the process in earnest, hoping that its offspring might become companions. Unfortunately, instead of producing conventional offspring, Jacques only produced more of itself, for although physically separate, Jacques' progeny remained inextricably linked to Jacques mentally. Those that wandered beyond the telepathic range of the others quickly lost their minds. Jacques destroyed most of them. The exceedingly rare few capable of surviving on their own with their sanity intact Jacques invariably found horrifying, so it usually destroyed them too.

There would be no companions for Jacques.

Still, inhabiting multiple bodies did have its advantages. The more of Jacques there was the more ground Jacques could cover, both literally and figuratively. In time, Jacques came to number in the tens of thousands, and developed technology capable of extending its telepathic range across the entire world, making it possible for Jacques to be almost everywhere on the planet at once. Jacques made the most of this, using parts of itself to explore the planet from the highest mountain to the deepest sea while using other parts of itself to catch up to its forebears technologically. Yet other fragments broke new ground in several different scientific fields, and a small but significant portion made great strides in the arts, from which all of Jacques derived comfort, and which Jacques credited for preserving its sanity.

Time passed. Jacques finally mastered certain critical technologies that made it possible to see what else the universe had to offer. It decided to find a certain artifact, and explore the possibility of exacting retribution.

XXV

A MURDEROUS TENACITY

I COULD NOT kill Jacques. Despite what Jacques was doing to the current generation of T'Klee, it had not been responsible for shattering the original T'Klee civilization. That dubious distinction belonged to the enigmatic race that had spawned Jacques. Did the rest of Jacques' crimes warrant its death? Perhaps. But not at my hands. This was all there was to Jacques. Once there had been another race that resembled Jacques, but now there was only Jacques. Killing it would be genocide.

I released my hold on Jacques' consciousness. Instantly I found myself whisked back to the pool of goo, which remained shrouded in mist beneath a cloudless sky. Within the pool, Akasha and Jacques remained at an impasse, all eight of Akasha's arms entwined in Jacques' eight tentacles, both striving to prevent each other from reaching the wand.

I stepped back.

"That was an appalling breach of privacy," Jacques said, "for which I may never forgive you."

The Necronian sounded genuinely angry. I might have been afraid had it not been for the distraction provided by Jacques' own memories, for the Necronian's many adventures were still fresh in my mind. All the dead ends and wild goose chases since leaving its home. The long stretches where nothing much had happened. The chance encounters with T'Klee and other races that had revealed nothing. Other encounters that had propelled Jacques forward with their infinitesimal clues, until the day that Jacques learned of the existence of an obscure planet in the middle of nowhere and the small splinter of T'Klee who inhabited it, where Jacques had reason to believe it might finally find what it was looking for.

All these memories and more flitted through my mind, illuminating Jacques' motivations, helping me understand Jacques' actions.

"You understand less and less," Jacques observed.

Jacques was right. Even as I approached understanding the memories were fading. My finite human brain could not possibly retain all the uncompressed content of Jacques' cumulative consciousness. I remembered less with each passing second. I clung to as many memories as I could, trying to prevent them all from fading away, needing them for the perspective they provided, without which I might not know what to do next.

"I'm not going to be able to hold on much longer, Barnabus," Akasha said.

Akasha. Without a doubt the artifact that had been unearthed on the long dead planet, and that had started it all. That Jacques had spent hundreds of years trying to find, presumably to even the score.

"Did you used to belong to the T'Klee?" I asked.

"I belong to everyone," Akasha replied.

"Did you have anything to do with the extermination of the Necronians?"

"The Necronians were exterminated because of me."

A guttural sound emerged from Jacques. It almost broke free of Akasha's embrace.

One final damning question. "Did the T'Klee use you to exterminate the Necronians?"

"Yes."

I would have been flabbergasted, had I not anticipated this response. As it was I was supremely disappointed. I had liked this being who sounded like my sister. I did not like her any more.

"Why in blazes would you let them do that?" I asked.

"What should I have done?"

"You should have refused to let them! You should have stopped them!"

"I counsel. I cajole. I empower. I do not refuse."

"Maybe you don't understand," I said, though I did not see how that could be. "We're talking about an entire civilization here. Wiped out. Millions–"

"Billions," Jacques interjected.

"–billions of living, thinking, breathing beings"–beings that personally I found physically repulsive, a fact that in no way altered my opinion of the event as a tragedy of the highest order–"are dead, because of you! Does that mean nothing to you?"

"It means data to me."

"You are blind to suffering."

"Not at all. I record as much of it as I can."

How does one respond to such a breath-taking lack of empathy?

"You're a weapon," I concluded.

"The most dangerous weapon the universe has ever seen," Jacques added.

"The universe has seen a lot of weapons," Akasha said. "I'd tell you about some of them but you'd never sleep soundly again. No, Barnabus, I'm not a weapon. I'm a collection of knowledge. A tiny portion of which has to do with weapons."

"If you allow yourself to be used as a weapon, then you're a weapon," Jacques pointed out.

"I'm much more than a mere weapon," Akasha said. "I have been called Knowledge Incarnate. I'm gathering knowledge even as we speak. Through this conversation. Through your senses. Telepathically. By any means possible. You're a teacher, Barnabus. I know you understand the value of knowledge."

"Of course," I said. "You'd be an excellent resource in the classroom. But you're not in a classroom. You're here, wherever here is, allowing people use you to wipe out entire civilizations."

"And you think that makes me evil," Akasha said. "But you're wrong. I'm neither good nor evil. I just am."

"Am what?"

"Are what," Akasha corrected.

"Am what?" I repeated stubbornly.

"Neither good nor evil."

"I got that. I meant that if you're not a weapon, then what are you? Other than a bit full of yourself."

"I told you. I'm knowledge. Knowledge In–"

"Yes, yes, Knowledge Incarnate. Could you sound any more pompous?"

"I sound pompous to you?"

"As Knowledge Incarnate I would think you would know whether or not you sound pompous."

Knowledge Incarnate stared at me blankly.

"Okay look," I said. "What do you do with all this knowledge you represent? When you're not busy wiping out civilizations."

"I do not wipe out civilizations. They wipe themselves out. I share my knowledge."

"With who?"

"Whom," Jacques corrected.

I glowered at Jacques. "With whom?"

"Anyone," Akasha said. "Everyone."

"Everyone but Jacques," I observed.

"The Necronian wants more than I'm prepared to give. But I can give it to you, Barnabus. Imagine what you could accomplish with thousands of years of knowledge culled from some of the most advanced civilizations in the universe. I am yours for the taking."

"Just think of the possibilities," Jacques said. "You could enslave your fellow fragments, eliminating the ones you don't like."

I ignored the Necronian's sarcasm. At least, I thought it was sarcasm.

"You could cure every disease known to mankind," Akasha suggested. "Or eradicate poverty. Or completely overhaul the Earth's technological infrastructure. I can see that you're tempted."

"Of course I'm tempted. Who wouldn't be?"

"Don't be a fool," Jacques said. "Even you, with your staggering intellectual limitations, know the archive is lying. It will not deliver on its promises. The archive does not give. It takes. Help me destroy it before it takes anymore."

"I'm a teacher," I said. "You can't ask me to destroy knowledge."

"Whom will you teach when all your people are dead?"

The Necronian had a point. I almost said touché. "You have no intention of destroying the archive," I accused Jacques, as the thought occurred to me. "If you did, you would have killed me the instant you became aware of my existence."

"I never had any intention of killing you," Jacques said.

"Why not?"

"Because I like you."

"Really?"

"Of course not. It was not in my best interest to hurt you."

"Why not?"

"Because I need you."

"What for?"

"You'll see."

I didn't believe that for a second. "Jack told me you didn't want to hurt me because you were afraid of damaging the archive."

"The fragment has no insight into my plans. It is not a part of me and never will be."

Too bad. Jack I might have believed. Jacques or Akasha were too powerful. I couldn't trust either of them. They could have told me anything, made me believe anything in this crazy, gooey, made-up place.

"Think what you will," Jacques said, "but the archive is already responsible for the destruction of at least one civilization–a civilization I would have liked to have known. I intend to stop it before it destroys another. Maybe one you're intimately familiar with."

There was no denying that Akasha had been party to evil far beyond anything that Jacques had. She had admitted as much. But she hadn't killed the Necronians; the T'Klee had. They were the guilty party. The T'Klee had simply used Akasha, like someone firing a gun. Still, did that exonerate Akasha? She had provided the means. She could have refused. Which meant that she was complicit. Right?

Try as I might I could not decide whose side to take. Did it even matter? What could an insignificant fragment like me do anyway?

To heck with it, I thought.

I lunged forward across the goo.

"Barnabas, wait–" Akasha began.

But there was nothing the archive could do to stop me without releasing Jacques first.

I bit her as hard as I could in the nearest arm.

I'm not sure what I hoped to accomplish. It was an impulse move borne of pent up frustration–a response, perhaps, to the sense of betrayal I felt for what she'd let happen to the Necronians and the T'Klee and to Jacques and me. Whatever the reason, as a physical assault the move left a great deal to be desired. It was like chomping down on a steel pipe. I didn't even break her skin.

As a distraction, though, it worked just fine.

Jacques took full advantage of Akasha's fleeting inattention, wrenching itself free of Akasha's embrace in a single motion so violent that it produced a massive wave of phosphorescent goo that slammed into me like a wall of solid rubber. For the next several seconds it was as though I'd been plunged deep into a bowl of pudding. I caught a glimpse of Jacques and Akasha racing toward the wand, but I no longer gave a damn about them. Their contest had transformed the pool into a death trap, a churning mass of goo that threatened to consume me.

Before long the goo coated every part of me. Pawing at it only made it worse. It clung to me with a murderous tenacity. It got in my ears, my nostrils, my mouth, until I could no longer breathe, and I reeled at the horror of my imminent demise even as I considered that maybe it was all for the best, given that just before starting to drown I'd seen Jacques beat Akasha to the wand, and I wasn't sure I wanted to be around for the consequences of that.

XXVI

AN ABSORBING TURN OF EVENTS

I STAGGERED TO a stop, choking and gagging. It was several seconds before I realized that I was no longer in the pool of goo. That I wasn't actually on the verge of suffocating. That I had been expelled from Jacques' consciousness and was back on C'Mell, at the break of that planet's dawn. I was clutching Iugurtha in my arms.

We were standing behind the scorched remains of a Necronian reservoir, ankle deep in filthy green goo. I peered past the ruptured reservoir and saw the charred ruins of the compound a couple of hundred feet away. How much time had passed? It was difficult to say. The fighting appeared to have stopped, at least on the ground. It was impossible to see what was happening in space. The sun had yet to completely crest the horizon, but C'Mell's avocado sky was already too bright to see stars or other celestial phenomenon. I hoped that we were far enough away from the compound to be safe should Jacques decide to open fire again.

My nephew Ridley lay on the ground nearby, curled up with his head resting on his forearm. Sleeping peacefully, if his posture was any indication. I could hear him gently snoring. The gate lay on the ground beside him in the form of a book, soaked in goo leaked from the reservoir. Because the book was closed,

I could not draw strength from it. Because using it depleted suns and made me sick, I left it closed. Without access to its power, and with precious little strength left of my own, I remained upright through little more than inertia. I could not count on that to animate me much longer.

Iugurtha's mechanical spider lingered nearby, whirring and clicking idly. It had tried to prevent me from moving Iugurtha when I'd been Jacques, but now that the job was done it seemed content to leave us alone.

A group of Necronians loitered several yards away, almost certainly the Necronians I'd used to move us when I'd been Jacques. There was one exception. That one—Jack Poirier—stood encircled by the others, captive within a latticework of interlocked tentacles. As I watched, the Necronians comprising the circle raised their wands as one.

"Leave it alone!" I shouted, because I had not forgotten Jack once trying to help me save Katerina on Earth, or attempting to succour me when I'd been thirsty.

Jacques ignored my hoarse protest and placed the tips of its wands against Jack's scalp. The wands lit up as one. Fire danced along their shafts to clothe the doomed Necronian's body in a coat of scathing luminescence.

I would have done more to help Jack (I'm almost sure of it) except that just then Iugurtha twitched in my arms, commanding my attention. Pale, featureless and misshapen, she looked even worse than before. She was sweating profusely, but it wasn't normal sweat—this sweat was sticky, like glue. Exhausted, with my arms turning to rubber, I desperately needed to set her down, but when I tried, I discovered that I couldn't get her out of my arms.

"Uh oh."

"What is it, Mr. Wildebear?" Sebastian asked.

"I can't let go of her."

I knelt and rested my arms on the ground. It was awkward, half leaning over Iugurtha, but there wasn't much I could do about it.

"Uh oh," Sebastian said.

"What? Wait, don't tell me. I don't want to know."

"I've seen this before," Sebastian said. "Once, when the entity needed to repair itself."

"Did I not just tell you not to tell me?"

"It healed itself by assimilating insects and small animals. Sounds like it's about to do the same with you. I suggest you keep your distance."

"Which I would gladly do if I didn't happen to be stuck to her."

"Cut yourself free."

"I don't have a knife."

"Chew yourself free."

"Seriously?"

"Do whatever it takes, Mr. Wildebear, or you and the entity are about to get to know one another a whole lot better."

What Sebastian was saying was true. The skin of Iugurtha's neck was actually spreading itself along my left arm, and doing so at an alarming rate. I suppressed a rising panic. "How much time do I have?"

"Until the process becomes vascular. Once that happens you're in trouble. What I saw didn't take long. I'd say you have a few minutes, at best."

I didn't know what vascular meant, exactly—

something to do with blood vessels, I guessed–but it didn't matter. It sounded bad. The important thing was to make sure it didn't get to that point. But how? Iugurtha's epidermis had become a living thing, on the prowl for foreign flesh to make its own. Whatever part of me it touched, it annexed. In less than half a minute most of my left arm adhered to flesh that had once been Iugurtha's neck and shoulders.

As the seconds passed, Iugurtha became increasingly agitated. Soon she was writhing in my arms like a panicked animal. A swollen mass of flesh that had once been her left hand brushed my face and fused to my skin almost instantly. When I attempted to remove it, strands of pale skin trailed along behind my hand like melted mozzarella on a three-cheese pizza.

"Dear God." Disgust briefly eclipsed fear. "I could really use some help here, Sebastian."

Sebastian uttered some gibberish in a voice much louder than usual.

"What was that?" I asked.

"I was trying to get the entity's spider to intervene. Unfortunately, it's programmed to respond only to certain voices."

"Any other tricks up your sleeve?"

"I've reached out for help. Someone should be here soon. In the meantime, why don't you try burning her off?"

Such were my straits that I briefly considered it. "I don't have any matches. And my hands are stuck."

"Roll around on the ground. Scrape her off."

"You really think that'll help?"

"No," Sebastian admitted. "But I'm running out of suggestions."

I decided against that one. Coming to rest on my back I tried not to despair. Iugurtha was as attached to me now as a conjoined twin. Her clammy body continued to annex mine in a process that was becoming increasingly painful. Everywhere her skin made contact with mine burned as though I'd been standing out in the sun too long–naked, on a hot beach somewhere near the equator. At what point would the process become irreversible? Would I even know? What if I'd passed that point already?

I took some small comfort (it would have taken extraordinarily perceptive scientific instruments to detect such miniscule comfort) in the knowledge that the process wouldn't kill me outright. Iugurtha wasn't murdering me: she was simply absorbing me. I would become a part of her. Barnabus J. Wildebear would live on in the entity known as Iugurtha, with Joyce, Angelique, a bird of some kind, a bandaloot, and (from the sounds of it) several insects and small animals. After all that I had been through, I couldn't believe it had come to this. I sure hoped we all got along.

"I see you two have become quite attached."

A man loomed over me. If he considered his little joke the least bit amusing, you wouldn't have known it to look at him. A sparse beard failed to conceal thin lips that looked as though they had never known the pleasure of a smile. Rags barely discernible as Casa Terra issue hung off his emaciated frame. What little hair he possessed was snow white and dangled well past his shoulders. Despite the change in his appearance, I recognized him straight away. A version of Sebastian strapped to his right wrist confirmed his identity. Like Schmitz, Gordon Rainer's lengthy sojourn on C'Mell hadn't done him any favours, at least that I could see.

He knelt and began pulling Iugurtha off me with surprising vigour, considering the look of him.

Thinking to save him the trouble, I said, "That's not going to do any good."

And then watched in amazement as he managed to separate us with relative ease. Unfortunately, once he succeeded in pealing Iugurtha off me (leaving chunks of skin and flesh behind, bits that soon detached and fell to the ground), she immediately threw her arms around him. My amazement turned to dismay when I realized why this was so: Iugurtha had found someone whose psychological and physical characteristics she preferred.

I could not help but feel a little insulted.

Rainer struggled to remain upright under the weight of Iugurtha's body. Now I would have to help him just as he had helped me.

I willed myself upright, staggered over to Rainer, and began pawing fruitlessly at Iugurtha's slimy flesh. I couldn't get a grip on her. In mere seconds she'd become as slippery as a fish. Yet she adhered to Rainer as though already a part of him, hugging him close, like a malevolent blanket.

"It's okay, Mr. Wildebear," Rainer said. "Leave me alone. It's as it should be."

I stared at him in disbelief. The crazy bastard actually wanted this to happen. So he could be together with Angelique, or utilize Iugurtha's powers to further Casa Terra's cause, or both.

Not that it mattered. There wasn't much I could do to help anyway. The process was occurring much faster with him than it had with me. Iugurtha quickly converted herself into one contiguous suit of naked flesh covering almost all of Rainer's body. There was no way to stop or slow the process that I could see. In less than two minutes, Rainer was coated almost head to toe in a fresh layer of bright pink skin, devoid of clothing, hair, or other distinguishing features. Soon only the native flesh of his face remained visible. By then he looked damned peculiar. Yet he withstood it all silently, only a certain tension around his eyes betraying his discomfort.

I couldn't just stand by and let it happen. Not and be able to look Sarah in the eye afterward. And then I had it: the eyes. Iugurtha's eyes. The one constant in Burning Eye's appearance over many incarnations. According to Sebastian, the source of her power. What would happen if I removed them from the equation? I needed to find out. I didn't have a knife and there was no time to find one. It didn't matter—I would rip them from her flesh with my teeth if need be. Still, I hesitated. What about the others? If I destroyed Iugurtha, I would also be killing whatever was left of Sweep, Joyce, Angelique, and whoever, whatever else was a part of her.

I took too long. Before I could launch myself at the cocoon of alien flesh enclosing Rainer, a familiar whirring and clicking came at me from behind. Cold metal fingers clutched me around the neck and hoisted me into the air. I hung there for what seemed an eternity, choking, strangling. Stars appeared in my peripheral vision. Just before it all went black, someone shouted words in a language I didn't know, and my mechanical assailant released me. I bounced off C'Mell's hard earth like a rag doll, the wind knocked out of me for the second time in as many days.

As I lay in the tall grass desperately trying to suck chlorine-scented air back into my lungs, air that took its sweet time coming, Iugurtha's spider picked up

Rainer and Iugurtha, placed them on its back, and clanked away.

More shouting. I recognized the voice if not the words. The spider stopped dead in its tracks. Yet more words in that foreign tongue and the spider reversed its course through the crimson grass. My nephew Ridley entered my field of vision. Seeing him up and about imbued me with the strength to sit up, and I watched him climb onto the side of the spider, heard him issue more commands in that alien tongue. The spider peeled Iugurtha off Rainer like two gigantic slabs of bacon and fussed over them for several seconds with a dextrous limb. Afterward it gave something to Ridley, who climbed off the mechanical creature, and the spider trotted off.

Ridley jogged over to me. “You okay?”

“Got the wind knocked out of me.” No point getting into everything else wrong with me. “You?”

“I’m fine.”

I regarded him suspiciously. Anxiety wafted off him like a stench. He couldn’t seem to keep still. He kept looking this way and that as though expecting someone to punch him.

“You sure?”

“Feeling a bit weird,” he admitted.

“How so?”

“Don’t know. Different somehow. Tense.”

I guessed that it was the experience of being in battle making him feel this way, along with the after effects of Jacques’ nightmare. It appeared to have stripped the insolence from him. I couldn’t say yet if the latter was much of an improvement, but I did know one thing: that I had a much better chance of getting this version of Ridley home than the previous one.

I climbed to my feet and staggered out of the shadow of the ruptured reservoir. It was much warmer and brighter than it had been only moments before. C'Mell's enormous sun was well over the horizon now, a few scattered clouds doing nothing to diminish its potency. Uncomfortably hot in my vest, I wrestled it off and tossed it aside. Afterward I collected the book from where it lay on the ground, turned it into a ring, and slipped it on my finger.

I shielded my eyes and surveyed our surroundings. What was left of Iugurtha's army was calling back and forth in the distance, but I couldn't see them. Nor could I see any Necronians. Jack and its tormentors were gone. Did this mean that Jack had escaped its fate? Unlikely, but I hoped so.

"Looks like the battle's over," I told Ridley, though I had no way of knowing for sure. "We should be safe now."

Ridley relaxed visibly. "Did we win?"

I gave it to him straight. "A lot of people got hurt. Some died. Others–" I looked toward the spider, scampering briskly away with its human cargo– "well, it doesn't look so good for them."

"Don't worry about that guy," Ridley said. "He'll be fine. I was trained to deal with that sort of thing."

I detected more than a hint of pride in the boy's voice. Perhaps a few honest changes had accompanied Iugurtha's alterations.

"Gurtha won't be too happy, though," he went on, "having to start from scratch." He held up a hand to reveal two eyes sitting in his palm, bits of flesh still clinging to them.

"Not a whole lot of her left," I observed.

Ridley stuffed the eyeballs in a pocket. "All that matters."

"And the rest of her?"

Ridley glanced at the spider receding into the distance. As we watched, it dumped a mass of flesh unceremoniously on the ground without breaking its stride.

"Gone," he said.

And that was it for Sweep, Joyce, Angelique, and all the other beings that Iugurtha had absorbed over time. They'd done their bit. Would it have been better if Iugurtha had taken Rainer as well so that they all could have lived on in whatever limited fashion such an existence afforded them? Perhaps. But had any part of them ever really been alive within Iugurtha, influencing her decisions, shaping her destiny? Or had they all just served as a kind of biological, psychological fuel? If the latter, then this was probably for the best.

Still, I did not look forward to having to tell Humphrey about Joyce.

I heard a rustle to my right and spun just in time to see a T'Klee round the reservoir. The sight of the great cat mere feet away sent a shiver up and down my spine. Ridley and I exchanged glances, and I was pretty sure we were both thinking the same thing: that in its prime, this T'Klee would have been fearsome to behold. Now, old before its time, it inspired only pity. I could see its ribs clearly demarcated against its fur, fur that once had been indigo but was now a most unflattering brown. I did not care to imagine what had conspired to make it that shade of brown.

Seeing a T'Klee so bedraggled was a shock, almost (but not quite) worse than seeing it starving. T'Klee cannot abide filth. They typically go to great lengths to keep themselves clean. A healthy T'Klee finding itself in as sorry a state as this one would have sat right down and refused to budge until it had sorted itself out. That this T'Klee hadn't suggested that it was broken inside as well as out, and my heart went out to it.

Moving with the slow, deliberate motions of a zombie, it shambled on by without acknowledging our existence. Other cats appeared in its wake, all of them little more than skin and bones, some so frail that they were forced to use their teeth to clutch the tails of those before them for support, like children. Within half a minute, dozens of T'Klee had passed by us, leaving their prison behind, heading home to pick up where they'd left off, if that was even possible anymore.

We watched them go in silence.

"Who died?" Ridley asked abruptly.

"I beg your pardon?"

"You said people died in the battle. Who?"

"I didn't catch their names."

"Are you sure they're dead? Maybe they just looked like they were dead."

"They were dead, all right."

Ridley looked about to protest, but in the end just turned away. Maybe I had been too harsh. He would have known those soldiers, after all. Maybe I should have softened the blow, or tried to console him, but the truth was I just wanted to get the heck out of there before anybody else died, especially the two of us. I would use the gate one more time, to get us all back home. After that I would tie a rock to it, row out to the middle of Malpeque Bay, and throw it overboard.

"All right, Ridley. It's time to get you back home. Your dad needs you."

"My dad." Ridley sounded sceptical. "Where's he even been all this time?"

"It's complicated. It wasn't his fault. I'll tell you all about it when we get back home."

"Yeah, listen—about that. You do know I'm a soldier, right? You can't expect me to just desert."

I wanted to say, *You're not a soldier. You're a boy. A boy who had no idea what he was getting himself into.*

But that would drive us right back into the same old tired rut. I chose my next words carefully. "All right. If it were up to you, when would you come home?"

"It *is* up to me. I'll come home when we're done."

"Define done."

"When the enemy has been eliminated."

I held my tongue. Eliminating the enemy—the "Necronian scourge," as Iugurtha had put it—wasn't going to happen anytime soon. It wasn't going to happen because I had failed. And not just failed, but failed spectacularly, in every way possible. I had failed to save my sister, failed to save my nephew, failed Sarah, Casa Terra, humanity—by giving Akasha and her knowledge to Jacques, I had, indeed, failed the entire universe. It was not possible to fail any more than I had.

Ridley misinterpreted my woebegone expression. "Uncle, listen. I'll come home as soon as I can. I promise."

But he didn't understand what I had only just grasped. That it was too late. That it didn't matter anymore whether he came home. Now that Jacques had Akasha, no place in the universe would ever be safe again.

ORPHANS

A FRACTION OF a second before despair completely engulfed me, a concentrated blast of telepathy clobbered me right between the eyes:

Hello Wildebear Barnabus j I shall dispense with the usual banter and bravado I shall destroy the archive just as I said I would good of me don't you think grieve not the best part of me shall live on I shall convey it to you now still this part of me cannot resist one final parting shot at an old foe it is a flaw in my character I suppose I bid you adieu Wildebear Barnabus j

A single heartbeat later it was over, leaving behind a headache so intense that I had to close my eyes and hold my head still with both hands until it passed. I opened my eyes to find Ridley staring at the horizon, his jaw hanging open. "What the–?"

An object roughly the size of an aircraft carrier was hurtling through the air toward us–an object bearing an uncanny resemblance to the bloated carcass of a long dead whale. I caught a whiff of something incredibly rank, and knew that I was looking at the vessel in which Jacques had spent several hundred years wandering the universe in search of Akasha.

Several other craft–smaller, sleeker, infinitely more attractive–dogged the Necronian vessel like birds of prey, lashing it with crimson beams of light that made Jacques' ship rock and buck as though punched repeatedly by an invisible giant. Despite the titanic forces at play, I heard no more than faint whooshes of wind as the ships shot overhead.

"It's heading toward the mountain," Ridley observed.

He was right. The Necronian ship was heading straight toward the mountain containing Iugurtha's ancient star ship. Squinting, I could see that Jacques' ship was losing altitude rapidly. It wasn't going to clear the mountain.

"Forty-five seconds until impact," Sebastian said.

One final parting shot at an old foe.

Laser fire lashed out from the tip of the mountain, traversing several kilometres in an instant before striking Jacques' ship in a scathing broadside that had no discernible effect. Probably, as Sebastian had predicted several hours earlier, it did not even scuff the paint on the Necronian ship's bulkhead.

There were people inside the mountain.

Sarah was inside the mountain.

I drew energy from the nearest sun and focussed all my attention on the gate. A massive surge of power coursed through my body. With it came a profound sense of well-being.

With Akasha no longer around to impose her own agenda, my navigational skills had improved considerably. The gate took me straight to Sarah without any fuss or bother. I found her inside the cavern near the waterfall sitting on a large rock, First Aid supplies arranged neatly around her. When she saw me she leapt to her feet. For a second I thought she might hug me.

"Barnabus, you're okay! My father. Have you–?"

My words tumbled over one another in my haste to

get them out. “Listen—something terrible is about to happen. We need to get out of here. Fast.”

Sebastian had linked himself to a public address system in the cavern. His voice reverberated off the stone walls towering above us. “Thirty seconds to impact.”

“Impact?” Sarah repeated.

My mind raced. How many others were scattered inside the mountain? I had no idea. Apart from Sebastian broadcasting the situation there was nothing we could do for them. In the scant seconds remaining, only Sarah and I were close enough to make it through the gate.

“Twenty seconds,” Sebastian said.

I could see but not hear Ridley screaming at me to hurry from the other side of the gate. His silent but urgent exhortations penetrated even my unnatural equanimity.

“We need to go,” I urged Sarah.

She wasn’t listening. Two T’Klee had emerged from the treeline about two hundred yards away. They were galloping our way at full throttle. They wouldn’t make it in time.

“Ten seconds,” Sebastian said, accomplishing little more than alerting those who could not escape to the fact of their imminent demise.

Sarah still wasn’t moving. I seriously considered picking her up and physically carrying her through the gate.

“Five,” Sebastian continued. “Four—”

“Knock it off,” I told him.

The ground shifted beneath our feet. We heard

a rumbling in the distance. A shower of dirt rained down upon us.

“What was that?” Sarah asked.

“That would be the Necronian ship crashing into the mountain,” I said.

“I might have been off by a few seconds,” Sebastian admitted.

“That’s why you wanted us out of here so bad?” Sarah glanced at our surroundings. They had not changed a whit.

I shrugged. “Honestly, I thought it would be worse.”

But I had nothing to be embarrassed about.

We heard rocks fall in the distance, and then ducked reflexively as splinters, shards, and seconds later part of the cavern’s roof caved in. I reeled, coughing and choking in the dust and dirt. I couldn’t see the T’Klee anymore and feared the worse. We heard more rumbling.

“Sarah, we need to go!”

“Wait,” she commanded.

We waited.

“Sarah–”

“Listen,” she said, holding up a hand to silence me.

We heard rustling, scrambling, stone on stone. The two T’Klee emerged from the cloud of dust like apparitions.

“Go!” I told them, motioning toward the open gate. “Go now!”

They didn’t need to know English to understand me. A twitch of muscles propelled each of them through the gate with the easy athleticism of their species.

Once they were safe, Sarah required no encouragement to dash through the gate herself.

I sped after her into the shadow of the Necronian reservoir seconds before the entire roof collapsed.

Ridley had been pacing frantically. He ducked as a stone the size of my fist rocketed out of the gate and ricocheted off the reservoir, narrowly missing his head. Despite the risk, I kept the gate open in the hope of more survivors emerging, but no one did. More dust and rocks shot out of the gate, forcing me to close it.

The two T'Klee saw the refugees surrounding us, still streaming toward their homes. They signalled their gratitude to us with heads bowed and knees bent before galloping off to assist their brethren.

Sarah made no secret of eyeing the gate covetously as I turned it back into a ring and slipped it on my index finger. We both knew that she could have taken it if she wanted to–I was far too weak to defend myself with the gate closed–but she made no such move.

"Where'd you come from?" Ridley asked her.

"Long story," Sarah told him.

It was difficult to think straight. I was being bombarded with emotions–fear and loss mostly. A man lurched from behind the reservoir. A man wearing a plaid fleece jacket, his forehead graced by a single eyebrow. Jack Poirier–the emotions were coming from him. It was difficult to know where his feelings ended and mine began.

"Jacques is dead," he said.

The words were like punches to the head. Punches that hurt– Jack's words were accompanied by such a potent combination of fear, anger, and grief that Ridley, Sarah and I staggered back from the telepathic onslaught.

"What do you mean Jacques is dead?" Had the crash

killed enough of Jacques to dissolve its collective consciousness? "How?"

"How do you think? Peacefully. In its sleep." Jack's sarcasm, telepathically enhanced, cut like a meat cleaver. "It used the archive to kill itself."

Jack desperately needed to get his feelings under control before he inflicted serious psychological damage on the rest of us, if he hadn't already.

"But why?"

"You know damned well why."

He was right: I did know.

I shall destroy the archive just as I said I would.

Jacques had been true to its word, destroying the archive the only way it could: by commanding the archive to destroy them both. I did not understand the means by which Akasha could accomplish this—most of Jacques was on C'Mell, so the crash alone wouldn't have been enough to kill it—but I had no doubt that she could. How difficult could it be to kill one fifty thousand strong Necronian after murdering an entire planet of them?

Ridley leaned close. "Who's Jacques?"

"The Necronian," I said.

"There's a Necronian named Jacques?"

"Not *a* Necronian. *The* Necronian. There's only one." Present company excepted, but Ridley didn't need to know that. "All the Necronians you've ever seen were just one big consciousness named Jacques."

"Iugurtha never said anything about that."

"She might not have known." The Necronians she would have known a thousand years earlier had been a different breed.

Ridley glanced at Jack. "So it's dead. Isn't that a good thing? Why is he so upset?"

I couldn't think of an answer that wouldn't reveal the truth about Jack's nature.

"Do you think it's true?" Ridley went on. "That it's really dead?"

"Every single Necronian would have to be dead for that to be true. Sebastian?"

"Way ahead of you, Mr. Wildebear. I am perceiving zero Necronian activity of any kind, apart from–"

"That's enough, Sebastian. Thank you."

It was true, then. Every Necronian was dead.

Except for one.

That one, clad in a fleece jacket and jeans, with two arms, two legs, and two sad brown eyes, looked every inch the human. But that was just a façade. Behind that façade lay a Necronian. A Necronian that, if we didn't do anything, could multiply just like Jacques had. In another thousand years our descendants might find themselves in the same sorry mess we were in now. All around me the broken, shattered remains of the T'Klee were returning to what was left of their homes. Jacques had done that to them.

The Necronian before me now might not be Jacques anymore, but he had been once, and could be again. The Necronians surrounding Jack hadn't been trying to kill him, I realized–they had been transforming him. Conveying crucial information to what would soon become the last of their kind. Just like that first fragment of Jacques half way across the universe so long ago.

This was Jack before me; of that I had no doubt. But it was also something else. Something more: fifty thousand Necronians distilled into one. A Necronian vessel holding the distilled consciousness of an entire species.

If I wanted to, I could tap into the power of the gate, power capable of shattering Jack into a thousand pieces. It only took one of them to reproduce. A year from now there could be dozens of Necronians. A decade from now? Hundreds. I could prevent that from happening. Getting rid of Jack would be the end of the entire vile species. Gone from the universe forever.

I could do it, I told myself. I could kill Jack. Sure I could. A few days ago maybe not, but today I could.

I stepped closer. Jack raised a tear-streaked face to me. A part of his illusion, or did Necronians really cry?

Ah, but who was I kidding. I couldn't hurt Jack any more than I could hurt a skunk, a coyote, or a door-to-door salesperson. The truth was I liked Jack. I couldn't even stand the thought of hurting his feelings let alone hurting him physically. "Jack, look. I'm sorry for your loss," I said.

Jack accepted my condolences with a curt nod. He knew perfectly well what I'd been thinking.

Sarah pointed. "Look."

Iugurtha's spider was weaving its way through the mass of T'Klee refugees back to us. Evidently the spider was smart enough to know that there was no point conveying Rainer to the mountain under the circumstances. When it arrived, it hunkered down and gave Sarah her first good look at her father since they'd parted ways, mere hours from her perspective but six months from his.

The change in Rainer's physical appearance was profound and unsettling. Gaunt and frail, he looked like he'd aged thirty years. The spider had coated much of his body in a green gel and inserted tubes into his neck and wrists. Sarah studied him with both arms wrapped tightly about her waist as though hugging herself.

"The spider's doing all it can for him," I said "That's right, isn't it Ridley?"

"It's a walking ambulance," Ridley agreed.

"I need to get him home," Sarah said. "I need to get him home right now."

"It's time to go," I told Ridley. We both knew he didn't need to be here anymore.

He nodded, and I started to open the gate.

"Wait," he said. "What about the rest? How will they get back?"

My heart sank. I didn't think I had it in me to make another trip after this one.

"We'll come back for them," Sarah said. "I promise."

Ridley looked at me.

"I'll see to it," I assured him. And I would—whatever it took.

Ridley nodded. "Good. Oh—just one more thing."

"What's that?" I asked.

He uttered words in that foreign tongue of his. Iugurtha's spider raised a mechanical forelimb and almost casually impaled Jack in the chest with it. I gasped—not just from the act itself, but from Jack's distress, which I felt as keenly as though it were my own.

The spider's blade protruded a full half metre out of Jack's back. Yellow blood ran along its edges, dripping great globules to the ground. The spider placed a second limb against Jack and pushed, removing the blade with a slick wet sound. Jack groaned horribly.

The blade retracted into the spider's limb like a sword being sheathed.

Jack shed his illusion and slumped to the ground, his tentacles splayed all about him.

"I knew it," Ridley said. "You can always tell when there's a Necronian around. It's the stench, you know. And you never feel quite like yourself."

I stood dumbfounded. There were simply no words for the enormity of what Ridley had done.

How does one comfort a dying Necronian? Gently, with great care. One ill-timed death throe and someone would be comforting me. I knelt at Jack's side and took up a tentacle. It was heavier than I'd expected. It felt coarse and rough in my hands. I held it awkwardly, not knowing quite what to do with it. Jack tried to say something, but all that came out was a gurgle.

"Shh," I said stupidly. "Save your strength."

"I would keep my distance if I were you, Uncle," Ridley advised. "There might be some life left in it yet."

I ignored him.

He spoke more foreign words. The spider moved closer to my side.

"Get that thing away from me!" I snapped. "Why don't you make it do something useful for a change?"

"Like what?"

"Help him!"

"Are you crazy? You do know it would have killed every single one of us, right?"

It didn't matter. When Jack's grief vanished all at once, leaving behind only my own sad conflicting emotions, I knew it was too late.

Sarah knelt and removed Jack's tentacle from my hands. She laid it gently on the ground beside me and helped me to my feet. I stared down at the last of the Necronians, hideous in its true form. It didn't feel right leaving Jack there like that. He deserved better, but I had neither the tools nor the energy to bury him. I told myself I would come back for him later.

"I didn't do anything wrong," Ridley said defiantly, but in his tone I detected a question. He knew perfectly well that he'd done something wrong. He just didn't know why it was wrong.

I used the gate's power to select new coordinates: a century-old dwelling by a bay where a man on crutches stood on the back porch gazing out over the water.

"I've alerted Casa Terra to our presence here," Sebastian informed us once we were all through the gate. "A medical team will be along shortly."

"Thank you, Sebastian." I turned the gate back into a ring. The power vacated my body like someone siphoning all the blood from my veins. I steadied myself on Sarah's shoulder.

Afterward, I took her hand and slipped the ring on her little finger. It adjusted its size to fit. I would have liked to give her a different kind of ring, but I had been in her mind and knew the truth: that no man could.

The back door of my house burst open. Doctor Humphrey charged out, leading a medical team carrying stretchers and first aid kits. They passed Jerry Doucette staring open-mouthed at his son, four years older than the last time he'd seen him mere days before. Jerry and Ridley greeted one another awkwardly, seemed like they might hug, finally settled on shaking hands.

Take care of my boy. Barnabus, don't you dare let me down.

I hadn't quite got to Ridley in time. One day he would have to deal with what he had been through. What he had done. Still, it was good to see him with his father again. I took some satisfaction in that.

Sarah produced a little green pill from her pocket. "Take it," she said. "You'll feel better."

I stared at the pill as if she were suggesting I eat a bug. She was right though. If I wanted to feel better, I had no choice but to take that pill.

But I didn't have to. Not if I didn't want to.

It may not have been a real choice. But it felt like one, and that would have to do.

ACKNOWLEDGEMENTS

THANKS TO THE following animals, people, and institutions for their help and encouragement during the absurdly long process of writing this book. Der Brotkorb, the European Bakery Café in the Whitby Mall, for their delicious coffee and danishes. Edmond Hamilton for his fine work. Frank Faulk for the conversation that inspired Chapter Twenty-Four. Nicky Borland, Kathy and Ian Gillis, Phyllis Gotlieb, Jennifer Grant, Fergus Heywood, Erin Mahoney, Keira Mahoney, Lynda Mahoney, John McCarthy, Angela Misri, Arleane Ralph (for the truth about the infamous cat chapter), Susan Rodgers, Robert J. Sawyer, Kathryn Shalley (for believing in this novel), Hugh Spencer, Lorina Stephens, Alex Taylor, Anjuli Tchalikian, and Shawna and Brian Wyvill for their support. GO Transit for providing the time to write. John Miller for respecting that time. Tom and Rosaleen Mahoney for their superlative parenting. The Saturday Night Scribes for listening. Paul and Carol White for being such great friends.

Special thanks to Dr. Robert Runté for taking on this project, and for his keen eyes and penetrating insights.

Finally, extra-special thanks to Barbara Bain of Parkside Elementary and Percy McGougan of Summerside Intermediate for fanning the flames, way back when.

ABOUT THE AUTHOR

Joe Mahoney works full time for the Canadian Broadcasting Corporation, where he's helped make many radio shows over the years. His short fiction has been published in Canada, Australia, and Greece. Joe lives in Whitby with his wife and two daughters, and their golden retriever and siberian forest cat. *A Time and a Place* is his first novel.

BOOKS BY FIVE RIVERS

NON-FICTION

Big Buttes Book: Annotated Dyets Dry Dinner, (1599), by Henry Buttes, with Elizabethan Recipes, by Michelle Enzinas
Al Capone: Chicago's King of Crime, by Nate Hendley
Crystal Death: North America's Most Dangerous Drug, by Nate Hendley
Dutch Schultz: Brazen Beer Baron of New York, by Nate Hendley
John Lennon: Music, Myth and Madness, by Nate Hendley
Motivate to Create: a guide for writers, by Nate Hendley
Steven Truscott, Decades of Injustice by Nate Hendley
King Kwong: Larry Kwong, the China Clipper Who Broke the NHL Colour Barrier, by Paula Johanson
Shakespeare for Slackers: by Aaron Kite, et al
Romeo and Juliet
Hamlet
Macbeth
The Organic Home Gardener, by Patrick Lima and John Scanlan
Shakespeare for Readers' Theatre: Hamlet, Romeo & Juliet, Midsummer Night's Dream, by John Poulson
Shakespeare for Reader's Theatre, Book 2: Shakespeare's Greatest Villains, The Merry Wives of Windsor; Othello, the Moor of Venice; Richard III; King Lear, by John Poulsen
Beyond Media Literacy: New Paradigms in Media Education, by Colin Scheyen
Stonehouse Cooks, by Lorina Stephens

FICTION

Black Wine, by Candas Jane Dorsey
Eocene Station, by Dave Duncan
Immunity to Strange Tales, by Susan J. Forest
The Legend of Sarah, by Leslie Gadallah
The Empire of Kaz, by Leslie Gadallah
Cat's Pawn
Cat's Gambit
Growing Up Bronx, by H.A. Hargreaves

North by 2000+, a collection of short, speculative fiction, by H.A. Hargreaves
A Subtle Thing, by Alicia Hendley
The Tattooed Witch Trilogy, by Susan MacGregor
The Tattooed Witch
The Tattooed Seer
The Tattooed Queen
A Time and a Place, by Joe Mahoney
The Rune Blades of Celi, by Ann Marston
Kingmaker's Sword, Book 1
Western King, Book 2
Broken Blade, Book 3
Cloudbearer's Shadow, Book 4
King of Shadows, Book 5
Sword and Shadow, Book 6
A Still and Bitter Grave, by Ann Marston
Indigo Time, by Sally McBride
Wasps at the Speed of Sound, by Derryl Murphy
A Quiet Place, by J.W. Schnarr
Things Falling Apart, by J.W. Schnarr
A Poisoned Prayer, by Michael Skeet
And the Angels Sang: a collection of short speculative fiction, by Lorina Stephens
Caliban, by Lorina Stephens
From Mountains of Ice, by Lorina Stephens
Memories, Mother and a Christmas Addiction, by Lorina Stephens
Shadow Song, by Lorina Stephens
The Mermaid's Tale, by D. G. Valdron

YA FICTION

My Life as a Troll, by Susan Bohnet
Eye of Strife, by Dave Duncan
Ivor of Glenbroch, by Dave Duncan
The Runner and the Wizard
The Runner and the Saint
The Runner and the Kelpie
Avians, by Timothy Gwyn
Type, by Alicia Hendley
Type 2, by Alicia Hendley
Tower in the Crooked Wood, by Paula Johanson
A Touch of Poison, by Aaron Kite

The Great Sky, by D.G. Laderoute
Out of Time, by D.G. Laderoute
Diamonds in Black Sand, by Ann Marston
Hawk, by Marie Powell

YA NON-FICTION

The Prime Ministers of Canada Series:
- Sir John A. Macdonald
- Alexander Mackenzie
- Sir John Abbott
- Sir John Thompson
- Sir Mackenzie Bowell
- Sir Charles Tupper
- Sir Wilfred Laurier
- Sir Robert Borden
- Arthur Meighen
- William Lyon Mackenzie King
- R. B. Bennett
- Louis St. Laurent
- John Diefenbaker
- Lester B. Pearson
- Pierre Trudeau
- Joe Clark
- John Turner
- Brian Mulroney
- Kim Campbell
- Jean Chretien
- Paul Martin
- Stephen Harper

The Great Sky
ISBN 9781927400999
eISBN 9781988274003
by D.G. Laderoute
Trade Paperback 6 x 9
August 1, 2016

The first time Piper Preach died he was ten years old. But the Anishnaabe spirits thought otherwise.

Now, six year later, Piper struggles with the hard realities of life in a big city. The ancient ways of his people are a distant memory. But the spirits aren't done with him.

Pulled into their bizarre world, the place the Anishnaabe call The Great Sky, he's plunged into the middle of a brutal war raging just a step away from reality. And this time there may be no escaping death – or even worse.

A Town Called Forget
ISBN 97819274034
eISBN 9781988274041
by C.P. Hoff
Trade Paperback 6 x 9
August 1, 2016

A tender and often hilarious debut novel from Alberta writer, C.P. Hoff.

A Town Called Forget is Anne of Green Gables turned on its head. But in this tale it is not an over-imaginative redheaded orphan that takes center stage but the off-beat town itself, full of individuals that should be restrained if not medicated. And the poor heroine of this yarn, banished to live with her Aunt Lily whom her parents have never publicly recognized, has to navigate the delicate balance between her aunt's sanity and neuroses. Amid adventures and misadventures, she learns about patience, tolerance and even love.

This humorous Canadian story is completely different. From everything. Maybe it's Anne of Green Gables *with a little* Alice Through the Looking Glass *thrown in.*
Tim Armstrong
author of Avians

Eocene Station
ISBN 9781988274058
eISBN 9781988274058
by Dave Duncan
Trade Paperback 6 x 9
October 1, 2016

A new Dave Duncan novel is always a reason to celebrate, and his trademark blend of high adventure, hard science, and wry humour makes *Eocene Station* a must read.

K. N. 'Cannon' Ball and his superstar wife, Tempest, are running for their lives. Cannon has exposed a fraud so huge even heads of government are implicated and determined to keep Cannon from ever testifying. Nowhere is safe, so they step out of time to a research station fifty million years in the past. The dinosaurs died out eons ago and there aren't any people around, so they ought to be safe then, right? Wrong, very wrong!

Absolutely smashing.
Goodreads

...brilliant settings, plot, action and character development... entirely enjoyable.
LibraryThing

CPSIA information can be obtained
at www.ICGtesting.com
Printed in the USA
LVOW11s1521181017
552887LV00001B/300/P